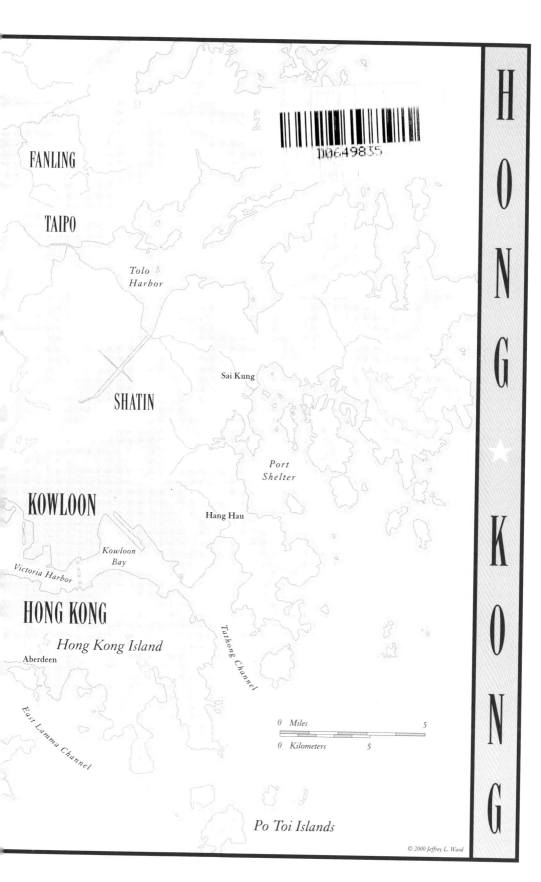

FANLING

TAIPO

Tolo Harbor

Sai Kung

SHATIN

Port Shelter

KOWLOON

Hang Hau

Kowloon Bay

Victoria Harbor

HONG KONG

Hong Kong Island

Aberdeen

Tathong Channel

East Lamma Channel

| 0 | Miles | | 5 |
| 0 | Kilometers | 5 | |

Po Toi Islands

H
O
N
G

★

K
O
N
G

HONG
KONG

Nonfiction books by Stephen Coonts

The Cannibal Queen
War in the Air

Novels by Stephen Coonts

Cuba
Fortunes of War
Flight of the Intruder
Final Flight
The Minotaur
Under Siege
The Red Horseman
The Intruders

STEPHEN COONTS

HONG KONG

A Jake Grafton Novel

ST. MARTIN'S PRESS  NEW YORK

www.stmartins.com

Library of Congress Cataloging-in-Publication Data

Coonts, Stephen.
      Hong Kong : a Jake Grafton novel / Stephen Coonts.—1st ed.
      p. cm.
      ISBN 0-312-25339-7
      1. Grafton, Jake (Fictitious character)—Fiction. 2. Americans—China—Fiction. 3. Hong Kong (China)—Fiction. 4. Conspiracies—Fiction. 5. Kidnapping—Fiction. 6. Admirals—Fiction. I. Title.

PS3553.O5796 H66 2000
813'.54—dc21

                                                                        00-031766

First Edition: September 2000

10 9 8 7 6 5 4 3 2 1

To John and Nancy Coonts

ACKNOWLEDGMENTS

Doing background research for a novel like this is always an adventure. Friend and neighbor Gilbert Pascal, engineer and physicist, read and offered valuable suggestions on draft chapters as the tale developed. Paul K. Chan read and commented upon the manuscript.

The plot of this tale was a collaboration between the author and his wife, Deborah, who delights in dreaming up literary tangles.

Revolutions and revolutionary wars are inevitable in class society, and without them it is impossible to accomplish any leap in social development and to overthrow the reactionary ruling classes and therefore impossible for the people to win political power. . . .

The seizure of power by armed force, the settlement of the issue by war, is the central task and the highest form of revolution. This Marxist-Leninist principle of revolution holds good universally, for China and for all other countries.

—Mao Tse Tung

HONG KONG

CHAPTER ONE

One tiny, red, liquid drop of blood was visible in the center of the small, neat hole in China Bob Chan's forehead an inch or so above his right eye. Chan's eyes were wide open. Tommy Carmellini thought his features registered a look of surprise.

Carmellini pulled off his right latex glove, bent down, and touched the cheek of the corpse—which was still warm.

Death must have been instantaneous, and not many minutes ago, Carmellini thought as he pulled the glove back onto his hand.

The diminutive corpse of China Bob Chan lay sprawled behind his Philippine mahogany desk in the library of his mansion on the south side of Hong Kong Island.

When Carmellini had eased the library door open a few seconds ago, he had seen the shod foot protruding from behind the desk. He scanned the room, then entered the library.

The side of the room opposite the door consisted of a series of large plate-glass windows accented with heavy burgundy drapes. Through the windows was a magnificent view of the harbor at Aberdeen. Beyond the harbor was the channel between Hong Kong Island and Lamma Island. A few lights could be seen on sparsely populated Lamma, and beyond that island, the total darkness of the South China Sea. Tonight the lights of the great city of Hong Kong, out of sight on the north side of the island's spine, illuminated a low deck of stratus clouds with a dull glow.

The band at the party on the floor below this one was playing an old American pop hit; the tune was recognizable even though the amplified lyrics were muffled by overstuffed furniture and shelves of books that reached from floor to ceiling.

Tommy Carmellini looked around, trying to find the spent cartridge. There, a gleam of brass near the leg of that chair. In the subdued light of the library he almost missed it.

He stepped over, bent down, looked.

7.65 millimeter.

That cartridge was designed for small, easy-to-conceal pocket pistols. Difficult to shoot accurately, they were serious weapons only at point-blank range.

Standing in front of the desk, he put his hands on his hips and carefully scanned the room. Somewhere in this room Harold Barnes hid a tape recorder eleven days ago when he installed the wiring for a satellite dish system.

Presumably Chan had ordered the system so that he could watch American television. Perhaps he was a fan of C-Span, which was broadcasting the congressional hearings concerning foreign—i.e., Chinese—donations to the American political parties in the last election; in the past ten days his name had certainly been mentioned numerous times in those hearings.

Alas, Barnes had left no record of where he hid the recorder. He had been shot in the head the night after he completed the installation.

Carmellini was certain Barnes would have used a recorder, not a remote transmitter, which would have been too easy to detect and find. One reason he was certain was that he had known Barnes, a quiet, careful, colorless technician who had gone through the CIA tradecraft course with Carmellini. Who would have suspected that Barnes would be the first of that class to die in the line of duty?

The mikes ... Harold ostensibly spent four hours on the television satellite dish system, a system he should have been able to install in two. If he followed normal practice, he would have hardwired at least two tiny microphones, one for each track of the recorder.

The chandelier over the mahogany desk caught Tommy's eye. Ornate, with several dozen small bulbs, it would attract Harold Barnes like sugar attracts a fly.

Carmellini studied the chain that held the chandelier. There was a wire running down it ... no, two wires—one black wire and the other smaller, carefully wound around the chain.

Barnes could have put a mike in the chandelier, another anywhere in the room—maybe the desk or over by the reading area—and hidden the recorder behind some books, perhaps on the top shelf. Surely there were tomes that didn't get removed from the shelves once a decade.

Carmellini stepped to the nearest bookcase, studied the spines of the books that filled the thing. Not a flake of dust.

A diligent maid would not be good.

So ...

He pulled a chair over under the chandelier, then stood on it.

Aha! There it was, taped in the junction of the main arms of the chandelier. With the bulbs of the chandelier burning brightly, the tiny recorder would have been almost impossible to see from the floor.

Carmellini reached. In seconds he had the two reels out. Maybe three-quarters of the tape had been used, about six hours' worth.

Back on the floor, he was tempted to put the reels into his pocket, then thought better of it. He pulled up a trouser leg and carefully shoved them down into one sock.

He had a new tape in his other sock, but with China Bob dead, the recorder seemed superfluous. Should he cut the wires and remove the device?

How much time did he have?

If China Bob Chan killed Harold Barnes, why was the recorder still there? Was he waiting for someone to come for the tape?

Suddenly aware that time was fleeing, Tommy Carmellini pushed the chair back to its former position. He vigorously rubbed the uphol-stered seat of the chair to remove any marks his shoes had made.

As he straightened, he heard a noise. It seemed to come from the secretary's office. When he stepped in that direction the light in the smaller office came on.

Carmellini moved swiftly and flattened against the wall. The door to the secretary's office was to his right. He listened intently for foot-steps.

Carmellini desperately wanted to avoid being caught in this room with a dead man on the floor and a tape in his sock. True, he had diplomatic immunity as the assistant agricultural officer at the consulate, but the publicity and hullabaloo of an arrest and interrogation, not to mention expulsion from the country, would not be career-enhancing.

He heard the scrape of a chair being moved.

Coiled, ready to lash out if anyone came through the door, he approached it, staying back far enough that he remained away from the glare of the light.

Someone was sitting behind the secretary's desk, someone small. My God, it was a kid! A boy, perhaps ten or twelve.

Carmellini stepped back so he would be out of sight if the youngster glanced this way.

Now he heard a computer boot up.

There was one other exit from this room, at the far end. Carmellini didn't know if the door was locked, but it led to another suite of offices which opened into the hallway near the elevator.

He walked toward the door, moving quietly and decisively.

The knob refused to turn. Locked. There was a keyhole, but he could not see the brand name or type of lock.

He removed a leather packet from his pocket and unfolded it, revealing a carefully chosen selection of picks. He took one, inserted it in the lock.

As he bent down to work on the lock, he saw for the first time the heads of the bolts in the door. They had been painted the same dark color as the door to make them less noticeable.

Even if he got the lock open, the door was bolted shut.

He put the pick away and stowed the packet in an inside jacket pocket as he walked back toward the secretary's open door.

Standing at least six feet from the door, he moved so he could see inside.

The kid was at the computer, typing.

Now he sat back in the chair, waiting . . .

In seconds a naked woman appeared on the screen, a woman holding what appeared to be a giant penis in her hand. Now she—

Jesus, the kid is into porno!

Just what the woman was going to do with the penis, Tommy Carmellini never discovered, for at that instant the door from the hallway opened and a woman walked in. The boy took one look at the intruder and closed the screen, but not before the woman got a good look at it.

She cuffed him once, said something in Chinese.

The boy ran through the icons, closed the Internet connection as the woman spouted Chinese as quickly as her lips would move.

Carmellini stepped back against the wall and waited.

He heard the computer go off, heard the scrape of the chair and footsteps, then the door to the hallway close firmly.

He peered into the office.

Empty.

He opened the hallway door a crack, just enough to see the woman and boy disappear into the elevator at the end of the hallway.

He paused for a second, then went back into the library and scooted the chair under the chandelier. Installing the new tape in the recorder took about thirty seconds; then he found the on-off switch and turned off the recorder. He put the chair back where it belonged and rubbed the seat again.

At the door in the secretary's office, Carmellini checked to ensure no one was coming, then stepped into the hallway and pulled the door shut until it latched. Strains of Gershwin's "An American in Paris" were audible here.

As he walked toward the staircase that led to the rooms below where the party was being held, Carmellini stripped off his latex gloves and put them in his pocket.

Downstairs he found Kerry Kent sipping champagne and talking animatedly with a long-haired intellectual type who was gazing hopefully at her. Kerry was a tall English woman with a spectacular mass of reddish brown hair who spoke both Cantonese and Mandarin fluently. On most working days she labored as a translator at the Greater China Mutual Aid Society, an insurance firm, but in reality she was an officer in the British Secret Intelligence Service, the SIS. Tonight she was wearing an elegant dark blue dress that just brushed her ankles and a modest borrowed diamond necklace.

"Oh, there you are, darling," she said lightly, laying a hand on Tommy's arm. "I have been talking to this brilliant playwright—" She said his name. "His new play is opening next week in the West End. My sister told me quite a lot about it, actually. What a coincidence! When we get back to London we must see it."

Carmellini shook hands with the scribbler and gently led Kerry away. "Did anyone watch me come in?" he asked, just loud enough for her to hear over the hubbub of cocktail party chatter and music.

"I don't think anyone was paying much attention. What were you doing up there?"

"Watching porno on the Internet. Fascinating stuff! I'll tell you all about it later. Who is this sicko stalking you?"

He was referring to a Chinese man who was standing six feet away and openly staring at Kerry. When she moved, he moved.

"An admirer from the provinces, obviously, hopelessly smitten. All my life I've had this devastating effect on men. It's such a bore. I'm thinking of having chest reduction surgery to end these unwanted attentions."

That comment was intended as a joke, for Kerry had a slim, athletic figure.

Carmellini snarled at the staring man and guided Kent away by the elbow.

"Did you get it?" She meant the tape.

"It wasn't there. China Bob is stretched out behind his desk with a hole in his head."

"Dead?" A furrow appeared between her eyebrows.

"Very."

"You found the recorder?"

"In the chandelier. But the tape was missing."

Kerry Kent sipped champagne as she digested Carmellini's lie. Just why lying to her was a good idea he couldn't say, but his instinct told him not to trust anyone. Someone shot Harold Barnes, and another someone, perhaps the same one, put a bullet in China Bob Chan's head—and Carmellini had known Ms. Kent for precisely three days, not exactly a long-term relationship.

There were at least three ways to get from this floor of the mansion to the floor above: two staircases and an elevator. Carmellini had slipped up one set of stairs after he went to the men's room, which was out of sight of the ballroom, just down the hall toward the back stairs. Anyone in this room could have done precisely the same thing in the last few hours, and probably several of them had.

Perhaps the tape held the answer.

Carmellini scanned the crowd one more time, trying to fix the guests in his mind. The cream of Hong Kong society was here tonight.

"Tell me again," he said to Kerry Kent, "who these folks are."

She scanned the crowd, nodded toward a man in his sixties in the center of a small crowd. "That's Governor Sun Siu Ki, surrounded by his usual entourage—officials and bureaucrats and private industry suck-ups. The gentleman of distinction talking to him is Sir Robert MacDonald, the British consul general. The tall, blond Aussie semi-eavesdropping on those two is Rip Buckingham, managing editor of the *China Post*, the largest English-language daily in Hong Kong. Beside him is his wife, Sue Lin. Over in the far corner is the American consul general, Virgil Cole, talking to China Bob's sister, Amy Chan. Let's see, who else?"

"The fellow in the uniform with the highball, standing by the band."

"General Tang, commanding the division of People's Liberation Army troops stationed in Hong Kong. He's been in Hong Kong only a few weeks. The papers ran articles about him when he arrived."

"The man talking to him?"

"Albert Cheung. Educated at Oxford, the foremost attorney in Hong Kong. Smooth and silky and in the know, or so I've heard."

She continued, pointing out six industrialists, three shipping magnates, and two bank presidents. "These people are the scions of the merchant and shipping clans that grew filthy rich in Hong Kong," she said, and named names. "If ever a group mourned the departure of the British, there they are," she added. "Never saw so much of the upper crust chatting it up together."

Any person in the room could have gone upstairs and popped China Bob, Carmellini reflected. All of them had probably excused themselves and gone in search of the facilities once or twice during the evening. Or someone could have ridden the elevator from the basement or walked to the library from another area of the house. The field was wide open. Still, Tommy Carmellini took one more careful look at each of the people Kerry had pointed out, then said, "Perhaps we should leave now before the excitement begins."

"A marvelous suggestion. Let me say a few good-byes as we drift toward the door."

Five minutes later, as they stood waiting for the consulate's pool car to be brought around, Carmellini asked Kerry, "So what's on the agenda for the rest of the evening?"

"I don't know," she said lightly and turned toward him. He accepted the invitation and kissed her. She put her arms around him and kissed back.

"You are such a romantic," she said when her lips were free.

"And single, too."

"I haven't forgotten."

"I don't recall mentioning my marital status before."

"You didn't. Your reputation preceded you. Tommy Carmellini, unmarried burglar, thief, second-story man . . ."

"And all-around good egg."

"James Bond without the dash and panache."

"Don't knock the recipe until you've tried it."

"You'll have to sell me."

"I'm willing to give it a go, as you Brits say."

"Tell me about the Internet pornography. Little details like that spice up action reports, make them interesting."

The consulate pool car pulled to a stop in front of them, and the valet got out. "I was saving that morsel for later," Carmellini said as he tipped the man and accepted the keys. "After all, the night is young."

CHAPTER TWO

The morning sun shone full on the balcony of the fifth-floor hotel room when Jake Grafton opened the sliding glass door. The bustle and roar from the streets below assailed him, but he grinned and seated himself at the small, round glass table. As he sipped at a cup of coffee he sampled the smells, sights, and sounds of Hong Kong.

His wife, Callie, stepped out on the balcony. She was dressed to the nines, wearing only a subtle hint of makeup, with her purse over her shoulder and her attaché case in her left hand.

As she bent to kiss Jake he got a faint whiff of scent. "You smell delicious this morning, Mrs. Grafton."

She paused at the door. A furrow appeared between her eyebrows. "What are you going to do today?" she asked.

"Loaf, read the morning paper, cash some traveler's checks, and meet you for lunch."

"When are you going to start on your assignment?"

"I'm working on it this very minute. I know it doesn't look like it, but the wheels are turning."

Today was the third day of the conference, an intense seven-day immersion in Western culture for Chinese college students. Callie was one of the faculty.

"I'm soaking up atmosphere," Jake added. "This trip was billed as my vacation, as you will recall."

Perhaps it was the rare sight of her husband in pajamas at eight on a weekday morning that bothered her. She smiled, nodded, and said good-bye.

As Jake worked on the coffee he surveyed the old police barracks immediately across the road from the hotel. The barracks was surrounded by a ten-foot-high brick wall, which hid it from people on the street. Three stories high, it was constructed of whitewashed brick or masonry in the shape of a T. The windows in the base of the T, which was parallel to Jake, revealed rooms with bunks, lockers, showers, laundry rooms, and a kitchen and dining hall, all set in from outside balconies that ran the length of each floor, much like an American motel. The top of the T was an administration building, apparently full of offices. Police cars filled the parking spaces around the building.

The lawn, however, was a military encampment, covered with troops, tents, fires, and cooking pots. Here at least five hundred People's Liberation Army, or PLA, troops were bivouacked, covering almost every square yard of greenery. Pencil-thin columns of smoke from the fires rose into the still morning air.

In colonial days the Royal Hong Kong police force must have been a nice life for single British men who wanted to do something exotic with their lives, or at least live their mundane lives in an exotic locale and make a very nice living in the process. Like most colonial police forces, the Royal Hong Kong force was famously corrupt, had been since the first Brit donned a uniform and strolled the streets.

Today Chinese policemen and soldiers scurried to and fro like so many ants. Jake wondered if there were any British policemen still wearing the Hong Kong uniform.

Jake Grafton drained his coffee cup and turned his attention to the English-language newspaper, the *China Post,* which had been slid under the door of the room early this morning.

The financial crisis in Japan was the lead article on the front page, which contained lengthy pronouncements from the Chinese government in Beijing. The article also contained a quote from the American consul general, Virgil Cole.

Jake read the name with interest and shook his head. He had flown with Cole on his last cruise during the Vietnam War, and the two of them had survived a shootdown. And he hadn't seen the man since. Oh, they corresponded routinely for years after Cole left the navy, but finally in one move or other the Graftons lost Cole's address, and the Christmas cards stopped. That was ten or so years ago.

Tiger Cole. After his broken back healed, he had gotten out of the navy and gone to grad school, then got into the high-tech business world in Silicon Valley. When he was named consul general to Hong Kong two years ago, *Fortune* magazine said he was worth more than a billion dollars. Of course, he was also a generous donor to political causes.

Maybe he should call Tiger, ask him out to dinner. Then again . . . He decided to wait another day. If Tiger didn't call, he would call him.

On the second page of the paper was a column devoted to a murder that apparently happened last night. The body was discovered just before press time. Jake recognized the victim's name—China Bob Chan— and read the article with a sinking feeling. As the key figure in a campaign finance scandal in Washington, China Bob had been getting a lot of press in the United States of late, most of it the kind of coverage that an honest man could do without. Chan's untimely demise due to lead poisoning was going to go over like a lead brick on Capitol Hill.

On the first page of the second section of the newspaper Jake was pleasantly surprised to find a photo of Callie with two of the other Americans on the seminar faculty, along with a three-paragraph write-up. Amazingly, the reporter even spelled Callie's name correctly. He carefully folded that page to keep.

All in all, Jake thought, the newspaper looked exactly like what it was, a news sheet published under the watchful eye of a totalitarian government intolerant of criticism or dissent. Not a word about why the PLA troops were choking the streets, standing at every street corner, every shop entrance, every public facility, nothing but the bare facts about China Bob's murder, not even an op-ed piece about the implications of his death vis-à-vis Chinese-U.S. relations.

Jake's attention was captured by several columns of foreign sports scores on the next-to-the-last page. Australian football received more column inches than the American professional teams did, Jake noted, grinning.

He tossed the paper down and stretched. Ahhhhh . . .

Someone was knocking on the door to the room.

"Just a minute!"

Jake checked his reflection in the mirror over the dresser—no need to scandalize the maid—then opened the door a crack.

A man in a business suit stood there, a westerner . . . Tommy Carmellini.

"Come in." Jake held the door open. "I'm not going very fast this morning, I'm afraid."

"Have you seen the morning paper?"

"China Bob?"

"Yes."

"I saw the story."

"It's true. Chan's as dead as a man can get."

"Let me take a shower, then we'll go downstairs for some breakfast."

"Okay." Tommy Carmellini sat down in the only chair and opened his attaché case.

When Jake came out of the bathroom fifteen minutes later, Carmellini was repacking his sweep gear in the attaché case. "No bugs," he told Jake.

"The phone?"

"Impossible to say. I have no idea how much impedance and resistance on the line are normal."

"Okay."

"How did you know the story was true?"

"Alas, I met China Bob last night a minute or two after he had joined the ranks of the recently departed. He was warm as toast and the hole in his head was brand-new. There was a spent 7.65-millimeter cartridge under a table a few feet away."

"Who shot him?"

"I didn't. That's all I know for sure."

"Do you have the tape on you?"

Carmellini sat and removed it from his sock. He passed it to Jake Grafton, who examined it cursorily and put it in a trouser pocket.

After they had ordered breakfast in the hotel restaurant, the two men talked in general terms about the city in which they found themselves. Jake told Carmellini that he and Callie had met in Hong Kong, in

1972. "Haven't been back since," Jake said, "which was a mistake, I guess. It's a great city, and we should have come every now and then to watch it evolve and grow."

Carmellini was only politely interested. "How come," he asked the admiral, "they sent me over here to help you out? You're not CIA."

"You sure about that?" Jake Grafton asked. Carmellini noticed that Grafton's gray eyes smiled before he did. His face was tan and lean, although the nose was a trifle large. The admiral had a jagged, faded old scar on one temple.

"Few things these days are exactly what they appear to be," Carmellini agreed. "As I recall, when I met you last year you were wearing a navy uniform and running a carrier battle group. Of course, the agency is going all out on cover stories these days."

Jake chuckled. "I was pushing paper in the Pentagon when they were looking for someone to send over here to snoop around. Apparently my connection to Cole from way back when got someone thinking, so . . . Anyway, when they asked me about it, I said okay, if my wife could come along. So here I am."

Carmellini frowned. "How did I get dragged into this mess? I had a pair of season tickets to see the Orioles and a delightful young woman to fill the other seat."

"I asked for you by name," Jake replied. "The new CIA director tried to dissuade me. Carmellini is a thief, he said, a crook, and last year when someone murdered Professor Olaf Svenson, Carmellini's whereabouts couldn't be accounted for. Seems that you were on vacation at the time, which is not a felony, but it made them do some digging; of course nothing turned up. No one could prove anything. Still, your record got another little smirch."

"He said that?"

"He did. Apparently your personnel file is interesting reading."

"You know how football players talk about adversity?" Tommy Carmellini remarked. "I've had some of that, too. And smirches. Lots of smirches."

"Uh-huh."

"So if you know I'm smirched, how come you asked for me?"

"My aide, Toad Tarkington, suggested you. For some reason you impressed him."

"I see."

Their breakfast came. After the waiter left, Jake said, "Tell me about last night. Everything you can remember."

Carmellini talked as he ate. "They have me working with this woman from SIS, a Brit named Kerry Kent. She's a knockout and speaks Chinese like a native. I've known her exactly three days and an evening."

"Uh-huh."

Carmellini explained about the party, about how Kent got two in-vitations and took him along as her date. Two hours into the evening, he explained, he saw his chance and sneaked upstairs.

"I was pretty spooked when I found China Bob all sprawled out. I got the tape out of the recorder and installed a new one, so anyone checking the machine would think the original tape didn't work. That was my thinking, which wasn't very bright on my part. I did have the presence of mind to turn the recorder off, so maybe anyone finding it will buy that hypothesis. Then again . . .

"By the time I got downstairs the thought occurred to me that I didn't know beans from apple butter. Anybody in Hong Kong could have killed China Bob, for any conceivable reason. Including, of course, my companion for the evening, Kerry Kent. She spent fifteen minutes in the ladies' just before I went upstairs, or so she said. Just to be on the safe side, when I got downstairs after retrieving the tape I told her it wasn't in the recorder."

Jake Grafton looked up from his coffee. "And . . ."

"And damn if she didn't frisk me when we were outside waiting for the valet to bring the car around. Gave me a smooch and a hug and rubbed her hands over my pockets."

"You sure she was looking for the tape?"

"She patted me down."

"Maybe she was trying to let you know she was romantically inter-ested," Jake suggested with a raised eyebrow.

"I had hopes," Carmellini confessed. "She's a nice hunk of female, tuned up and ready to rumble. But she had me take her straight home. She didn't even invite me up for a good-night beer."

"I thought secret agents were always getting tossed in the sack."

"I thought so, too," Carmellini said warmly. "That's why I signed on with the agency. Reality has been a disappointment." Another lie, a little one. Carmellini joined the CIA to avoid prosecution for burglary and a handful of other felonies. However, he saw no reason to share the sordid details with his colleagues in the ordinary course of business, so to speak.

"Did she find the tape on you?"

"No. I had it in my sock."

"Did she have a pistol on her?"

"She didn't have a pistol in her sock, and believe me, there wasn't room for one in her bra."

"Her purse?"

"A little clutch thing—I gave it a squeeze. Wasn't there. Of course, whoever shot China Bob probably ditched the pistol immediately."

"So who are your suspects for the killing?"

"It could have been anybody in Hong Kong. Anybody at the party or anybody who came in off the street and went straight upstairs. Still, Kent or the consul general are high on my list. As I mentioned, she camped out in the ladies' just before I went upstairs. I saw Cole coming down the stairs five minutes before I went up."

Virgil Cole, the perfect warrior. Jake was the one who had hung the nickname "Tiger" on him, back in the fall of 1972 when Cole became his bombardier-navigator after Morgan McPherson was killed. This morning Grafton took a deep breath, remembering those days, remembering Cole as he had known him then. Those days seemed so long ago, and yet . . .

The Chinese employees of the Bank of the Orient had known the truth for days, and they had told their friends, who withdrew money from their accounts. As the news spread, the queues in the lobby had grown longer and longer.

This fine June morning a crowd of at least two thousand gathered on the sidewalks and in the manicured square in front of the bank, waiting for it to open. The bank was housed in a massive, soaring tower of stone and glass set in the heart of the Victoria business district, between the slope of Victoria Peak and the ferry piers. Its name in English and Chinese was of course splashed prominently across the front of the building in huge characters. In still larger characters lit day and night mounted on the side of the building at the twenty-story level so they would be visible from all over the island, from Kowloon, indeed, on a clear day from mainland China itself, was the name of the bank in Japanese, for the Bank of the Orient was a Japanese bank and proud of it.

After urgent consultations and many glances out the window at the crowd, which was growing by the minute, bank officials refused to open the doors. Instead, they called the Finance Ministry in Tokyo. While the president of the bank waited by the telephone for the assistant finance minister for overseas operations to return his urgent call, someone outside the bank threw a rock through a window.

One of the cashiers called the police. The police took a look at the crowd and called the governor, Sun Siu Ki. Sun didn't go look; he merely called General Tang Tso Ming, the new commander of the division of the People's Liberation Army that was stationed in Hong Kong.

A half hour later several hundred armed soldiers arrived. They spread themselves two deep across the street on each end of the crowd. They also surrounded a park across the street from the bank where many people were waiting. There really weren't enough soldiers to physically prevent the crowd from moving, so the soldiers did nothing but stand in position, waiting for orders. Then four tanks clanked up, ripping up asphalt, and stopped with their big guns pointed at the crowd.

General Tang arrived with the tanks. He looked over the crowd and the soldiers, had his officers adjust the placement of the troops, then went to the door of the bank and pounded on it with his fist. When it didn't open, he pulled his pistol and rapped on the door sharply with the butt.

Now the door opened.

General Tang and two of his colonels marched into the Bank of the Orient and demanded to see the president.

As they walked along the sidewalk toward the Star Ferry, Tommy Carmellini said, "Admiral, I'm really flying blind. The people at Langley sent me over here with orders to help you out, but they didn't tell me what this is all about."

"They sent me over here," Jake Grafton told the CIA officer, "because I knew Tiger Cole in Vietnam. Apparently I'm one of the few people in government who know him personally. Washington wants to know what in hell is going on in Hong Kong."

"What do they think is going on?"

They each bought first-class tickets on the ferry and went up on the top deck. As the ferry pulled out, Jake Grafton said, "China is coming to a crisis. The whole country is tinder ready to burn. One spark might set it off. The Communists want to stay in power by delivering economic prosperity, which can come only if the economic system changes. They are trapped in this giant oxymoron; they want economic change without social and political change. On the other hand, the United States wants a big piece of the China pie. So the American establishment has traded technology and capital for access to Chinese markets and low-cost labor. In other words, they have invested in the political status quo, which is the dictatorial Communist system."

Tommy Carmellini nodded his understanding.

Jake continued. "The Communist system distorts and corrupts everything. The only way a Chinese importer can get goods into the country is to obtain a government import license. These licenses are restricted to prevent private entrepreneurs from competing against state-owned enterprises. Enter China Bob Chan and a thousand like him. If you are an enterprising Chinese businessman, for a fee Chan will obtain for you an import license from a government official—in effect, he splits the bribe. This system ensures that the bureaucracy is corrupted from top to bottom. Every single person in government is on the take, party members, officials of every caliber and stripe, army generals, everybody. This system generates enormous profits that go into their pockets, and the industrialized West gets to sell high tech to China."

"Only the public loses," Carmellini murmured.

"Precisely. Anyway, to get specific, the Chinese government used China Bob Chan to make political contributions in America and grease the wheels to get American export licenses for restricted technology, some of it military. As a general rule, government licenses always create opportunities for graft of one sort or another, in China and America. In this case the PLA, the People's Liberation Army, wanted the American military technology. Unfortunately, China Bob pocketed about half the money the PLA paid him to do all this American greasing. The guy who dealt with China Bob on behalf of the army was General Tang, now the PLA commander here."

"Uh-huh."

"The story is that Tang was sent here to find and apprehend a political criminal, Wu Tai Kwong. Remember the man who stood in front of the tank in Tiananmen Square in 1989?"

"I thought he was dead."

"He may be. But dead or alive, he's public enemy number one; he gave the Commies the finger. These people are paranoid."

"That's an occupational hazard with absolute dictators," Tommy Carmellini said lightly.

"Anyway, that is what the army says it's doing here. In reality, Tang and the army are here to prevent a political uprising in Hong Kong. The CIA thinks China Bob Chan washed the money to finance the revolution."

"He was working both sides of the street?"

"The CIA thinks so. The politicians in Congress wanted someone to come over here and root around and give an independent assessment of how deep the consul general is in all this. The White House picked me, for lack of someone better."

"Virgil Cole?"

"That's right."

"Why you?"

"Well, basically, I got the impression that I'm supposed to worm my way into Cole's confidence and get him to say things to me that he wouldn't say to anyone else. That was the thinking in Washington, anyway. It stinks, but that's the sordid truth."

"Maybe it's all bullshit," Carmellini suggested. "Rumors go round and round. I'm an expert on rumors."

Grafton had his arms on the railing of the boat. "Cole is apparently having a relationship of some type with Amy Chan. Her father was a British soldier and her mother was a Chinese girl who came to Hong Kong when the Nationalist cause collapsed and Mao took over on the mainland. The mother got in just before the door slammed shut, took up prostitution to feed herself. She was supposedly really good-looking, became a high-class hooker, ended up falling for this Brit soldier and having Amy by him. Of course the soldier was a shit and went tooling off to Britain when his tour was up—seems he had a wife there, too.

"Anyway, Amy's mother saved her money and sent her daughter to America for an education. She had a degree from UCLA and was working at the American consulate processing visa applications when Cole arrived. They hit it off right from the start."

"Uh-huh."

"Her half brother was China Bob Chan. He used Cole as his poster boy to advertise his influence with the Americans. Amy had him over to the mansion every other night. China Bob paraded him in front of government toads, General Tang, everybody and anybody who came down here from Beijing. This has been going on about a year. Cole has been talking to congressional investigators, so he is aware of the intricacies of all this. Still, the Tiger Cole I remember from way back when wouldn't give a good goddamn what anybody thought about his love life."

"That's my impression of him, too," Carmellini mused. "I've seen his dossier and spent an hour or so with him, and I'd say you are pretty close to the mark."

"We're here to find out what Cole and China Bob have been up to," Jake said. "I want to listen to that tape you brought over. Callie will help me with the Chinese." He had the thing in *his* sock just now.

"I'll have to get a player out of the communications room at the consulate," Tommy Carmellini told Jake as they joined the throng waiting to get off the boat when it slid into its dock in the Central District. "It takes a special machine to play the thing."

"Let's get bugs in Cole's office in the consulate. Search his desk, see what you can learn. As soon as you can, open the safes and start going through the files. I want to see anything that implicates Tiger Cole in a conspiracy to overthrow the Chinese government. If there is not a shred of physical evidence, I want to know that, too."

"Jesus! Where'd you learn how to do investigations?"

"We don't have time for subtleties. I want to know what in hell is going on in Hong Kong, and I want to know *now*. If representatives of the American government are members of a conspiracy to overthrow the lawful government of China, that could be construed as an act of war."

As they walked out of the Star Ferry terminal, Tommy Carmellini nodded at the admiral and set off for the consulate on Garden Road.

The president of the Bank of the Orient was Saburo Genda. When General Tang and his officers were escorted into his office, he was on the telephone with Governor Sun, trying to explain the situation.

"We do not have money on hand to pay all the depositors waiting outside," Genda explained as patiently as he could.

He listened to a burst of Chinese, which he spoke reasonably well, then answered, "Of course the bank is solvent. Yes, we have reserves. Unfortunately, we just do not have sufficient cash in the vaults to pay all the people waiting outside. . . . Yes, we will open in a few hours. You have my assurances, sir."

He hung up the telephone and wiped his forehead.

Tang wanted to know why the bank wasn't open.

Genda ran through it all again.

"Get some money," General Tang said.

"We are trying, General, but since we don't have printing presses in the basement, we must obtain currency from other banks. We are in the process of doing that now."

Tang disliked being patronized, which he thought a slight on his dignity and his position, and he told Genda that in no uncertain terms.

He was just winding up when the telephone rang. Genda answered.

"Sir, the Finance Ministry in Tokyo is on the line."

Genda switched to Japanese and began talking into the telephone, leaving the general to stew. Tang felt out of place in this huge, opulent office decorated with tropical hardwoods and designer furniture, four stories high in a grand temple dedicated to the gods of money.

Tang Ming was a peasant's son, born during World War II, whose earliest memories were of his family fleeing before advancing Japanese troops.

He had spent his adult life in the army. From skin to backbone he was a soldier. A firm believer in the social goals of communism, he was, like a majority of his fellow countrymen, a cultural and racial xenophobe. Before his assignment to Hong Kong he had actually seen foreigners on only two occasions in his life, both official visits to Beijing. He had seen the foreigners at a distance, not talked with them.

Sitting in this huge office and watching an impeccably attired senior Japanese executive babble in a foreign tongue about matters he didn't understand made General Tang Ming restless and irritable.

Someone with a cellular telephone called the editor of the *China Post*, Hong Kong's leading English-language newspaper, and informed him about the restless crowd in front of the Bank of the Orient. The editor, Rip Buckingham, had heard rumors for the past two days about the possible collapse of the bank, so as he listened to the caller describe the crowd and the troops, his gut told him, *This is it*.

Rip called the newsroom and ordered four reporters and two photographers dispatched to the scene immediately. Then he extracted an eyewitness account from the caller while he jotted notes.

When he finally let the caller go, Rip automatically glanced out the window of his corner office at the giant Coca-Cola sign on top of the Bank of the Orient building, an imposing seventy-story skyscraper in Hong Kong's Central District. In a typical Hong Kong deal, the developer of the building played off competing consumer giants, one against the other, for the honor of having their logo prominently displayed on the masthead of the new bank building, the biggest one in the colony. Reportedly the local Coke bottler had paid a fee in excess of ten million dollars U.S. to the developer just for the privilege of putting a sign up there. That was in 1995, two years before the British turned over the colony to the Chinese Communists.

No one is building buildings like that in Hong Kong now, Rip thought bitterly.

Rip was an Australian who had enjoyed a wonderful, vagrant youth. He repaired slot machines in Las Vegas, worked as a motorman on San Francisco trolleys, sailed the Pacific and Indian oceans in the forecastles of rusty Liberian tramps, and bicycled across most of China, including the entire route of the ancient Silk Road, from Tyre on the eastern edge of the Mediterranean to Sian in central China. Finally, in his late twenties, Rip Buckingham came to rest in Hong Kong, where he got a haircut and traded his sandals for leather shoes. He even married a local girl.

Rip turned to the computer sitting on a stand beside his desk and began writing. He wanted to get the eyewitness account down while it was fresh and immediate. He was still working on it when his reporters began calling in on their cellular telephones. He folded the facts they had gleaned into the story he was writing and asked questions.

Unlike a reporter operating in a Western nation, Rip did not telephone the governor's officer or the police or the PLA to elicit comments or give those officials a chance to dispute the accounts his reporters were getting. He had done that years ago when he first took over the managing editor's position, and before long was told by some government functionary, "You can't print that." The police then came to the newspaper office to ensure that he didn't.

So far he had managed to avoid the wrath of the Communist officials who ruled Hong Kong. It hadn't been easy. He was, he often thought wryly, becoming a master at damning with faint praise. I'm the king of innuendo, he once grumped to his wife. Actually, as he well knew, he had escaped censorship only because his paper was published in English, a language that few government officials spoke with any fluency. All the Chinese-language newspapers had a squad of resident apparatchiks from the New China News Agency who had to approve everything.

As Rip worked on the story, a sense of impending doom came over him. There were several hundred banks in Hong Kong, most of them privately owned, yet China had no Federal Deposit Insurance Corporation. Chinese banks outside of Hong Kong were owned by the state and theoretically could not fail. Of course, if those state-owned banks were examined using Western accounting standards, all were insolvent.

The problem was the desperate financial straits of the Chinese government, which saw the privately owned banks in Hong Kong as a source of low-interest loans for noncompetitive state-owned industries that would collapse without cash infusions, industries that employed tens of millions of mainland workers.

The Japanese who owned the Bank of the Orient had refused to make those loans to the Chinese government. Now the bank was failing, and thousands of people were going to be flat-ass broke after a lifetime of work and saving.

What was the Chinese government doing to prevent that outcome, if anything?

As luck would have it, after he left the Star Ferry terminal Jake Grafton wandered along with the crowd, lost in thought. When he at last began paying attention to his surroundings he found himself in the square outside the Bank of the Orient, shoulder-to-shoulder with several thousand other people. The doors of the bank were apparently locked. From time to time people came out of the crowd to try the doors, which refused to open.

Armed soldiers in uniform were visible here and there, but they were well back, away from the crowd, and seemed to be making no attempt to disburse it or prevent people from approaching the door of the bank to rattle it, pound on it, or press their foreheads against the glass and look in.

Here and there knots of people argued loudly among themselves, waved passbooks, and stared openly and defiantly at the soldiers.

For a moment, Jake thought of wandering on, finding another bank to cash his traveler's checks. Surely they all weren't closed today.

Yet something made him linger. He found a few empty inches on a flower bed retainer wall and parked his bottom.

Meanwhile, in the executive suite of the bank, President Saburo Genda was getting bad news from the assistant finance minister in Tokyo.

"We will not loan the bank additional funds. I'm sorry, but the prime minister and the finance minister are agreed."

President Genda's forte was commercial loans to large companies. He had spent much of his adult life dealing with wealthy businessmen with a firm grasp of economic reality. He fought now to keep his temper with this obtuse government clerk.

"You don't understand," he said, his voice tightly under control. "We are experiencing a run on the bank. There is a crowd of several thousand depositors outside demanding their money. Without additional cash, the bank cannot pay them. Without more money, the bank will collapse."

"I am sorry, Mr. Genda," said the bureaucrat. "It is you who do not understand. The government has decided to let the bank fail. It would simply cost too much to save it."

"But—"

"The Bank of the Orient made far too many real estate loans in Hong Kong at astronomical evaluations. As you know, the market collapsed after the Communists took over. It may be twenty years before the market recovers. Indeed, it may never recover."

"Mr. Assistant Minister, your ministry has known about the bad loans for years. Your colleagues were working with us. We have the assets to pay our depositors, but the assets are in accounts in Japan and you have frozen them. Those funds belong to this bank! Make them available for us to pledge and we will borrow the cash we need locally."

"I am sorry, Mr. Genda. The government has decided to offset the bank's assets against the amounts the bank owes the government."

"You can't do this," Genda protested. "This isn't the way things are done. You are violating the banking regulations!"

"The decision has been made."

"Have you discussed the failure of the bank with the governor of Hong Kong or the Chinese government in Beijing?"

"We have. Since the bank is not Chinese, they did not choose to guarantee its debts."

Genda continued, almost pleading, trying to make the bureaucrat see reason. "This is a Japanese bank! Many of our senior people are former Finance Ministry officials. We have close ties with the government, extremely close ties."

"I am sorry, Mr. Genda," the civil servant said politely. "As I said, the decision has been made. We here in the Ministry expect you to take personal responsibility for the condition of your institution. Good-bye."

The assistant minister hung up, leaving Saburo Genda standing with the telephone in his hand, too stunned to hang it up, too stunned to speak to his subordinates standing around the room waiting for a report. He felt as if his head had just been separated from his body. In two minutes of conversation, the civil servant at the Finance Ministry had ruined him: He could never work in a bank again; his whole life had just been reduced to rubble.

"Open the bank," General Tang said in Chinese. "I order you to open the doors of the bank."

"The bank is ruined," Saburo Genda told the soldier, his lips barely able to form the words. "Tokyo refuses to guarantee our borrowings of cash to pay the depositors."

Tang Ming tried to understand. Foreigners! "But this is a bank. You have much money in the vault. Give it to the people who want it, and when you run out, tell them they will have to come back another day."

"Then the riot will occur in our lobby."

"You must have money!" Tang gestured to the crowd. "What have you done with all of their money?"

Genda had had it with this fool. "We loaned it out," he said through clenched teeth. "That is the function of banks, to accept deposits and make loans."

Tang Ming stretched to his full height. He looked at Genda behind his great, polished desk, a whipped dog, and his two colonels and Genda's secretary and the crowd beyond the window.

"Come," he murmured at the colonels and strode out.

The tangible anger of the crowd made Jake Grafton uneasy. He sensed it was high time for him to be on his way, time to be out of this group of angry Asians who were working themselves up for a riot.

Still he lingered. Curiosity kept him rooted.

Although he spoke not a word of Chinese, he didn't really need the language to read the emotions on people's faces. A few people were openly crying, weeping silently as they rocked back and forth in sitting positions. Others were on cellular phones, presumably sharing their misfortune with family and friends.

The number of wireless telephones in use by the crowd surprised Jake—China was definitely third or fourth world. There was money in Hong Kong, a lot of which had been invested in state-of-the-art technology. Still, most of the people in this square existed on a small fraction of the money that the average American family earned.

As Jake sat there with two thousand American dollars' worth of traveler's checks in his pocket that he could get cashed at any bank in town, the vast gulf between the comfortable, middle-class circumstances in which he had lived his life and the hand-to-mouth existence that so many hundreds of millions—billions—of people around the world accepted as their lot in life spread before him like the Grand Canyon.

He was no bleeding heart, but he cared about people. Always had.

He found people interesting, could imagine himself in their circumstances; this was one of the qualities that made him a leader, a good naval officer, and a decent human being.

General Tang Ming climbed into a small van with public address system speakers mounted on the roof. Sitting in the passenger seat of the van holding a microphone, the general explained the facts as he understood them: The bank had loaned all the money it had and had no more to pay to the people in the crowd. It would not open its doors.

Since waiting for an event that would not happen was futile, Tang ordered the crowd to disperse. The language he used was Mandarin Chinese, the dialect of northern China, of Beijing, and of most of the soldiers under his command. Unfortunately, it was not the language of the people in the crowd, most of whom spoke Cantonese or English.

As General Tang harangued the crowd in the street outside the Bank of the Orient over a loud, tinny PA system in a language few understood, the crowd became more boisterous. Some people began shouting, others produced stones and bits of concrete from construction sites that they threw toward the bank windows. Several men nearest the main entrance to the bank pounded on the door with their fists, shouting, "Open up and pay us!"

Others in the crowd, sensing approaching disaster, tried to leave the area by passing through the cordon of soldiers. Almost by reflex, the greatly outnumbered soldiers tried to hold the crowd back. They struck out with billy clubs and rifle butts. Inevitably the conflict panicked onlookers, many of whom gave in to their urge to flee all at the same time. Those in the center of the crowd began pushing those on the fringes toward the soldiers.

A shot was fired. Then several shots.

General Tang was still holding forth on the PA system from the passenger seat of the van when the first fully automatic burst was triggered into the crowd by a frightened soldier.

People screamed. More shots were fired into the crowd, random insanity, then the soldiers were either trampled or ran before the fear-soaked mob trying to escape.

A sergeant in one of the tanks on the edge of the park tried to aid the escape of his fellow soldiers, who ran past the tank in front of a wall of running civilians who were also desperate to escape. The sergeant opened fire at the civilians with a machine gun mounted on top of the main turret. The bullets cut down several dozen people before the gun jammed.

In three minutes the sidewalk and street in front of the bank contained only dead, dying, and wounded people, many of them trampled. More than a hundred people lay on the pavement and grass and in the flowerbeds, some obviously dead, some bleeding and in shock.

General Tang climbed out of the public address van and stood staring uncomprehendingly at the human wreckage. He hadn't recognized the muffled pops as shots since the public address system was so loud, and he was initially pleased when the people he could see from the van began to move. Alas, by then the situation was out of control. Surprised by the panic evident among the civilians he could see through the van's windshield, Tang stopped speaking and heard, for the first time, the shooting, the shouting, and the screaming.

Staring now at the people lying in the otherwise empty street, he became aware that several officers were beside him, shouting questions.

The thought that ran through the general's head was that the crowd should not have run. It was their fault, really. He certainly hadn't given orders for the soldiers to shoot.

"Pick them up," he said and gestured toward the dead and wounded. The officers beside him looked puzzled.

"Pick them up," General Tang repeated. "Take them to the hospital. Clear the street."

When the first shot was fired, a nervous Jake Grafton raked two old ladies from their perch on the retaining wall and shoved them onto the ground. Then he threw himself on top of them.

He didn't move until the shooting was completely over and most of the people on their feet had fled. Only then did he stand and look about him at the bodies, at people bleeding, at people like himself who had taken what cover they could find.

He helped the two old women to their feet. Neither was hurt. They looked about them with wide, fearful eyes. Without a word they walked away, away from the bank and the soldiers and the gunshot victims.

Jake Grafton lingered a moment, watching the soldiers check the people lying on the concrete. Then, with his hands in his pockets, he walked through the troops and along the street away from the square.

The soldier who fired the first shot was from a fishing village on the northern Chinese coast. Eighteen years old, he had been in the army for nearly two years. He had been in Hong Kong for two weeks and two days—he was counting the days so he could accurately report to his family when he next sat down with a scribe to dictate a letter. His name was Ng Choy, and now he was crying.

Sitting on the hard, clean, bloody pavement of the bank square, he couldn't stop the tears. The body of the man he had shot was lying beside him. In his panic Ng had triggered a burst of seven shots, all of which hit this middle-aged man in the chest. By some fluke, after the man was shot his heart continued beating for almost half a minute, pumping a prodigious quantity of blood out the bullet holes. The sticky mess was congealing now and turning dark.

Ng Choy didn't understand any of it. He didn't understand why he was here, what everyone had been shouting about, what the sergeant had wanted him to do, why this man had tried to wrestle him out of the way, and he didn't understand why he had shot him.

So he sat there, crying uncontrollably, while his fellow soldiers walked around him, carrying away the wounded and the dead.

Finally two soldiers picked up the corpse beside Ng, leaving him on the cold pavement with his rifle and the pool of sticky blood.

Rip Buckingham cradled the telephone automatically between his cheek and shoulder. "How many dead?" he asked the reporter on the line.

"Fifteen, the soldiers say. One woman died as they loaded her into the ambulance. At least forty more were injured by bullets. I estimate a dozen or two were trampled—it will be impossible to get an accurate count of the injured."

"Get to the bank officials. Find out why they wouldn't open the doors of the bank."

The story would be front-page news around the world, with a big, bold headline: 15 KILLED IN HONG KONG BY PLA TROOPS. The teaser under the main headline would read, *Crowd at Japanese Bank Fired Upon.*

Ten minutes later Rip was told, "I talked to a cashier. The officers of the bank are in a meeting and unavailable. The bank is insolvent. Tokyo refused to loan it any more money."

"*What?*"

"Yes. The Japanese are letting the bank fail. The word is Tokyo already poured twenty billion yen into it. Apparently that's the limit."

This story is growing by leaps and bounds, Rip thought.

He called a man he knew on a Japanese newspaper and asked for help. In twenty minutes the Tokyo newsman called back with confirmation from the Finance Ministry. The government of Japan had decided not to save the Bank of the Orient, a Japanese-owned bank headquartered in Hong Kong. After consultations with Finance Ministry officials, the Chinese authorities had elected not to intervene.

Rip looked at his watch. There was still time. He grabbed a notebook and his sports coat and headed for the door.

The army was cleaning up the mess in front of the Bank of the Orient, loading bodies in ambulances and the backs of army trucks. Rip stood watching for several minutes. There were few onlookers; the soldiers standing around didn't seem in the mood for gawkers. Yet because he wasn't Chinese, it was several minutes before the nearest soldier gestured for him to move on.

Rip went to the office tower entrance of the bank building and showed his press pass to the security guard. It took some talking and several hundred Hong Kong dollars, but eventually he managed to get into the executive suite on the fourth floor.

He explained to the receptionist that he wanted to talk to the president of the bank. He gave her his card: "Rip Buckingham, Managing Editor, *China Post,*" with the *China Post* lettering in the company's trademarked style.

The receptionist told him to take a seat.

He looked at the art on the walls and at the magazines on the table. He really didn't expect to see any bank officer. He thought it would be helpful to see the street in front of the bank again, see it knowing it was an important place, so he could visualize the scene the reporters were describing to him. And he had the time before deadline. So he was surprised when the receptionist appeared in the doorway and said, "Mr. Genda has a few minutes. Come this way, please."

Saburo Genda had a corner office. Through the window Rip caught a glimpse of the last army truck leaving. Except for a few police guards, the square was empty.

Genda was slumped in a large stuffed chair beside the desk with his back to the square. He didn't look up as Rip entered, didn't pay any attention to him until the Australian was seated across from him. He had Rip's card in his hand. He glanced at it.

"So, Mr. Buckingham," Genda said in accented English, "ask your questions."

The Japanese executive looked, Rip thought, like he had slept in his clothes. He had the fashionably gray hair, the dark power suit and tie, the trim waistline . . . and he looked exhausted, worn out.

"What happened, Mr. Genda?"

"They killed the bank."

"They? Who is they?" Rip asked as he wrote down the previous reply in shorthand.

"The Finance Ministry. They seized our assets in Japan. They refused to let us draw on those assets for the cash we need to operate on a daily basis. The news leaked out, there was a run on the bank . . . We are out of business, insolvent. The bank has," Genda took a deep breath and exhaled, "collapsed." He raised his arms and let them fall to the arms of the chair. He looked at his hands as if he had never seen them before.

"You are saying the Finance Ministry chose to put you out of business?"

"Yes."

"Do you know why?"

"They said it was the bad real estate loans."

"But I thought they have known about those loans for years."

"They have."

"Then . . ."

"Someone in Japan made a decision, Mr. Buckingham. I don't know who or why. The decision was to make the bank fail."

"Make it fail? You mean allow it to fail."

"No, sir. When the Finance Ministry seized our Japanese assets, the

Ministry forced the bank to close its doors. There was no way it could stay open. They took a course of action that made the failure of the bank inevitable."

Rip made a careful note of Genda's exact words.

"Mr. Genda, I have heard that the Bank of the Orient refused the Chinese government's demands for low-interest loans. If the bank had made those loans, would it have failed today?"

Genda tried mightily to keep a straight face. He started to answer the question, then thought better of it. He lowered his head. He seemed to be focused inward, no longer aware of Rip's presence.

Rip tried one more question, then rose and left the office. He pulled the door shut behind him.

CHAPTER THREE

"Tell me again about Tiger Cole," Callie Grafton said to her husband. They were eating lunch on the balcony of their hotel room. Jake had related his adventure at the bank square this morning and the fact that Tommy Carmellini had dropped by for breakfast.

"I remember you and Tiger flew a plane from the carrier into Cubi Point during the final months of the Vietnam War," Callie said, "and I went to the Philippines to meet you. I remember meeting him at the airport when you showed me the plane before you left."

Jake nodded. He, too, remembered. "A few weeks after that we were shot down," he said.

"As I recall," Callie said, "he was tall, silent, intense."

"That was Tiger. He never had much to say, but when he did, people listened."

She had been a junior translator at the U.S. consulate in Hong Kong in those days. And now Tiger Cole was the consul general. Who would have guessed?

"Tiger broke his back in the ejection," Jake continued, recalling days he hadn't thought about in years. "After we were rescued he spent a long time in the hospital, then they sent him to Pensacola for rehabilitation. He finally said to hell with it and pulled the plug. I think he went back to college in California, got a master's in something or other, then got involved in the computer industry."

"I lost his address about ten years ago," Callie explained. "He sent us Christmas cards, then we moved or he moved or whatever."

Jake Grafton chuckled. "Sometimes life deals you an ace. Last month *Fortune* magazine said he was in on the ground floor of three big high-tech start-ups."

"And now he's the consul general," Callie said distractedly. "Why do you want me to translate this tape?"

Jake summarized his morning conversation with Carmellini while Callie finished her salad. "The tape may contain something worth knowing. China Bob was a rainmaker, a wheeler-dealer who played every angle he could find. Something on that tape might shed some light on what is happening in this town."

"You mean on what the Americans are doing to help make it happen?"

"If they are."

"This CIA officer, Carmellini? Do you trust him?"

"I met him last year in Cuba," Jake explained. "He was working with a CIA officer who was subsequently killed. The dead officer told me Carmellini was a safecracker before the CIA recruited him."

"That doesn't sound like anything I'd want on my résumé," Callie shot back.

"It may not take all kinds, but we sure as hell got all kinds."

"Are we going to do this tonight?"

"I don't know. Whenever Carmellini shows up with a tape player."

"I certainly don't want to sit around this hotel room all evening waiting for him."

"I didn't say we should."

"Why don't you call Tiger Cole, invite him to go to dinner with us?"

"You think he'd go?" Jake asked dubiously.

"For heaven's sake, of course he'd go! Unless he has another commitment, then he'd probably want to set something up for tomorrow. Call him. Tell him you're in town and want to have dinner. I always thought you saved his life after you two were shot down."

"That's true," Jake admitted. "But he's the consul general and pretty busy and—"

"You're a two-star admiral in Uncle Sam's navy, Jake Grafton. You can buy a drink anywhere on this planet."

Rip Buckingham was about ready to send the bank story to the makeup room when he received a telephone call from the governor's office.

"This is Governor Sun's assistant, Mr. Buckingham. Your newspaper is running story about tragedy in front of Bank of Orient? This morning?"

"Yes."

"Governor Sun Siu Ki has issued statement. Statement go in story."

The aide's English was almost impossible to follow, so Rip replied in Cantonese. "Read it to me," he said, trying to keep the dejection out of his voice.

"A crowd of justly outraged citizens gathered this morning at the Bank of the Orient to withdraw their money panicked when bank officials shamefully failed to open their doors," said the aide, reading slowly. "In the rioting that followed, several people were killed by the gallant soldiers of the People's Liberation Army while they were restoring order. The officials of the Bank of the Orient will be held responsible for this tragedy. . . ."

There were several paragraphs more, and as the governor's assistant dictated in Cantonese, Rip wrote it down in English, in his own private shorthand. He read it back to ensure he had it, then quickly typed out the statement on his computer. He put a note above the statement for the front-page editor, directing him to put the governor's statement in a box in the center of the page. However, he didn't change a word of his story, which gave the facts, without comment, as they had been gathered by his reporters.

When he had sent the story for the *China Post* on its electronic way, he called it up again and made some changes. His fingers flew over the keyboard, changing the slant of the story, trying to capture the despair of Saburo Genda and the hopelessness of the crowd waiting for money that rightfully belonged to them and would never be paid. He also tried to capture the callousness of the soldiers who used deadly weapons on defenseless people.

When he had finished this story, he E-mailed it and the governor's statement to the Buckingham newspapers worldwide. The *China Post* was owned by Buckingham Newspapers, Ltd., of which Rip's father, Richard, was chairman and CEO. Richard Buckingham started with one newspaper in Adelaide at the end of World War II, and as he liked to tell it, with hard work, grit, determination, perseverance, and a generous helping of OPM—other people's money—built a newsprint empire that covered the globe. Richard still held a bit under sixty percent of the stock, which was not publicly traded. A series of romantic misadventures had spread the rest of the shares far and wide; even Rip had a smidgen under five percent.

Thirty minutes after Rip E-mailed the story to Sydney, the telephone rang. It was his father.

"Sounds like Hong Kong is heating up," Richard growled.

"It is."

"When are you going to pack it in?"

"We've had this conversation before, Dad."

"We have. And we are going to keep having it. Sometimes in the middle of the night I wake up in a sweat, thinking of you rotting in some Communist prison because you went off your nut and told the truth in print about those sewer rats."

"All politicians are sewer rats, not just ours."

"I'm going to quote you on that."

"Go right ahead."

"So when?"

"I don't know that my wife or mother-in-law will ever leave, Dad. This is their place. These are their people."

"No, Rip. *You* are their people. You are the husband and son-in-law, and in China that counts for just about everything. You make the decision and they will go along with it. You *know* that."

"What about the *Post?*"

"I'll send someone else to run it. Maybe put it up for sale."

"Nobody is going to pay you serious money for a newspaper in Communist China, Dad. Not here, not now."

"We'll see. You never had a head for business, Rip. You are a damned good newspaperman, though, a rare talent. You come to Sydney, I'll give you any editorial job in the company except mine, which you'll get anyway in a few years."

"I'll think it over."

"The thought of you in one of those prisons, eating rats . . . Oh, well." Without waiting for a response, his father hung up.

The massacre in front of the Bank of the Orient was the hot topic of conversation among the American Culture conference attendees during the afternoon break. One of Callie Grafton's fellow faculty members told her about it as she watched the attendees whispering furiously and gesturing angrily. Three or four of them were trying to whisper into cell phones. Callie didn't tell her informant that Jake had been in the crowd in front of the bank and had given her an eyewitness account at lunch.

At least twenty people were killed, the faculty member said, a figure that stunned Callie. Jake hadn't mentioned that people were killed, only that there had been some shooting. Obviously he didn't want her to worry. "Ridiculous to worry, after the fact," he would say, and grin that grin he always grinned when the danger was past.

Through the years Jake had wound up in more than his share of dangerous situations. She had thought those days behind her when he was promoted to flag rank. An admiral might go down with his ship, it was true, in a really big war, but who was having really big wars these days? In today's world admirals sat in offices and pushed paper. And yet . . . somehow this morning Jake wound up in the middle of a shooting riot!

Perhaps we should go home, Callie mused, and then remembered with a jolt that Jake was here for a reason and couldn't leave.

She tried to forget riots and bodies and her husband's nose for trouble and concentrate on the conference.

Unfortunately, one of the attendees was a government official, a political officer sent to take notes of the questions and answers and jot down the names of any Chinese who might be "undermining the implementation of the laws," in the phrase the official used to explain his presence to the faculty.

This official was a bald, middle-aged party apparatchik, a generation removed from most of the attendees, who were students in their early to mid-twenties. The first day Callie Grafton found herself fixating on the man's facial expressions when any student stood to ask a question.

Angry at herself for feeling intimidated, she still had to carefully phrase her comments. While she could not be prosecuted for political deviancy, her participation in the conference could be terminated by this official on the spot. That sanction was used the very first day against a political science professor from Cornell. Callie was ready to pick up her notebook and follow him out the door, then decided a precipitous leave-taking would not be fair to the students, who came to hear her comments on American culture.

That first evening Callie remarked to Jake, "Maybe taking part in this conference was a mistake."

"Maybe," he agreed, "but neither of us thought so when the State Department came up with the invitation." State had procured a conference faculty invitation for Callie as a cover for the Graftons' presence in Hong Kong. "Don't be intimidated," Jake continued. "Answer the students' questions as best you can, and if the organizers give you the boot we'll see the sights for the rest of our stay. No big deal."

Today after the break, the questions concerned the American banking system. Hu Chiang had asked questions often during the last three days, and he was ready when the room fell silent.

"Mrs. Grafton," he asked in Chinese, the only language in use during the conference, "who decides to whom an American bank will lend its money?"

Hu was tall, more muscular than the average Chinese youth, Callie thought, which made him a fairly typical Hong Kong young adult, most of whom had enjoyed better nutrition while growing up than their mainland Chinese peers.

"The bank lending committee," Callie answered.

"The government gives the committee guidance?"

"No. Government sets the financial standards the banks must adhere to, but with only minor exceptions, the banks loan money to people and enterprises that are most capable of paying back the loan with interest, thereby earning profits for the owners of the bank."

This colloquy continued for several minutes as the party boss grew more and more uncomfortable. Finally, without even glancing at the listening official, Hu asked, "In your opinion, Mrs. Grafton, can capitalism exist in a society that lacks political freedom?"

The official sprang from his seat, turned to face Hu, and pointed his finger. "I can sit silently no longer. That question is a provocation, an insult to the state. You attempt to destroy that which you do not understand. We have the weapons to smash those who plot evil." He turned toward Callie. "Ignore the provocations of the criminal elements," he ordered peremptorily, closing the discussion. Then he sat heavily and used a cloth to wipe his face.

Callie was trembling. Although she could speak the language, she felt the strangeness of the culture acutely. She was also worried that she might somehow say something to jeopardize the conference or the people who had invited her.

"Mr. Hu merely asked my opinion," Callie said, trying to hold her voice steady. "I will answer the question."

The official's face reddened and his jowls quivered. "Go," he roared at her, half rising from his seat and pointing toward the door. "You insult China with your disrespectful attitude."

Callie gathered her purse and headed for the door. As she walked she addressed her questioner, Hu Chiang, who was still standing in the audience. "The answer to your question, Mr. Hu, is no. Political freedom and economic freedom are sides of the same coin; they cannot exist independently of each other."

"I got thrown out," she told Jake when she unlocked the hotel room door and found him on the balcony reading.

"I thought you would, sooner or later," he said and grinned broadly. "Still glad we came?"

She slumped on the side of the bed and held her head in her hands.

Jake put his arms around her. "Hey, I called the consulate. Tiger Cole wants us to come to dinner tomorrow night."

"I told you so," Callie Grafton said through her tears, then tried to smile.

Removing the tape player that would play the miniature tape he had taken from China Bob's library from the tech shop in the basement of the consulate presented Tommy Carmellini with several problems, the most intractable of which was that the device could not be in two places at once. Kerry Kent had access to the office. Carmellini thought that if she chose to look for the player while it was missing, she would realize that Carmellini had lied to her, that he didn't trust her. She might even conclude that she was a possible suspect in China Bob's murder.

The problem was that the tape player was a unique device that played a nonstandard small tape that held up to eight hours of recording, so Carmellini couldn't hope to buy one over the counter at a gadget shop.

Tommy Carmellini thought about all of this as he stood in the small shop staring at the one serviceable tape player. Or was there only one? The room was chock-full of electronic components and gizmos, perhaps he just didn't know what was there. He began searching under the workbench, then worked his way to the large steel filing cabinets that stood against the back wall.

Aha! On the top of the cabinet behind an obsolete commercial Sanyo reel-to-reel tape player was another small player that looked as if it could handle the tape from China Bob's. He got it down, blew the dust off it, sat it beside the first one. Yes. The same model, controls, etc. He plugged the thing in and found a tape in one of the drawers that looked like it would fit. When he had the tape properly installed on the reels, he pushed the Play button.

Nothing. The thing was broken.

Without a qualm, he put the working machine in his attaché case and left the broken one in its place. There were several headsets lying around, so he selected one and tossed it into the case, too.

He found Kerry writing a report in the office the CIA officers used. The senior man was there, Bubba Lee, schmoozing with two of the other permanent men, George Wang and Carson Eisenberg. All three were Chinese-Americans; Lee and Wang had two Chinese parents, Eisenberg had a Chinese mother. All could speak perfect Cantonese and pass for natives, which they often did. This morning they wanted to shoot the breeze about Harold Barnes, who had been in Hong Kong for only a couple of months before he was killed.

"I went to the police department this morning," Eisenberg told Tommy, "to see if they have developed any leads on Barnes. They were all atwitter over China Bob's murder last night. You and Kerry got out of there just in time. They kept everyone else until dawn, including Mr. Cole."

"Did they ever find the murder weapon?"

"Little automatic, nickel-plated?"

"Could have been."

"Found it in the secretary's office just outside the library, in the trash can."

"That makes sense," Kerry Kent said. "If I had just shot someone, I would want to get rid of the weapon as soon as possible."

Tommy Carmellini stared at her in amazement. She was either ditsy or had more brass than any broad he had ever run across.

Lee and the others spent a very pleasant half hour going over the Chan layout with Tommy, speculating about motives, generally rehashing everything, and reaching no conclusions.

Then, finally, the men returned to their offices, closed their doors, unlocked their private safes, and got on with the business of covert and overt espionage, leaving Carmellini to the gentle company of the British transplant, Kerry Kent.

"I wonder who has the tape," she said. "Barnes was always such a careful workman. One must assume the device worked and someone swiped the tape."

Carmellini shrugged.

"One has to assume," she continued, "that the tape is the key to the mystery."

"If you think I have it, you're barking at the wrong dog," he said.

She came over to the desk where he was sitting, squatted so her face was level with his. No more than twelve inches separated them. "You can trust me, you know."

"So you think I have it."

"I don't think you trust me."

"Whatever would give you that impression? I've known you three whole days . . . no, four now. Four delightful days of humdrum work and one evening of romance lite. You kissed me what? Twice? I trust you as much as you trust me."

"I never mix business and pleasure."

"So there's no hope for us? Wait until my mother hears the news; she had such high hopes. Now get up off the floor and go sit in a chair. A woman kneeling before me will give people the wrong impression and create a tragic precedent."

Kerry did as he asked.

"What I'd like to know," he said, "is how many people paraded through that library before and after me, looked over China Bob's corpse, then went back to the party and didn't say a word to anyone."

"This morning a request came in from the chairman of the congressional committee," she informed him. "Congress invited China Bob to Washington to testify."

"All expenses paid, no doubt."

"The poor man is probably better off dead," Kerry said firmly. "His position between the Chinese and the Americans was going to get scorching hot."

"Whoever shot him did him a real favor," Carmellini agreed. He picked up his attaché case and walked out of the office.

"I had just graduated from college when I first came to Hong Kong," Callie Grafton told her husband as they walked the streets of Kowloon, taking in the sights, sounds, and smells. "I felt like I had finally come to the center of the earth's civilization, the place where all the currents and tides came together.

"I remember my first ride on the Star Ferry as if it were yesterday. The white-and-green boat was *Morning Star*, very propitious, you must agree, for a girl making her way in the world for the very first time. All of the thirty-nine-ton double-ended diesel boats are named for stars, and between them made four hundred and twenty crossings a day between Kowloon and Central. Each crossing took about ten minutes, regardless of the weather or sea conditions. The boats began running at six-thirty in the morning and stopped at eleven-thirty at night. There were two classes of passengers—first class, which rode on the upper deck, and second, which rode on the main deck.

"Everyone who lived or worked or visited Hong Kong rode on these ferries. On days off I would ride the ferries a dozen times a day, looking at the people and listening to them talk, laugh, cry, giggle. . . . Chinese laborers and wealthy merchants and sons and daughters and wives and mistresses and teenage toughs, English civil servants and nannies, Australian adventurers, tourists from everywhere on earth, Europeans, Russians, American sailors, Malays, Filipino maids, Japanese businessmen, Hindus, Sikhs—everyone came to Hong Kong, to make money and a new life for themselves or just to see it, to learn the truth of it. All the roads of the earth lead to this place.

"I loved the city. It was British, colonial, civilized, grand and trivial, yet it wasn't. It was Chinese, but not quite. It was timeless, yet everyone was in a hurry and the city was being transformed before my eyes.

"From this city I could feel the power of China, the thousand million people, the ancient and the new, the way of the seeded earth. I came to think of China as a giant oak, deeply rooted and enduring through the centuries while the lives of men changed like the seasons.

"In this city I can still feel the pulse of the earth. I can stand in the crowded places and listen to the hundreds of voices, all babbling about the things that fill human lives. I can hear the generations talking of the things that never change, the dreams, ambitions, and concerns that make us human."

Jake Grafton squeezed his wife's hand, and they walked on.

Rip Buckingham's brother-in-law, Wu Tai Kwong, was a delivery driver for the Double Happy Fortune Cookie Company. Rip was happily married and living in Hong Kong when he learned that his wife's younger brother was involved in the anti-Communist movement in Beijing. The whole thing seemed innocent enough . . . until that same brother-in-law stood in front of the tank in Tiananmen Square in 1989 and had his photo plastered on every front page in the world. That incident made him a criminal. And a dedicated revolutionary.

Now, of course, he was a fugitive . . . and living in Rip's basement. Although he was a notorious political criminal and the object of the greatest manhunt in Chinese history, the government had no idea what Wu looked like now, where he was from, who his family was, or what name or names he might be using. Perhaps this was to be expected in a nation where public records were spotty at best, a nation where a significant portion of the population was illiterate and without identity papers of any kind, a nation with more than a hundred million migrants who roamed at will, looking for work.

Still, the Chinese authorities knew with an absolute certainty that sooner or later they would get their man. They had offered a large reward for Wu Tai Kwong. Human nature being what it is, they had merely to wait until someone betrayed him.

Wu Tai Kwong, being who he was, was not hiding. True, he wasn't broadcasting his whereabouts and he was using a false name and false identity papers, but he had no intention of stopping his political activities. He hated the Communists and intended to destroy them or be destroyed by them, whichever way fate spun out the story.

The tale could go either way, he realized. Someone who knew or suspected who he might be would tell someone, and so on, and the rumors would spread like ripples in a pond. Still, Wu had to talk to his friends, had to plan, to plot, to conspire against those he hated. He did so knowing that any day could be his very last, for he knew that once the Communists caught him they would execute him quickly, then broadcast the news of their triumph.

This afternoon he stopped his delivery van at various corners on Nathan Road and picked up the solitary people standing there waiting. He picked up four men and a woman in this manner, then found a quiet place to park near the old Kai Tak airport. These people knew him, knew his real name, knew the risks he took, and he trusted them with his life. Since they literally held his life in their hands, they also trusted him.

Today this "gang of six" discussed the current situation, the public anger at the failure of the Bank of the Orient, the predictable resentment against the PLA for shooting into an unsuspecting crowd.

"Is this the spark? Is now the hour?"

They debated the question hotly.

To overthrow the Communists, Wu Tai Kwong had argued for years, two things must come to pass. The great mass of people must be aroused against the government, and the army must refuse to fight the people.

"There are things still to be done," Hu Chiang argued. "We are almost ready, but not quite."

"The police know far too much," the woman replied. Alas, keeping the existence of a large subversive organization a total secret was impossible. People whispered, some tried to sell information to the authorities, others wanted to betray their colleagues and the movement for reasons that ran the gamut of human emotions. "There are too many leaks, too many people talking. We must wait no longer. Every day we wait the danger grows, yet we grow only marginally stronger."

"We are bribing the police," one man pointed out when his turn to talk came. "Every day the number of people who want money grows. It is inevitable that someone will take a bribe and turn us in . . . if they haven't called Beijing already. We must act now!"

Wu waved them into silence. "There is another factor. The Americans suspect that the American consul, Cole, has moved money into Hong Kong. They are trying to trace the money, find out where it went. China Bob Chan is dead, but the trail is not cold. If we wait too long, the Americans may decide to tell Beijing what they know . . . or suspect."

"So that is the decision?" Hu Chiang demanded.

"I will not make the decision," Wu told them. "We will vote. Now."

Only Hu Chiang voted to wait.

"Then it is decided," Wu told them. Even Hu looked relieved that the waiting was over, he thought.

"The longest journey begins with the first step. Let us begin."

As he started the van to drive away, Wu remarked, "We must win or die."

"Win or die," they murmured.

The house where the Buckinghams lived perched precariously on the side of the mountainous spine of Hong Kong Island, just below the Victoria Peak tram station. From it one had a magnificent view of the central business district, Kowloon, and the harbor.

The roof of the building was flat. Paved with tile and equipped with lawn chairs and sun umbrellas, it made a wonderful patio on almost any day clouds did not obscure the sun. At the head of the staircase was a small room with large windows that Lin Pe, Rip's mother-in-law, used as a greenhouse.

When he got home, Rip found his wife, Sue Lin Buckingham, on the roof sitting under an umbrella, reading. He removed a cold beer from the refrigerator in the greenhouse and sagged into a lawn chair beside her. As he summed up the events of the day, his wife put down her book and listened in silence.

Sue Lin was a rarity, a highly educated Chinese woman. She had never known her father, who died before she was born. Her mother made a small fortune in fortune cookies and insisted that her daughter get an education. Sue Lin spent her teenage years at a private school in California, then got bachelor's and master's degrees from the University of California at Berkeley.

Rip Buckingham, Australian bum and Chinese aficionado, fell for her the very first time he saw her. She had not been similarly smitten, but he persisted. Eventually he won her heart, a triumph that he still regarded as the great accomplishment of his life. She was, he thought, the most gracious lady he had ever met.

This evening she listened in silence to Rip's narrative of the Bank of the Orient debacle and his summary of Governor Sun's statement.

"The statement was really an order telling you how to write the story, wasn't it?"

"Yes, I suppose." Rip took a big swallow of beer, then stared glumly at his toes.

"The government may shut down the newspaper. You've been expecting it."

"I know. I just kept hoping it wouldn't happen." He swept his hand at the city before them. "This is our city, our place. We have done nothing wrong. The paper merely prints the news in a fair, unbiased manner. What's wrong with that?"

Sue Lin didn't reply. "Perhaps they won't shut you down."

Rip sipped some more beer. "It's time we thought about leaving."

"We can go anytime," his wife responded without enthusiasm. They both held Australian passports. "But I don't want to go without Mother. You know that. And Mother won't leave Hong Kong."

"She always said she wouldn't leave, sure, but this place is going to explode," Rip argued. It was hell trying to use logic on women who didn't want to hear it. "This isn't the city that it used to be. She *must* see that! And she had money in the Bank of the Orient. In the middle of listening to the reporters and writing the story, that thought ran through my head."

"Money or no money, she won't leave without my brother. Absolutely not."

"I guarantee you he won't leave alive. Not a chance in hell."

"He's all she has from her early life."

"Bull! She has both of you! I know there were three other children, but that was thirty-some years ago. They are adults with children of their own or they're dead."

"Rip, you don't understand."

"I *do* understand. And I think it's time your mother listened to reason. When this place explodes, your brother is going to be leading the revolution. The government is going to figure out who he is—who his mother is, who his sister is, who his brother-in-law is. While Wu is busy answering destiny's call, the Communists are going to put you, me, and your mother against the wall and shoot us dead. *We're running out of time!* If we don't leave we'll die here. We've *got* to get the hell out of China!"

"Don't be ugly."

"Why don't you listen to reason?"

Sue Lin held out her hand. He took it.

"Our world is coming apart," Rip told her. "Everything is cracking, breaking, shattering into thousands of pieces. I feel helpless, doomed. At any second the great quake will come and this little world where you and I have been so happy is going to cease to exist."

Tears ran down her cheeks. She turned her back on him and wiped them away.

They were sitting side by side, holding hands and looking at the city, when the cook called from the greenhouse and told them dinner was ready.

CHAPTER FOUR

Tommy Carmellini was waiting in their hotel room when the Graftons returned after dinner. He was sitting in the darkness well back from the window.

"Did the maid let you in?" Jake asked sharply.

"No, sir. I let myself in. I didn't want the staff to know I was here."

"Next time wait in the lobby."

"Right."

"Callie, this is Tommy Carmellini."

"Mrs. Grafton, you can call me Jack Carrigan. That's the name I travel under."

"So you have two names, Mr. Carmellini?"

"Sometimes more," he admitted, grinning.

"Most people are stuck with only one," Callie said, "the one their parents picked for them. It must be nice to have a name that you pick yourself and can toss when you tire of it."

"That *is* one of the advantages," Carmellini agreed cheerfully.

"I brought the tape player." He gestured toward the bed, where the device rested. "I don't speak Chinese. To me it just sounds like a bunch of birds twittering."

Jake flipped on the rest of the lights as Callie seated herself on the bed across from Carmellini. She eyed the tape player distastefully. "What's on the tape?" she asked.

Carmellini leaned forward and looked into her eyes. "A CIA officer was murdered just hours after he planted two bugs and a recorder in the library of a man named China Bob Chan. Two nights ago China Bob was shot and killed in that library by a party unknown. I got there before the body cooled and took the tape from the recorder. That tape is probably the best evidence of the identity of the person who killed Chan. In fact, it may be the only evidence we'll ever get. It also might shed some light on who killed the CIA officer."

"You told Jake that Tiger Cole, the consul general, might have killed Chan."

"Mrs. Grafton, anyone in Hong Kong could have gone into that library and shot China Bob."

Callie glanced at Jake, who said nothing.

"The recorder was voice-activated," Carmellini explained, "so that valuable space on the tape wouldn't be wasted recording the street noises that penetrated an empty room. When the sound level dropped below the electronic threshold, the tape would play on for a few seconds, then stop. Places on the tape where the recorder stopped were marked as audible clicks."

"We'll play it later," Jake Grafton said in a tone that settled the issue.

"Sure." Carmellini rose to go. "Nice to meet you, Mrs. Grafton."

Callie merely nodded.

Buckingham Lin Su, or as she wrote it in the Western style, Sue Lin Buckingham, found her mother, Lin Pe, in her study consulting her fortune book. Lin Pe lived in her own three-room apartment in the Buckinghams' house. Just now she was smoking a cigarette which she had fixed in a short black plastic holder. The smoke rising from the cigarette made her squint behind the thick lenses of her glasses.

Sue Lin broke the news. The Bank of the Orient had collapsed, failing to open its doors today. Depositors trying to withdraw their money had been fired upon by soldiers.

Lin Pe took the news pretty well, Sue Lin thought, considering that her company kept all its accounts at the Japanese bank because it paid the highest interest rates in Hong Kong.

Lin Pe listened, nodded, and when Sue Lin left, got the accountant's latest summary from her desk and studied it.

The Double Happy Fortune Cookie Company, Ltd., was a profitable international concern because of one person—Lin Pe. Thirty years ago when she came to Hong Kong from a village north of Canton, she found a job in a factory that baked fortune cookies for export to America. Before she went to work there she had never even heard of a fortune cookie. The little fortunes printed on rice paper inside the cookies charmed her. She wrote some in Chinese and one day showed her creations to the owner, an alcoholic old Dutchman from Indonesia who also mixed the cookie batter and cleaned up the place at night, if he was sober enough. He translated a few, they went into the cookies, and Lin Pe had found a home.

When the Dutchman died five years later of cirrhosis of the liver, she bought the company from his heirs. It thrived, because Lin Pe was a very astute businesswoman and because the fortunes she put into her cookies were the best in the business.

About three dozen fortunes were in use at the cookie factory at any one time. Writing good fortunes was a difficult business. She was hard put to come up with three or four good new ones per month, which meant some of the old ones had to be used again. Lin Pe kept a book, her "book of fortunes," in which was recorded every fortune she had ever written and notations on what months it had been used. She changed the fortunes going into the cookies on a monthly basis.

Just now she put down the accountant's summary and consulted the fortune list she had constructed for use next month.

"Happiness will find you soon." She had used this fortune before and thought it one of her best. Other cookie people wrote "You will find happiness," but that was bland, without wit or snap. Lin Pe sent the happiness searching for you.

"Your true love is closer than you think." Love, Americans seem enamored with it. Many of the letters she received from restaurant owners in America pleaded with her to use more love fortunes in her cookies. Lin Pe had never been in love herself, so to write these fortunes she had to imagine what it might be like. This was becoming more and more difficult as the years passed.

"Beware . . . use great care in the days ahead." When she saw this fortune in her book, she inhaled sharply.

It was her fortune.

One cookie in three thousand contained that fortune. Yesterday she plucked a cookie off the conveyor belt as it was about to go into the packing machine, and that was the fortune inside.

She closed the book, unable to continue. She shivered involuntarily, then sat staring out the window.

Rip Buckingham disliked the Communists, and her son Wu hated them. Neither knew them like Lin Pe did, for she had lived through the Great Cultural Revolution. Occasionally she still awoke in the middle of the night with the stench of burning houses and flesh in her nostrils, listening for the shouts, the sobs, the screams. She had fled to Hong Kong to escape that madness; now the storm seemed to be gathering again out there in the darkness. She could feel its presence.

The money. Its loss was a disaster, of course, but perhaps the Japanese could be shamed into paying it back. The neat little men with their perfect haircuts and creased trousers must know the importance of keeping faith with their customers, even if the law didn't require it.

The cookie company could run a few days without writing checks. Lin Pe began considering whom she might borrow money from to meet the payroll. Rip and Sue Lin had plenty of money and would have loaned her all she wanted without giving it a thought, but Lin Pe was too proud even to consider that course of action. Amazingly, the possibility never crossed her mind. From her desk drawer she removed a private list of her fellow businesspeople and studied that.

Rip Buckingham's idea of the perfect way to spend an evening was to loaf in a lawn chair on his roof reading newspapers from all over the world as he sipped beer and listened to music. Occasionally he would pause to watch a ship slip through the harbor on its way to or from the open sea.

Hong Kong didn't have enough dock facilities, so many of the freighters had their cargo on- and off-loaded onto lighters, which were towed back and forth between their anchorages and the ships by tugboats. Flotillas of ferryboats were in constant motion crossing and recrossing the strait, fuel boats cruised for customers, tour and party boats dashed about, here and there someone sculled a sampan through the heaving ridges of waves and wakes.

Rip was not enjoying the view tonight.

He finished with a Beijing newspaper and threw it onto the pile with the Hong Kong dailies. He grabbed a Sydney paper and started flipping though it.

The problem was that he liked being a newspaperman. He liked going to the office, saying hello to everyone, reading the wire service stories, tapping away on his computer as the cursor danced along, then seeing it all in print. He liked holding the paper in his hand, liked the heft of it, liked the way that it felt cool to the touch. He liked the smell of newsprint and ink, liked the idea of trying to catch the world every day on a pound of paper. A newspaper was worth doing, and Rip Buckingham didn't want to do anything else.

And he wanted to keep doing it here. In Hong Kong.

He was still stewing, and trying to get into last Sunday's *Washington Post*, when his wife came through the greenhouse leading two men. Rip recognized them immediately—Sonny Wong and Yuri Daniel.

Wong Ma Chow, "Sonny," was a gangster, the leader of the last of the tongs. He made a huge fortune in Hong Kong real estate, then lost it in the collapse that followed the British departure. Since then he had returned to the service business. Whatever service you wanted, Sonny could provide . . . for a price.

Rip had seen Yuri Daniel, Sonny's associate, around town for four or five years. Rip had never before had any dealings with him, nor had he wanted to. Yuri was a Russian or Ukrainian or something like that, reportedly from one of those hopelessly poor, squalid villages in the middle of the vast Eastern European plain. Rumor had it that he left the mother country in a large hurry with a suitcase full of money taken at gunpoint from a Russian mobster. How much truth was in the rumor was impossible to say, but it was a nice rumor.

Yuri's expressionless face, with its cold, blank eyes and pallid features, certainly didn't inspire trust. Inspecting it at close range, Rip idly wondered why Sonny chose to be in the same room with Yuri Daniel.

"Hey, Sonny."

"Hey, mate. What do you hear on the Bank of the Orient thing?"

"At least fifteen dead."

"The lid is gonna blow off this place. People aren't going to take this lying down. Even I had money in that goddamn thing."

"Tea? Beer?"

"Beer would be great."

Sue Lin was still there, and now she nodded at Rip and went for the refrigerator.

"First time I've been up here," Sonny said, surveying the view from a chair beside Rip. "Hell of a view you got here, yessir. Hell of a view. You're right up here with the upper crust, looking down on the world."

Yuri sat on Sonny's other side, turned slightly away from the two of them. He hadn't yet said a word.

Sue Lin brought the beer, then left them. She paused at the door of the greenhouse and looked back, catching Rip's eye. She raked her windblown hair from her eyes, then went in, closing the door behind her.

"... owned a building just below here some years back," Sonny was saying. He pointed. "That one right there, with the little garden on the roof. The value of that building went up to four times what I paid for it. I was collecting fabulous rents every month, then it all just ... just melted away, like ice cream in the noonday sun."

"Yeah."

"One day, the whole thing ..." He sighed.

Rip sipped a beer. Sue Lin had brought one for each of them. Yuri was looking at the ships in the harbor to the west.

"I always liked this view," Sonny said. "Always."

"Yeah."

"These are the last days of Hong Kong, Rip. It's coming to an end."

Rip didn't say anything to that. What was there to say?

"Got your message that you wanted me to drop by. So what can Wong and Associates do for the scion of the Buckingham clan?"

"China Bob Chan."

"Too bad, huh?"

"Got any ideas on who might have done it?"

"It wasn't me, Rip."

"Hey, Sonny. If I thought there was the slightest possibility, I would have respected your privacy. What I'm after is any background or insight you might be able to provide, not for attribution, of course. What was China Bob into?"

"You've been following the American thing ... ?" Sonny began. "The PLA was giving him money to contribute to American political campaigns. Don't ask me why. The generals think the American po-

liticos are as crooked as Chinese politicians. And they may be right—
there was a guy in the American embassy in Beijing who was handing
out visas to the United States to anyone who said he would go over
there and contribute to the president's reelection campaign."

"Uh-huh."

"Chan was into the usual stuff here. And he was big into smuggling
people, which I won't touch. It's too dirty for me, Rip, but not for
China Bob."

"Where to?"

"Anywhere. Malaysia, Australia, America, anywhere people wanted
to go, China Bob would do the deal. Course he didn't always deliver—
it's a smelly business."

"Did he do passports?"

"S.A.R. passports, but no one wanted those," Wong said. Hong Kong
became a Special Administrative Region of China in 1997 when the
British turned over the colony. "I heard that for the right price—and
the right price was very high—China Bob could produce genuine passports. That's not generally known around, I believe."

"Was he doing that a lot, do you think?"

"No country I know about is granting visas to people holding S.A.R.
passports, so there isn't a lot of demand for those. The refugee problem
has these other countries scared silly. The old British colonial passports
are a dreg on the market—you can't get into America or Australia or
Singapore or Indonesia or anyplace I know with one of those. Even
Britain is worried about tens of thousands of Chinese refugees flooding
in. No one is granting entry visas."

Rip sipped some more on his beer and waited.

"Guy like China Bob had a lot of deals going," Sonny said, thinking
aloud. "The guy who sold China Bob blank American passports will
deal with me, if you want. Faking an Australian visa on an American
passport shouldn't be a problem."

"You and China Bob were sorta competitors, weren't you?"

Sonny bristled slightly at that remark. "Our businesses paralleled
each other at times," he admitted. "There was room for both of us."

"You're talking a forged passport?"

"Genuine. The real thing, right out of the lock box at the consulate.
The source is very reliable."

"Uh-huh."

"He's not honest, you understand, but he is reliable. That's a critical difference in business, one so few people appreciate."

"I think I see it," Rip told Sonny, who nodded as if he were pleased.

"I put the passport with Australian entry visa in your hands," Sonny explained. "You take your Chinese relative to the airport, put her on Qantas to Sydney. She breezes through immigration at both ends. Guaranteed."

"How much?"

"Twenty grand American. Cash. Half in advance, half on delivery of the documents."

Rip whistled. "Is that what China Bob was into?"

"He did a little of that. And he brought stuff in. He could get import permits for darn near anything; anything he couldn't get a permit for he could smuggle in. Money, import, smuggling—those were his main businesses, but he did some people, too. For fifty grand he could put your cousin on a freighter going to the United States. The Philippines were a real bargain, though, only about four thousand. Your cousin would be in a locked container with some other passengers. He'd have to take his own food and water with him, but he wouldn't get a sunburn. About eight days at sea, five hundred a day. Hell, Rip, it would cost more money than that to send him on a cruise ship."

"The passengers didn't always get there, though," Rip pointed out.

"Rip, I just couldn't say. Dumping the cargo at sea—something like that the people involved don't talk about. Oh, you hear whispers, but people like to whisper. Gives them something to do."

Rip waved away that possibility. He knew those kinds of things were happening, but he really didn't believe China Bob had gotten his hands that filthy for the paltry dollars involved.

Rip glanced at the Russian. On the other hand, Yuri looked like he would cheerfully cut your throat for cigarette money.

"Was Bob into Chinese politics, do you think?"

"Hey, Rip, I don't think the guy intentionally set out to die young."

"Well, he figured wrong somewhere, that's for sure."

"Everyone makes mistakes occasionally. Even China Bob."

"Think someone double-crossed him, one of his associates maybe?"

"I doubt if somebody shot him to get his wife. Wives being what they are, not too many people kill to get one. To get rid of one, yes." Wong snorted at his own wit. When the noises stopped, he said, "A double cross is likely. Though if I were a betting man, I would put my money on the PLA. Rumor had it Bob might go to America, embarrass a lot of important people." He shrugged.

"Thanks for coming by tonight, Sonny."

"Okay. Now tell me the real reason you called."

"I enjoy seeing your smiling face."

"I didn't shoot him, Rip. Bob and I did a lot of business together. His death leaves me scrambling, trying to salvage some things we had going. I'm not saying his death will be a net loss to me—I figure over time everything will balance out. You gotta be philosophical. These things happen."

"Uh-huh."

Sonny Wong gave up. "Great view you got here, Rip."

"Yeah."

"You ever want a passport for your mother-in-law, call me."

"I'll keep that in mind."

"Come on, Yuri. Let's go find some beds."

With her husband's help, Callie Grafton got the small tape reels properly installed on the player and pushed the play button. She was wearing the headset Carmellini had brought. Before her was a legal pad and pen on which she made notes and summarized the conversations as she listened. She made no attempt at a word-by-word translation. Occasionally she had to rewind the tape and listen to portions of conversations several times to make sure she had the meaning right.

Midnight came and went as she listened intently, occasionally jotting notes.

Finally she took a break, stopped the tape, and took off the headset. After she had helped herself to water, she muttered to her husband, who was out on the balcony watching the lights of the city; "What are you going to do with the tape after I finish with it?"

"I don't know. Depends on what's on it."

"I'm about halfway, I think. I don't understand everything I've heard, but Chan was apparently laundering money."

"For whom?"

"For the PLA. The money was going to America."

"Okay."

"The congressional investigators might be able to put voices and facts together to make something of all this."

"Perhaps."

She stood silently, stretching. Finally she lowered her arms and massaged his neck muscles. "Do you think Tiger killed him?"

"Hon, I don't know. I'm waiting for you to tell me what you think."

"What are you going to do if he did?"

"I don't know that either."

She went back inside and put on the headset.

It was three in the morning when Callie Grafton removed the headset and turned off the tape player. Jake was curled up on the bed, asleep.

She went out on the balcony and saw that rain had fallen during the night. Just now the air was almost a sea mist, which made the lights of the city glow wondrously.

She had listened to the ten minutes prior to the gunshot, which the tape captured, three times.

China Bob Chan had been a human, and presumably somewhere there was someone who cared for him, perhaps even loved him. Try as she might, Callie could work up no sympathy for the murdered man. He was gone and that was that.

She turned off the lights and lay down on the bed. She was so exhausted she wondered if she could relax enough to sleep. Then her eyes closed and she was out.

The sound of morning traffic coming through the open sliding-glass door woke Jake. Callie was asleep on the bed beside him.

Being as quiet as possible, he got up and put on running shorts, shirt, and shoes, made sure he had a key to the room, then slipped out and made sure the door locked behind him.

Down on the street the day was in full swing. People filled the sidewalk, all in a hurry, all rushing somewhere. Jake tried to stay out of their way until he got to Kowloon Park, with its semi-empty sidewalks. As he jogged through the park he passed morning exercise classes engaged in slow, stylized calisthenics that reminded him of ballet.

He ran the entire length of the park and out onto the sidewalks of

Austin Road, where he headed for the docks on the western side of the peninsula.

He had gone only a few dozen yards along Austin Road when he realized that he was being followed. Someone was jogging behind him, huffing loudly. And there was a car on the street, creeping along.

Jake Grafton glanced back over his shoulder, taking in the car and the man in casual pants who was running behind. He was a couple hundred feet back, and running was obviously not a sport with him. The guy was wearing the wrong shoes and carrying too much weight, for starters.

The thought of Callie asleep in a hotel room with the tape of China Bob's last hours on the bed beside her flashed through Jake's mind.

When he reached the street that ran beside the dock area, Canton Road, he turned left, south, to head back toward Tsim Sha Tsui on the southern tip of the peninsula. He kept his pace steady and tried not to look over his shoulder, though he did glance back once to make sure his tail had not collapsed on the sidewalk.

He veered left onto Kowloon Park Drive, just loping along.

Ahead was a ramp up to an overpass that went across the street and into the lobby of a major hotel. Looking neither right nor left, Jake took the ramp, made the turn at the top, and slowed just enough to go through the glass doors, which reflected the early morning glare.

His tail came thudding up the ramp, made the turn, charged for the door with his head down, inhaling deeply as he tried to get enough air to ease the pain in his chest. On the street below the car that had been keeping pace with the runner accelerated away.

Jake Grafton caught the tail by the throat as he came through the door and slammed him into a marble pillar, where the man collapsed, too stunned to move.

Glancing around to be sure no one was paying too much attention, Jake picked the man up by his pants and shirt and shoved him back out the door onto the ramp. There he slammed the man's head into the ramp railing, and the man passed out.

After he eased the heavy man to the concrete, Jake patted him down. He had a small automatic in a holster in his sock, so Jake relieved him of that and pushed it down inside his own athletic sock. A wallet . . . he didn't need that anymore, either. A few keys, matches, an open pack of Marlboros . . .

Grafton spent no more than ten seconds searching the man, then he straightened and went on into the hotel, leaving one middle-aged Western woman staring open-mouthed at him. No one else seemed interested.

Callie was still asleep when Jake let himself into the hotel room. The tape was still in the player.

Jake examined the pistol, a Chinese-made automatic, loaded. He put it in his luggage.

The wallet he had taken from the tail contained Hong Kong dollars and a variety of cards, all displaying Chinese characters.

He was toweling off after his shower when Callie awoke.

"Hey, beautiful woman, did you sleep okay?"

She sat up in bed, looked around at the bright room and the daylight streaming through the gauzy drapes.

"I don't know who killed that man, Jake."

"Couldn't tell from the tape?"

"Impossible to say. But China Bob was into everything. Everything! He smuggled people, money, dope . . . he was even bringing in computers and guns."

"Computers?"

"I couldn't make much sense of it."

"Was Cole on the tape?"

"I don't know. I don't know his voice."

"You'll meet him again tonight."

"I don't know that I want to."

"Hey, kiddo. We're the first team, okay? What say we have breakfast and see some sights?"

CHAPTER FIVE

The governor of Hong Kong, Sun Siu Ki, sat at his desk in City Hall puffing a cigarette as he listened to an interpreter translate Rip's story of the fatal riot in front of the Bank of the Orient from the *China Post*. A copy of the offending paper lay on the corner of the desk in front of him, out of his way. Spread out where he could read them were the front pages of three Chinese-language newspapers.

Sun couldn't believe his eyes or ears: Every editor in Hong Kong had apparently decided today was the day to tell the most outrageous lies about the government.

The copy of the leading Chinese-language paper had been hand-delivered to the governor's office by one of the newspaper's censors, who was horrified when he saw the paper rolling off the press. The lead headline and story on the Bank of the Orient failure was certainly not the one he had approved, and he wrote a note to the governor stating that fact.

The headline and story reported that Beijing had ordered the Bank of the Orient to close its doors since it had refused to lend money at superlow rates to customers designated by Beijing. The unspoken inference was that bribes in Beijing were the price of access to easy credit.

The censor had the presses stopped, but not before a truckload of the libelous papers had already left to be installed in vending machines in the northern area of Kowloon.

The other two papers carried slightly different versions of the same story. According to them the bank failure was the direct result of lending to unnamed politically connected entities who were unable to repay the loans, which had been made at ridiculously low rates. The morning editions of these papers had been distributed. The governor's aide bought these copies from vendors at the Star Ferry terminal on his way to work.

Everyone in Hong Kong was reading these lies.

The aide was in the next room, talking to the censors involved. Apparently both of them swore the stories were not the ones they approved for publication.

If the newspapers weren't enough, already this morning the governor had received a call from army headquarters: Several thousand people were sitting in the plaza outside the closed Bank of the Orient. They were peaceful enough, but they were there, a visible, tangible, unspoken challenge to the Communist government. As he listened to the interpreter, Sun Siu Ki was thinking about those people.

Behind his desk was a large window. Through that window, when he bothered to look, the governor could see a breathtaking assortment of huge glass-and-steel skyscrapers—one of which was the Bank of the Orient—designed by some of the world's premier architects. These buildings were the heart of one of the most vibrant, energetic cities on earth, a city as different from the old, decaying Chinese cities of the interior as one could possibly imagine. This difference had never impressed Sun Siu Ki.

A career bureaucrat, he was governor of Hong Kong because of his family's political connections in Beijing. He knew little about capitalism, banking, or the way Western manufacturing, shipping, and airline companies operated, and nothing at all about stock markets or the international monetary system. The wealth and dynamic energy of Hong Kong struck him as foreign . . . and dangerous.

A wise person once observed that Hong Kong was China the way it would be without the Communists. Nothing resembling that thought had ever crossed Sun Siu Ki's mind or caused him a moment's angst.

Baldly, he was in over his head. He didn't see it that way, however.

Sun believed that he knew what he needed to know, which was how to surf the political riptides of the Communist upper echelons in Canton Province and Beijing.

The problem du jour was the defiance of the government's authority by the people in the streets . . . and the newspapers. As bad as the uncensored stories were in the Chinese press, the headline in the *China Post* was the most outrageous: 15 MASSACRED AT BANK OF ORIENT.

Sun Siu Ki had replaced a governor who didn't attack pernicious foreign ideas with sufficient vigor. If people saw that the Communists were too soft to defend themselves, they were doomed: They would be swept away, eradicated as thoroughly as the Manchus. Being human, the party cadres were doing their damnedest to prevent just such a disaster.

Many of the readers of the *China Post* were not Chinese. The newspaper's reactionary stories inflamed the foreign devils, and they wrote outrageous, incendiary letters to the editor, which that fool published. All this caused faraway officials of the foreign banks to fear the loss of their money. Foreigners thought only of money. The culpability of the *China Post* was plain as day to Sun Siu Ki.

He gestured the interpreter into silence and seized a sheet of fine, cream-colored paper with the crest of Hong Kong on the top. There were still many boxes of paper bearing this logo in the attic of Government House. Thrifty Sun saw no incongruity in using paper bearing the likeness of the British lion. He wrote out an order for the offending newspaper to cease publication and signed it with a flourish. After further thought, he wrote out an order for the arrest of the editor. A few weeks in jail would teach him to mind his tongue.

While he was at it, he wrote out arrest orders for all of the editors involved. The time had come, Sun told himself, to whip these people back into line and show them who was in charge.

With the newspaper editors dealt with, Sun began to ponder the best way to handle the protesters in front of the bank.

The CIA contingent was summoned to the consul general's office just minutes after they arrived at work.

"What's going on?" Tommy Carmellini asked Kerry Kent, because she was more fun to talk to than the three men. Prettier, too.

"Didn't you see the crowd in front of the Bank of the Orient when you came in this morning? The ferry from Kowloon was packed; the only topic of conversation was the demonstration they were on their way to join."

The consul general's office was large and sparsely furnished, apparently reflecting the taste of the current occupant. Virgil Cole was several inches over six feet, with wide shoulders and short blond hair that was suspiciously thin on top. Ice-cold blue eyes swept the people who trooped in and stood in front of his desk.

Carmellini had spent a few moments with the consul general when he checked in last week. Cole had said little, merely welcomed him to Hong Kong, shook hands, muttered a pleasantry or two, and sent him off. He had also attended a meeting that Cole had chaired.

Cole stood behind the desk now, looked into each face. "There's a crowd gathering in front of the Bank of the Orient this morning," he said without preliminaries. "Tang and the army will probably run them off before long."

No one disputed that assessment.

"I want to know what's going on in City Hall."

"We have some excellent sources there, sir," Bubba Lee began, but Cole waved him into silence.

"They are marvelously corrupt—I know that. The problem is our whisperers are too low on the totem pole. I want to know what Beijing is telling Governor Sun and General Tang and what those two are telling Beijing, and I want to know it now, in real time."

Lee took a deep breath and said, "The only way we can get that information, sir, is to tap the telephones."

"While you are at it, bug Sun's office. Do it today." Cole nodded curtly at Lee, then seated himself in the chair behind his desk and picked up the top document in his in-basket.

Apparently the spooks had been dismissed. Lee turned without a word and led his colleagues from the room.

Out in the hallway with the doorway closed, Lee faced them. "You heard him. He's the most garrulous man I ever met."

"A dangerous blabbermouth," Carson Eisenberg agreed.

"Nevertheless, he's given us our marching orders, so let's dive in. Carmellini, your star is rising."

As they walked toward the CIA office, Carmellini said, "Can anyone get us a couple of telephone company trucks and some uniforms?"

"Tommy, you are in a city where money doesn't just talk, it sings like Pavarotti. You can get anything in Hong Kong; the only question is the price."

"We need a floor plan of City Hall. Blueprints would be better."

"Blueprints, yes," said George Wang. "We bought them from a butler when the British were still in residence." He waggled his eyebrows at Kerry Kent, who stayed deadpan.

"Okay," said Tommy Carmellini, "this is how we're going to do it. . . ."

Rip Buckingham was in his office on the second floor of the newspaper, closeted with the newspaper's headline writer, when he heard a commotion on the stairs. By the time he got to the door the policemen were up the stairs and shouting fiercely at two reporters who were trying to keep them from coming in. One of the policemen, a sergeant, tired of a zealous reporter's interference and threatened to chop him in the side of the neck.

"Ng Yuan Lee, what are you doing?" Rip shouted in Cantonese, which froze the sergeant. He snarled at the reporter, who drew back.

"Rip Buckingham, I have a warrant."

"You're kidding, right?"

"No," the sergeant said, extracting a piece of paper from his pocket. "They have issued a warrant for your arrest, signed by the chief judge. The governor demanded it."

Rip Buckingham threw up his hands in resignation. He didn't, however, argue with the sergeant and his colleague, who were merely doing their jobs.

"I'm sorry, Rip," Marcus Hallaby, the headline writer, told him from the office door. "God, I'm sorry! I just didn't think the headline was that big a deal, and . . ." Marcus was crying. He was also half soused, precisely the same condition he had been in yesterday afternoon when he wrote the massacre headline, precisely the same condition he had been in for the last ten years. He covered his face with his hands and sagged against the wall.

"Hey, Marcus, it wasn't your fault," Rip said, trying to sound like he meant it. After all, he had been the one who always refused to fire Marcus when headlines irritated people he couldn't afford to irritate.

These little storms blew in several times a year. For a day or two there was lightning and thunder, then the sky would clear and Marcus would still be there, contrite, apologetic, slightly drunk.... The damn guy just couldn't handle life sober and Rip had never been able to condemn him for that.

"It was the story," he told Marcus. "And the governor . . ."

"We must shut down the newspaper, Buckingham," the sergeant said gently. "We have our orders. Everyone must leave the building. We will put a guard on the doors."

"Who gave these orders?"

"Governor Sun Siu Ki."

"May I see the paper, please?"

The order was in Chinese. Buckingham read it while the sergeant wiped his hatband and ran his hand through his hair. He ignored the curious staffers standing nearby and turned his back on Marcus, who was sobbing audibly. Rip folded the document and handed it back to the officer.

"Perhaps it will help if I tell all the staff in English what they must do." He said it easily, without even a hint of temper, and the sergeant agreed again. As a very young man touring China, Buckingham had learned the fine art of self-control.

Some of the staffers wanted to argue with the officers, but Buckingham wouldn't permit it. With sour looks, muttered oaths, and tears, the staffers—two-thirds of whom were Chinese—turned off the computers and office equipment and vacated the building. Buckingham remained the epitome of gracious affability, so he was given permission to have a private conversation with an assistant before the policemen took him away. Most of the staff milled helplessly on the sidewalk as the police car disappeared into traffic.

Jail held no terrors for Rip Buckingham. He had been incarcerated on several occasions in his footloose past when local policemen didn't know quite what to make of a six-foot-three Australian bicycling through forbidden areas, that is, areas in China off the beaten track, in which tourists were not permitted. He usually talked his way out of their clutches, but now and then he spent a few nights in the local can.

Fortunately his gastrointestinal tract was as impervious to bacteria as PVC pipe. Had his GI tract been more normal, one suspects he would not have strayed so far from tap water. He would probably be in Sydney now, married to one of the local sheilas, with one and a half blond kids, holding down some make-work position in his father's worldwide newspaper empire while the old man groomed him to follow in his footsteps, et cetera, et cetera.

As he rode through the streets of Hong Kong in the police car, wedged in the backseat between Sergeant Ng and his colleague, Rip Buckingham thought about the et ceteras. He also thought about his father, Richard Buckingham, and what he would say when he heard the news. Not the news his son had been arrested, but that the paper had been shut down.

Amazingly, for a man who owned fifty-two newspapers located in six countries, his father never really understood the romance of the printed word. Richard Buckingham saw newspapers as very profitable businesses with enviable cash flows. "Newspapers," he liked to say, "are machines for turning ink and paper into money."

Measured on Richard's criteria, the *China Post* had once been one of his best. B.C. Before the Communists.

Strange, Rip thought. He was thinking about the paper as if it would never publish again. Well, perhaps its day was over. For that matter, perhaps Hong Kong's day was over.

The Brits just turned over the keys and walked away. They went home to their unimpressive little island on the other side of the world and pretended Hong Kong never happened.

Maybe that was the wise thing to do.

Rip Buckingham shook his head, angry at himself. He was becoming demoralized. This was his city, his and Sue Lin's. She was born in Hong Kong, grew up here; he had adopted it.

Sue Lin loved Hong Kong.

Well, he thought defensively, he did, too. The city belonged to everyone who loved her. God knows, there were millions of people who did.

Despite his best efforts at keeping his spirits up, he was glum when the police car rolled through the gate of the city prison.

Damn Communists!

Sue Lin Buckingham told her mother that Rip was in jail, on a warrant demanded by Governor Sun Siu Ki. Policemen had arrested him, closed the newspaper. And this morning another riot was developing in front of the Bank of the Orient.

"Rip was foolish," Lin Pe told her daughter in Cantonese, the only language in which she was fluent. She spoke a little English, but only when she had to. She acquired most of her English from American movies which she watched on a VCR, running scenes over and over until she understood the dialogue.

The news about Rip annoyed her. He had no respect for authority! "He has been baiting the tiger with his news stories and editorials, and now the jaws have snapped shut. Only a fool spits in the eye of a tiger."

"The paper was losing circulation, Mother, and advertising." Sue Lin was tense, unhappy over the news of her husband's jailing, and her mother's simplistic reaction angered her. As if this lifelong capitalist didn't understand the dynamics of the marketplace! "The *Post* used to make money because it was *the* newspaper for Hong Kong bankers and businesspeople to read. Rip knew that he had to address the concerns of the people he wanted as readers or he would lose them. And when he lost them, he would lose the advertisers who wanted to reach them. It's that simple."

"Apparently Sun Siu Ki isn't concerned about Rip's advertisers," the mother snapped.

"Sun Siu Ki is an extraordinarily stupid bastard." Rip Buckingham's Chinese wife was no shrinking violet.

"That may be," her mother agreed evenly. These young people! "But he represents the government in Beijing, in precisely the same way that the old governor represented the queen in her palace in London. The difference, which dear Rip chooses to ignore, is that the English queen never laid eyes on a copy of the *China Post*. She didn't give a"—she snapped her fingers—"what Rip Buckingham said in his silly little newspaper in Hong Kong, on the other side of the planet. The people in Beijing don't share Queen Elizabeth's indifference. They apparently do read Rip's scribblings. They're a lot closer, their skin is a lot thinner, and Sun is their long right arm."

Sue Lin sank into a chair. "Oh, Mother, what are we going to do? Rip is in jail. No one knows how long they intend to keep him. They may even send him to a prison on the mainland."

Her mother's expression softened. "The first thing to do," she said, "is to call Albert Cheung, the lawyer. He knows everything. He will know what to do."

Lin Pe made the call. After talking to three people who pretended they never heard her name before in their lives, she got through to Albert Cheung, an illegal refugee from mainland China who was so smart that he won a scholarship to study law at Oxford. When he returned to Hong Kong, with a trace of a British accent and a fondness for tweeds, he managed to elbow his way to the top of the legal heap and into the inner sanctums even though he had no family in the colony. He had had a finger in every big deal in Hong Kong for the past twenty years. He was filthy rich and slowing down, yet he was too smart to pretend that he didn't remember Lin Pe.

"It has been years since I've heard from the chairman of the Double Happy Fortune Cookie Company, Limited," Albert Cheung said.

"You've been getting your dividends every quarter," Lin Pe told him. Albert took stock instead of a fee when she floated the initial public offering for her company on the Hong Kong exchange.

"Yes, indeed," he said. "I was wondering, have you ever thought of selling the company? Retiring to a life of leisure? Travel the world, see the Great Pyramids, the Acropolis—?"

"I've had some other things on my mind, Albert. Like getting my son-in-law out of jail."

"Rip Buckingham? See, I keep up. But I didn't know he was in jail. What has he done?"

"Sun Siu Ki closed the *Post* today and arrested him. Could you find out how long they intend to keep him?"

"So the tiger has him in his jaws?"

"Yes."

Cheung sighed. After a few seconds he said, "Many things are possible if you are willing to pay a fine. Would you—?"

"Within reason, Albert. I will not be robbed by anyone."

"I saw the headline in the morning *Post*: '15 Massacred at Bank of Orient.' And the PLA did the shooting. That headline was not wise, Lin Pe."

"I think Sun Siu Ki was just fed up."

"Perhaps the bank closing had—"

"Rip Buckingham's world is collapsing. He's been fighting back the only way he can."

"I'll see what I can do, Lin Pe. Give me your telephone number."

She did so, asked about his wife and children, then hung up.

"He'll see what he can do," Lin Pe told her daughter. "It will cost money."

"The newspaper will pay."

"The newspaper is finished," said Lin Pe. "It will never publish again."

"Richard Buckingham is a powerful man."

"Sun Siu Ki and the people in Beijing probably never heard of Richard Buckingham, and if they have heard, they don't care," Lin Pe said, which was, of course, true. To see beyond the boundaries of China had always been difficult. Even the queen of England, she reflected, knew more about the outside world than the oligarchy in Beijing.

"The next thing to do," Lin Pe said, "is to call your father-in-law. Someone from the newspaper has probably called him already, but you should do so now."

As her daughter walked from the room, Lin Pe added, "Don't forget, all calls out are monitored." She went back to writing fortunes.

Well, there it was. A way to get some money and get out before Wu Tai Kwong set China on fire. Sell the fortune cookie company to Albert Cheung!

The traders at the Hong Kong stock exchange had expected a wild ride in the aftermath of the collapse of the Bank of the Orient, but the ride was worse than anyone imagined it might be.

At the opening bell the traders were faced with massive sell orders, while the buy orders were minuscule. Prices went into freefall. Ten minutes went by before exchange officials finally learned that the computer system was at fault. Most—but not all—of the sell orders had an extra zero added just before the decimal, increasing the size of the orders by a factor of ten. On the other hand, some—not all—buy orders had their final digit dropped somewhere in cyberspace, shrinking them to a tenth of their original size.

The result was chaos. Since not every order was affected, the orders had to be checked by hand, which drastically limited the number of orders that could be processed. Unable to cope, officials closed the market.

Exchange officials quickly determined that they had a software problem, but finding the cure took most of the day. While they were working on it, one of the exchange officials was called to the telephone. The governor's aide was on the line demanding an explanation. For the first time, the exchange official mentioned the possibility of sabotage.

"Sabotage?" the governor's aide asked incredulously. "How could anyone do that?"

"Probably a computer virus of some type," he was told.

"Are you certain that is the case?"

"Of course not," the exchange official snapped.

Sun Siu Ki was on the telephone to Beijing when the phones went dead. He tried another line, couldn't even get a dial tone, so he motioned to an aide that there was a problem and handed the instrument to him.

Sun turned to General Tang, explained that Beijing wanted the bank demonstrators dispersed and, if possible, wanted to avoid a bloody incident that the press would publicize around the world, inflaming foreign public opinion. "Remove the press from the area," Sun advised, "before you remove the hooligans. That way the foreign press will be unable to use provocations as propaganda. Still, first and foremost, these hooligans must not be permitted to flout the authority of the state. That is paramount."

Tang understood his instructions and the priorities they contained. Both men firmly believed that the state could ill afford to give an inch to anyone challenging its authority or resolve. Perhaps they were right, because both men knew Chinese history and their countrymen.

In any event, they were determined men who believed that the party and the government could and should use every weapon in the arsenal, indeed, every resource of the state, to fight for the survival of the revolution. And if pushed, they were fully capable of doing just that.

The telephones had been off for ten minutes when Tang left the governor huddled with his aide, who tried to explain that the computers at the stock exchange had been sabotaged. As Tang rode out of the City Hall parking area in his chauffeur-driven car, two telephone repair vans passed him on their way in.

Three men wearing one-piece telephone company jumpers and billed caps climbed from the vans. Tommy Carmellini removed an armload of tools and equipment from the van he came in while Bubba Lee talked to the security guard in Chinese. Carson Eisenberg unloaded the equipment they needed from the other van. The men strapped on tool belts. When Lee motioned to them to follow, they picked up their equipment and trooped along in single file into City Hall.

Tommy Carmellini was worried. He was an obviously non-Chinese worker who didn't speak a word of the language. The other two spoke Chinese, of course, and they had assured Tommy that there would be no problem, but still . . .

When he walked into City Hall, Carmellini took the bull by the horns. The very first Chinese he saw, he brayed, as Australian as he could, "G'day, mate. Where's your switchbox?"

Carson Eisenberg repeated the question in Chinese, the official pointed and said a few words, and they were in!

The CIA officers went to work on the telephones. Since the system was an ancient government one, this involved picking up each handset and using a noisemaker that allowed a colleague in a manhole just up the street to identify the line and tap it. After each line was identified, there was much shouting in Chinese into the instruments for the benefit of the watching civil servants.

As the crew worked their way from office to office, Carmellini inspected the building and its security system. He did this as one of the uniformed guards stood beside him quietly observing his every move. Carmellini smiled at the guard, nodded, then ignored him.

The building looked modern enough. The hallways and rooms were spacious, with hardwood floors, but, like government offices the world over, looked crowded and cramped.

Carmellini was in the foyer of the governor's office examining the door locks and alarms when one of the staff began staring at him. Carmellini glanced at the man . . . and recognized him: It was the guy who had stared at Kerry Kent at China Bob Chan's party the other night!

The man's brows knitted; he knew he had seen Carmellini before but couldn't quite remember when or where. His puzzlement was obvious.

Carmellini headed for the hallway with his escort right behind.

The staffer followed.

Uh-oh!

He had seen a men's room a moment ago and he headed for it now, his entourage in tow. Inside he went into a stall and shut the door.

He listened as the staffer and the security escort chattered away, their remarks totally unintelligible.

Carmellini unzipped his overalls, shrugged them off his shoulders, and sat.

He sat listening for almost fifteen minutes, then flushed noisily and rearranged his clothing.

When he opened the stall door, the room was empty.

Carmellini was listening at the door of the men's room when he heard footsteps. He got away from the door just in time. It swung open, and the man, wearing a PLA officer's uniform, looked startled. Tommy nodded pleasantly and walked out.

The hallway was empty. He went down a flight of stairs, walked toward the service entrance, passed the table with the two security guards, and went out into the parking area. The other three men were still inside. Carmellini got behind the wheel of one of the vans and sat staring at the side of City Hall, waiting.

Everybody in Hong Kong seemed to be on their way to the Central District this morning. Public transportation facilities were packed, with long lines of people waiting to board subway trains, buses, taxis, and the Star Ferry at Tsim Sha Tsui. PLA soldiers at the Central District subway station, the MTR, tried to prevent people leaving the trains at that stop, but there were too many people and the soldiers were overwhelmed. Taxis and buses were directed not to discharge passengers when they stopped at the usual stops, so they stopped in the middle of city blocks and opened their doors. By ten in the morning at least ten thousand people were in the square in front of the Bank of the Orient and on the surrounding sidewalks.

That was the situation when General Tang arrived direct from the governor's office in City Hall. He became angry with his officers, whom he felt should have made greater efforts to prevent the crowd from gathering.

"Since we failed to prevent the crowd from gathering, now we must make it disperse," he instructed the staff, only to be told that the officers doubted they had enough soldiers present to make much of a show. Ordering the crowd to leave without sufficient soldiers to enforce the order would make the PLA appear ridiculous, an object of scorn.

"In accordance with your instructions, sir, we have used our men to prevent news media from congregating here."

"Why not prevent everyone from congregating?"

"We tried, sir, but we simply did not have enough men."

Tang lost his temper. "Why did you wait for me to tell you to get more men? This demonstration is a direct affront to the government. It is a crime against the state and will not be tolerated! Order the police to send all available men here. They should have been here already, preventing this crowd from gathering in an unlawful assembly."

"Sir, we have discussed this matter with the police, who say they have no spare men to send. All are engaged in law enforcement and traffic control duties elsewhere."

"Get more soldiers, as many as you need. Have them brought here by truck as soon as possible."

"Yes, sir."

Tang found a vantage point in a third-floor office of a nearby building. The civilians who worked for a shipping company were ejected and the soldiers moved in. From here Tang could see that the crowd below consisted of men, women, and children, all well behaved. People sat visiting with each other and, as the noon hour approached, ate snacks brought from home. Water and food vendors worked the crowd.

"Why have you allowed these vendors to congregate here?" Tang demanded of his staff. "Run them off."

The soldiers tried. The vendors promptly gave away everything on their carts and obeyed the soldiers, who laughed along with the crowd. Watching from above, Tang was coldly furious.

"Two hours, sir. We will have another two hundred men here within two hours."

"By truck?"

"Yes, sir. The trucks must go through the Cross-Harbor Tunnel, which is crowded at this hour."

Tang could contain his fury no longer. He stormed at the staff, berated them at the top of his lungs. When he had vented his ire, he retired to a private office and slammed the door.

Jake and Callie Grafton spent the morning cooped up with a flock of middle-aged British and American tourists riding a small tour bus around the coast of Hong Kong Island. They visited the mandatory jewelry factory—they looked but didn't buy—and rode a sampan to a fish restaurant in the harbor at Aberdeen.

A barefoot old woman in a loose cotton shirt and trousers, brown as a nut, with a lined, seamed face, sculled the tourists over. The restaurant was one of a half dozen in the harbor, all built on barges. Permanently anchored, covered with Victorian gingerbread painted in bright, gaudy primary colors, the restaurants somehow still managed to bear a faint resemblance to a pagoda.

These much-photographed temples of capitalism made Jake smile. Callie's mood, however, was somber; she hadn't smiled all morning.

After they had given the waiter their order—the waiter seemed to know an extraordinary amount of English, although Callie chatted with him in Chinese—Jake and Callie Grafton were left in semiprivacy with glasses of wine. They were seated in a booth by a window that looked across acres of fishing boats and the residential sampans of the boat people. Beyond the harbor were rooftops and high-rises, all the way up the mountain.

"You don't seem too happy about your glimpse into China Bob's affairs," Jake said tentatively.

"I'm sorry. I've got no right to be such a stick in the mud."

"Not your fault. The guy was a probably a shit."

"Sssh! People might be listening."

"I hope not."

"Let's just say he was a foul, evil man who made his living on the misfortunes of others."

"That would be fair."

"The tape was really hard to figure out," Callie explained, "and I don't think I've got it yet. I would say that at least half of the tape is made up of his side of telephone conversations. When he was silent too long, the tape stopped and one hears that infuriating beep, and the first few words of his next sentence are missing.

"Of course, he also had conversations with people in his office, and sometimes during those conversation he would take telephone calls.

"The tape is full of beeps, missing words, mumbled words, incomprehensible garble, and Chinese spoken too fast for me. Sometimes Chan and a visitor would both speak at the same time . . . sometimes they both shouted at the same time. Everyone around here smokes, have you noticed that?"

"Yes."

"They talk with cigarettes dangling from their mouth. . . ." She sighed. "The tape needs to be gone over by experts. All I got were snatches of conversation, words and phrases, sometimes a bit of give and take, usually just bits and pieces."

"And you don't know who killed Chan?"

"No. There is a beep—which means the tape was stopped—then a bit of a phrase, incomprehensible, and the shot. Nothing after that. The tape stops."

"Before that, what was on the tape?"

"Someone talking about an import permit for computers."

"Okay."

"And before that, an argument about money. It seems someone gave Chan money to give to people—I think in America—and he pocketed at least half of it, according to the man who shouted at him."

"You said Chan was into human smuggling?"

"That was the subject of several conversations, I think. Hard to be sure. I got the impression that it would be better for everyone if the cargo didn't survive the voyage."

"You aren't crying for China Bob?"

"I wouldn't mind throwing a shovelful of dirt in his face."

"Hmm." Jake took a sip of wine.

"Where's the tape now?" Callie asked. "Did you leave it in the room?"

"It's in my pocket."

"Oh. Okay."

"Along with a pistol I took off a guy who was following me this morning when I went jogging."

"You're kidding me."

"Nope. A little automatic. Loaded." Jake removed the man's wallet from another pocket and passed it to Callie. "See if you can figure out who this guy is."

She ignored the money, Hong Kong dollars equivalent to about forty dollars American, and examined each of the cards. "I don't know many Chinese characters," she said tentatively, "but none of this stuff looks like an official ID card. I would think that in Hong Kong everything is in English and Chinese."

She returned the documents to the wallet and passed it back. Jake took out the money and put it in his shirt pocket, so he could leave it on the table after lunch as a tip.

As they were eating lunch he realized that two people were watching him and Callie from the kitchen door and whispering together. One was a man who didn't look like he was kitchen help.

After a few minutes the man took a seat at an empty table by the door and devoted himself to studious contemplation of the menu.

"When we get back to the hotel," Jake said to his wife, "I want to see if I can get you a flight back to the states."

"I don't want to go back alone."

"And I don't want you in the middle of a civil war. I'm going to have a heart-to-heart talk with Cole, and then I think I'll go back, too. Sending me over here to root around was a bad idea from the get-go."

"You're worried about the man who followed you this morning, aren't you?"

"I'm getting worried about everything. We're in way over our heads."

As they rode the sampan back to the tour bus, he slipped the wallet into the water. When no one was looking, he did the same with the pistol.

Callie reached for Jake's hand. "Come on, Romeo, hold my hand. We're smack in the middle of an exotic city and I could use a little romance."

Lin Pe rode the tram down Victoria Peak. It was but a short walk from Rip and Sue Lin's house to the tramway, and the motorman always stopped on the way down when he saw her standing there. She stepped aboard and wedged herself in among a carful of plump, rosy-pink Germans. With barely a lurch the car continued its descent of the steep grade.

At the bottom she set off on foot, walking quickly, her small purse clutched tightly in her left hand.

Huge buildings rose on all sides, towering palaces of glass and steel. Around them traffic swirled on multilane streets that could be crossed only at over- or underpasses. Hiking the concrete canyons was strenuous, but Lin Pe could remember dawn-to-dark days in the rice paddies from her youth. Nothing could be as strenuous as those lean times, with too much work and not enough to eat.

The human sea thickened as she approached the bank square. Acres of people crowded the sidewalks and spilled into the streets. Most seemed content to stand right where they were since the bank square wasn't all that big. Still, Lin Pe pressed forward, worming her way through.

There were some soldiers about, but they were standing back, well out of the way. Lin Pe walked right by them and edged her way carefully into the middle of the square, where she finally found a tiny area of unoccupied concrete and sat.

The bank loomed before her like a dark, black cliff, blocking out the sun. When she looked straight up she could see a patch of blue sky.

She folded her hands in her lap and spoke to the woman beside her. They chatted politely for a moment—both had money in the closed bank—then fell silent, each lost in her own thoughts.

When Lin Pe had been very young there had been a man. He had worked hard and given her six children. One died in infancy; the three eldest she left behind with his parents after he died. The two youngest, Sue Lin and Wu, she carried away, one in each arm, when she decided she must go. Without her man, burdened with the children and his parents, both of whom were vigorous enough then but growing older, she would never be able to make it. She had too many children ever to attract another man. So she left.

She sat in the square thinking about the children she left behind, as she did for a few minutes every day. Finally her mind turned to fortunes. Thinking up fortunes had been the most important thing in her life for many years now, and she returned to it whenever the world pressed in.

"Go always toward the light" had been one of her favorites. The words seemed to mean more than they said, which was why the fortune appealed to her. She thought about it now, about what inner meaning might be hiding in the words.

By midafternoon Tang's officers believed they had enough soldiers to force the crowd to leave, so they sent a staff officer to man the loud-speaker mounted on a van.

Like a thick, viscous liquid, the thousands of people began slowly flowing outward from the bank square. The crowd was orderly and well behaved and obeyed the soldiers with alacrity.

Thirty minutes after the order was given, only a few hundred civilians were still in sight from Tang's third-story window.

He turned to his officers. "Wait for more soldiers, you said, so we waited. And when told to go, the people went like sheep. For hours they sat here illegally, in open and notorious defiance of the government. They have made fools of us again."

One of the senior colonels tried to argue that the reason the crowd dispersed in an orderly fashion was because there were so many troops in sight, but Tang was having none of it. The government had been defied; he could feel it.

"Another crowd may return tomorrow," Tang said, "so I want enough troops stationed on the streets to deny access to this square. And put four tanks in the square. We will advertise our strength."

One of the people who did not leave the square was Lin Pe. She was sitting against a curb with a flower bed behind her, and she was very small. The soldiers ignored her.

When she was almost the last civilian left in the square, Lin Pe slowly levered herself erect and turned her back on the bank.

Eighteen-year-old Ng Choy watched her leave. He didn't know her, of course. She was just a small, old woman, one of thousands he had seen in and around the square that day.

Ng Choy turned his attention back to the stain on the concrete where the man he had shot yesterday had fallen.

His rifle was heavy in his hands.

There were three of them, and they would probably have killed Tommy Carmellini if he hadn't been scanning the faces in the crowd. He was walking from the consulate toward the Star Ferry, trying to go with the ebb and flow of packed humanity. He was renting a room by the week in a cheap hotel in Kowloon until he found an apartment, and he was on his way there after work. Hordes of people jammed the sidewalks and spilled into the streets this afternoon, even more than usual for Hong Kong, a notoriously crowded city.

The eyes tipped him off. The man was fifteen feet or so away, standing by a power pole, when he saw Carmellini. His eyes locked on the American, who happened to glance straight at him. The man was several inches shorter than Carmellini and powerfully built. He left the spot where he had been standing on an interception course.

Instinctively, Carmellini turned and started the other way. And saw another set of brown eyes staring into his as a man closed in from the direction of a street vendor's cart.

Carmellini didn't hesitate. He leaped for this second man, so quickly that he took his assailant by surprise. Carmellini knocked the man down as he went over and through him and kept on going.

As he turned a corner he looked back, and that was when he realized there were three of them pushing and shoving people out of the way as they chased him.

Oooh boy!

Tommy Carmellini stepped off the jammed sidewalk and began running along the gutter, between the sidewalk and the traffic coming toward him. Behind him the three thugs did the same.

Of course he was unarmed.

Carmellini was carrying a thin attaché case that contained a Hong Kong guidebook, a Chinese-English phrasebook for tourists, and a Tom Clancy paperback. After he got through the first intersection he glanced behind him. His pursuers were successfully dodging traffic, still coming, so he tossed the case into the street and settled down to some serious running.

He loosened his tie and the top button of his shirt.

After three blocks the street became limited access and separated from the sidewalk. Carmellini stayed in the street.

The three thugs following had lost some ground.

As he went under an underpass a speeding truck grazed Carmellini and bounced him off the concrete abutment. He kept his feet but he lost a step or two. When he topped the underpass his pursuers were closer.

Oh, man! That damned tape. He didn't have it and he didn't know what was on it! Of course the guys behind him wouldn't believe *that*! No doubt they were out to get the tape and permanently shut his mouth.

A few more blocks and he was into the Wanchai District, today as tame and touristy as North Beach in San Francisco, but in its day home to some of the raunchiest whorehouses east of Port Said.

But how did they know about the tape?

As he ran he worked on that problem in a corner of his mind.

The crowd here was only a bit thinner than the throng in the Central District, but the night was young.

Running down the street in his suit and tie pursued by three thugs, looking futilely for a cop, Tommy Carmellini was a victim looking for a crime site. Twice he ran by knots of armed soldiers standing on street corners, and the soldiers made no move to stop him or the three men following.

Insane! Like something from a pee-your-pants anxiety nightmare.

He considered possible courses of action and rejected them one by one. Dashing through a nightclub, darting into a building, jumping on a moving truck . . .

When he saw the entrance to the MTR, the subway, he didn't hesitate. He charged down the stairs and hurtled the turnstile.

He went around two sharp turns . . . and there was his opportunity. About nine feet or so over his head was a scaffolding on the side of a wall, for repairing light fixtures or something.

Without even pausing, Carmellini launched himself. He caught the bottom pole—the scaffolding was of bamboo poles—and swung himself upward. He hooked a leg and was up, flat on the walkway, when the three men chasing him rounded the corner and shot underneath.

This wasn't the time or place for a breather.

Quick as a cat, Tommy Carmellini swung down and charged back up the stairs, fighting the stream of people coming down. Out on the street he slowed to a walk and joined the crowd flowing along Hennessey Road.

Kerry Kent. As he walked he remembered how she hugged him at the party as they waited for the car, subtly ran her hands over him. Could she be the rotten apple?

And if she wasn't, who was?

CHAPTER SIX

Jake and Callie Grafton had dinner in Tiger Cole's private apartment at the consulate. Jake wondered if he would have recognized the consul general if he had seen him on the street. Cole was several inches over six feet, with wide shoulders and thinning, sun-bleached hair. No doubt the hair was graying. . . . His eyes were as blue as ever and still seemed to look right through you, or perhaps it was only Jake's imagination, a trick of memory from years ago.

Small talk wasn't Cole's forte. He listened politely to Callie, who tried to fill the silence with the story of the conference fiasco, impressions of Hong Kong, and a running commentary on Jake's career through the years. She told him about Amy and about Jake's current assignment at the Pentagon, and wondered about Cole's life. His answers were short, almost cryptic, but he looked so interested in what she was saying that she kept talking. Finally, over the main course, she fell silent.

"You two are very lucky," Cole said, "to have found each other. You seem very happy together."

"We are," Jake Grafton said and grinned at his wife.

"I was married three times," Cole continued, speaking softly. "Had a girl by my first wife and a boy by my second. The boy died two years ago of a drug overdose. His heart just gave out. He'd been in and out of rehab facilities for years, could never kick the craving." Cole stirred his dinner around on the plate with his fork, then gave up and put the fork down. He sipped at the wine, which was from California.

"I wasn't a good father. I never understood the kid or the demons he fought. I thought he was stupid and I guess he figured that out."

"Jesus, Tiger!" Jake Grafton said, "That's a hell of a thing to say!"

Cole looked at Callie. "Now *that* is the Jake Grafton I remember. Was never afraid to say what was on his mind."

Grafton finished the last of his fish and put his silverware on his plate.

"I wondered about you," Cole continued. "Wondered if you were still the way I remembered, or if you had turned into a paper-pushing bureaucrat as you went up the ladder."

"I see you're still the silver-tongued smoothie who charmed your way through the fleet way way back when," Jake shot back.

"Yep, still an asshole." Cole flashed a rare grin. "My presence in the diplomatic game is a stirring testament to the power of political contributions. I knew you were wondering—that's the explanation in a nutshell."

"You owe Callie an apology for sitting there like a bump on a log letting her carry the conversation."

Cole bowed his head toward Callie. "He's right, as usual. I apologize."

She nodded.

"When I saw the newspaper article a couple years ago announcing your appointment, I had a chuckle," Jake said. "You're so perfectly suited for the diplomatic corps, why'd you take this appointment?"

"After the kid died I needed to get the hell out. I was wasting my life with people with too much money and not enough humanity. I didn't like them and I didn't like the man I had become. When this opportunity came I grabbed for it like a drowning man going after a rope."

"You certainly had some interesting experiences in Silicon Valley," Jake commented. "You helped design key networking software, you started a company that got one of the biggest contracts to make the Chinese telephone and air traffic control systems Y2K compliant.... Certainly sounds as if you had your plate full."

"You did some checking on me before you came to Hong Kong."

Jake Grafton chuckled. "I did. I made some inquiries when I got the chance to come to the conference here with Callie."

"The company did the bulk of the Y2K China stuff after I left."

"You were over here then, weren't you?"

"That's right. I had to put my shares in a blind trust."

"So just how advanced are the Chinese computer systems?"

Cole made a face. "They've bought some state-of-the-art stuff. Hong Kong is as wired as any American city. On the mainland it's a different story; only the most obvious public applications have been computerized. The reason their growth rate is so high is that they are leapfrogging tech levels. For example, the first telephone system some cities are getting is wireless."

Cole fell silent. It was obvious he didn't want to talk about computers or high tech, so Callie changed the subject. "Tell us about Hong Kong," she said.

A glimmer of a smile appeared on Cole's face, then quickly vanished. This was a subject that interested him. "The rich are getting richer and the poor are getting left farther behind. That happens throughout the industrial world, but in China there is no social mobility mechanism. If you are born a poor peasant you can never hope to be anything else. In an era of rapid change, that hopelessness becomes social dynamite. The reality is that the forces of social, economic, and political change are out of everyone's control, and the dynasty of Mao Tse Tung is numbered. Every day the tensions are ratcheted tighter, every day the pressure builds."

"These demonstrations in the Central District that the government is dispersing with troops—what is that all about?"

"A Japanese bank failed and the depositors lost their money. The Chinese government doesn't want to attempt to overhaul the banking system, which is state-owned and insolvent. The government has used the banks to fund bad loans to state-owned heavy industry. They can't fix the system, so they ignore the problem."

"Isn't that dangerous?"

Cole shrugged. "The state-owned industries and the banks are insolvent. To wipe out all the debts is to admit that socialism is a failure and fifty years of policy has been one massive error. To make that admission is to forfeit their mandate to rule."

"So there's no way out?"

"The crunch is inevitable."

"Since Callie got thrown off the platform at her conference and these demonstrations keep getting bigger and bigger, we thought we might go home early," Jake said, stretching the truth only a little. "I called the airlines this afternoon with no luck. There are no seats at any price. Everyone and their brother is trying to get out of Hong Kong."

"A lot of people are worried. They certainly ought to be."

"Someone said the troops are after a political criminal."

"The troops are hunting a man named Wu Tai Kwong, public enemy number one, which is a measure of how paranoid the government has become. The man who stood up to them in Tienanmen Square in 1989 has become a symbol of resistance and must be ruthlessly crushed."

"One brave man," Jake commented.

"Ah, yes. Courage. Courage, daring, the wisdom to wait for the moment, and the wit to know it when it arrives. That's Wu Tai Kwong."

"You speak as if you know him," Callie observed.

"In some ways, I think I do," Tiger Cole replied thoughtfully.

"So you think communism will collapse in China?"

"Communism is an anachronism, like monarchy. It's died just about everywhere else. It'll die here one of these days. The only question is when."

"What does Washington say about all of this?" Jake wondered.

Tiger Cole chuckled, a dry, humorless noise. "Wall Street doesn't like revolutions, and the market is the god Americans worship these days." He talked for several minutes of the politics driving Washington diplomacy.

Later, as they stood at the window staring up the unblinking commercial signs on the tops of the neighboring skyscrapers, Cole said, "The industrial West is operating on the same fallacy that brought the British to Hong Kong a century and a half ago. They think China is a vast market, and if they can just get access, they will get rich selling Western industrial products to people so poor they can barely feed themselves. 'It will work now,' the dreamers say, 'because the Chinese are going to become the world's premier low-cost labor market, earning real money manufacturing goods to be sold in the industrial West.' " Cole threw up his hands.

Callie asked, "Do China's Wu Tai Kwongs have a chance?"

"I think so," Tiger Cole said. "The little people have everything to gain and nothing to lose. The king has everything to lose and nothing to gain. There is only one way that contest can end."

"It's going to cost a lot of blood," murmured Jake Grafton.

"Lots of blood," Tiger agreed. "That too is inevitable. In China anything worth having must be purchased with blood."

Tommy Carmellini didn't go to his hotel in the evening; he went back to the consulate. He found the equipment he wanted on the shelves in the basement storage room, signed it out, then went upstairs to steal an attaché case. He found a leather one he liked in the CIA spaces under one of the desks. It was a bit feminine for his tastes, yet Kerry Kent would never miss it. Her desk was locked, of course, but the simple locks the furniture manufacturers put on the drawers could be opened with a paper clip. Carmellini settled down to read everything Kent had in her desk.

Letters from England—he gave those only a cursory glance. Lots of travel brochures, letters from girlfriends, two from men—lovers, apparently—a checkbook. He went through the checks, used her pocket calculator to verify that she was indeed living within her income, examined the backs and margins of the check register to see if by chance she had jotted down a personal identification number. Indeed, one four-digit number on the back of the register was probably just that. Tucked under the checks was a bank debit card.

Well, it was tempting. She had caused him a bad moment this evening. Either she sent the thugs or someone she reported to made the call, he felt certain.

Her desk took an hour. He checked his watch, then began on the desks of his CIA colleagues. All the classified documents were supposed to be locked in the fireproof filing cabinets or the safe. Tonight didn't seem like the evening to open those, but perhaps tomorrow night or the night after.

He was working on the boss's desk when he heard someone coming. He closed the drawers, went to his own desk, and selected a report from the in-basket. He had it open in front of him when one of the marines from the security detail stuck his head in.

"How's it going, sir?" the lance corporal asked.

"Just fine. Everything quiet?"

"As usual."

"Terrific."

"Gonna be much longer?"

"Couple hours, I think."

Twenty minutes per desk was sufficient for each of the three men. Other than personal items of little significance, Carmellini found nothing that aroused his curiosity.

Since he was doing desks tonight, he decided he might as well do Cole's. The consul general's office was locked, of course, but Carmellini had the door open in about eighty seconds.

A reasonable search of the bookcases, desk, and credenza would take a couple of hours. He checked his watch. The night was young.

Tommy Carmellini picked the locks on Cole's desk, opened the drawers, and began reading.

Tiger Cole had just said good-bye to the Graftons when his telephone rang. "Tiger?"

He recognized the voice. Sue Lin Buckingham. She didn't waste time on preliminaries. "I know Rip would want you to know, so I called. He's in jail. The authorities shut down the *Post* today and arrested him."

"Have you called a lawyer?"

"Lin Pe called Albert Cheung. I think Albert will get him out of jail tomorrow."

"Tell Rip to come see me."

"I'll tell him."

Cole hung up the phone and poured himself another glass of California Chardonnay.

He snorted, thinking about Jake Grafton and the innocent grin that had danced across his face when he admitted he had "made some inquiries." Yeah. Right. Grafton had probably read his dossier cover to cover.

So he already knew that Cole's company did all the Y2K testing and fixing on some of China's largest networks. . . .

Hoo boy. Talk about irony! He had thought the U.S. government would take months to figure out what happened in Hong Kong. It turned out some dim bulb in Washington who didn't have one original thought per decade decided to send Jake Grafton to look around.

Cole took another sip of white wine and contemplated the glass. He had spent most of his professional life around very bright people, some of them technical geniuses. Jake Grafton was a history major, bright enough but no genius, the kind of guy many techno-nerds held in not-so-secret contempt.

Grafton's strengths were common sense and a willingness to do what he thought was right regardless of the consequences. Cole remembered him from Vietnam with startling clarity: No matter what the danger or how frightened he was, Jake Grafton never lost his ability to think clearly and perform flawlessly, which was why he was the best combat pilot Cole ever met.

Yes, Cole thought, recalling the young man he had flown with all those years ago, Jake Grafton was a ferocious, formidable warrior of extraordinary capability, a precious friend and a deadly enemy.

Perhaps it was Cole's good fortune that fate had brought Grafton here. His talents might be desperately needed in the days ahead.

Cole checked his watch, then walked out of the apartment, locking the door behind him.

The sign on the door said, "Third Planet Communications." Cole used his key.

The office suite was on the third floor of a building directly across the street from the consulate. As luck would have it, Cole could look out his office window directly into the Third Planet suite.

With several hundred of the brightest minds in Hong Kong on its payroll, Third Planet was an acknowledged leader in cutting-edge wireless communications technology. In the eighteen months it had been in business it had become one of the leading wireless network designers and installers in Southeast Asia. Although Cole had put up the capital to start Third Planet, he didn't own any of the stock. In fact, the stock was tied up in so many shell corporations that the ownership would be almost impossible to establish. Cole was, however, listed on the company disclosure documents as an unpaid consultant, just in case any civil servant got too curious about his occasional presence on the premises.

Tonight Tiger Cole walked through the dark offices to a door that led to a windowless interior room. A man sitting in front of the door greeted him in Chinese and opened the door for him.

The lights were full on inside the heavily air-conditioned room, which was stuffed with computers, monitors, servers, routers—all the magic boxes of the high-tech age.

Five people were gathered around one of the terminals, Kerry Kent, Wu Tai Kwong, Hu Chiang, and two of Third Planet's brightest engineers, both women. Cole joined them.

"We're ready," Wu said and slapped Cole on the back.

Another warrior, Cole thought, shaking his head, a Chinese Jake Grafton.

"Is the generator in the basement on?" Cole asked. Through the years he had noticed that these kinds of petty technical details often escaped the geniuses who made the magic.

Yes, he was informed, the generator was indeed running.

"Let's do it," Cole said carelessly, trying not to let his tension show.

One of the female engineers began typing. In seconds a complex diagram appeared on the screen. Everyone watching knew what it was: the Hong Kong power grid. The engineer used a mouse to enlarge one section of the diagram, then did the same again.

Finally she sat looking at a variety of switches.

The other engineer pointed with a finger.

The mouse moved.

"Now we see if the people of China will be slaves or free men," Wu said.

Months of preparation had gone into this moment. If the revolutionaries could control China's electrical power grids, they had the key to the country. Hong Kong was the test case.

The engineer at the computer used one finger to click the mouse.

The lights in the room went off, then came back on as the emergency generator picked up the load in the office suite. The computers, protected from power surges and outages by batteries, didn't flicker.

Cole and the other witnesses rushed from the room, charged across the dark office to the windows that faced the street.

The lights of Hong Kong were *off!*

Tears ran down Cole's face. He was crying and laughing at the same time. He was trying to wipe his face when he realized Wu was pounding him on the back and Kerry Kent was kissing his cheeks.

When Cole got his eyes swabbed out, he looked across the street at the consulate. The emergency generator there had come on automatically, so the lights were back on.

Tiger Cole wondered how long it would be before it occurred to Jake Grafton to ask if Cole's California company had worked on the computers that controlled the Hong Kong power grid.

As they rode the ferry back to Kowloon, Jake asked Callie, "Did you recognize his voice?"

"Yes. He talked to Chan about computers. Chan was trying to cheat him."

"But you don't know if he killed Chan?"

"The identity of the killer is impossible to determine by listening to the tape."

"May I send it off to Washington?"

"Jake, do whatever you think is right."

"Well . . ."

"You didn't tell Tiger why you are here."

"I thought I'd call him tomorrow. Before we got down to business I wanted a social evening."

"I'm not going with you for that."

"I should see him alone," Jake agreed.

They had just gotten off the ferry on the Kowloon side and were walking toward their hotel when the lights went off. One second the city was there, then it wasn't. The effect was eerie, and a bit frightening.

Callie gripped Jake's arm tightly.

When the electricity went off all over the city of Hong Kong, it also failed at the new airport on Lantau Island. And in the air-traffic-control rooms at the base of the tower complex. Fortunately there were only a few airplanes under the control of the Hong Kong sector, and those were mostly freighters on night flights.

The air-traffic-control personnel worked quickly to get the emergency generators on so that the radars could be operated and the computers rebooted. The computers were protected by batteries that should have picked up the load but for some reason didn't. The emergency generators were on-line in three minutes and the radars sweeping the skies in three and a half.

The computers, however, were another matter. When the controllers finally got one of the computers on-line, the hard drive refused to accept new data via modem. Manually inputted data was changed in random ways—flight numbers were transposed, altitude data were incorrect, way points were dropped or added, and the data kept changing. It was almost as if the computer had had a lobotomy.

The second computer had the same problem as the first, and so did the third. The controllers worked the incoming flights manually, but without the computers they were in a severely degraded mode.

Inside the new, modern, state-of-the-art terminal, conditions were worse than they were in the tower. The restoration of power via emergency generators brought the lights back on, but the escalators wouldn't work, the automated baggage system was kaput, none of the flight display screens worked, the people-mover train refused to budge—its doors were frozen in place—and the jetways that allowed access to and from the planes could not be moved. Fortunately there were few passengers in the terminals and concourses, but those who were there were trapped until service personnel could get to them.

When power was finally restored from the main feeds, the computers still refused to work. The airline companies' reservations computers, fax machines, and Internet terminals seemed to be working fine, but the airport had ceased to function.

The technicians in the Hong Kong harbormaster's office were also having problems. The radars that kept track of the myriad of ships, barges, tugs, and boats of every kind and description in Victoria Harbor and the strait were working, but the computer that processed the information and presented it to the harbor controller was no longer able to identify or track targets. When the technicians tried the backup computer, they found it had a similar disease.

The people who had caused these problems sat and stood in front of the computer monitors at Third Planet Communications in a merry mood. Someone opened a bottle of Chinese wine, which they drank from paper cups.

The virus programs they had written and loaded on the affected computers seemed to be working perfectly. As Cole explained to Wu and Kent all those months ago, "Remember the chaos that was supposed to happen when Y2K rolled around, and didn't? We must make it happen now. Revolutions are about control, which is essence of power: We must take control away from the Communists. When the Communists lose their power they lose their leadership mandate. It's as simple as one, two, three."

Tonight Cole told Wu, "The revolution has begun."

He shook hands all around and headed for the door with a light step. Tomorrow would be a hell of a day and he needed some sleep.

Tommy Carmellini hailed a taxi in front of the consulate. The driver took him back to his hotel via the Cross-Harbor Tunnel, creeping along through the blacked-out city with a solid stream of cars and trucks.

The rear door of the hotel was locked. To discourage thieves, no doubt, Carmellini thought as he opened it with a pick. The job took less than a minute. With the electricity off, of course there was no alarm when the door opened. There wouldn't have been an alarm even if the power had been on—the door wasn't wired, a fact Carmellini had ascertained fifteen minutes after he checked into the place.

He went up the back stairs and carefully unlocked his room. A old-fashioned metal key, thank God, because the card scanners in use at the new hotels would not be working, leaving all the patrons locked out of their rooms.

No one was in the room waiting for him.

Carmellini changed into black trousers, a long-sleeved dark shirt, and tennis shoes. The equipment from the consulate went into a knapsack, as did a roll of duct tape, a small flashlight, a glass cutter, a few small hand tools, and an extensive assortment of lock picks: everything necessary for a quiet night of burglary.

Kerry Kent lived in an apartment house on a side street off Nathan Road, a mile or so north of the Star Ferry landing at Tsim Sha Tsui. The building was about ten stories high, filled the block, and was ten or fifteen years old, Tommy Carmellini thought.

The street was unnaturally quiet. A few people were up and about at two in the morning, but without electrical power to drive the gadgets, the night was very still. Carmellini could hear traffic on Nathan Road and, from somewhere, the rumble of a train.

He checked the scrap of paper where he had written the apartment number.

Kent's pad should be on the seventh floor, he decided, and went into the building to examine the apartment layout. The elevators weren't working so he climbed the dark staircase. Okay, the first floor was the one above the ground floor, so she would be on the eighth floor.

He walked along the hall until he found the apartment that corresponded to hers, which was twenty-seven.

Back outside on the sidewalk he examined the windows and balconies, counted upward. Okay, Kent's was the balcony with the two orange flowerpots and the bicycle chained to the rail.

He stood on the sidewalk just a moment, adjusting his backpack, listening, looking. . . .

When he was sure no one was observing him, Tommy Carmellini leaped from the sidewalk and grasped the bottom of the wrought-iron slats in the railing on the first-floor balcony. He could tell by the feel that the iron was rusty. Would it hold his weight?

Using upper-body strength alone, he drew himself up to the edge of the balcony floor and looked. And listened.

When he was convinced it was safe, he pulled himself up hand over hand until he could hook a heel over the rail, which squealed slightly in protest.

In seconds he was balanced on the rail, still listening. . . .

He straightened, examined the underside of the floor of the balcony above him. He reached up for the rails, grasped them, and gradually gave them his weight, making sure the slats and railings were not too rusty or broken.

Up the side of the building he went, floor by floor, silently and quickly. Two minutes after he left the street, he was crouched on Kerry Kent's balcony examining the door, which was ajar. For ventilation, probably, since the night was warm and pleasant. As he listened for sounds from inside the apartment, he examined the windows of the apartments across the street, looking for anyone who might have watched him climb the side of the building.

Only when he felt certain that he was unobserved did he remove two tiny remote microphones, bugs, from his backpack, and a roll of duct tape. Using a knife, he trimmed two pieces of tape about two inches long from the roll and stuck them on the front of his shirt, where they were accessible. Then he returned the knife and tape roll to the backpack.

Due to the low probability that Kent routinely swept for bugs, these would transmit to a recorder as long as their batteries lasted, a time frame that depended on how many hours a day noise was generated in the apartment. They should last a couple of weeks if she didn't watch too much television or leave the radio on continuously. Months if electric power wasn't restored to the building.

The recorder had to be nearby, outside if possible, where Carmellini could get at it without too much effort. He planned to find a place to install it after he got the microphones in place.

Just to be on the safe side, he removed the backpack, which contained the burglary tools he wouldn't need since she left the sliding glass door ajar, and placed it on the floor out of his way.

Now he got to his feet, crouched to present as small a silhouette as possible to any casual observer, and inched the door open with his latex-clad fingertips. Applying steady pressure, he got the door moving and kept it moving, as slowly as possible.

When he had it open enough, about fourteen inches, Carmellini stood, turned sideways, and stepped in.

Moonlight was the only illumination. As his eyes adjusted to the gloom Carmellini could see that the apartment consisted of just one room and a bath. The kitchen area, a sink and stove, was located in the inside corner of the room to the right of the door. The area to the left of the door was the bathroom. The rest of the apartment, which was about the size of a standard American motel room, contained a Western-style bed, a few chairs, and a dresser. A television sat atop the dresser. Posters of famous paintings adorned the walls.

And in the bed, asleep apparently, were Kerry Kent...and a man. From this angle Carmellini could see only his hair—the man appeared to be Chinese. Kent's bare leg stuck out from under the sheet and light blanket that covered them.

Carmellini stood in the darkness listening. Heavy, deep, rhythmical breathing.

From where he was standing he examined the apartment, looking for a place for the bugs.

The head of the bed certainly looked inviting. It was some kind of wooden latticework; he could reach in and stick a bug on the back of the top of the headboard. It should be out of sight there and safe enough, unless someone moved the bed and examined the headboard.

The other one . . . perhaps under the bedside nightstand that held the telephone.

The decisions made, Tommy Carmellini stepped forward with bugs and tape ready.

Like a silent shadow he moved to the edge of the bed and bent down. He reached up under the nightstand and was affixing the first bug when Kerry Kent's deep breathing stopped.

She was facing away from him, thank God, but she might turn over. He froze.

Yes, she was turning toward him. He waited until she had completed her move and was breathing regularly again, then he felt to make sure the tiny transmitter's antenna was hanging down freely. It was. Now he slowly stood, staying perfectly balanced, moving at the speed of a glacier, making no noise at all.

To get the other bug behind the headboard meant that he had to reach across her, above her face, and put it in place without jiggling the headboard in any way, for the movement of the headboard would be transferred to the bed.

He didn't let his limbs come to a stop but stayed fluidly in motion, each move thought out and planned so that he stayed balanced on both feet.

He got the tape, with the bug in the center of it, in the proper position and pressed firmly so that it would stick to the wood. The antenna seemed to be hanging in place behind one of the lattices.

He had pulled his arm back and was ready to turn when her breathing changed abruptly and she awoke. One second she was asleep, the next she was awake. Just like that.

Carmellini stood frozen. He was about eighteen inches from her head. If she decided to get up to go to the bathroom, this was going to get very interesting.

Can a person feel the presence of another human being, one absolutely silent and motionless?

There are those who swear they can. Tommy Carmellini believed that some people could, and he stood now willing his heart to beat slowly lest she hear it.

For the first time he was also aware of the faint voices and traffic rumble that could be heard through the open balcony door, which had of course been almost closed before he arrived. Would she notice the noise? Or the coolness of the night air?

She turned in bed again, rubbed against the sleeping man.

Oh, great! She'll wake him!

She mumbled something in Chinese . . . and the man stirred.

He turned, put his arm around her.

Seconds passed, his breathing deepened.

Tommy Carmellini realized he was sweating. Perspiration was trickling down his nose, down his cheeks. He dared not move. . . .

If I don't relax, she's going to smell me!

The seconds dragged. She adjusted her position in the bed . . . and finally, little by little, her breathing slowed and grew deeper.

Carmellini began moving toward the open door. He didn't walk, he flowed, gently, steadily, smoothly. . . .

On the balcony he debated if he should close the door. If it made a noise now . . . no! The risk was too great.

After scanning the other balconies and the apartment buildings across the street to ensure he didn't have an audience, Carmellini went over the rail. He leaned back, checked the balcony below as best he could, then lowered himself onto the railing. Balancing carefully, he released his grip on the wrought-iron slats above and coiled himself to go down another floor.

In half a minute he was standing on the street. He was wiping his hands on his trousers when the electrical power was restored to the neighborhood, bringing the lights on. Televisions and radios that had been on when the power failed blared into life.

What is it his mother used to say? "You're going to get caught, Tommy, one of these days. Sneaking around like you do ain't Christian. People'll get mean when they catch you sneaking, one of these days."

One of these days, he thought. *But not today.*

He began looking for a place where he could hide the recorder.

As Tommy Carmellini walked south on Nathan Road toward his hotel, a van whipped to the curb and a man jumped out with a bundle of paper in his arms. He put the stack on top of a newspaper dispenser, cut the plastic tie that bound it together, then got back in the van, which rocketed off down the street.

Carmellini paused by the stack and took a sheet off the top. A flyer of some type. In Chinese, of course.

He folded it and put it in his pocket.

Wonder what that is all about?

CHAPTER SEVEN

Governor Sun Siu Ki didn't have newspapers to worry about this morning; he had shut down the politically incorrect rags and jailed the editors. No, the rag du jour was a flyer that had been distributed by the tens of thousands throughout the Special Administrative Region, the old colony, of Hong Kong.

The flyer, titled *The Truth,* was a single sheet of paper printed on both sides with Chinese characters. It contained a highly critical account of the Bank of the Orient debacle and shooting, blaming the entire incident on the Chinese government's attempted looting of the bank and on the overaggressiveness of the People's Liberation Army. The sheet called for mass demonstrations to demand that the authorities cease requiring bribes from banks, release the jailed newspaper editors, and allow the publication of uncensored news. The sheet was signed by a group calling itself the Scarlet Team.

"This is outrageous, inflammatory, antirevolutionary criminal propaganda," the governor told his assistant, who agreed completely with that assessment. "Have the police find the people who did this and arrest them." Sun hammered on the desk with his fist as he added, "I will not tolerate these criminal provocations! Find these people!"

"Yes, sir," said the aide.

The governor wadded up the offending flyer and threw it into the wastebasket beside his desk.

He took a deep breath, then tackled the next item on the morning's agenda. "Has electrical power been restored throughout the city?"

"Yes, sir. Apparently so. The engineers are still trying to determine why the load was lost in the first place. Unfortunately power fluctuations apparently caused extensive damage to the computer systems at Lantau Airport and Harbor Control."

"When will the systems be operational again?"

The aide didn't know the answer to that one. He would find out and report back, he said, which didn't please the governor.

Everything seemed to be going wrong all at once. As if to emphasize that fact, the secretary came in to announce that the ministry in Beijing was on the telephone.

The minister was worried. Questions were being asked at the highest levels. Did Sun need more help handling the situation in Hong Kong?

"No, certainly not," Sun replied. "Criminal elements are taking advantage of events that are out of anyone's control, but the government is firmly in charge."

Because Albert Cheung was somebody important, the warden of the prison had Rip Buckingham brought to his office. There was a room in the prison for lawyers and clients to meet, but it consisted of a long table with chicken wire down the middle and a guard at each end. There was no privacy.

Albert had known the Chinese warden a long time—he slipped him a handful of currency when they shook hands. After the guards brought Rip, the warden and guards left together, leaving Rip and Albert alone.

"I thought Lin Pe might call you," Rip said, sinking into a stuffed chair. "You'll have to excuse my odor. They're having trouble with the showers and soap."

"Lin Pe called me yesterday. Yesterday I went to see Governor Sun. We negotiated. I went back this morning and we negotiated some more. To make a long story short, he wants a hundred thousand Hong Kong." Actually Sun Siu Ki had wanted two hundred thousand, but Albert had beaten him down. This he didn't mention. He didn't like to discuss money with his clients, except when absolutely necessary. Discussing money offended his sense of dignity.

Rip grunted noncommittally. He was thinking how clean and comfortable Albert Cheung looked. Wearing an impeccable gray suit and conservative silk tie, he looked as if he had just stepped out of the Pall Mall Club in London. Rip was wearing filthy khaki chinos, a nondescript blue shirt, and penny loafers without socks. His clothes looked like he had worn them day and night for a month, although it had been only two days.

"Your wife wants you home," Albert said tentatively.

Rip Buckingham didn't want to talk about his wife. She had come to visit him yesterday and the prison staff had refused to let her in unless she paid a bribe. That, Rip knew, was pretty much standard procedure these days. Sue Lin refused to pay. Or so one of the guards told him last night. That certainly sounded like her, Rip reflected. She was tough, and Rip liked that a lot.

He picked up a pencil from the warden's desk and stroked it with his fingers as he asked, "What do I have to do to reopen the paper?"

"Sun and I did discuss that matter," Albert acknowledged.

"How much?"

"Well, it's not that simple. Apparently people in Beijing have been talking to the governor."

"Uh-huh."

"You'll need to sign a contract with Xinhua for editorial services. That will cost you so much a month." Xinhua, the New China News Agency, was the Communist government's propaganda organ.

"How much?" Rip asked idly.

"I don't know. It probably won't be nominal."

"We sometimes run Communist government press releases as news," Rip told the lawyer, "but only if they're newsworthy. My staff decides. You'd be amazed at the reams of trash bureaucrats generate. My readers aren't interested."

"You don't have to print anything you don't wish to print. However, the agency will assign an editor, who must approve anything that you do want to print."

"Censorship."

"Call it that if you like."

"For Christ's sake, Albert!"

"Rip, be reasonable. This isn't a comfortable little chunk of England anymore, with British judges and British law. *This is China!* You have to go along to get along."

Buckingham said a dirty word.

"Give me the authorization to pay Sun and I'll get you out of here. You think about the paper. We'll talk later."

Rip broke the pencil in half and tossed the pieces on the warden's desk. "I won't publish the paper under those conditions," he said. "I can tell you that right now. But it isn't my paper. It belongs to Buckingham News, Limited, which may soon be looking for a new managing editor."

"Buckingham News, that's your father, right?"

"Rich owns about sixty percent of it, I think. My sisters and I own small pieces, some of the stock is in executive compensation plans, and the rest is owned by some hot dollies Dad took a fancy to. He gave them stock certificates instead of diamonds."

"Does that work?" Albert asked curiously.

"Dad says it depends on how many shares you give them," Rip said, his face deadpan. He shrugged. "Buckingham News pays no dividends, there's no market for the stock, and Dad has absolute control. About all a shareholder can hope for is that the certificates will be worth real money someday. One might think of it as a sort of pension plan for the women."

"What does Mr. Buckingham do with the profits if he doesn't pay dividends?" asked the Hong Kong attorney. "I assume there are profits."

"He buys more newspapers, cable television networks. He got into satellite distribution of television signals years ago. He said that technology would ultimately have a greater impact on the human race than the invention of movable type. Certainly it's going to have a greater impact on the third world."

Rich may be a noxious old fossil, his son reflected, but he had vision. Rip told the lawyer, "As a matter of fact, I think Buckingham News owns the company with about fifty percent of the satellite dish business in Hong Kong."

"Very progressive," said Albert Cheung.

"In any event, the women seem happy and Dad appears to be doing all right."

"Wonderful, wonderful."

"Quite. But I don't know what Dad will do about the *Post*. The only principle to which he is irrevocably and totally committed is making money."

"Yes."

"A lot of money."

Albert Cheung looked interested. "I like money myself," he remarked blandly.

"Go pay the man and get me the hell out of here," Rip Buckingham told the lawyer. "The company in this place is fascinating but the food isn't anything to brag about."

"Mr. Cole, there's a Rear Admiral Grafton on line one."

"Thank you," Cole said to his secretary and picked up the phone. "Hello, Jake."

"I just called to thank you for last night. It was good seeing you again."

"And you."

"I was wondering if I could drop by today and have a chat about government business? Could you give me an hour or so?"

"Come at lunch and I'll buy."

"About twelve?"

"See you then."

When Sue Lin heard her brother, Wu, come in, she went downstairs to his room and knocked. He immediately opened the door. He was here to change clothes, which was about all he ever did at this house.

"We need to talk," she said softly in English, worried as always that the domestics would overhear.

Only two years older than Sue Lin, Wu had always awed her, ever since she could remember. Never had she met a man with his inner calm, a man whose strength radiated like heat from a fire. He was, she thought, the most masculine of men, a man so strong emotionally and spiritually that nothing on this earth could shake him.

Of course he attracted people, men and women, like a magnet attracts iron filings. In a reflective moment Rip had compared Wu to Christ. "If he was preaching a new religion he could convert the world," Rip said, and Sue Lin thought Rip was probably right.

As Wu looked at her his face softened. "Of course," he said, nodding gently. "May I continue to change, or would you like to go upstairs?"

"Go on," she said, motioning toward the closet, and told him about Rip being arrested and the newspaper closed.

"I have heard," Wu said. "I am sorry for Rip."

"Albert Cheung will get him out, but the paper . . . the governor will probably keep it closed."

She sat in the only chair in the small room. "The day has almost arrived, hasn't it?"

"Its coming was inevitable," Wu replied calmly. Sue Lin had never seen him excited—she didn't think anything could disturb his inner peace.

"Rip is worried. If the authorities finally learn that you are my brother, Lin Pe's son, Rip thinks they will take their frustrations out on us."

"Rip is probably correct," Wu said softly. He rarely raised his voice. "His understanding of the scope of the official mind seems quite complete."

"He wants us to leave Hong Kong now."

"Sister of mine, I advise you to obey your husband."

"Mother will not leave."

"Her destiny is not yours."

"Wu, for God's sake, you must tell Mother to leave! She will listen to you! She ignores my pleas."

Wu sat on the bed and took his sister's hand. "Leaving China would cost Lin Pe her life. *This* is who she is. On the other hand, you have your husband, your life together, which you can live anyplace on the planet. Lin Pe does not have that."

"Are you saying that Rip and I should leave you two here?"

"This country, these people, they are my life also."

Sue Lin Buckingham jerked her hand from his grasp. "I think the new maid is suspicious of you. She watches you from the window, pretends she knows no English when it is obvious she understands some of it. She may be a police spy."

"What would you have me do?"

At that Sue Lin threw up her hands and left the room.

Albert Cheung drove Rip to the building that housed the newspaper. It was raining again, a steady drizzle. Albert wanted to take him home but Rip insisted on going to the office.

There were two policemen with shotguns standing under an overhang outside the building.

Albert pulled his Mercedes into the alley that led to the parking area in back. "Thanks, Albert," Rip said and released his seat belt.

As Rip reached for the door handle, Albert put a hand on his arm and said, "Wait a minute, Rip. I want to give you some advice, if you'll listen."

"I'll listen. I won't pay for your advice, but I'll listen."

"It's time for you to go. Take your wife, go back to Australia. That is your place. That is where you belong."

Rip growled and reached for door handle.

"Listen to me," Albert said sharply. "The British are gone. For one hundred and fifty years this city was a part of Britain. It was as English as tea and toast. No more. Those days are *over*. And everyone has to adjust to the new reality."

"I've adjusted. I just don't like it."

"Like it or not, Hong Kong is now part of China, and China is an absolute dictatorship. The British ways—free speech, democracy, open, honest government, a tolerant, pluralist society, the rule of law, open debate about the public's business, fair play—all that is dying or dead. People here must jettison the old ways and adopt the new. They have no choice—*they have to do it!* I've been reading your paper: You rail against the incoming tide."

Rip tried to rebut Albert Cheung. "I have tried to fairly—"

" 'Fairly'? Don't be ridiculous. *Fair* is a British concept, not Chinese. There is nothing you can do."

"This is my home, too," Rip said savagely.

"Stop playing the fool. Get on a plane."

Rip sat for a moment listening to the slap of the windshield wipers. "Why don't you leave?" he asked the lawyer.

"I happen to be Chinese, you may have noticed. And there is money to be made here."

"There are six million people in Hong Kong without anyplace else to go."

"You're wasting your breath trying to save the world, Rip. You won't get a halo. You won't even get a thank-you."

"Don't charge me for this advice, Albert." Rip got out of the car, shut the door firmly behind him.

Albert Cheung sped away without another look at Rip.

Maybe the cops would have let him in the building, maybe not; Rip didn't try. He went around back and unlocked his motorcycle, an old Harley-Davidson he had imported from Australia.

Motorcycles were popular in Hong Kong—mainly Japanese bikes, fast and fuel-efficient—but not as ubiquitous as they were in Singapore or Bangkok. The British always discouraged motor vehicles for private use by making it expensive to register one or get a driver's license. The Communists continued that policy. Still, a lot of people today had the money or political connections, so there were more and more motor-cycles. Those who couldn't afford to go first-class rode Chinese iron. With no demand for forty-year-old Harleys, thieves weren't interested, or so the theory went. Rip always locked his anyway.

He turned on the fuel cock, adjusted the choke, and started kicking. The engine caught on the third kick.

He was warming the engine when the woman who ran a small newsstand across the street came looking for him.

"Rip, why have the police closed the building?" Originally from Hunan Province, she had lived in Hong Kong at least twenty years. Rip had deduced that one time by questioning her closely about Hong Kong news stories she could remember.

"The governor has ordered the paper closed, Mrs. Guo," Rip told her. "He didn't like what he read."

"You did not go to jail? I heard they arrested you."

"I went to jail." He gave her a brief summary, then said good-bye. "My wife is waiting for me. She worries."

"Yes, yes. Go home to her." Mrs. Guo went back along the alley with her head down, as if she were walking against a storm. Hard times . . .

The Chinese are used to hard times, Rip reflected. They've never known anything else.

He put the motorcycle in motion.

The streets were still crowded. Traffic sprayed water on Rip, who had to concentrate to keep his motorcycle under control.

Rip had first seen Hong Kong as a teenager in the mid-eighties, when there were still vestigial traces of the nineteenth-century city, and large swatches remained unchanged from the days of World War II. Back then many people could talk for hours about the Japanese occupation from their personal experience. Not many of those old people were left, of course, and few people now asked about the old days. Nobody cared anymore.

That was the way of the world, Rip knew. Certainly the way of China. The past—good or bad—was soon forgotten. There was always today to be lived through and tomorrow to prepare for. Venerable ancestors were, of course, worthy and honorable and all that, but, alas, they were quite dead.

It was that Chinese focus on the now that intrigued Rip Buckingham. For the Chinese, he thought, all things were possible. Coolies and peasants from the rice paddies had built this modern city, were constantly transforming it, and in turn were transformed by it. It was an extraordinary metamorphosis.

Today not a single building remained from the nineteenth century. The commercial buildings were fifty-story-plus avant-garde statements in steel and glass. Mile after mile of high-rise apartment buildings housed more than six million people. The thought of living in one was a daunting prospect for Westerners, but the fact remains, six million people were decently housed.

As he rode the Harley through traffic and tried to ignore the drizzle and road spray, Rip Buckingham marveled again at the raw power of this great city. Chinese signs were freely intermingled with the logos of international corporations and brand names. Rip thought this mixture symbolic of Hong Kong, where East and West met, transforming both.

Hong Kong was a vast human stew, and by choice Rip was right in the middle of it.

He inched his way up the narrow, twisty roads that grooved the northern face of Victoria Peak, then guided the motorcycle into a driveway and triggered a radio-controlled garage-door opener in a house glued to the side of the peak. Buckingham News actually owned the place, which was a good thing since Rip could never have paid for it on his salary.

As he was getting off the machine inside the garage his wife came through the door.

"You're soaked," she said.

"Doesn't matter. I stunk from jail."

She kissed him.

He hit the button to close the outside door, then led her up the stairs to the living room. A large window looked out on the Central District and Kowloon across the strait. As Rip told his wife about jail and the governor, he automatically glanced outside. Kowloon was almost hidden in the rain and mist.

"I called your father."

"What did he say?"

"Just that you should call when you could. I asked him if I should hire Albert Cheung, and he said yes."

Rip stretched and nodded. "I need to take a shower, put on some dry clothes. I'll call him later."

"What are we going to do, Rip?"

"I don't know," he said, meaning it. "This place is our life. Sun Siu Ki just took it from us."

"They won't let you keep publishing the *Post*."

"I know."

"Things are changing."

"I know. *I know!* You told me. The police told me. Albert Cheung told me. I know, I know, and *goddamn,* I resent it."

"Mother won't leave without my brother."

Rip took his wife's hand. "I know that, too," he said gently and kissed her.

An hour later, after he had a long, hot shower and put on fresh clothes, Rip called his father's office in Sydney. Soon Rich's voice boomed through the instrument.

Rip told him about the cease publication order and the demands of Sun Siu Ki.

"Dad, I don't think we should run the paper under these conditions. It's censorship. Knuckling under to the Communists will cost Buckingham News its standing in the international community, and that ultimately will mean loss of ad revenue all over the globe."

"That paper is worth a hundred million," Richard Buckingham thundered into the telephone.

Rip had to hold the instrument away from his ear. The old man sounded like he was in the next room.

"Bloody Chinks! A hundred million!" Rich ripped off a couple oaths, but the volume was going down. "All the bloody lies they've told the last fifteen or twenty years, about how great it was going to be in Hong Kong when they took over . . . Makes me want to puke!"

"Yessir," Rip agreed.

"And the bloody Brits." Richard added them to his list. "Believing those lies . . ."

"Maybe it's time to pack it in," Rip said reluctantly, trying to get back to the business at hand. "Maybe in a few years the government here will see the benefits of a free press."

"They don't really have a choice," Richard rumbled. "The world has outgrown censorship. But you're right—we can't buck the bastards head-on. Pay off the *Post* employees. Send me the names and qualifications of everyone who wants to work for another Buckingham paper and is willing to move. We'll see what we can do." There was a second of dead sound, then he added, "Move at their own expense, of course."

"Yes, sir."

"I'd like to see you and Sue Lin. Come on home."

"In a few weeks. We have to wrap up some things here."

"Righto, mate."

"And Dad? Thanks."

"For what?"

"For seeing this my way."

"See you in a few weeks."

Richard Buckingham hung up the telephone and sat staring out the window at the artsy-fartsy roof of the Sydney Opera House. He called in Billy Kidd, who had been his number two since Richard was the publisher, editor, and sports writer of the *Wangeroo Gazette*.

"The Commies have shut down the *Post* in Hong Kong," he began. After Richard told Billy what he knew, he added, "I want a story about the shutdown and I want it on the front page of every paper I own. Call Rip at home and have him write it. Use a file photo of him."

"Righto."

"Top of the front page, Billy." Richard picked up a legal pad and pencil from his desk and handed it to Billy, who could take a hint. He began taking notes.

"Billy, someday those Commie bastards are going to regret screwing with me. Bad press is the only lever I have, and by God, I'm going to use it."

Richard Buckingham got out of his chair and paced the office. "Put the one-baby story on the telly chat shows again. More Falun Gong persecution stories. Bang the drum every day. And I mean every day, Billy. A new, different, bad slant each and every day."

"Whatever you want, Richard. But I don't think that—"

"And I want something about those hundred million migrants roaming around China that the Commies are cracking down on. I'm tired of reading about these lawless vagrants threatening the economic prosperity of the new China. The corrupt, venal Communist regime is threatening the economic prosperity of the new China. They are prosecuting the harmless kooks in the Falun Gong movement, jailing people whose only crime is to want a little bit of life's sweetness. Massive pollution, sweatshops, child labor—China's the last big sewer left on earth, and that's the way we'll write it from now on. Fax it to the managing editor of every paper."

Billy finished taking notes and asked sourly, "Anything else?" He had been with Richard Buckingham too long to cower.

"Communism is as dead as Lenin. The Buckingham newspapers and television networks are going to trumpet that news loud and clear. Find a politico to write it, somebody important or somebody who wants to be important."

"You—"

"And why does the free world tolerate the crimes against humanity that the Chinese government perpetrates on those who can't defend themselves? Maybe an article, 'Tiananmen Square Revisited.' "

Billy scribbled furiously. "You're the boss," he said.

"You're damn right I am," Richard roared. "Those bloody Chinks didn't like the coverage they got from the *China Post*—they're going to shit when they see the press they're getting from now on. When anybody anywhere says anything bad about Red China, I want to read it in the papers and hear about it on the telly news shows. From this day forward Buckingham News is the world's foremost voice urging the overthrow of the Communists in Beijing."

Rich punched the air and sat down. "You and I are going to do at least one good thing before we go, Billy-boy," he said conversationally.

Billy Kidd launched himself from Richard's office. Billy knew that when Richard was on a tear you didn't get many openings, so he bolted at the first one he saw.

An hour later Richard called Billy on the intercom. "Don't we own a big piece of a direct TV company in Hong Kong?"

"That's right. China Television, Limited. Very profitable."

"Sell it as fast as you can. Maybe a competitor will buy it. Get what you can and let's move on."

"Richard, I know you're angry, but China Television is worth serious money. Satellite television is here now; China is on its way to becoming the largest market on earth. Those little dishes are selling like Viagra."

Richard Buckingham's answer was matter-of-fact. "I'm going to piss on a lot of Commies, Billy. I don't want something of mine hanging out where they can cut it off, throw it in the dirt, and stomp on it. Get rid of China Television—we'll take the loss out of their hides."

Billy refused to quit. "No one will pay what it's worth," he insisted.

Richard was patient. "Billy, with the Communists in power, nothing in China is worth real money. That's the lesson the Americans and British and Japanese are going to learn the hard way."

A man was waiting on the street when Jake stepped out of the hotel. He was standing under an overhang to stay out of the rain. As Jake walked along the sidewalk with Callie's umbrella, the man got into a car that had been parked in the taxi space in front of the building.

Jake ignored the tail. He was acutely aware of the Chan tape in his pocket. For some reason he was relieved that he had ditched the wallet and pistol he had taken from the man who had followed him yesterday.

As he entered the ferry terminal, the car outside pulled to the curb, and two men got out of the rear seat.

Jake saw them board the *Star of the West* just before the gangplank came over. The second man aboard had a bandage on his head; this was the fellow whom Jake had relieved of wallet and pistol. He boarded on the lower deck. The other man came to the upper deck, where Jake was, but he stayed well away from the American.

Exiting the Central District ferry terminal, Jake hailed the only taxi he saw. He didn't bother checking to see what the men following him did.

When Jake entered Cole's office, Cole came around his desk and shook hands. "We have a choice," he said. "We can have lunch served here, go to the cafeteria, or slip down the street to a restaurant with wine and all the trimmings. What will it be?"

"Here, if that's okay with you?"

"Here it is. Have a seat and let me talk to the secretary."

In a few minutes Cole was back. He sat in one of the black leather guest chairs beside Jake.

"I guess I should have leveled with you last night," Jake said. "I'm here on official business. A lot of Washington bigwigs are getting nervous about the situation in Hong Kong. More to the point, they are getting nervous about China Bob Chan and your relationship to him. They managed to talk the White House into sending me over here to talk to you, see what I can find out, and report back."

A look of puzzlement crossed Cole's face. "Why you?"

"Someone found out that we flew together way back when, the politicians are embarrassed about China Bob, I was getting on a four-star's nerves at the Pentagon, someone with some stroke at the National Security Council thinks I can work miracles. It all happened at once, so here I am."

"Uh-huh."

"When this trip got suggested, I initially said no. Then Callie was asked to do the culture conference, sort of as a cover. . . ." He shrugged.

"Ask your questions."

"Are you or your friends having me followed around town?"

"You're being followed?"

"Two men followed me here this morning. Presumably they're outside somewhere, waiting for me to come out."

Cole looked genuinely surprised. "Jake, I have no idea."

"I guess it all boils down to this: Are you or are you not a member of a conspiracy to overthrow the government of China?"

Cole whistled. "Jesus! You flew all the way over here from Washington to ask me that question?"

Jake Grafton scratched his head. "Well, I think the folks in Washington expected me to be a bit more circumspect, but, essentially, yeah. If the answer to that question is no, the next question is, Have you ever given advice or anything of value to anyone whose goal is the overthrow of the government of China?"

Cole pinched his nose, looked at Grafton, and grinned. The grin started slowly and spread. Jake knew he didn't grin often.

Finally Cole broke into a laugh. He was still chuckling when the secretary came in with a tray. On the tray were two bowls of soup, several sandwiches, and a couple cans of Coke. Tiger Cole's face returned to its normal detached expression. As the man left the room the consul general muttered, "I always serve American drinks to guests. Today is Coke day. Tomorrow is Pepsi."

Cole tasted the soup. "You are a rare piece of work, Grafton. When they taught you to go straight for a target way back when, you learned the lesson well."

Jake tried the soup himself. It was something Chinese, a watery vegetable, okay but nothing to write home about. No crackers in sight. He popped the can of Coke and took a sip. At least the drink was cold.

Cole pointed his spoon at Jake, then decided to use the spoon on the soup. Once a chuckle escaped him.

They ate in silence. Finally Cole finished soup and sandwich and leaned back in his chair to sip on the soft drink.

"Do you know how ironic this is, that of all the people on this planet, you, Jake Grafton, are the one who comes flying out of my past to ask about my future."

"I haven't asked about the future," Jake shot back. "It's the present the weenies in Washington are worried about."

"Ah, yes. The present."

Cole walked around the desk and stood at the window looking out. He couldn't see much, merely a gloomy forest of skyscrapers with glass sides on a dreary, rainy day.

"This warm front is supposed to get out of here tonight," he said. "The next three or four days will be bright and sunny."

"Uh-huh." Grafton finished his Coke and set the empty can on the tray along with the dirty dishes.

Cole returned to the desk, sat in his regular chair, folded his arms on the desk, and looked Jake Grafton in the eye. "Some ground rules. We'll play this game my way or not at all."

Grafton adjusted his position in his chair. "What are the rules?"

"I'll answer your questions completely, frankly, truthfully, but you can't tell a living soul for one week."

Jake thought about that. "The problem," he said after a bit, "is that you are in the diplomatic service of the United States. If a private citizen wants to saddle up and ride off to a revolution, that's between him and whoever is running the universe this week. If a diplomat does it, that's a different case altogether."

"A point well taken," Cole said. "I gave this some thought while we ate. Let's do this: If you will agree to the conditions I stated, complete silence for a week, I'll write out a letter of resignation, leave the date blank, and give it to you. You fill in the date anytime you wish and see that the people in Washington get it—no sooner than a week from today."

Now it was Jake Grafton's turn to go to the window and look out. "Why don't you just tell me some lie to get me out of your hair?"

"Ooh boy, that's rich! Coming from you. When they asked you way back when whether or not you had ever bombed an unauthorized target, what did you say?"

"I said yes."

"Indeed you did. You were the rarest of rarities, a truly honest man. Sorry, but I don't have it in me to lie to Jake Grafton."

"Listen, Tiger. I can't stay silent for a week. Not if you tell me you're up to something you shouldn't be up to."

Cole cocked his head and looked at Jake with an odd expression. "What should I be up to?"

"Don't give me that!"

"Do you know what these Communists are? Do you know what they represent?"

Jake Grafton leaned across the desk toward Tiger Cole. "If the government of the United States told me to pull the trigger," he whispered hoarsely, "I'd be willing to personally send every Communist in the world straight to hell. But as long as I'm in the United States Navy I don't have the luxury of choosing that course of action without orders. Neither do you when you're representing the United States of America. Write out that resignation and date it today. I'll send it in for you."

Cole leaned back in his chair and rubbed his eyes.

After a bit he asked, "When are you going to send it in?"

Grafton threw up his hands. "I don't know!"

Cole spun around to the PC that sat on a stand near the desk, turned it on, put stationery in the printer tray, and started typing. Three minutes later a letter rolled off the printer. Cole read it through, signed it, then handed it to Grafton.

Jake took his time reading the letter, then folded it carefully. "Got an envelope?"

Cole got one from a drawer and handed it across the desk.

Jake put the letter in the envelope, then stowed it in an inside breast pocket of his sports coat.

"Any more questions?" Cole said.

"Want to tell me why?"

Cole leaned back in his chair and stretched. He looked out the window at the slabs of skyscraper glass while he collected his thoughts, then turned his attention back to Grafton.

"I should have died that December day in 1972 when I was lying in the jungle muck in Laos with a broken back. Would have died, too, if I had been flying with an average mortal man. But no! As fate would have it I was flying with Jake Grafton, the warrior incarnate. Jake Grafton wasn't leaving that jungle without me—it was both of us or neither of us. So he fought and we both lived. I can close my eyes and remember it like it was yesterday. That moment was the most important of my life."

Cole turned toward the window and the gloomy, rainy day. "And I remember the day I became a millionaire," he continued, speaking softly. "We did an initial public offering. I went from owing thirty-three thousand dollars in student loans and two thousand on an old Chevy to a net worth of twenty-three million bucks just like *that!*" He snapped his fingers, turned back toward Jake, and snapped them again.

"One day in September three years ago I became a billionaire. The tech stocks were going up like a rocket, the valuations were . . . but you know all that. You see, we designed software for complex data networks and wireless telephone systems and burglar alarms and car security systems and toys that talk . . . magic technoshit. Stuff. In a world full of stuff, we were the kings of the new magic stuff. The world beat a path to our door.

"So there I was, filthy rich, able to buy anything on the planet . . . and none of it meant pee-squat. My boy died of dope, and I got the hell out. That was where I was when I was asked to help overthrow the Communists."

Tiger Cole leaned forward in the chair. "I've been in Hong Kong two years and gave a hundred million or so to the revolution, and the value of my stock holdings has just kept climbing. I'm worth *two* billion dollars, Jake. *Two billion!* I've squandered my life on bad marriages to stupid women. Wasted it, and the system gave me *two . . . billion . . . dollars.*"

Cole spread his hands, as if that explained everything. Obviously he thought it did.

"Who asked you to help overthrow the Communists?" Jake Grafton said.

"Ahh . . ." A trace of a smile appeared on Cole's face. "You already know or you wouldn't have asked."

Jake Grafton stood, went to the door of the office, and pulled it open several inches. He looked back at Cole, still sitting behind the desk. "Some dreams are bigger than others," he said.

Cole nodded.

"The sandwich was okay. The soup's terrible."

Jake Grafton pulled the door completely open and walked out of the office.

CHAPTER EIGHT

Rip Buckingham was on a squash court batting balls against the wall when Tiger Cole arrived at the athletic club. "I heard the governor shut down the paper," Cole said after he closed the door to the court.

"Yep. I spent a couple of nights in the can."

"You've been begging for it for years."

"Already I feel cleaner, closer to God. I'm going to try to get arrested more often, work up to once or twice a month."

They played hard for twenty minutes, then returned to the dressing room. They were the only men in the shower. As the water ran, Rip told Cole, "The rain is supposed to stop tonight. Wu says tomorrow is our day."

"Okay."

"Kerry is counting on your help with the computers."

"I can't guarantee anything. We need another week to verify our methodology."

"We don't have a week."

"I didn't think he'd wait."

"Hard to believe the time has come."

Cole just nodded. He thought, life's transitions always come at the worst possible time.

"How about the governor? What is he saying to Beijing?" Rip knew that Cole had had the CIA bug City Hall.

"He doesn't have a clue," Cole said. "If the Chinese government knows what's going down, they haven't told him or Tang."

"I'd like to bring Sue Lin and her mom to the consulate," Rip muttered, barely loud enough for Cole to hear above the sound of running water.

"Rip, we've been all through that three or four times. Take them to the Australian consulate."

"If it goes bad the PLA will overrun the Australians. The Americans are the only people they don't have the balls to take on."

"Take the women to the airport tonight and put them on a plane to Sydney."

"The old woman won't go, can't go—doesn't have a passport—and the daughter won't go without the old woman."

"For Christ's sake! Have your father send a private jet; land them somewhere in the damned outback. There has to be at least one immigration official in Australia who can be bought."

"There are probably dozens, but the women don't *want* to leave."

"Rip, it's time to stop sweating the program. If we lose we'll all be dead. The women know that."

"Jesus, another philosopher!" Rip glowered at the older man.

Cole was right, of course. Still, Rip thought he would feel better if he had somehow managed to get Sue Lin and Lin Pe out of the line of fire. If that made him an unrepentant chauvinist, so be it.

"Had a talk with Sonny Wong a few nights ago," he told Cole. "The bastard says someone in your consulate is selling him genuine American passports."

"Think he was lying?"

"No."

Tiger Cole finished washing and went into the dressing area. When Rip joined him, he said in a low voice, "That explains a lot."

"A lot of what?"

"China Bob Chan knew far too much. He and Sonny did dozens of deals together through the years."

"So who's leaking?"

"Only two people have access to the passports. One of them has to be in on it, maybe both. One of them is a woman who sleeps with one of the CIA dudes."

"Didn't one of consulate staffers just in from the states get killed a week or so ago?"

"A CIA officer. Shot to death on the street after he planted bugs in China Bob's library."

They finished dressing in silence and left separately.

The bakery for the Double Happy Fortune Cookie Company was housed in a warehouse near the Chinese University in the New Territories. After the Dutchman died, Lin Pe moved the bakery here for a reason: Even though wages for cooks and laborers were low, wages for students were even lower. By paying students more than the going wage, Lin Pe managed to staff her business with some of the brightest, most talented workers in Hong Kong.

The cookie packaging and storage facilities for bulk bakery supplies were located on the first floor. The actual baking of the cookies and printing of Lin Pe's fortunes occurred on the second floor. In the company offices on the third floor where Lin Pe had kept the books by hand for many years, banks of computers manned by students studying computer and electrical engineering were operating around the clock. Behind the warehouse several delivery vans were parked, as well as a half dozen full-sized trucks that were used to transport overseas cookie shipments to the airport.

Wu Tai Kwong had taken the situation as he found it. The bakery employees were now one of the key cells of the revolutionary committee; threads ran from the bakery to dozens of cells in the university and in factories and offices all over town. From there, the threads ran all over China. Wu Tai Kwong well knew that a local uprising in Hong Kong was doomed; he was playing for much bigger stakes.

This afternoon he lingered on the loading dock with several of his key lieutenants smoking, watching the rain fall, and making last-minute plans.

The time for waiting was over. The spontaneous protests in front of the failed Bank of the Orient had deeply impressed Wu and his friends. The willingness of unarmed citizens to defy the PLA was, Wu thought, a direct measure of the depth of their antigovernment feelings. The Communists also understood that fact, which was the reason they reacted so violently to peaceful protests.

The conspiracy dynamic was also pressing mercilessly. As the organized circle of government enemies expanded, secrecy became nebulous. The enforcers who had ruthlessly punished security lapses when there were relatively few conspirators—and even executed government spies—became powerless as the group expanded exponentially. Whispers at the rank-and-file level became impossible to prevent. Absolute secrecy could be enforced only in a few key cells. Fortunately Virgil Cole, the American, had signed on a year ago and contributed vast sums of money, money that was used to bribe the regular and secret police and anyone else whose silence was deemed necessary.

The government in Beijing knew it had sworn blood enemies, of course, but Beijing was far away, with dozens of layers of corrupt officialdom between here and there. Still, even an absolutely corrupt government could bestir itself if the threat was perceived as grave enough.

Time, Wu told his friends, was running out. Now or never. Fight or submit. Fight or die.

Today his friends watched his facial features as he talked, listened intently to every word. Wu recruited them to his vision and held them enthralled with the power of his personality, nothing else. Energy radiated from him, life, *power* . . .

Some of the women who came within his personal orbit thought of him as a semireligious figure, a modern-day Buddha or Confucius. He wasn't: Wu Tai Kwong was a fierce, driven man of extraordinary personal courage who had ordered executions of traitors and occasionally pulled the trigger himself. He believed in himself and his convictions with a righteous fervor that ordinary people would label irrational. What the people who knew him well saw was a man with the wisdom, courage, determination, and titanic ego necessary to lead a nation as large as China into a new day.

Wu removed a cell phone from his pocket. "Do we go?" he asked them one last time.

Positive nods all around.

Wu dialed the number.

One ring, two.

"Hello." Cole's voice. How well Wu knew it.

"Go," he said and flipped the mouthpiece shut, severing the connection.

"The new day is almost here," Wu said now to his friends and laughed heartily. He would have laughed on Judgment Day. His laughter seemed to calm the taut nerves of those around him, some of whom forced themselves to smile.

Wu Tai Kwong took a last drag on his cigarette, tossed the butt into a rain puddle, got into the delivery van he normally used, and drove out of the Double Happy Fortune Cookie Company parking lot.

He joined the flow of traffic in the crowded street and crept along toward the first light. The windshield wipers fought a losing battle with the rain, which was coming down harder now than it had all day. Perhaps it was only his imagination.

Another van pulled out in front of him, inched its bumper out into the space between Wu and the vehicle ahead, and of course he had to let it in.

The driver got the van into the traffic stream ahead of Wu, and of course didn't make it through the first light.

Sitting behind the van, thinking of rain and soldiers and millions of angry people, Wu failed to take alarm when the back door of the van ahead opened and two men hopped out. They slammed the door closed, then one stepped to the passenger door of Wu's van and one to the driver's door. They jerked the doors open.

The man on Wu's side had a pistol in his hand, one that he seemed to produce from thin air. Wu looked left—the man climbing into the passenger seat also had a pistol, one pointed at Wu's midsection.

"Put the van in park," the man said standing beside him, "and move over. I'll drive."

Wu floored the accelerator. The van jumped forward, smashing into the back of the vehicle ahead. The man standing on the driver's side fell to the street while the man on the passenger's side who was half in and half out hung on to the door for dear life.

Wu slammed the vehicle into reverse and cranked the wheel over as he jammed the accelerator back down.

A bullet smashed the driver's window. Wu felt the thump of the wheel rolling over the fallen man just before the van impacted the vehicle behind. Wu kept the accelerator mashed down, the rear wheels squalled. . . .

The man on Wu's left was inside the vehicle now, swinging at his head with a pistol. Wu drove his right hand into the man's teeth, then slammed on the brake and tried to get the transmission in reverse.

The engine stalled.

In the silence that followed Wu could hear the gasping oaths of the man in the passenger seat. He was grinding on the starter when the man hit him a glancing blow in the head with the pistol.

Wu tried to elbow the man, punch him in the face, but he passed out when the man hit him in the head with the gun a second time.

Jake Grafton unlocked the door to his hotel room and couldn't believe his eyes. The room was trashed. The bed had been stripped, the mattress stuffing strewn everywhere, the furniture broken, the television smashed . . . every item of clothing he and Callie had brought to Hong Kong lay somewhere in the middle of that mess. Even the carpet had been peeled back around the walls.

"Callie?"

He walked into the room, checked to make sure she wasn't in the bathroom or closet or lying under the mess or behind the dresser.

"*Callie?*"

He knew what they had been searching for—the tape. They didn't find it because it was in his pocket.

Where was Callie? She could be downstairs, or shopping, or getting her hair done. . . .

"*Callie!*" He roared her name.

A woman peered through the open doorway from the hall. A Chinese woman, the maid. She asked something in Chinese.

"The lady who was here?" he replied. "Where did she go?"

The maid shook her head uncomprehendingly, stared in amazement at the sea of trash.

Jake Grafton brushed by her and hurried along the hallway. Unwilling to wait for an elevator, he charged down the stairs, trying to think.

He raced for the manager's office and blew by the secretary. The manager was a Brit. "Someone trashed my room"—he gave the man the number—"and my wife is missing! Call the police!"

The man stood gaping at Jake, so Jake repeated it, then went charging out of the office.

He had to find a phone.

Fumbling with the telephone book, barking at the operator, he finally got through to the American consulate. "Tommy Carmellini, please."

In less than a minute Carmellini was on the line.

"Grafton. This morning someone did a real messy search of my hotel room. My wife is missing."

Several seconds of silence followed as Carmellini digested the news. "The tape," he said. "Did they get it?"

"No. Who was it?"

"God knows."

"*I* want to know."

"Well, I sure as hell don't know what to tell you, Admiral. If they snatched your wife, you'll probably be hearing from them."

"Unless they have plans for making her talk."

Carmellini didn't respond.

"Is the consul general there this afternoon?" Grafton asked.

"I don't know."

"I'm coming over there. See you in about a half hour. Find me a weapon."

Jake Grafton slammed the telephone down and marched through the lobby to the street. He passed two uniformed police on their way into the building and didn't stop.

Tiger Cole was in his office. With Carmellini in tow, Jake stormed past the secretary and barged in. Cole was on the telephone. ". . . the trade agreements can be interpreted as—" One look at Grafton's face stopped the words.

"May I call you back, Mr. Secretary? A crisis has arisen here that I must deal with." He listened for a second or two, muttered something, then hung up.

"What in the world—?"

"Someone trashed my hotel room searching it and my wife is missing." Jake came around the desk and seized Cole's lapels. "If you know who has her or where she is, now is the moment to come clean."

"*Hey!*" Cole tried to pull Grafton's hands off.

The admiral held on fiercely and lowered his face toward Cole. "If anything happens to Callie I'll kill you," he snarled. "*Anything!* Do you understand me, Cole?"

The consul general became very still. "I understand, Jake."

Grafton released Cole and straightened.

"Who has her?"

"I don't know. Tell me about it."

Jake sat on the desk. He described the room. "When I left her to come here for lunch, she was fine. Going to go downstairs for lunch, but she said she would be waiting for me when I got back from the consulate. She wasn't, and the place had been violently trashed. Whoever did it was looking for this!" He pulled the tape from his pocket and showed it to Cole. "This is the tape from China Bob Chan's library, removed from the recorder within minutes after his death."

Cole's brow knitted. "How'd you get it?"

"Mr. Carmellini gave it to me. He was sent over here to help with my investigation. The death of Harold Barnes seemed a good place to start."

Jake turned to Carmellini. "Anything of interest on your searches or bugs?"

"No, sir. Not yet."

"What's he searching?" Tiger asked.

"Everything in this building," Grafton barked. "Safes, filing cabinets, desks, hard drives, databases, trash cans, everything. I want to know what the fuck is going on in Hong Kong and I want to know *now!*"

Cole took a deep breath. "Did you bug this office, Carmellini?"

"Yes, sir."

"Disable the bugs and leave us alone. Admiral Grafton asked a question and he deserves an unrecorded answer."

Carmellini took less than a minute to remove the hidden wireless microphones. One was stuck to the eraser of a pencil, one of a dozen pens and pencils protruding from a coffee cup on Cole's desk; another was pinned to the window curtain behind his chair.

When the door closed behind Carmellini, Cole said, "I don't know who kidnapped your wife."

"Did you know it was going to happen?"

"No. I'm amazed that it did."

"Let's take it by the numbers. What in hell are you mixed up in?"

"As you surmised at lunch, a group of revolutionaries is about to kick over the lantern. I'm one of them."

"Uh-huh."

Cole raised his hands questioningly.

"Did your group kill Harold Barnes, or have him killed?"

"To the best of my knowledge, no."

"Don't start that quibble shit with me, Cole! You are ten seconds away from a phone call to Washington. Did anyone in your group kill Harold Barnes? Tell me what you think."

"No."

"Who killed him?"

"I don't know. I thought at the time it might be someone in the CIA who was in bed with China Bob."

"Where did China Bob fit in all this?"

Cole took a deep breath and leaned back in his chair. "I wish I knew the correct answer to that. I was using him as a conduit to get untraceable money into Hong Kong to fund the revolution. About a hundred million American dollars went through his hands."

"Your money?"

"Yes."

"*Jesus,* Tiger! What in the hell are you doing, man?"

"Violently overthrowing the Communist government of China. I thought it was a great investment."

"Did the thought ever cross your mind that perhaps the best thing you could do for your fellow Americans was let the Chinese solve their own problems?"

"I'm not going to justify my actions to you or anybody else," Cole said coldly. "I've done what I believed was the right thing for my fellow man—all of them. You and the people in Washington can put that on my tombstone or stick it up your ass, I don't care which."

"Okay, okay." Jake held up his hands. "What else was Chan into?"

"He smuggled some computers into the country for me."

"Was he making campaign contributions to American politicians?"

"I believe so."

"Who supplied the money?"

"The PLA."

"What else was he up to?"

"Anything that would turn a dollar. Chan liked money and had a finger in every pie in town. That's probably what got him killed."

"Someone thought he knew too much about too many things?"

"I suspect that's the gospel truth."

"Did he know your money was going to fund a revolution?"

"I believe he thought I was in the drug business, but he may have guessed the truth at some point."

Jake Grafton held both hands to his head. "I can't believe this shit!"

Cole smacked the desk with the flat of his hand. "Don't give me any sanctimonious crap! I won't listen to it! Thirty years ago America's liberals refused to fight for freedom in Asia—now they're partners with the propaganda ministry of the Communist government as investors in China.com. Anything for a goddamn buck! Yeah, I'm funding a revolution. If the warm, well-fed, comfortable, educated establishment bastards in America lose some money or bleed a little, it'll break my slimy heart."

Jake Grafton took his time answering. "You can't give freedom to people, Tiger. It's something they have to earn for themselves. If they don't want freedom enough to fight for it, they won't value it."

"The Chinese are going to fight, all right," Cole shot back. "They're going to do their share of bleeding."

"Okay," Jake Grafton said.

When Cole calmed down, he asked, "Did Callie listen to the tape that Carmellini brought her?"

"Yes."

"All of it."

"She said she did."

"Who knew about the tape?"

"Carmellini, and whoever he told. He brought us a special player and earphones to listen to the thing. I presume he got them out of the closet here at the consulate."

Tiger Cole took a deep breath. "Let's make some assumptions, see where they take us. Let's assume that whoever grabbed Callie is interested in the contents of that tape."

Jake Grafton nodded.

"We know China Bob was taking money from the PLA to give to American politicians," Cole continued. "And we know he wasn't passing all of it along. The PLA has figured this out, too, but I fail to see why they would care what was on that tape. If a PLA officer killed China Bob, he wouldn't care if the American government knew it. The Chinese government doesn't care. Oh, Beijing might be embarrassed about the congressional revelations, but the government really doesn't *care*. Do you understand me?"

"I guess."

"For these people, Beijing is the center of the universe. What the Americans think or don't think is as important as the shape of the craters on the back side of the moon."

"Okay."

"The only reason the PLA would want the tape is because there's something on it that threatens them. If they knew about the revolutionaries, they wouldn't need the tape. Do you agree?"

"I'm listening."

"That leaves someone else Chan dealt with. Not me, because it's too late for you or anyone else to stop the train. The danger to the revolution is past."

"I accept that for now," Grafton said. "If the shit hits the fan tomorrow. If it doesn't . . ."

"The tape would be of value only to someone who doesn't know the timetable, someone who thinks that he can sell the information that's on it or use it for blackmail. He's assuming that the world he knows is still going to be there, otherwise the tape has no value."

Jake took the tape from his pocket and placed it on Cole's desk. "Do you have anybody who could translate this for me?"

"Yes. Kerry Kent."

"Is she in the building?"

"Yes." He pushed the button on the intercom and said his secretary's name. "Is Mr. Carmellini waiting out there?"

"Yes, sir."

"Please have him go to the CIA office and ask Ms. Kent to come see me."

When he released the intercom button, Cole told Grafton, "She's a British SIS agent on a foreign assignment. She works here."

"Do you want the Brits to hear this?"

"I don't think she'll pass it along to London."

"Think or know?"

"She's Wu Tai Kwong's girlfriend."

"I'm not going to sit here for six hours while she listens to the tape. Gimme your best guess. Who snatched Callie?"

"The first possibility that pops into my head is a local gangster named Sonny Wong. I have reason to believe that people in this building are feeding him information, maybe even selling him passports."

"Do you know who these people are?"

"Suspicion only."

"What else is Wong into?"

"His primary occupation is smuggling: refugees, dope, diamonds, guns, whatever will earn a buck."

"Where do I find this star of the social register?"

"You need to see a man named Rip Buckingham. He's a friend of mine. I'll give you his address. We won't call because the telephones might be tapped, but I'll write a note for you to take with you. Go over to his house."

"Does he know about the plan for revolution?"

"Yes."

"He's one of the inner circle?"

"Yes."

"What does he know?"

"As few of the specifics of my business as possible. Like all good conspirators, we compartmentalize all we can, just in case. Obviously he knows details that I don't. He's as familiar with the big picture as I am, of course."

Jake Grafton could sit still no longer. He walked to the window and back, rubbing his hands. "I need a weapon, a pistol. Got one you could loan me?"

Cole hiked a foot up on his lower desk drawer, pulled up a trouser leg, and pulled down his sock. He was wearing an ankle holster. "It's a five-shot Smith and Wesson thirty-eight with a two-inch barrel," he said as he unstrapped the holster. "The police will get real pissy if they catch you toting it around. About all it's good for is shooting yourself."

"Would you have done that if they arrested you?" Jake murmured.

"Hell no. I've got diplomatic immunity," Cole said.

"Is immunity bulletproof?"

"Nope. Which is why I carried the pistol."

Cole was writing down Rip Buckingham's address on a Post-it when the intercom buzzed. The secretary's voice came through the box. "Sir, Mr. Carmellini is back with Ms. Kent. And there is a call from a Mr. Wong. He says he has something that might be of interest to you."

Cole looked up and met the unblinking gray eyes of Jake Grafton.

"Send Carmellini and Kent in," he told the box, "and I'll take the call." When Carmellini and Kent were seated beside Jake Grafton, Cole pushed the speaker button on the telephone.

"Cole."

"Mr. Cole, my name is Sonny Wong. I don't think we have ever formally met, but you may have heard someone mention my name." Wong spoke decent English, but the accent was unmistakable.

"I have indeed heard your name."

"I have come into the possession of several items you may wish to redeem, Mr. Cole. One is an American lady named Grafton."

CHAPTER NINE

The color drained from Jake Grafton's face as Tiger Cole said, "I'm listening."

"You may remember our mutual friend, China Bob Chan? It seems that a tape recording was made in his library the evening he died."

Wong paused. Cole said nothing. Kerry Kent looked at Tommy Carmellini, who kept his gaze fixed on the telephone.

"Still there, Mr. Cole?"

"Yes."

"This lady has listened to the tape. I don't have the tape, mind you, just the woman. She heard you shoot China Bob, Mr. Cole."

"So?"

"You have diplomatic immunity in China, but the American State Department might take a dim view of murder. Conceivably, the American government could waive your immunity and turn you over to the Chinese for trial. A federal indictment in the United States is more probable. This woman could put you in prison for the rest of your life."

"I'm still listening."

"The other item I have is even more marketable. Amazingly, with the entire resources of the Chinese government devoted to the search for public enemy Wu Tai Kwong, I have managed to apprehend the criminal."

"Why are you telling me all this?"

"I think the authorities would be very interested in both of my prizes, Mr. Cole. As you know, they have offered a very tempting reward for Wu. I propose to sell both these people to you or to the Chinese government. Think it over."

"You son of a bitch! Who are you trying to bullshit? Sun will throw you in the same hole he's got waiting for Wu. If Wu won't talk, I will."

Sonny chuckled. "You underestimate the gratitude that will overflow Sun's hard little heart if I produce Wu Tai Kwong. Waving Wu's head in Beijing will make Sun's fortune—the bastard may wind up as our next premier."

"You're the biggest liar west of Little Rock."

"Everybody has a price."

"What's yours?"

"Fifty million American dollars."

"I think you're trying to hijack the revolution."

"Hijack it? I'm trying desperately to profit from it."

"Without Wu, there won't be a revolution."

"Crap," shot back Sonny Wong. "No one can stop it now. You'll lead it yourself. Or I will."

"I'd be a fool to pay."

"You'd be a fool not to. Your choice."

"Fifty million?"

"Yep. Transferred by you into a Swiss bank account. You have three days to make the transfer or I make a delivery to the People's Liberation Army."

Cole took a deep breath. "What account?"

"One of my colleagues will call you with the information, a Mr. Daniel. Should you decide to redeem one person and not the other, discuss that with Mr. Daniel."

"I'll want to talk with both parties right now to make sure they are alive and well cared for."

"Discuss the details with Mr. Daniel."

"If anything happens to them I—" Cole began but he was talking to a dead telephone.

He pushed the button to cut the connection.

They all sat staring at the telephone.

After a moment, Grafton said, "Callie said the tape is inconclusive.

She said anyone listening to it couldn't determine who fired the shot that killed Chan." He picked up the tape from the desk, fingered the reels, then laid it down again.

"It's money Wong's after," Cole muttered. "If he doesn't get money, he'll probably kill her."

"But he wants the tape," Jake objected. "Wants to know what's on it."

"Yeah. He and China Bob did a lot of business together. God only knows what the two of them talked about. He wants the tape, too."

"Wu Tai Kwong?"

"The political criminal."

"Why would you care about him?" Tommy Carmellini asked.

"Who do you think is leading the revolution?"

"I guess I hadn't put two and two together."

"Wu isn't his real name. As fate would have it, he's Rip Buckingham's brother-in-law. If we can overthrow the Communists and Wu lives long enough, he's going to be the first elected president of the new Republic of China."

"And Wong wants you to pay a ransom for him?"

"If I don't pay for Wu, Sonny Wong will indeed turn Wu over to the People's Liberation Army, which will pay Sonny the posted reward and execute Wu."

"Fifty million dollars is a lot of kale," Tommy Carmellini remarked, rubbing his chin.

"Callie and I have been pretty diligent savers and investors," Jake said, "and we have about one-fifth of one percent of that amount."

Cole waved a hand dismissively. "I'll pay it," he said.

"They may kill them anyway."

"We'll set up a trade. They produce Wu and Callie, I make the call authorizing a wire transfer of the money. When the money is in his bank, we leave."

Jake Grafton shook his head slowly. "He'll have to kill you and Wu after you make the call. Wong can't afford to let Wu live to send an army to hunt him down. Hell, he'll have to kill us all so nothing leaks out."

Cole's face wore a blank expression. His mind was obviously going at a mile a minute.

"How come this Wong knows so much about the revolution?"

"He's involved, obviously."

"Obviously. How is he involved? What's his role in all this?"

"Not now," Tiger Cole said, frowning. "I can't tell you now."

"*Goddamn you!*" Jake Grafton roared. "That asshole kidnapped my wife!"

"I'm sorry, Jake," Tiger Cole said.

The admiral struggled to get himself under control. He played with the pistol, checked it, then pulled up his trouser leg. When he spoke again it was in a normal tone. "If you had nothing to do with Callie's kidnapping, you have nothing to apologize for," he said as he strapped the ankle holster to his right leg. "If you did, I'll kill you, Cole. It's that goddamn simple."

"How did Sonny Wong capture Wu Tai Kwong?" Carmellini asked.

"Everyone in Hong Kong knows Wu is somewhere in the city," the consul general replied. "The revolutionary movement has more leaks than the *Titanic.*"

"So why hasn't Wu been arrested before?"

"Because we've paid off the police." Cole shrugged. "Everyone in the Chinese government is corrupt, all of them. This is the third world!"

"Can we get help from the police to get Callie back? Wu?"

"Beijing has posted a huge reward for Wu. The cops are corrupt, but you are fooling yourself if you think no one will call the PLA to turn him in. They will!"

"Okay," said Jake Grafton. "Let's talk about Callie. Only a few people knew she was going to listen to that tape. Carmellini, you're one of them. Who'd you tell?"

"No one, Admiral."

"Somebody figured it out."

"Kerry Kent," Tommy said bitterly.

"You ass," she hissed and went for him with her fingernails.

Carmellini grabbed her wrists. He was far too strong for her. "Don't play the injured lover with me," he sneered with all the contempt of a man who had never been in love. "I've heard that song before. You're the number-one suspect on my list."

"I trust her," Cole said, in a tone that ended the argument.

Carmellini pushed Kent away. If looks could kill, he would have received a fatal wound just then.

"The postmortem can wait," Jake Grafton said. "We've got other fish to fry." He picked up the tape from Cole's desk and put it in his pocket.

The maid brought Rip the cell phone. He was sitting on his roof under a dripping umbrella. The air was now a fine sea mist; occasionally a whisper of breeze tossed a handful of droplets on his face, almost like a kiss.

The maid didn't look at him, merely handed him the phone and left.

Rip pushed the button and answered.

"Rip, this is Sonny Wong."

"Hey, Sonny."

"Got some bad news for you, Rip. Hate having to deliver it like this, but the world is pressing in, if you know what I mean."

"Like what?"

"Like I have your brother-in-law as an unwilling guest."

"My brother-in-law?"

"Yeah. Wu. Remember him? Drives for the Double Happy Fortune Cookie Company? Is wanted by the government for political crimes? The million Hong Kong dollars reward? That brother-in-law."

"Jesus, Sonny, I thought we were friends."

"We are, Rip, but this is business. Hong Kong is about to blow up in our faces, no thanks to your brother-in-law, who has done everything within his power to light the fuse. It's been a grand party, but it's over. A guy has to look out for number one. You and I are not friends ten million American dollars' worth. That's what it will cost you to see Wu in one piece again."

"I don't have that kind of money, Sonny. You know that."

"Ah, but your father does. Call him! Tell Richard Buckingham that if I don't get the money, your brother-in-law Wu Tai Kwong will be turned over to General Tang Tso of the PLA, who will probably shoot him before he writes the reward check. Or strangle him. For some reason, those guys still like to strangle people. So old-fashioned and messy. Uncivilized too, but probably very satisfying on some level. Almost orgasmic."

"You're a perfect bastard, Sonny."

"Not quite perfect but I'm working on it. If I were Richard Buckingham's heir, like a certain person I know, I wouldn't have to be. You know what I'm saying? It's an accident of birth, really, that I was born in a sewer, poor as a flea on a starving rat, and I've been digging and scratching every minute since then to get out of it."

"Let me talk to Wu."

"You're going to have to take my word on this, Rip. Wu is sleeping right now; I don't want to wake him."

"How do I know you've got him?"

"If you're really worried about that point, I'll have someone drop by with a finger. What the hell, he's got ten. He'll never miss a few."

"Okay, okay."

"You talk to Richard. I'll call you back in a few hours, give you the particulars on a Swiss bank account that I'm trying to fatten up. You can plan on transferring the money there."

With that Sonny hung up.

Rip went inside looking for Sue Lin. He found her in the kitchen. "Where's the maid?"

"The new one?"

Rip nodded.

"After she gave you the phone, she went downstairs, got her umbrella, and left. Didn't say a word to me. I happened to look out the window and saw her walking toward the tram."

"Wu's been kidnapped."

"*What?*"

"Sonny Wong has him. He wants ten million American dollars or he'll turn him over to the government and collect the reward."

She sat and put her face in her hands. Rip put his arms around her shoulders and found she was shaking.

"Hey." He knelt in front of her, opened her hands. Tears streamed along her cheeks. "Hey."

"I've seen this Sonny Wong," she whispered. "He is evil."

"Sue Lin, I've known him for years. Yeah, he's a crook, but he's always been straight with me. He's just wants money. Unfortunately we looked like an easy mark."

"He'll kill Wu."

"We'll pay the money. I'll bet he'll let him go."

"With the city full of people who worship Wu?" she protested, shaking her head. "Sonny Wong will kill him and take the first plane out before anyone finds out the truth."

The sound of a man groaning woke Callie Grafton. She opened her eyes and looked around. It took several seconds before she realized what she was looking at. She was in a small stateroom, perhaps on a ship, lying on a narrow bed, a lower bunk. Across the aisle, almost within reach, lay a man with his back to her. He was the one groaning.

Blood stained his shirt and the sheet on which he lay.

She extended her arm . . . and felt a sharp pain roar through her skull. Slowly she put her hands to her head and pressed. She had the mother of all headaches.

Her head throbbed with every heartbeat. Gradually the pain seemed to ease somewhat, and once again she extended her hand to the groaning man.

His back was warm.

Callie moved, painfully, until she could touch the man.

She swung her feet over the edge of the bunk and sat up, which almost split her head with pain. In a minute or so the pain lessened and she could see and function.

Ever so slowly, she stood, turned the man over, and examined him.

His left hand was bloody. She looked. His little finger was missing, leaving only an oozing, partially scabbed wound.

She tore at the sheet, finally got a strip off it, and wrapped the strip around the man's hand as a crude bandage.

He had stopped groaning. When she finished she realized his eyes were open and he was looking at her with intelligent brown eyes. He was Chinese, in his mid-thirties perhaps.

"You've lost a finger," she said in Chinese.

"They cut it off."

She sat back down on her own bunk, put her aching head in her hands. It was coming back: the knock on the hotel room door, the voice—she thought it was the maid or bellman. When she opened the door, several men rushed in. They grabbed her mouth to keep her from screaming and threw her on the bed and one of them produced a hypodermic.

That was all she remembered. That and the fear.

Now she was sitting in a stateroom . . . she could feel the boat rocking in the waves. It must be a small ship to rock like this. There was a round porthole with the glass painted over; a bit of light leaked through the scratches in the paint. That light was all that illuminated the tiny room.

When she turned her head she could see that the man on the bunk had rolled over. Now he was looking at her.

"Does your hand hurt?"

"Not too much," he said.

"Who are you?"

"You wouldn't know me."

"Do you have a name?"

"Wu."

"I'm Callie."

"Callie." He said it experimentally.

"Where are we?"

"I think we have been kidnapped. They knocked me out, so I don't know."

"Me, too."

She still had her watch, which was unexpected. Almost three o'clock. The men had burst into the hotel room about ten A.M.

She wondered if it were the same day.

She lay down and thought about her husband.

"Commander Tarkington?"

"That's right." Tommy Carmellini pressed the telephone to his ear to help himself concentrate. The voice that sounded in his ear from the other side of the Pacific was certainly clear enough.

"My name is Tommy Carmellini. We met last year in Cuba. Do you remember?"

"Yes." Tarkington sounded sleepy. The telephone call had awakened him.

"Admiral Grafton asked me to call you. He needs your help." Tarkington was Jake Grafton's aide.

"I got a pencil. Shoot." Now Toad was alert.

"His wife has been kidnapped," Carmellini said.

"Callie Grafton? *Gawd damn!*" The Toad-man whistled through his teeth.

Carmellini glanced around the office. Kerry Kent and the three CIA dudes were all staring at him, listening to his every word.

"We believe the man behind it is a Hong Kong citizen named Sonny Wong," Carmellini continued. "I don't know his real name. He is associated with a Russian national named Yuri Daniel. The admiral asked me to call you. He wants the CIA to run those two through the computers and see what they can come up with. Wong may have some bank accounts in Switzerland or some other bank haven. Look for passports, visas, travel records, wire transfers, anything."

"Okay." Toad's voice was crisp and businesslike.

"Have the National Security Agency set up a study of telecommunications traffic in the Hong Kong area. Obviously we are interested in the Graftons, Sonny Wong, Yuri Daniel, kidnapping, ransom, anything along those lines."

"I'll talk to them in a few hours. Tell the admiral I'll go through the agency director's office. Shouldn't be a problem. Anything else?"

"That will do it for now."

"Heard anything about Callie? Is she okay?"

"We don't know."

"Does this Wong dude want money or what?"

"Money."

"Wow!" said Toad Tarkington. "That Wong must have really bad karma—I can smell it from here. Jake Grafton is the last man on the planet I'd want blood-crazy mad at me. You tell the admiral I'm on my way to the office as soon as I get my pants on."

Jake Grafton sat at the conference table in Cole's office and tried to clear his thoughts. There was stationery in the trays under the computer printer, so he helped himself to a couple of sheets. He took a U.S. government black ballpoint from his shirt pocket and clicked the point in and out while he collected his thoughts.

The National Security Adviser had sent Jake to Hong Kong to find out what was going on; the man was entitled to know.

Jake wrote quickly in a clear, legible longhand detailing what he had learned. The consul general was involved in a conspiracy to overthrow the Chinese government and had resigned. Cole had been in the building when China Bob Chan was killed, may have talked to him, and may have been somehow involved in his death. The enclosed tape was made in Chan's library by the recorder planted by Harold Barnes and should be listened to by Chinese-language experts.

He wrote two pages total, then put the handwritten sheets and the audiotape in a large padded envelope, which he sealed. He wrote the National Security Adviser's name on it and handed it to Cole.

"I want you to send this to Washington in the next diplomatic pouch. The Chan tape is in there."

"Okay."

"I'm relying on your honor, Cole."

"I am well aware of that fact, Jacob Lee, and will try not to take offense at the fact you felt the need to point it out."

"I'm all out of apologies," Grafton replied coolly.

"I'll put the envelope in the pouch," Cole said. "The problem is the airlines—nothing is coming in or going out of Lantau since the air traffic control computers crapped out."

"Did you have anything to do with that?"

"I certainly hope so."

Jake scratched his head, trying to make up his mind. "I want the tape in the bag and on its way," Jake said finally, "so I won't be tempted to trade the damned thing to this Wong asshole for Callie."

"Okay."

"And the time has come for you to resign." Jake took Cole's letter of resignation from his pocket and tossed it on the desk. "Fax that thing to Washington."

"Now?"

"Right now."

Cole took a deep breath. "Okay," he said.

The intercom buzzed. "Mr. Cole. There's a small package here for you. The sergeant at the gate brought it up. He says you should see it."

"Is he still there?"

"Yes, sir."

"Have him bring it in."

The marine was square as a fire plug and togged out in a khaki shirt and blue trousers with a red stripe up each seam. He looked pale.

"Did you X-ray the package, Sergeant?" Cole asked.

"Yes, sir. There's no bomb. Looked like a bone."

"A bone?"

"Well, three little bones. Jesus, sir, it looks like a finger."

Cole cut the brown wrapping paper away from the box with a letter opener, then cut the tape that held the top on.

Jake Grafton was looking over Cole's shoulder when he opened the box. It was a finger, all right, freshly severed, if the still-soft blood was any indication.

"Thank you, Sergeant," Cole said softly and sent the marine on his way.

Jake Grafton stood still as a statue, staring at the finger.

"It isn't Callie's," he said.

"Probably Wu's," Cole muttered and used the intercom to ask the secretary to have Kerry Kent come up to the office.

While they were waiting Jake walked around the office looking at Cole's memorabilia. He was thinking of Callie, wondering how he was going to get her back, when he realized he was looking at an old photo of himself and Tiger Cole. The thing was in black and white, framed, sitting on an out-of-the-way shelf behind the conference table. He and Cole were standing in front of a bomb-laden A-6 in their flight gear, obviously on a flight deck. Neither man was grinning.

Those were simpler days.

Kerry Kent knocked, then came charging into the office. She looked into the box, and clapped her hand over her mouth.

"Those bastards," she said between clenched teeth. "Those fucking bastards."

Victoria Peak and the tops of the buildings were wreathed in fog when Jake Grafton walked out the front entrance of the American consulate. The rain had stopped, leaving the air tangibly wet, thick, warm, and heavy.

He walked slowly, taking his time, watching for people who might be paying attention to him.

He had to will himself to walk slowly, to analyze and think logically about the situation and what he could do to affect it.

The tension in everyone he met was visible—all the pedestrians were on edge, regardless of age, sex, race, or how they were dressed. Without smiles or nods, the people walked briskly with their heads down, avoiding eye contact, avoiding each other, hurrying toward the great unknown.

He stood in line and bought a ticket on the tram, then waited a minute or two with the crowd for the tram to descend the mountain. He let other people board the car in front of him, arranging it so he was one of the very last aboard, and told the motorman where he wanted off.

The car got underway almost noiselessly as the cable pulled it up the tracks. The only sound Jake could hear was the faintest rumble from the wheels, or perhaps he was only feeling the vibration of the steel wheels on the steel rails. The grade was about thirty percent, he estimated. A series of stairs ran alongside the cable car's track for those in the mood for a serious climb.

No one in the car spoke. All studiously avoided looking at each other as the car silently climbed the steep grade. The buildings slid past and the fog thickened.

The car stopped at a tiny platform about three-quarters of the way up the side of the mountain. Jake got off, then the car resumed its journey and disappeared into the fog.

He walked along the street, found the right house, rang the bell.

A man opened the door, a man in his late thirties, perhaps even forty.

"Rip Buckingham?"

"Come in, please."

When the door closed behind him, Jake said, "I suppose Wong called you."

"Yes. My wife is upstairs. Wu is her brother."

They sat at a table in the kitchen, with a window beside them that gave a view of some nearby housetops amid the gloom.

"Cole said they took your wife."

"Yes."

"Sonny won't be able to stay in Hong Kong after this."

"If he gets fifty million from Cole, he won't want to."

"He also wants ten million from me. From my dad, actually, Richard Buckingham."

"Buckingham News?"

"Yeah."

Jake considered the situation in silence as he sized up Rip Buckingham and tried to figure out how much steel was in him. Finally he said, "Wong won't be able to live comfortably anywhere if he releases Callie and Wu alive to testify against him. Switzerland isn't an extradition haven."

"After Wong gets his money, he'll kill everybody who might cause him trouble," Rip said heavily. "A man once told me that four hundred Chinese each paid Sonny fifty grand American to go to America. The ship sailed away and was never seen again."

"Twenty million dollars," Jake muttered after doing the math in his head.

"I don't know if the story is true," Rip continued, "but I know Sonny. He doesn't take unnecessary chances."

Tommy Carmellini had his equipment set up in the attic of the consulate. He had worked for three nights bugging and wiring selected offices, one of which was the CIA office. Another was the consul general's. Grafton wanted to know what was going on—Carmellini intended to find out.

Just now he settled into the folding chair he had stolen from the immigration office and donned a headset, which was plugged into the amplifier. The tape recorder was recording all the microphone inputs simultaneously for later study. Without interfering with the recording, he flipped through the channels, listening to various bugs in turn, sampling the audio.

The CIA office was his main concern. He listened to them chat, matched up voices with the faces in his memory. They were still squeezing the juice from the kidnapping. Well, an admiral's wife doesn't get snatched every day.

Kent also knew that Sonny Wong claimed he had Wu. She wasn't sharing that tidbit with the others, Carmellini noticed. In fact, she was sharing very little.

A remark of Bubba Lee's set the tone. "Man, calling Washington and telling NSA to get on the case—that Grafton *is* somebody."

"Yeah, but who?" That was Eisenberg.

"An admiral in the navy. Don't they sometimes get posted to the intel community?"

"Sometimes."

"Well, that sailor has some stroke, or thinks he has."

"Thinks he has, yeah."

"Do you buy it about Sonny Wong? Does a snatch sound like something he would do?"

"Never can tell, man. Things are getting twangy tight around this town. Riots, people shot in the streets, power off half the night..."

"Did you hear about the airport?" Was that Bubba Lee? "The computers out there rolled over and died. People trapped on the concourses, no water in the fountains or toilets, flights canceled. I heard someone went crazy and threw a chair though a plate-glass window."

"Whole goddamn town is falling apart."

"Hey, the whole goddamn *country* is falling apart, if you ask me."

There was more of it, thirty minutes or so. At some point Carmellini realized that there were only two men talking. Eisenberg had been silent a long time, as had Kerry Kent. Maybe they were no longer in the room.

Didn't Cole say Eisenberg knew the woman in the passport office?

Carmellini flipped to that microphone. A loud conversation in Chinese drowned out everything else in the room.

Disgusted, Tommy Carmellini turned the selector to listen to the mike in the consul general's office.

Yep, there was Kent.

"—might kill him. I've been saying for months that he should have an armed bodyguard around the clock. Does anyone pay any attention to the fears of a woman? What does *she* know? What could *she* possibly contribute to this—"

"He didn't want a bodyguard! You know that. Stop this goddamn whining."

"Whining? They may *kill* him!"

"Indeed. He's been a fugitive for a dozen years, with his life hanging by a thread. The revolution continues regardless. The world keeps turning, the tide is coming in...at last!"

"What are you doing to get him back alive?"

"I'm paying the damned ransom."

"What else?"

"What else do you think I should do?"

"I don't know!" she moaned. "I only know that I want him *alive*! I need him, China needs him—*everything* depends on him. *Everything!*"

"Tell me some more about Sonny Wong," Jake Grafton said to Rip Buckingham, "everything you can remember." They were still in Rip's kitchen, seated in front of the window. The rain had stopped and the fog was lifting, revealing the skyscrapers of the Central District.

"Sonny's the head of the last of the old-line Hong Kong criminal gangs, or tongs," Rip told the American. "He's sort of an anachronism, a fossil from the wilder days."

"Kidnapping isn't anything new," Jake said sourly.

"No," Rip admitted. "I thought Sonny was above poopy little capers like this, but apparently not."

"I want to know everything, who his associates are, what he does for money, where he lives, what he eats, his habits—vices, women, kids, everything."

"What's on your mind?"

"I want my wife back."

"That may be impossible."

Jake Grafton gripped the edge of the table and squeezed as hard as he could. All these years, ups and downs and ins and outs, good times and hard times, the tiny triumphs and disasters and little victories that fill our days . . . to have her life end here, now, snuffed out by a criminal psychopath who wants money?

When his muscles began quivering from the exertion, Jake Grafton released the table. He rubbed his hands together, thought about Callie, about their adopted daughter, Amy. "Let's hope not," he said to Rip, so softly that the Australian almost missed the response.

CHAPTER TEN

British consul general Sir Robert MacDonald spent a long afternoon with his staff writing a situation report for the Foreign Office. While so engaged he received a telephone call from the foreign minister in London, who was worried.

"The PM wants to know what in the world is going on out there," the foreign minister said after the usual pleasantries.

"The authorities are having some public relations difficulties," replied Sir Robert, never one to overlook the obvious. He had gone to school with the PM, who loathed him. Forced to accept Sir Robert into the government, the PM had sent him as far from London as he possibly could. "A few technical problems too, I'm afraid," the consul general continued. "Rather inconvenient when the power goes off at odd hours."

"The Buckingham newspapers published a provocative piece in today's U.K. and American editions," the foreign minister informed Her Majesty's Hong Kong representative. "I wonder if you've seen it?"

"Afraid not. The locals shut down the *China Post,* which was Buckingham's little rag hereabouts. Of course, they shut down all the newspapers—I'm sure my staff sent you that information in the morning report."

"Richard Buckingham signed this piece himself. He says that a revolution is about to sweep China, one that will overthrow the Communists."

"His son was the editor of the *China Post*," Sir Robert replied. Rip had been a thorn in MacDonald's side since the day the man arrived from London. "Governor Sun tossed him in jail," he said, unable to keep the satisfaction completely out of his voice. "He's out now, of course. Perhaps he had something to do with the article."

"I see," the FM said slowly.

"It's always a mistake to quarrel with a man who buys ink by the barrel," Sir Robert continued, repeating a comment his wife had made to him on several occasions when he took offense at *China Post* editorials. "Richard Buckingham can say anything he wants in his newspapers and there's jolly little the Chinks can do about it. But talk of revolution is rot, pure rot. The Communists are firmly in control. They have a division of troops in the colony."

Sir Robert still referred to Hong Kong as a colony, which it had ceased to be in 1997, even though his staff and the Foreign Office had repeatedly requested him not to.

"The Orient Bank fiasco was very poorly handled," the consul general told the foreign minister now. "I expressed our dismay at the senseless loss of life. Appalling. I told Sun that myself. Still, the Chinese brook no nonsense from dissenters." That was a serious understatement. The authorities were positively paranoid about dissenters, which caused them diplomatic problems throughout the Western world, including the U.K.

The FM was not so sure about the Communists' control of the political situation. "The world turns," he said. "I seem to recall that a few years ago everyone thought that the Communists in Russia had a firm grip—"

"China is not Russia," Sir Robert shot back, quite sure he was on solid ground. "The conditions are completely different."

"I'll convey your views to the PM," the foreign minister said wearily.

"Do that," Sir Robert said. "Good-bye."

He was amazed at the credulity of the people in London. Of course, they were eight thousand miles from the scene of the crime, but still . . . a revolution? Here? Because Richard Buckingham said so in his newspapers?

Governor Sun also had a busy afternoon. Between calls from Beijing demanding detailed facts he didn't have and issuing directives that made little sense, Sun huddled with key members of his staff, who were trying desperately to establish why the electrical power had failed last night throughout the S.A.R. and why so many of the computers that controlled critical government functions were on the blink.

"Could it be sabotage?" Sun demanded. Like so many of the bureaucrats in Beijing, he had a healthy respect for the unvoiced anger of the people. Baldly, he feared the people he ruled. Repeatedly throughout Chinese history rioting mobs had overthrown dynasties and warlords. Anger and frustration could transform peasants into fierce giants capable of slaying dragons, and Sun well knew it.

Like so many Chinese officials who had held office as the dynasties rose and fell through the millennia, Sun instinctively wanted to control the people he ruled, ensure they stayed in their place, obedient and quiet. For that to happen in this day and age living conditions in China had to improve, which inevitably caused expectations to rise faster than they could be met. It was a vicious cycle with a bad ending; Sun didn't want to be the man on the spot when the music stopped and whole thing exploded.

Then there were the reactionary capitalist forces that the Communists had struggled against since the first day of the Long March. Always the reactionaries were there, waiting for a misstep, a mistake. Waiting.

Sun's aides knew his fears, and they thought they knew the seething maelstrom that was Hong Kong. They soothed him now, told him that there was no evidence of sabotage, when in fact they had no knowledge of why the computers had failed. "A voltage spike, the engineers think," the aides told the governor, who wanted to believe.

"A voltage spike" was the message he gave to Beijing.

American consul general Virgil Cole was not telling his government the truth either. Unlike Governor Sun and Sir Robert MacDonald, who thought they were reporting the truth to their superiors, Cole was lying and knew it. He knew precisely why the power went out last night in Hong Kong and he knew why the airport and harbor computers had failed. He knew what had happened and he knew the plan for going forward.

Of this, he told the United States government precisely nothing.

The Chinese desk at the State Department wanted reports and updates and answers to specific questions, all of which Cole farmed out to his staff. He told the staff more or less what he wanted them to tell Washington, which was the truth as far as it went, but not the complete truth, not by a long shot.

Cole blamed the crisis on the Chinese government's demand for loans at nominal interest rates, loans the government had no intention of ever paying back. The nongovernment stockholders in Hong Kong banks were taking their money and clearing out, which was the root cause of the Bank of the Orient failure. The shootings of unarmed civilians were directly due to the incompetence of the officers of the People's Liberation Army and a government that was paranoid of any dissent whatsoever.

Subsequent problems—power and equipment failures—Cole cavalierly blamed on technical incompetence. When the CIA resident, Bubba Lee, told him of Sun's "voltage spike" explanation to Beijing, Cole tossed that into his latest report to Washington.

During his tenure in Hong Kong, Virgil Cole had repeatedly told the American government that the Chinese government was a corrupt tyranny, with a gross disregard for human rights. The ruling oligarchy was paranoid, cowardly, greedy, technically incompetent, and devoid of personal honor. Cole had said all this so many times the people in Washington laughed about it, yet in the past he had made sure he didn't make himself so obnoxious that the powers that be would fire him. Oh no.

He referred his staff now to some of his past missives on governmental incompetence. When they returned with drafts of the reports Washington demanded, Cole read them with interest, made a few corrections, signed the things, and sent them off.

Lying to the government was a bad business, of course, and he had fretted over it for a year. When you put garbage in, you got garbage out. His conscience used to trouble him more than it did now, although it still twinged him a little.

This evening his lies didn't even make the long list. He was thinking of Wu Tai Kwong, Callie Grafton, and all the things that had to be done. The letter of resignation was also on his mind. It had been faxed off hours ago, and he was now awaiting an explosion from Washington.

It was time to go. He didn't need the consulate anymore.

If the Chinese arrested him, they knew far too much and the revolution was doomed. But they didn't know. So there was a chance, a good chance, he believed.

Time was running out. Lives were at stake, millions of lives. Tens of millions. *Hundreds of millions!*

He looked out the window. The frontal clouds had dissipated; blue sky was visible up there between the towering glass skyscrapers. Across the way was the Third Planet office. With the sky the way it was, the windows there were opaque.

Although Cole didn't know it, inside those offices Kerry Kent and Wu Tai Kwong's top lieutenants were holding a council of war. There were seven of them, each in charge of a specialized group of fighters. They were Wu's friends . . . although perhaps disciples might be a better description.

They took the news of Wu's kidnapping badly. Three of them were for finding Sonny Wong and demanding Wu's immediate return as the price of Wong's life.

Kerry Kent tried to dissuade them. "Sonny Wong has thought of that move," she argued. "Virgil Cole will pay the ransom. If he doesn't, we'll get Wu back in pieces. Do you want Wu alive or Wong dead?"

"That's Wong's choice," Hu Chiang said tartly.

"No, it's ours," Kerry shot back. "We've a revolution to fight. I want Wu back more than anyone in this room, but first and foremost, we must continue the fight that is his life. And ours. That is our first priority."

Hu was not persuaded, but two of Wu's other friends took up Kerry's argument. "The hour is *now,*" Wei Luk argued. "Wu Tai Kwong is a general in our army, it is true, but even generals are soldiers. Our cause is more important than any one person. We must not jeopardize it by taking sides in an internal squabble."

"Internal squabble?" Kent said incredulously. "Sonny Wong wants fifty million American dollars from Virgil Cole. That's ransom."

"Cole should have donated his money to the cause," Wei Luk replied stoutly. "If he had, he would not now need us to stop the revolution to save his pocketbook."

"His pocketbook? You fool! Wu Tai Kwong's life is at stake. Sonny Wong is threatening to murder him!"

"Perhaps he merely threatens. I think Cole is too worried about his money."

Hu Chiang managed to stop this fruitless argument. "Enough!" he shouted. "*Enough!* Kerry Kent said the revolution must be our first priority, and I agree. We cannot stop the revolution to search Hong Kong for one man. We must strike now. If we do not, for any reason, we endanger the lives of every member of the Scarlet Team. Let Cole pay the money. There will be time later to deal with Sonny Wong. There is nowhere on this earth he can go to escape us."

Wei Luk agreed with that, and so did the others.

Around sunset two men came to the door of the stateroom—it *was* a stateroom, Callie had decided, in a yacht or small ship. She and Wu had tossed and turned on their bunks all afternoon. Worried as she was, she still fell asleep for an hour or two, which she attributed to the drug they had injected her with. She still felt groggy, unable to focus properly.

One of them stood in the door and motioned to Callie. "Come with us," he said in Cantonese. She went. Pretending she didn't know Chinese would require some serious acting. She didn't feel up to the effort, so she didn't try.

One in front, one behind, they led her along a narrow passageway lined with doors. She got a glimpse out a porthole, saw that this deck was six or eight feet above the waterline and that the yacht was tied to a pier. It was some kind of yacht, she decided, an old one, though still maintained in excellent shape.

The man in front opened a door off the passageway, held it and motioned her through.

A man sat behind a small desk. He was not Chinese; European, perhaps, of medium height and weight, perhaps a hundred and fifty pounds. With a bony head and thin face and pinched nostrils.

"Sit," he said in English, and she took the only empty chair.

The two men who had brought her came into the small room—

which was no bigger than the stateroom where she had spent the day—and stood with their backs to the door.

"Mrs. Grafton," the man said and pushed a sheet of paper and ball-point pen an inch or two toward her. "We wish you to write a statement."

Russian. With that accent, he was a Russian.

She made no effort to pick up the pen.

The Russian waited a few seconds, then said, "Pick up the pen. You will write with it."

When Callie failed to obey he reached across the desk and slapped her, a stinging slap. He was remarkably quick with his hands.

Tears came to her eyes, which infuriated her. She sat there staring into his face through her tears.

"Perhaps I should explain. Pick up the pen or we will break your left arm."

She reached for the thing, got it in her right hand, put both hands back in her lap.

"Very good," the Russian said. "A first step. We make progress."

He leaned back in his chair and made a steeple with his fingers. "Before you begin writing, I will explain what we want. You listened to a tape that was recorded in the library of China Bob Chan the evening that he died. There were various conversations on the tape. Who were the people talking and what did they say?"

She looked at the pen in her right hand, so she didn't see the slap coming. God, the man was quick as a cat.

"Look at me, Mrs. Grafton. I am not nice. Nice is not a thing I have. I want something from you and I will hurt you to get it. I will cut your face, break your bones, break your head, cut out your eyes, watch men rape you . . . whatever it takes. I do not care if you live or die. Do you understand me?"

She nodded.

"Good. Very good!" the Russian said. He folded his hands on the table in front of him. "Did you listen to the tape?"

She decided not to talk. If you don't resist evil you become a part of it, she told herself. She saw the slap coming and went with it, but still the blow numbed her face. And another. And yet again.

She felt herself starting to go out, slipping away. Her eyes refused to focus.

Hands grabbed her roughly, held her in the chair. When she could focus again Wu was there, with a man on each side holding him. Wu's hands were bound by plastic ties and the ties were secured to his belt.

"Mrs. Grafton," the Russian said carefully. "Listen to me. I want to know what you know. If you do not talk, I will kill this man who spent the afternoon with you." That said, he drew a knife and inserted the point into Wu's arm. The color drained out of Wu's face, but he said nothing.

"He is very tough," the Russian said, grinning at Callie. "But he bleeds." He made a lengthwise cut in the man's arm about four inches long and wiped the knife on her blouse. "If you do not answer my questions I am going to cut him into little pieces and feed him to the fish."

He was as good as his word. He slowly inserted the knife into Wu's bicep, at least an inch deep, and slowly drew it down toward his elbow as the blood welled from the cut.

"I'll talk," Callie said, unable to watch.

"Where is the tape now?"

"My husband has it."

"Who brought you the tape?"

"Tommy Carmellini."

"Is Carmel—is he CIA?"

"Yes."

"Does your husband work for CIA?"

"Navy. He is in the navy."

"Why did Carmel bring him the tape?"

"Because I speak Chinese and Carmellini doesn't."

The Russian thought about that for a moment, then went on. "Did you hear China Bob Chan on the tape?"

"I think so."

"Virgil Cole?"

"Yes."

"Who else?"

"I don't know."

He lunged for her, his hand swinging, and she jerked back. One of the men behind her grabbed her hair.

The Russian slapped her, then said again, "Who else?"

"I didn't recognize the other voices."

The Russian glanced at the man behind her, and he released her hair.

She had cut her tongue on the inside of her mouth. The blood tasted coppery and felt slimy, and she had to swallow it.

"I am going to ask a question, Mrs. Grafton. I want the truthful answer. No lies, please. Lies will be very bad for you. Do you understand?"

"Yes." This time it came out a whisper. Blood was still streaming from Wu's wounds and dripping on the deck.

"Who killed China Bob Chan?"

"I don't know."

"Oh, Mrs. Grafton, I hoped I would not need to hurt you, and now you lie to me. Too bad, too bad."

The Russian came around the desk and reached for her. Callie spit blood in his face. When he blinked and drew back to avoid it, she slashed at his face with the ballpoint.

One of the men behind her jerked her half out of the chair, turned her, and hit her so hard she passed out.

When she came to she was in a cold, cold place, in absolute darkness. She felt around her . . . and felt something cold, like cold, dead flesh.

She was in a meat locker.

And she was freezing. Sore, not completely conscious, she curled up in a fetal position to try to conserve her body heat.

Rip Buckingham wanted to talk. He had been carrying this great burden in his breast for months and months and finally here was someone he could tell, someone who also had a huge stake in how the tale would end, someone with whom he could share his fears.

He started by telling Jake everything he knew about Sonny Wong, and then he couldn't stop. He told him about Lin Pe and Sue Lin and Wu Tai Kwong, about Wu's romance with the British SIS agent Kerry Kent, told him how Kerry approached Virgil Cole and asked for his help, how Cole agreed to help fund the revolution and teach key cell members the fundamentals of cyberwarfare.

"Soon," Rip said. "Very soon. The revolution will start and the world as we know it will come to an end."

Jake Grafton listened without saying a word. He knew some of it, surmised more, but Rip filled in the gaps and made the story whole.

"They are going to find out who Wu really is and come for Lin Pe and Sue Lin. They are going to drag them off to prison, strangle them. The Chinese think like that. If I can't shoot you I'll piss in your well and strangle your mother."

"And the women refused to leave," Jake suggested.

"How did you know?"

"If they had agreed you wouldn't still be here, would you?"

"I suppose not."

"How soon is soon?"

"Tonight maybe. Tomorrow. Tomorrow night. I don't know, but it's got to happen quickly."

"Does this Sonny Wong know the timetable?"

"Only if he has a spy at the very top levels of the Scarlet Team. Each cell has a name. The top one is the Scarlet Team."

"How do you start a revolution, anyway?"

"Wu never told me. He didn't want me to know too much."

"Well, let's you and me go see if we can find Mr. Wong."

Rip didn't think much of that idea. "He won't have Callie or Wu with him," he objected.

"I want to see him."

"Why?"

"I want to talk to the man," Jake explained. "Give him a reason not to harm Callie."

"Sonny isn't the kind of man who is easily convinced of anything," Rip explained. "Especially where money is involved. Talking won't do any good."

"That depends on what we say," Jake said patiently. "And how we say it. You'll see. I'm fairly good at delivering messages."

"I can't see how this will help," Rip protested, but Jake's mind was made up.

They rode the tram up the mountain—because the first cable car was going up—and got a taxi at the visitors' center on top. "Wong has a floating restaurant in Aberdeen," Rip told the admiral, who wondered if it was the same one that he and Callie had eaten at yesterday. He hoped not. The thought that Wong might have made a dollar off him rankled.

"Whenever I want to talk to the guy I leave a message there," Rip continued. "For all I know, Sonny sleeps there sometimes. One other thing I forgot to mention: He has an associate, not a partner, but a chief lieutenant. The man is Russian, Yuri Daniel. Avoid him if you can. Just being around him makes my skin crawl."

To Jake's relief, Wong's was not the restaurant where he and Callie had eaten. It was the next one down, gaudy as a painted whore, sporting enough lights to decorate the White House Christmas tree.

Jake and Rip lined up at the same little wharf and took a sampan across the choppy black water to the restaurant. The main dining area was almost empty.

"With air traffic screwed up and all the electrical problems, the tourists are staying in their hotels," Rip opined.

The maître d' let them have their pick of window seats, then left them.

"I'm not hungry," Jake said. "Let's go see if Wong is around. Where are the offices?"

"The second floor, or deck, I think." Rip pointed to a small black door near the kitchen entrance.

"Lead on."

The door was unlocked. Rip pushed it open. There was a man sitting inside. Rip spoke to him in Chinese, asked if Wong were around.

The man looked Rip over, asked his name, then went upstairs.

In about a minute a medium-sized Chinese man in his fifties came down the narrow stairs. He broke into a grin, which revealed crooked teeth. "Rip Buckingham, as I live and breathe," the man said in English. "This is a surprise. Who is your friend?"

"Jake Grafton."

"I'm Sonny Wong," the Chinese man said but didn't offer a hand. "Come upstairs. We'll talk there." He turned and led the way back up the narrow staircase. Rip and Jake followed. The man who had been sitting in the foyer also came along.

Wong's office was roomy enough, furnished with a practical desk and some overstuffed chairs, and decorated with the stuff curio stores sold to tourists, stuff that looked valuable but probably wasn't—carved elephants, ivory pagodas, here and there a hand-carved chess set.

Sonny Wong turned to face his guests. "So, Mr. Grafton, did you come to buy your wife back?"

"I came to explain why you should release her unharmed."

"Oh, no harm come to her if Virgil Cole pay the money I asked. If not . . ."

"Cole will pay," Jake said, looking around, then focusing on Sonny. "You got a nice life here in Hong Kong. Rip tells me you've got a lot of stuff, a restaurant, houses, apartments, boats, money, women. . . . Virgil Cole is going to pay you. If you send my wife back alive and in the pink, you can continue to live your good life here in Hong Kong. We'll chalk this little episode up as an adventure and go on down the road."

Sonny smiled. He looked at Rip. "Do you think Cole would pay more to get you and Mr. Grafton back alive?" He turned toward the telephone on his desk. "Why don't we ask him?"

Jake Grafton drew Cole's .38 snub nose from his right trouser pocket, turned, and shot the guard at the door square in the heart. The shot was like a thunderclap in that small space.

Wong turned, quick as a cat, but too late.

Jake Grafton rammed the barrel of the snub nose against his lips.

"If you even twitch, I'm going to blow your brains all over that desk." He stared into Wong's eyes, trying to see if the man would do something stupid. Then he felt his pockets.

Rip Buckingham was standing frozen, staring at the dead man by the door, his jaw slack.

Jake marched Wong backward around the desk, opened and closed drawers. Sure enough, in one he found a pistol, a small automatic. It felt heavy enough.

"Rip."

Buckingham turned toward him. Jake tossed him the automatic with his left hand.

"See if this is loaded."

"I don't know . . ."

"Pull the slide back, see if there is a shell in the chamber."

Rip bent over slightly, his long hair falling across his face. He used both hands on the pistol. "It's loaded," he reported.

"Find the safety, put it to the off position."

After several seconds, Rip said, "Okay."

"Fire a shot into that chair."

Rip extended the pistol to arm's length, aimed, and pulled the trigger. The shot wasn't as loud as the boom from the snub nose, but it was loud enough.

"You're armed," Jake told him. "Go search all the rooms on this deck. Make sure Callie and Wu aren't here. Shoot anyone who looks at you cross-eyed. No conversation, just shoot them. Go!"

To his credit, Rip Buckingham went.

Keeping the snubbie against Wong's teeth, Jake began searching his desk. The papers were written in Chinese, which was no help to Jake. He tossed the stuff all over as he scanned it, looking for . . . well, anything. Anything at all.

"You want to call the police?" Jake asked Wong.

Wong didn't reply.

"We can tell them about the kidnapping, have them call the American consul general, who will verify that the wife of an American flag officer was kidnapped by you and you personally demanded a ransom. American trade being what it is with China, I think the authorities might take a damn dim view of your activities, Mr. Wong."

Jake didn't call the police because Callie would probably be dead by the time the police got to her. He didn't say that, of course, but that was the nub of it.

He marched Wong back around the desk and made him sit in a chair while he searched the dead man. This man was also armed, another small automatic. Jake pocketed it.

He sat across from Wong, kept the .38 in close to his body, and pointed right at Wong's solar plexus.

"I misjudged you, Mr. Grafton."

"If I knew where she was, Wong, I'd kill you here and now and go get her."

"I believe you."

Jake sat silently, staring at the Chinese. For his part, Sonny Wong kept his mouth shut and didn't move.

The minutes crawled by. The telephone rang. Jake didn't answer it. After four rings the noise stopped.

Jake heard no shots, no shouts, no loud noises. Which was a good thing for Sonny Wong, because he would have been the first to die. Jake thought the man knew that, for he sat silently and still.

Eight minutes later, Rip returned. He had put the automatic in his pocket. "There were some living apartments," he told Jake, "some men who looked at me curiously, but your wife and Wu aren't here."

"Let's go," Jake said, rising from his chair. "Wong, you'll lead the parade. The thing you'll feel in your back is the barrel of this pistol. Honest to God, if there is any trouble from anyone, I'm going to empty this thing into your back. Now let's go."

Down the stairs they went. They went out into the dining room, then into the kitchen. Five people were there, four men and a woman, preparing dishes for the patrons. Jake stood so they couldn't see the pistol he had on Wong and had Rip get everyone out of the kitchen.

When all five had left, Jake told Rip, "Go out into the main dining room. Announce that there is a small fire in the kitchen and everyone should leave in an orderly way. Customers and employees, everyone. Don't let them panic. Just herd them off this barge."

"A fire?"

"A small fire."

Rip looked around the kitchen, looked at Sonny standing there with a blank face, looked at Jake. "What about the people upstairs?" he asked.

"Working for Sonny Wong, they take their chances. If they have time to get out, good for them. If they don't, too bad. Now do as I say."

"What about Wong?"

"He can leave with me or die here. His choice."

Rip Buckingham took a deep breath. "When you deliver a message, you really deliver, Grafton."

Jake walked Wong over to the stove, a large gas burner with blue flames from several of the jets. Nearby was a deep-fat fryer full of hot grease. Jake turned the flames under it up as far as they would go.

He traced out the gas lines, which were routed along the junction of the deck and bulkhead. Through a door, into a storage room. There it was, a tank of bottled gas or propane, Jake couldn't tell which.

Jake led Wong to the door to the dining area. He pushed it open a crack, watched Rip getting the small crowd off the floating restaurant onto sampans. Some of the employees kept looking toward the kitchen, but Rip insisted that Sonny himself wanted everyone to leave.

"Give me your shirt," Jake said to Wong.

The Chinese unbuttoned the short-sleeve shirt and handed it over. With the pistol right against Wong's neck, Jake marched him to the deep fat fryer and dipped the shirt in. When it had absorbed a fair amount of grease, he tossed it onto the stove. The grease flared up.

Taking a step sideways to get a good view, Jake thumbed back the hammer of the revolver and aimed at the gas line. He missed with the first shot, but his second was rewarded with a loud hissing of escaping gas.

Jake eared back the hammer one more time, put the pistol against Wong's lips.

"There is no place on this planet you can hide, Mr. Wong. If any harm comes to my wife, I'm declaring war on you."

Then Jake ran. Out the kitchen door, across the dining room as fast as he could scramble toward the sampan dock at the main entrance. He heard Sonny Wong running behind him.

The kitchen exploded with a dull boom.

Rip Buckingham was standing alone on the dock. There were no boats.

The fire came out the kitchen door; the dining room quickly filled with smoke.

Jake said, "Shall we?" to Rip, took a last look at Wong, then dove into the black water. Rip was right behind him.

CHAPTER ELEVEN

When the van brought Eaton Steinbaugh home after his radiation treatment, his wife, Babs, was waiting by the curb. He felt like hell. Babs helped him inside. He wanted to go to the study and lie down on the couch, and today she let him. Usually she insisted he go to the bedroom and get in bed, but not today.

"You got an E-mail," she told him.

"Did you print it out?" he whispered.

"Don't I always?"

She handed him the sheet of paper. The message was from Hong Kong, somebody in Hong Kong—he had never before seen that E-mail address. The body of the message was a series of letters, arranged as if they were a word. He counted the letters. Twelve of them.

The letters appeared to be a code. And they were, but the code wasn't in the message. The twelve letters *was* the message.

He handed the sheet of paper back to Babs.

"Want to tell me what that means?" she said sharply.

"Within four hours."

"Cole?"

"Yes."

"Really, Steinbaugh, I don't know about you. Sick as you are and you're messing in other people's business. All away around the world, in China, no less."

"Umpf."

"They could prosecute you."

"For what?"

"How would I know? Something, that's for sure."

"They already did that," her husband replied. "Years and years ago." When he was twenty he spent two years in a federal penitentiary for hacking into top-secret Pentagon computer files. Of course he was thrown out of the university and ended up never going back. That was over ten years ago.

"Prison didn't teach you a damned thing, obviously," she snapped, and walked out with her head down.

A husband dying of cancer was a heavy load, and he appreciated that. Not much left for Babs to smile about.

Virgil Cole!

It was really happening.

Cole promised him it would. "Have faith," he said. "The time will come."

"I might be dead by then," Eaton Steinbaugh told Cole. He hadn't been diagnosed with cancer then. Maybe it was a premonition.

"Hey, man, the Lord might call us all home before then. Just do your best to make it work when the hour comes."

"They might change the codes. They might change the system."

"If they do, they do. That's life. I don't want you to guarantee anything. Just do the best you can and we'll all live with it, however it turns out."

Babs was sure as hell wrong, he reflected wryly, about what he learned in prison. While doing his time he taught a computer course for the inmates. Every day he had hours alone on the machine, hours in which he was supposed to be preparing lesson plans. He spent most of those hours hacking into networks and databases all over the globe. What he didn't do was tamper with the data that were there, so no one came looking for him. Locked up with nothing to occupy his mind, the hacking kept him sane.

That was then. Today just getting into a network was tougher, and a lot of the security programs had alarms that would reveal the presence of an unauthorized intruder. System designers finally were waking up to the threat.

But Eaton Steinbaugh had also learned a few things through the years. One was that getting in was a lot easier if you had access to the software and constructed a back door that you could use anytime you wanted.

He became a back door specialist. As soon as he was released from prison he was heavily recruited by software companies. Through the years he took jobs that interested him, and the demand for his skills forced the companies to pay excellent wages. For his own amusement, when he designed or worked on networks, he put in a trapdoor for his own use.

He was working for Virgil Cole's company when Cole called him in one day. Cole found one of the back doors, which was the first time anyone ever managed that trick.

That Cole! He was one smart cookie, shrewd and tougher than cold-rolled steel. Steinbaugh had never met a man like him.

Cole didn't fire him. Just told him to do a better job on the back doors or take them out.

He was working for Microsoft when Cole telephoned him eighteen months ago, wanted him to accept a job with Cole's company, which Cole was no longer with, go to China to do some Y2K remediation.

Steinbaugh had always refused Y2K remediations, which he regarded as mind-numbing grunt work, but he did it because Cole asked.

On his way to Beijing he went through Hong Kong and dropped in to see Virgil Cole at the consulate. Cole took him to the best restaurant in town, which was French of course, where they ate a five-star gourmet dinner on white linen in a private alcove and sipped on a two-thousand-dollar bottle of wine.

"You didn't have to do this for me, you know," Eaton Steinbaugh told Virgil Cole.

"I needed an evening out, and you're a good excuse."

They were sipping cognac and sucking on Cuban cigars after dinner when Steinbaugh remarked, "When you stop and reflect, life's contrasts are pretty amazing, aren't they?"

"What do you mean?"

"Well, I grew up in blue-collar Oakland, Dad worked on road-paving crews, we never had a whole lot. Then I wound up in prison, which was a bummer. Since then I've been all over the world, married, had a kid, and here I am in Hong Kong having a five-star dinner with a billionaire, just like I was somebody. You know?"

Cole laughed. Later Steinbaugh realized that Cole had hoped for this reaction, indeed, had played for it.

"I spent a lifetime working to get here, too," he said. "The low point in my life was a night in Vietnam. I was a bombardier-navigator on A-6 Intruder aircraft. One night near the end of the war the gomers shot us down."

"I didn't know that," Steinbaugh said.

Cole continued: "I remember lying in the jungle with a broken back waiting for the North Vietnamese to find and kill me. I was absolutely certain I had come to the end of the road. And I was wrong." He lifted his glass in a silent toast to Steinbaugh, and drank. Steinbaugh did likewise.

When he had his glass back on the table, Cole said, "If the Chinese people can get rid of the Communists, who knows, perhaps in the fullness of time they too will have some of the same opportunities that have enriched our lives."

"Yeah," Steinbaugh agreed, for the comment seemed innocuous enough.

"I want your help to make it happen."

Steinbaugh wasn't sure how to answer that.

"I want you to install some of your back doors," Cole said, looking him straight in the eyes.

"Where?"

"On some systems in Beijing. You're going to be working on some systems in the Forbidden City, the Chinese Kremlin. I want you to install back doors so that when the time comes, you can get into those systems and control them, screw them up, or disable them."

"When will the time come?"

"When the revolution starts."

"Jesus Christ!" Steinbaugh's eyes got big in surprise. He had sort of suspected that Cole had something on his mind when he asked him to come to see him in Hong Kong on his way to Beijing, but in his wildest imaginings he hadn't envisioned anything like this. "A revolution! Me screwing with government computers to help a revolution—wouldn't that be an act of war or something?"

"I'm no lawyer," Cole said, "but I suspect you're right."

The consul general's cigar had gone out, so he fussed over it, scraped off the ash, and got the thing smoldering again. When he saw that Eaton Steinbaugh was still listening, he went into specifics, some of which were very technical.

Steinbaugh was even more amazed, then he wasn't. Cole didn't do anything by guess or by God. He had thought about this, about what he wanted.

"Cyberwarfare," Steinbaugh said.

"That's right. We must divert the government's attention, confuse them all to hell, make it as difficult as possible for them to figure out what the threat is. That's the first goal. Second, we want to make it difficult for the Communists to respond militarily to the real threat when they figure out what it is. Third, we must deprive them of control over the people, the economy, the course of events. If we can deprive them of the power to make things happen, we will win."

"We?"

"You and me."

"Oh, come on."

"The revolutionaries."

"You're one of them?"

"Yep."

"Goddamn," Steinbaugh said.

Of course he agreed to do it.

Eaton Steinbaugh had pretty well finished the Beijing assignment when he got sick and had to go home to California. He was just thirty-five years old, and the doctors said he had terminal cancer. He mailed Cole a note, told him he'd better hustle the future right along, make it happen soon. Cole knew what he meant.

Now, today, this message arrived.

Within four hours.

One more message to go.

Steinbaugh got up from the couch and turned on the computer. He had set up the E-mail system so it would notify him immediately of any incoming mail.

Babs heard the computer noises and came to the door.

"You're really going to do it, aren't you?"

"Yes."

"You're a damned fool, Eaton. As if you don't have troubles enough, a dying man about to face the Lord and answer for all you've done, bad and good. I don't know how many felonies you're going to commit now."

"Neither do I. This is sort of fun, huh?"

She shook her head and went back to the kitchen.

Well, Babs was Babs. She was a good woman, although she knew absolutely nothing about computers, which were his passion. Truthfully, she didn't know much about men, either, or at least Eaton Steinbaugh—didn't know why he did what he did, made the choices he made. She thought him a fool for hacking as a young man and for his back doors, which he had made the mistake of mentioning a few years ago when they were talking about how fascinating his work was. Practical and unimaginative as always, she thought him a complete flaming idiot for helping Cole. He knew that, and somehow it didn't matter. She had never had any romance in her soul. Still, he loved her and she loved him, each in their own way, and that was good enough for this life.

When Jake Grafton got back to the consulate with Rip Buckingham, Tiger Cole's office was in an uproar. Even though it was almost midnight the lights were on, the secretary and two hovering aides looked white as ghosts, and Cole was on the phone. Since it was midnight here, it was noon in Washington.

Cole was standing beside the desk holding the telephone to his ear, looking out the window.

Although Jake didn't realize it, Cole was looking straight at the windows of the office of Third Planet Communications. There was a man at the window looking this way, but with the lights behind him, Cole didn't recognize him. Cole hoped the man was Hu Chiang on a break—Third Planet was going to be a busy place a bit later tonight.

On the telephone an undersecretary of state was demanding to know what the hell Cole had been up to in Hong Kong. The fax of Grafton's letter to the National Security Adviser had apparently found its way to his desk, and the undersecretary was shouting.

"A gross breach of trust, Cole. Outrageous! I have called the Justice Department. The lawyers there are recommending that the FBI investigate you for a possible treason prosecution. Do you hear me? *Treason!*"

"I don't know what to say, Mr. Podgorski. I suppose this incident will be an embarrassment to the administration."

"An embarrassment? You suppose? It'll be a nightmare, Cole. How could you? You know the president is on a tightrope over China, and now *this!*"

"Darn. What was I thinking? A public discussion of the administration's willingness to deal with tyrants won't win you any friends, I fear."

"Public discussion? Is that a threat?"

"You don't think I'm going to plead guilty to some trumped-up political charge or refuse to talk to the press, do you?" Cole asked dryly. "Prosecutions are political acts. I promise you that you will be reading my repeated requests that the administration stand up for the human rights of China's enslaved citizens in *The New York Times.* This whole issue is going to get a full, complete, open airing. Perhaps my friends in Congress will decide to hold hearings."

"Asshole! You asshole! I'm sending the FBI to arrest you. They'll be on the next plane."

"I'll pack my toothbrush," Cole told Podgorski and hung up the telephone.

"Sounds like it hit the fan in Washington," Jake Grafton said.

"They are agitated. My resignation was sudden, unexpected. After mature reflection, I suspect they will claim executive privilege covers my resignation and the reasons for it. They may even refuse to acknowledge I was an appointee of the administration."

Cole grinned. He did it so rarely that the effect was startling, as if a powerful light had been turned on. And as suddenly as it appeared, it was gone.

"Why are you dripping on my carpet?" Cole asked. His gaze went to Buckingham. "Both of you?"

"Little fracas at Sonny Wong's restaurant in Aberdeen," Jake said.

Rip added, "Grafton started a fire. We had to swim for it."

"Did you kill him?" Tiger Cole asked, referring to Sonny.

"No." Jake sighed. "I was sorely tempted. I almost wish I had.

Wanted to put the fear in the bastard. Maybe he'll send her back. Even if he doesn't, maybe he'll keep his hands off her."

The secretary looked at the admiral like he was insane. Both the aides were trying to keep control of their faces, with little success.

Rip Buckingham was beside himself. He shooed the secretary and aides from the room. When they were gone, he whispered hoarsely at Cole, "This man's crazy. He shot a man dead in Wong's office. Pulled a gun from his pocket and shot him right in the bloody ticker. Didn't say a bloody word, just . . . bang."

Cole shook his head. "That sure sounds like Jake Grafton."

Jake pulled the pistol from his pocket, opened the cylinder, and picked out the empties. "Need some more shells. Some gun oil too, if you have any. Salt water isn't good for these things."

Buckingham sank into a chair and put his head in his hands.

"I called my attorneys in California," Cole said. "They need a day to sell some stock, raise some cash. They will be ready to wire-transfer the money to that Swiss account the day after tomorrow."

"The day after tomorrow," Grafton echoed. "When Wong calls, why don't you tell him that he has to take them to a neutral place? I'll meet him there. When I see them safe and sound, I'll call you and you can wire the money. That way killing us won't solve his problem."

"It'll be a start."

"To be safe," Jake explained, "he has to kill Wu and you and everyone in the revolutionary movement who might oppose him or seek revenge. If all of you are in one place, after he gets the money he can just blow up the building and solve his problem."

"Okay. But how are you going to get Wu and Callie out of harm's way after he gets his money?"

"I don't know yet. I'll have to think about it."

"I don't think it can be done," Tiger Cole said softly.

"Sonny can't afford to be known as the man who killed Wu," Rip said. "Sure, a lot of people know that he kidnapped Wu. But if he kills him . . ."

Cole opened a desk drawer, extracted a small box, and walked to the chair where Buckingham sat. "This is your brother-in-law's finger," he told Rip. "Sonny Wong had it delivered this afternoon."

Buckingham looked in the box and turned pale.

"We need Wu alive. China needs him."

"Don't patronize me," Rip said crossly. "I'm a big boy."

"How about doing another story for your dad? The last one was very good—got 'em in an uproar in Europe and Washington."

"Okay," Rip said, brushing the hair back out of his eyes. He handed the box back to Cole.

"You can use a computer in the office across the street. More on the coming revolution, about the goings-on in Hong Kong. E-mail it to Richard for tomorrow's papers. We want to make damn sure the world knows who the guys are in the white hats."

Rip took a deep breath, his eyes still on the box.

"What do I say about Wu?"

"Don't mention him by name. 'Unnamed patriots' is the phrase. Nothing about Sonny Wong."

After Rip left, Cole used the intercom to ask the secretary to get Jake some clean clothes from his apartment. Then he asked the admiral, "Want a drink? I got some bourbon."

"Yeah."

"What did you tell Wong?"

"Not to harm Callie."

"I'm sorry, Jake. Sorry you and Callie got mixed up in this."

"Yeah."

Jake was buttoning one of Cole's shirts when there was a knock on the door. Tommy Carmellini stuck his head in.

"I thought I'd find you here, Admiral. You left a note on my desk asking for a report?"

"I did. Come in."

Carmellini dropped into an overstuffed chair and watched Jake put on his wet shoes over dry socks. "You want it here, where Mr. Cole can hear?"

"Yep. What have you found out?"

The CIA officer removed a small notebook from an inside jacket pocket and flipped it open. "The clerk selling the passports to Sonny Wong is a woman named Elizabeth Yeager." He spelled the last name. "She delivers the passports to her bedroom buddy, Carson Eisenberg, a CIA guy who is on Wong's payroll. She's been making false computer entries and writing up files to cover the thefts, so all the numbers will match when the department is audited."

"How did you find out this information?"

"I opened the safes down there, checked the logbooks, then went into the secured cabinets."

"Jesus!" Cole said. "And I thought this place was reasonably secure."

"Not even close," Carmellini shot back.

"Do you have Eisenberg's contact?" Jake asked.

"Name, phone number, and address. And I got his banking information, where he's been depositing the cash he got from Wong."

"What else?"

"Kerry Kent has been talking to some people in her apartment in Chinese. Don't know what it means without a translator, and don't know which translator around here I can trust. I sent the tape off to Washington."

"Uh-huh."

"The consul general uses English in his office, fortunately. He had a conversation earlier today with Kerry Kent about a plane that was supposed to arrive at seven this evening at Lantau Island. She was worried that with the airport closed, the plane couldn't land. Cole didn't think that would be a problem."

Carmellini looked at Cole. "Was it a problem, sir?"

"You're still taping conversations in this office?"

"Yes, sir. After you and the admiral had your little talk, I wired you up again."

"Goddamn you, Carmellini! I told you—"

"Can't fire me," Carmellini said smugly and grinned. "I work for him." He jerked his thumb at Grafton.

"Don't be a prick."

"It's genetic. Folks often remark upon that fact. You'd think I worked for the IRS or—"

"Can it," Jake Grafton snapped. "Anything else?"

"Yeah. Cole's been lying to you."

Grafton's eyes narrowed. He glanced at Cole, then concentrated on Carmellini. "Explain."

Carmellini extracted a sheaf of folded paper from another pocket. "The National Security Agency has been doing some intercepts on certain E-mail addresses, and they passed along some dillies that Cole had been sending and receiving."

Cole sat down behind his desk. He didn't look too upset.

"Seems that Mr. Cole has been E-mailing people in the states about something called York units. They are supposed to be on that plane."

"York?"

"York units. Don't know what those are, but it is obvious to me from reading this correspondence that Mr. Cole is not a traitor, that certain people in the United States government are cooperating with him and providing him with technical and logistical support. Six York units, tech manuals, computers, WB cell phones, the list goes on and on."

"I know what York units are," Jake muttered and glanced again at Cole. As usual the consul general's face revealed nothing of its owner's thoughts.

"Anything else?" Jake said to Carmellini.

"That about covers the waterfront, I think."

Jake looked at Cole. "What do you want to do about Eisenberg and the Yeager woman?"

"Can't prosecute them with illegally obtained evidence."

"They don't know how we got the evidence," Carmellini pointed out.

"Have the personnel officer call them in and fire them," Cole said to Carmellini. "Then give them a choice: They can go home and be prosecuted for theft and espionage, or they can stay in Hong Kong. If they want to stay, run them out of the consulate. Tell them if they ever show up in the states again they *will* be prosecuted."

"Yes, sir."

Jake frowned at Carmellini. "We're going to need some weapons that have a little more oomphf than this thirty-eight. Send the head marine up here and let me talk to him."

Carmellini nodded and headed for the door.

"Take the bugs with you," Jake added.

There were three of them, tiny things, cleverly hidden. Carmellini pocketed them, then left the room and closed the door behind him.

"Want to tell me about it?" Jake said.

"The administration wants the Communist era in China to end, and they are willing to help the rebels make it happen. But they don't want anyone to know they helped."

"You're the fall guy?"

"I suppose. They had to have someone to blame and I volunteered.

I thought you had figured that out. Life in California was getting to be a burden that I couldn't carry, and . . ." Cole shrugged.

Jake just nodded. He finished off his whiskey in one gulp and set the glass on the table by the couch.

"I guess the left hand and the right hand are still strangers in Washington," Cole added.

"Yeah," Jake Grafton replied. "They never tell all of it."

"Do you know these people who kidnapped us?" Callie Grafton asked Wu Tai Kwong between chattering teeth. He had used a piece of sheet to wash her wounds after she was brought back to the stateroom around midnight. He thought she had had a mild concussion, but she was shivering uncontrollably from her hours in the meat locker.

"I know them," he replied. He had ripped a sheet into strips and wrapped them around the cuts in his arm. The bleeding seemed to have stopped.

"They wanted to know what was on the tape. The CIA had a bug hidden in China Bob Chan's library and taped the conversations there the night he died. I listened to the tape."

"Sonny Wong is worried about what you heard."

"You think?"

"He might be on the tape."

"So who is Sonny Wong?"

"A gangster. Maybe the last big one in Hong Kong. There are many little gangsters, people who want to be big, but Sonny *is* big. Makes lots of money."

Callie wrapped herself tighter in the blankets. She couldn't stop shivering. Her face hurt like hell and she was bruised and ached all over, but the deep cold she felt was worse.

"Is this about money?" she asked. "Is that why we were kidnapped?"

"I think so." Wu sat down on his bunk. His hand and arm were hurting. He rested his elbow on his knee with the hand elevated. "Cole has so much. The temptation was too much for Sonny."

Callie waited for Wu to say more. She saw a broad-shouldered, medium-sized Chinese man of about thirty years, not handsome, not ugly, the kind of man who could melt into any crowd bigger than three. Or could he?

There *was* something . . .

"Sonny Wong is the security chief," Wu said. "Every revolution needs someone to enforce secrecy or the whole thing will collapse of its own weight. That is his job."

Callie began to see it. "So if someone talked to the police . . ."

"Sonny heard of it. He had people in every cell who reported to him. He plugged the leaks."

"He killed people who talked?"

Wu lowered his head. "Sometimes," he admitted. "Sometimes people saw the error of their ways and agreed to talk no more."

"He's a thug."

"An enforcer. It takes more than dreamers with stars in their eyes to make a revolution."

"He's the dirty end of the stick."

The metaphor threw Wu. Callie didn't feel like explaining.

"You trusted him that much?" Callie pressed.

"No one else wanted the job. No one wanted blood on his hands."

"How did you know this loyal murderer wouldn't betray you?"

"I didn't know. Anyone could have betrayed me, any hour of any day."

"Who is your thug in Beijing, Shanghai, et cetera?" Callie asked.

"Sonny has friends throughout most of China. Really, there was no one else who could do the job."

Callie was unwilling to leave the subject. "So you must have known that someday Wong might turn on you, take over the entire organization, put himself at the head? There is plenty of precedent, I believe. Saddam Hussein and Joe Stalin leap immediately to mind."

"That was a possibility," Wu Tai Kwong reluctantly admitted.

"So what did you plan to prevent that move from succeeding?"

"I planned to kill him before he killed me."

"Looks like you may have miscalculated," Callie snapped.

Thoroughly disgusted, she carried the blankets into the tiny bathroom and shut the door. The door had no lock.

CHAPTER TWELVE

Virgil Cole's daughter, Elaine, was an associate professor of mathematics at Stanford University. She was attending a women's political caucus in Washington, D.C., when she received a coded E-mail from her father. Like the message received by Eaton Steinbaugh, the E-mail consisted of a nonsense word, a dozen random letters, from an address in Hong Kong.

She received the message at noon when she checked her E-mail on her laptop in her hotel room. She got off-line, left the computer running, and gazed about her distractedly, the political meeting forgotten.

She opened the drapes on the window. Georgetown was visible but none of monumental Washington, which was out of sight to the right.

She had a small notebook in her computer case. She got it out now, opened it, and examined the notes she had written there. The handwriting was neat, almost compulsively so. She had made the notes the last time she was in Hong Kong visiting her father, over spring break.

Being Virgil Cole's daughter had always been a mixed blessing. He was quiet and unassuming, brilliant and rich. Somehow her mother's second husband never measured up. He was very nice, and yet . . . When she was young she had thought her mother was crazy for not staying with her father, but as an adult, she could see how difficult

Cole was, especially for her mother, who was neither brilliant nor quiet and unassuming.

Perhaps it had all worked out for the best.

Except for her half brother, of course, who had never come to grips with the fire in his father's soul.

A Chinese revolution. Yes, that was Virgil Cole. A great impossible crusade to which he could give all of his brains and energy and determination would attract him like a candle attracts a moth.

She had never seen him so full of life as he was in April during her visit.

A crusade! A holy war!

She had seen the fire in his eyes, so of course she said yes when he asked her to help. He didn't come right out and baldly ask. He explained what was needed, how the worm programs were already in place and at the right time needed to be triggered from a location outside of Hong Kong, triggered in such a way that the identity of the person doing it could never be established . . . beyond a reasonable doubt.

He explained the worms, how they were designed, and she carefully wrote down the instructions she needed to make them dance.

She played with her computer keyboard, checked the E-mail again.

So the revolution was *now*.

And she was going to help.

And she might never see her father again.

She was mulling that hard fact when the execute message came. She turned off the computer and stored it carefully in its carrying case. She left the case on the bed and took only the notebook with her.

She caught a taxi in front of the hotel and told the driver she wanted to go to the main public library.

Sure enough, the library had a bank of computers that allowed Internet access. The librarian at the desk near the computers was a plump, middle-aged woman. "The fee is a dollar," the lady told Elaine, who dug in her purse for a bill. "Such a terrible irony—the computers are here for people who can't afford their own, but the users must help defray the cost."

"I understand."

"Everything costs, these days," the librarian said. "We're fighting the battle with the library board to get the fee eliminated, but so far they won't yield."

"Yes."

"Our only rule is no pornography. If people keep calling up pornographic sites, I'm afraid the computers will have to be removed."

"Do you check to see what people are viewing on the Net?" Elaine asked, pretending to be horrified at this privacy intrusion.

"Oh, no," the librarian assured her. "But people do walk behind the cubicles, and they talk, you know!"

"Indeed they do. I'm here today to do some research for my thesis."

"Let me know if you need any help," the librarian said and turned to help the next person, a pimpled teen with unkempt long hair who looked as if he might be very interested in porno.coms. As Elaine walked away, the library lady began briefing this intent young man on the evils of cybersex.

With the notebook of passwords and computer codes on the table beside her, it took Elaine less than fifteen minutes to get through the security layers into the main computer of the central bank clearinghouse in Hong Kong. Once there, she began searching for the code that her father assured her would be there.

Virgil Cole answered the ringing cell phone on his office desk with his usual "Hello." He listened a moment, then broke the connection.

"The York units are in," he told Jake Grafton, who was stretched out on Cole's couch thinking about his wife. "Want to see them?"

"I thought Sergeant York was a paper program."

"It's hardware now."

"You got six?"

"That's right."

"Steal 'em?"

"No."

"Buy 'em?"

"Not quite. Let's say the American government retains legal title and I have custody."

"Let's go look." Jake reached for his shoes. "I was wondering how you red-hot revolutionaries were going to avoid being massacred by the division of troops the PLA has stationed in Hong Kong. This is it, huh?"

There was not much traffic on the streets at this hour, but Jake

Grafton paused in the entrance way of the consulate. Half hidden in the shadows, he restrained Cole with a touch on the arm while he scanned the street in both directions.

Only when he was sure there was no one waiting did he mutter at Cole and step through the entrance.

Cole led the way across the street and along the sidewalk for fifty yards. They went down the first alley they came to, then down a ramp to a loading dock under the skyscraper. A tractor-trailer rig was flush against the loading dock.

Cole climbed the stairs, nodded at two men sitting on the dock, and knocked on the door. A man carrying an assault rifle opened the door. Cole and Grafton went in.

The Sergeant York units were two-legged robots about six and a half feet tall. The legs had three knees—back, front, back—with three-pronged feet. They had articulated arms and, where human hands would be, three flexible grasping appendages, almost like jointed claws, which ended in sharp points. Two were hinged to close inward and one outward, almost like an opposed thumb.

Mounted on the right side of the torso on a flexible mount was a four-barreled Gatling gun that fired standard 5.56 millimeter rounds from a flexible belt feed. Capacity was two hundred rounds.

And the York units had heads mounted on flexible stalks that could turn right or left, be raised or lowered. Two Yorks were standing on the concrete floor back-to-back, turning their heads and looking about with an ominous curiosity.

"The best part," Cole said with more enthusiasm than Grafton thought he had in him, "is the tail. What do you think of the tail?" The prehensile tail was only about eighteen inches long, thick where it came out of the body and tapering quickly.

"It's cool." Jake could think of no other reply.

"The engineers wanted three legs, and the army absolutely refused to buy the thing if it had more than two—they were worried about their image. The tail was my compromise. It helps with stability, balance, agility, shock absorption. . . . With the tail the York is quicker and faster, and can leap higher. And it gives us room for more batteries, which are heavy."

"What were those soldiers thinking?"

"Yeah."

Three Chinese men were watching Kerry Kent walk a York out of the semitrailer. She used a small computer unit, much like a laptop. There were no wires. Like Grafton the Chinese men watched the Sergeant York robots and whispered to each other.

Jake Grafton felt mesmerized by the spectral stare of the robots that were outside the trailer. Their heads never stopped moving. They had no mouth or nose, but in the eye-socket position—the widest part of the head—were two cameras. The one on the right side had a lens turret on the face. As Jake inspected the nearest one, the turret rotated another lens in front of the left camera, if it was a camera.

"What the hell are these things looking at?" he asked Cole.

"Us, the room we're in, everything. They are learning their surroundings."

"Smart machines?"

"These things use a combination of digital and analog technology in their central processors so they can learn their surroundings without having to carry around computers the size of grand pianos. It's a neural network, modeled on the human brain. That breakthrough in computer design was one of the advances that took robot technology to another level."

"I see," Jake said as the third robot walked to a spot beside the other two and came to a stop. It tilted its head a minute amount, almost quizzically, as it scrutinized the two men.

"One of the fascinating things about neural networks," Cole continued, "is that the network needs rest periods or the error rate increases. Nap times."

"What is that thing looking for?" Jake asked, indicating the curious York.

"Just checking for weapons. When they're in a combat mode, they fire on unidentified persons carrying weapons."

"They can't shoot at everyone with a weapon. How do the Yorks separate the good guys from the bad guys?"

"It's a complex program, based on physical characteristics—such as size, clothing, sex, possession of a weapon—and aggressive behavior. Some behavioral scientists worked with our programmers to write it."

"Sex?"

"Most soldiers are men. That's a fact."

"I see."

"My main contributions to the Sergeant York project were some breakthroughs in ultrawide bandwidth radio technology. They communicate with their controller and with each other via UWB, which as you probably know has some unusual characteristics, unlike UHF or VHF.

"So these things talk to each other?"

"They are a true network—what one knows, they all know. Information is exchanged via UWB on a continuous basis, which means that these six are soon working from a very detailed three-dimensional database. Each unit also contains a UWB radar, so it can see through walls and solid objects. Very short-range, of course. The radars are off-the-shelf units, stuff being used to inspect bridge abutments for cracks and look for lost kids in storm sewers."

"What about the stalk on top of the head?"

"There is a flexible lens there for looking around corners. The sensor on the right side of the head works with visible light, the left with infrared. At night the sensitivity on the right sensor automatically increases so it can handle starlight."

The fourth York walked out of the truck and took a position beside the others but facing off at a ninety-degree angle.

"These units are prototypes," Cole explained, "not the refined designs the U.S. army will get as production units. These lack sensors in the rear quadrant, so they usually want to face in different directions so they will get the three-hundred-and-sixty-degree panorama."

"They 'want'?"

"Sergeant York has artificial intelligence. The operator can position the units, monitor their performance, override automatic features, approve target selection and the like, but these things can be turned loose on full automatic mode—then they fight like an army. They *are* an army. We developed them to fight and win on the conventional battlefield, the tactical nuke battlefield, and urban battlefields like Mogadishu. The Somali experience was the catalyst for their development."

Jake whistled, and two of the York units turned their heads to look at him.

"I guess I forgot to mention audio. They have excellent hearing in a much wider frequency spectrum than the human ear can handle."

"How much battle damage can they sustain?"

"A lot. They are constructed of titanium, the internal works are shielded with Kevlar, and Kevlar forms the outer skin. Still, mobility is their main defense."

"Two legs and a tail . . . how mobile are they?" the admiral asked.

Cole pointed to the Kevlar-coated areas on the nearest York's leg, the shapes of which were just visible under the skin. "The major muscles are hydraulic pistons; the minor ones are electromechanical servos—which means gears, motors, and magnets. A couple of ring-laser gyros provide the balance information for the computer, which knows the machine's position in relation to the earth and where the extremities are; it uses the pistons and servos to keep the thing balanced. York is extremely agile, amazingly so considering it weighs four hundred and nine pounds without ammunition."

"Power?"

"Alas, batteries. But these are top-of-the-line batteries and can be recharged quickly or just replaced in the field, a slip-out/slip-in deal. In addition, since the outer layer of each unit's Kevlar skin is photo-electric, outdoors on a sunny day the batteries will stay pretty much charged up as long as excessive exertion is not required of the unit."

Jake Grafton shook his head, slightly awed. "How much does one of these damned things cost?"

"Twice the price of a main battle tank, and worth every penny. They can use every portable weapon in the NATO inventory. Hell, they can even drive a hummer or a tank if you take out the seat and make room for the tail."

"Uh-huh."

All six were out of the semitrailer now. They arranged themselves in a circle, each facing outward. They made a small whining sound when they moved, a sound that would probably be inaudible with a typical urban ambient noise level.

"Preproduction prototypes," Cole said when Jake mentioned the noise. "The production units won't make those noises."

Kerry Kent came over, her wireless computer in her hand. "Let me introduce you to Alvin, Bob, Charlie, Dog, Easy, and Fred."

She was referring to the small letter on the back of each unit's head and on both shoulders. The nicknames were slight twists on the military phonetic alphabet system.

"The New York Net," Jake Grafton said. He wasn't trying to be funny because he wasn't in the mood: The thought merely whizzed through his cranium and popped out about as fast. Kent and Cole looked at him oddly without smiling.

She showed Jake the computer presentation. "Each unit can be controlled by its own computer, or one computer can control as many as ten units. When I'm in network mode, I can see what each unit is seeing or look at the composite picture." She moved an icon with a finger and tapped it. Jake leaned forward. The picture did have a remarkable depth of field, although it was presented on a flat screen.

She tapped the screen again. "As you can see, I can designate targets, tell specific units to engage it, or let the computer pick a unit. I can assign each unit a task, tell it to go to a certain position, assign targets, basically run the fight with this computer. Or I can go to an automatic mode and let the system identify targets in a predetermined order of priority and engage them."

"What if your computer fails or someone shoots you?"

"The system defaults to full automatic mode, which happens to be the preferred mode of operations anyway."

Jake shook his head. "The bad guys are going to figure out what they are up against pretty quickly. Maybe rifle bullets will bounce off these guys, but grenades, rockets, mortars, artillery?"

"Mobility is the key to the York's survival," Kerry rejoined. She tapped the screen.

Charlie York stirred. It tilted its head back to give itself a better view of the overhead, which was about twelve feet up. It crouched, swung its arms, and leaped with arms extended.

It caught the edge of an exposed steel beam and hung there, its tail moving to counteract the swaying of its body. Everyone in the room exhaled at once.

Jake stood there for several seconds with his mouth agape before he remembered to close it. The dozen Chinese men in the room were equally mesmerized. After a moment they cheered.

"The units can leap about six feet high from a standing position," Kerry Kent explained. "On the run they can clear a ten-foot fence. They normally stand six feet six inches high; at full leg extension they are eight feet tall."

"Very athletic," Cole said, nodding his head. He didn't grin at Jake, but almost.

"How long are you going to let Charlie hang from the overhead?" the admiral asked Kent.

Her finger moved, and Charlie dropped to the floor. The unit seemed to catch itself perfectly, balancing with its hands, arms, and tail. Now Charlie looked at Jake, tilted its head a few inches.

In spite of himself, Jake Grafton smiled. "Wow," he said.

A half dozen men began checking the Yorks, inspecting every visible inch. They had been trained at Cole's company in California as part of a highly classified program. One man began plugging extension cords into the back of each unit to recharge the batteries. The other men busied themselves carrying crates of ammunition out of the back of the semitrailer and stacking them against a wall.

"So tomorrow is the day?" Jake muttered to his former bombardier-navigator.

"Yep," said Tiger Cole.

"Another big demonstration in the Central District?"

"Yep. The army will be there. We'll strap them on with the Yorks."

"Jesus Christ! A lot of civilians are going to get caught in the cross fire."

Cole nodded once, curtly.

"Do it at night, Tiger. Maximize the advantage that high tech gives you. These Yorks probably see in the dark as well as they do in the daytime."

"This isn't my show." Tiger's voice was bitter. "I argued all that and lost. Revolution is a political act, I was told, the first objective of which is to radicalize the population and turn them against the government. Daytime was the choice."

"Explain to me the difference between your set of high-minded bloodletters and the high-minded bloodletters you are trying to overthrow."

"That's unfair and you know it. You know who and what the Communists are."

Grafton let it drop. This wasn't the time or place to argue politics, he decided. After a bit he asked, "Why only six of these things? Why not a dozen?"

"It will be a couple years before the first production models come off the assembly line," Cole told him. "We got all there are."

"I hope they're enough."

"By God, so do I," Tiger Cole said fervently.

"Here's a sandwich and some water, Don Quixote," Babs Steinbaugh said. She scrutinized the computer monitor. The E-mail program was still there, waiting.

Eaton Steinbaugh sipped on the water. The sandwich looked like tuna salad. Babs read his mind: "You have to eat."

He took the duty bite, then laid the sandwich down. Yep, tuna salad!

"China is so far away," she mused. "What can you do from here?" Here was their snug little home in Sunnyvale.

"Everything. The Net is everywhere." His answer was an over-simplification, of course. Steinbaugh didn't speak a word of Chinese, yet he knew enough symbols to work with their computers. He wasn't about to get into a discussion of the fine points with Babs, however, not if he could help it.

"This Cole . . . is he paying you anything?"

"No."

"Did you even ask for money?"

"We never discussed it, all right? He didn't mention it and neither did I."

"Seems like if you're going to do the crime, you oughta get enough out of it to pay the lawyers. For Christ's sake, the man's filthy rich."

"Next time."

She grunted and stalked away.

Babs just didn't appreciate his keen wit. Next time, indeed!

As he waited he thought about the trapdoors—sometimes he referred to them as back doors, because he had installed them—which were secret passages into inner sanctums where he wasn't supposed to go. While in Beijing he had worked on the main government computer networks in the Forbidden City. The powers that be didn't want to let him touch the computers, but Cole's company had the contract and the Chinese didn't know how to find the problems and solve them, so they were between a rock and a hard place. After much bureaucratic posturing and grandstanding, they let him put his hands on their stuff.

The network security system was essentially nonexistent. That was deplorable, certainly, but understandable in a country where few people had access to computers. Constructing and installing a back door was child's play once he figured out the Chinese symbols and Pinyin commands. A Pinyin dictionary helped enormously.

Installing back doors in other key government computer systems was not terribly difficult either, for these computers all were linked to the mainframes in the Forbidden City.

Like all top-down systems, the Communist bureaucracy with its uniform security guidelines and procedures was extremely vulnerable to cybersabotage. The best ways to screw with each computer system tended to be similar from system to system, but what worked best with railroad timetables and schedules usually didn't work at all for financial systems. Putting it all together was a sublime challenge, the culmination of his lifelong interest in logical problems. Eaton Steinbaugh enjoyed himself immensely and was bitterly disappointed when the reality of his cancer symptoms could no longer be ignored.

His illness did create another problem, however, one that he took keen interest in solving. The whole point of triggering the inserted code programs from outside Hong Kong was to prevent compromising the computer facility there—Third Planet Communications. But the person doing the triggering was going to leave a trail through the Internet, a trail that government investigators could later follow back to the guilty party.

Unless the guilty party disguised his tracks, made the trail impossible to follow. One way to do that was to use a generic computer, one dedicated to public use, so the identity of the user could never be established beyond a reasonable doubt. Due to his illness, Steinbaugh thought he might be unable to leave his home. He spent a delightful week working up a way to cover his trail through cyberspace and thought he had the problem solved. He wrote a program that randomly changed the ID codes buried throughout his computer's innards— called "cookies"—every time the codes were queried by another computer. He liked the program so much that when the China adventure was over he intended to post it on the Internet for the use of anyone seeking to screw with the commercial Web sites that were constructing profiles of visitors to sell to advertisers and each other, a practice that formed the slimy foundation of E-commerce. Of course, if he wasn't as clever as he thought he was, the FBI was going to be knocking on his door one of these days.

Not that it mattered. In or out of jail, Eaton Steinbaugh only had a few months to live, at the most.

Today, when the computer on his desk began signaling that he had an incoming E-mail, he began pecking at the keys in feverish anticipation.

Yes, there it was. From Virgil Cole. A series of numerals. He counted them.

Eleven.

That was right. Eleven random numbers. The guys at NSA would undoubtedly rack their brains for days trying to crack the code that wasn't there.

As soon as possible.

That was the message.

Start as soon as possible.

Too excited to sit, Steinbaugh got up, stretched, stared at the screen. Start with a bang, he decided.

He sat back down and began.

In less than a minute he was at the door of the main government computer in Beijing looking for his back door.

He typed. Pushed the Enter button.

Nothing.

Don't tell me those bastards have changed the access codes.

Not to worry. He had anticipated that possibility.

There! He found it.

He typed some more, inputting a code that no one else on earth knew.

And voilà!

In, in, in!

Ha ha ha ha ha!

Eaton Steinbaugh consulted his notebook, the one in which he had painstakingly written everything, just in case. A copy of the book was in his lawyer's hands, with instructions to send it to Cole when Steinbaugh died.

He found the menu he wanted, typed some more.

In three minutes he was face-to-face with a critical operational menu, one that gave him a variety of choices. He stared at the Pinyin, consulted his notebook, carefully scrolled the page . . . yes. Here it was.

He moved the mouse. Positioned the cursor over the icon just so. Clicked once.

Sure enough, the system now gave him access to yet another system, with another menu.

This menu had five choices: safe, arm, fire, self-destruct, exit.

He positioned the icon over the one he wanted, then clicked the button on the mouse.

Just like that. That was all it took.

Sue Lin Buckingham was waiting for Rip when he got home. He had written another story for the Buckingham newspapers predicting imminent revolution in Hong Kong and sent it to Sydney via E-mail. It would be published under his father's byline, of course, as the first one was.

"Your father sent an E-mail," Sue Lin said. "He will wire the money to Switzerland tomorrow."

Rip just nodded. All the members of the Scarlet Team had been in the Third Planet office except Wu and Sonny Wong. Amazingly, the team was going on with the plan despite the fact that one of their members had kidnapped the leader.

Wu had put it together, pushed the entire population of Hong Kong—and China, for the revolutionary movement was nationwide—toward this day with the force of his personality and leadership ability. Now he was a prisoner, held for ransom to enrich Sonny Wong, and nothing could be done!

Rip Buckingham stared at his wife's drawn features. "I don't know what to say," he told her. "I saw Wong earlier this evening at his restaurant. He has Wu, all right. Perhaps Wong will release your brother, perhaps he will kill him. Regardless, we march on."

"Can't the senior leadership force Wong to release Wu?"

"There isn't time for that distraction, they say." Rip's upper lip curled. "Some of them seem to think Sonny will share the money with them."

"You think?"

"I don't know what to think."

Rip threw himself in a chair. "I once saw an avalanche in the Andes," he mused. "It started slowly enough, but once it began to move no power on earth could stop it. The moving snow carried everything with it—trees, rocks, dirt, more snow. It got bigger and bigger and moved faster and faster. . . ."

He looked at his wife. "Perhaps they are right. Perhaps going forward is our only choice."

She poured him a glass of wine.

"Have you told your mother?" he asked.

"Not yet."

The military base in the arid lands of western China was not a garden spot. Too far from the ocean to receive much moisture, its weather was dominated by the Asian continental high. In the summer the area was too hot, in the winter far too cold, and too dry all the time. High peaks with year-round caps of snow were visible to the north and southwest. And always there was the wind, blowing constantly in a vast, clear, clean, open, empty sky.

The high desert was as physically different from the humid coastal lands of China as one could possibly imagine. Still, for the Chinese, the reality of the place was determined by a far different factor, one that had nothing to do with terrain or weather: The high desert was very sparsely populated.

For people who spent their lives in densely populated urban or rural environments, surrounded by relatives and cousins and lifelong friends, life in the empty desert was cultural shock of the worst sort. The isolation marked each and every one of the soldiers. Some it broke, some it made stronger, all it changed.

The primitive living conditions at the base didn't help. True, China had developed the high-tech industries that created the nuclear weapons and intercontinental ballistic missiles that were the reason the base existed, but the troop barracks were uninsulated and the men used latrines. The water was not purified, so minerals stained the teeth of the men who had been here for years.

Lieutenant Chen Fah Kwei hated the place. Tonight he was the duty officer in the underground bunker that housed the missile launch controls. There were six missiles in this complex, new ones outfitted with the latest fiber-optic ring-laser gyros and high-speed guidance systems.

Truly it was an honor to be the soldier in charge of this arsenal of national power, but Lieutenant Chen wished his transfer to Shanghai would come through soon. He had honor enough to last a lifetime, and he wanted to live someplace with eligible women, laughter, music, books, films. . . .

Tonight he thought longingly about these things while he inspected his teeth. He was using his knife blade for a mirror. As he studied the reflection of his open mouth in the highly polished blade, he decided that, indeed, the minerals were turning his teeth yellow. He tried to consume the minimum amount of water, swallowed it as quickly as he could, but still the minerals were ruining his teeth.

Glumly, he glanced at the monitors of the main computer, which displayed the status of the six missiles in their silos. Bored, sleepy, and homesick, he was playing with his knife when he felt the first thump, a physical concussion that actually rocked his chair.

At first he thought it was an earthquake, but nothing else happened. He glanced at the monitor.

Missile One. The status had gone red. Silo temperature was off the scale, hot. Now the fire light began flashing.

Stunned, he stared at the monitor for several seconds while he tried to comprehend the information displayed there.

A fire! There was a fire in Silo One.

He flipped a switch on the panel before him, and instantly a black-and-white television picture of the inside of the silo appeared on a monitor mounted high in the corner of the control room.

He stared at the picture. He couldn't see anything. The missile wasn't there. All he could see was . . . was . . .

Flames.

Flames!

He pushed the red alarm button on his console. He could hear the distant klaxon, which was ringing here, in the barracks, and in the fire station. Men to fight the fire, that was what he needed.

He looked back at the television . . . and the set was blank. The fire had burned up the camera or the leads.

The computer monitor . . . Still getting readouts, but they were cycling. The temperature was going through thirteen hundred degrees Fahrenheit. Missile fuel and liquid oxygen must be feeding the fire. At those temperatures the concrete of the silo would burn, the cap would rupture, and nuclear material from the warhead might be ejected into the atmosphere, to be spread far and wide by the wind.

Lieutenant Chen Fah Kwei pushed another alarm button on his panel. The wail of the siren warning of a possible nuclear accident joined the blare of the klaxon.

What had happened?

The missile must have ruptured, spilling fuel all over the interior of the silo, where it caught fire.

That must be—

Even as those thoughts raced through Chen's mind, he felt another thump in the seat of his pants.

The monitor. *Silo Two!*

His fingers danced across the controls, bringing up the camera.

A sea of fire.

Sabotage?

The telephone rang. Chen snagged it.

The colonel. "Report," he demanded.

"Sir, the missiles are blowing up in the silos. Two have gone."

Even as he spoke the third missile exploded.

"Impossible," the colonel told him.

"The silos are on fire!" Chen screamed. "I can see the fire on the television monitors. The temperatures are unbelievable. The concrete will burn."

"Activate the automatic firefighting system."

"Which silos?"

"All of them," the colonel roared.

Chen did as he was told. The firefighting system would spray tons of water into the silos as fast as the huge pumps could supply it.

The system was on and pumping as the missiles in Silos Four, Five, and Six exploded in order.

The control room was crammed with people shouting into telephones and talking to each other at the top of their lungs when Chen realized that one explanation of the tragedy was that the self-destruct circuits in the missiles had been triggered.

Of course, he had not triggered anything. The safety caps on the self-destruct switches were still safety-wired down. To destroy a missile in flight, the appropriate cap had to be forcibly lifted and the switch thrown before a self-destruct order was sent to the computer.

But what if the computer received or generated a self-destruct order without the button being pushed? Was that possible? It seemed to have happened six times!

Perhaps, Lieutenant Chen thought, *the thing I should have done after the first explosion was turn off the main computer.*

CHAPTER THIRTEEN

Ma Chao was a fighter pilot in the air force of the People's Liberation Army. Based at Hong Kong's new international airport at Chek Lap Kok on Lantau Island, across the runway from the main passenger terminal, his squadron was equipped with Shengyang J-11 fighters, a Chinese license-built version of the Russian-designed Sukhoi Su-27 Flanker, one of the world's premier fighters.

Major Ma's squadron came to Hong Kong in 1997 upon the departure of the British. For Ma Chao and his fellow pilots, the move to Hong Kong had been cultural shock of the first magnitude. They had been stationed at a typical base several hundred miles up the coast, across the strait from Taiwan. Ma Chao had grown up in Beijing and attended the military academy, where he was selected for flight training.

His first operational posting was to the squadron where he still served, almost twenty years later. When he first reported the squadron was equipped with the Chinese-made version of the Russian MiG-19, called the F-6.

The F-6 was the perfect plane for the Chinese air force. It was a simple, robust, swept-wing day fighter, easy to maintain and operate, adequately armed with three 30-millimeter cannon and two air-to-air heat-seeking missiles. Although the fuel capacity was relatively limited, as it was in all 1950s-era Soviet designs, the plane's single engine was powerful enough to give it supersonic speed.

Ma had loved the plane, which was a delight to fly. Unfortunately he didn't get to fly it often. The fuel and maintenance budget allowed each pilot to fly no more than two or three times a month, and then only in excellent weather. Fearful that the undertrained pilots might crash if they tried to fly aggressively, the generals insisted that the planes be flown as near to the center of their performance envelopes as possible. These doctrine limitations were universal throughout the air force.

Although the Chinese licensed the Su-27 design from the Russians for manufacture in order to upgrade the capabilites of their air force, the set-in-stone training limitations did not change. Ma and his fellow fighter pilots were strictly forbidden to perform aerobatic maneuvers or stress the airplanes in any way that might increase the risk of losing the plane. Consequently, their fortnightly training flights consisted of a straightforward climb to altitude, followed by a straight and level intercept under the control of a ground-based radar operator—a ground-controlled intercept, or GCI—then a return to base.

Ma Chao had spent his adult life with this system, never questioning it. The revelation occurred in Hong Kong a month after he arrived. One evening a woman he had come to know showed him a videotape of an Su-27 aerobatic performance at a Paris air show years before. Ma was astounded by the airplane's capabilities, which had been there all the time, waiting for the pilot with the courage to utilize them.

It seemed that all the assumptions upon which Ma Chao's life was based were equally suspect. Ma Chao soon discovered that Hong Kong, with its high-tech, high-rise, high-rent hustle and bustle and diversity, was as close to paradise as he would ever get. Every trip away from the squadron spaces was sensory overload, a cultural adventure that Ma and his friends found extraordinarily fascinating.

When he was finally approached by members of Wu Tai Kwong's Scarlet Team, he was an easy recruit. From the cockpit of an Su-27 he could see the future. Wu Tai Kwong was absolutely right: The great city of Hong Kong that Ma Chao flew over every two weeks was the future of the Chinese people; the rice paddies and poverty of the mainland were the past.

This June night Ma Chao was in the barracks preparing for bed when his cell phone rang. The cell phone was one of the wonders of the new age—Ma hadn't even known such things existed until he came to Hong Kong. This one was very special and could not be purchased commercially. This phone handled normal cellular telephonic communications well enough, but it also received covert wide bandwidth messages that were broadcast over commercial television signals. Since the WB signals degraded normal television reception slightly, this technology was never going to be approved for commercial use.

Tonight the message was a single line of traditional Chinese poetry. Ma Chao knew precisely what the code meant: Tomorrow!

Sonny Wong also knew what the message meant when he heard it. The senior leadership of the Scarlet Team had decided that the cause was more important than Wu Tai Kwong.

Sonny was certain that would be the decision, but it was nice to see events work out as he had predicted they would.

The government had provided the opening; the Scarlet Team would lead the revolution of the Chinese people. Sonny Wong would collect fifty million dollars from Virgil Cole and ten million from Rip Buckingham, a nice comfortable fortune that he would keep in Switzerland. This pile would be his safety net, his rainy day money, to be used if the Communists proved too tough to crack.

Once he had the money, he would eliminate Wu, Virgil Cole, and Hu Chiang. With these three out of the way, he would be in position to take over the Scarlet Team.

Yes, indeed, thought Sonny Wong, if he played his cards correctly, he could conceivably wind up as the next ruler of China. Emperor Wong. President Wong. Premier Wong. Whatever.

Or he could sell the Scarlet Team to the Communists and retire rich, rich, rich . . . live on the French Riviera, play baccarat at Monte Carlo. . . .

The loss of the restaurant this evening was an irritant, but only that.

He had dealt with brashness and disrespect before—and those fools were long gone. Jake Grafton was as good as dead: Sonny had already given the order.

Many of the students at the University of Hong Kong were not asleep this night. They were huddled together in apartments and bars all over the city. When the WB cell phones rang and they heard the coded message, a cheer went up.

Then they dispersed, went home to try to sleep a few hours and prepare for the day to come.

One of the people with a WB cell phone—made in California and smuggled in by China Bob Chan for Third Planet Communications—was Lieutenant Hubert Hawksley of the Hong Kong police. Hawksley had come to Hong Kong as a soldier in the British army way back when and liked it so much he wangled a police job when his army enlistment was up.

Other British policemen left when Hong Kong was turned over to the Communists, but Hawksley stayed. Through the years he had enjoyed a fine income, very little of which came to him in his pay envelope. He found the oriental way of life congenial and thought he understood the Chinese. Try as he might, he could not imagine that the Communists would be less corrupt than the colonial British. That opinion proved to be prophetic.

One of Hubert Hawksley's many professional acquaintances was Sonny Wong. Sonny had paid Hawksley quite a pile of money over the years. The thing about Sonny was that he was regular. Every month as regular as the post the money arrived. Cash.

One day a year or so ago Sonny had approached Hawksley at the floating restaurant, one of Hawksley's hangouts. He had joined the policeman at the bar, torn up Hawksley's tab, and ordered a beer himself.

"Are you hearing any rumors these days?" Sonny wanted to know when he finally got around to business.

"About what?"

"Sedition. Treason. Antirevolutionary goings-on."

"All the time," the policeman said genially. "The regime is vigilant. The secret police are on the job."

"They pass intelligence to you?"

"Of course. We keep them informed, they keep us informed."

"I was wondering if you might make me a copy of any information you receive along those lines. My friends and I would be willing to pay."

"How much?" Hawksley asked sharply.

"Five thousand Hong Kong a month."

"My risk is large," Hawksley replied.

"Six, then."

"Seven."

Sonny paused to think that over. "Of course," he said, "our long-standing arrangements would be unaffected."

"Of course."

"In addition to knowing what the state security people tell you, we would like to...shall we say...edit...any reports along these lines that the force passes to state security."

"Ahhh..."

Hawksley ordered another glass of stout while he thought about whom he would have to bribe to make that happen. He explained the organizational reality to Wong, then tried to estimate what the responsible people would need in the way of money to help Wong out.

"They mustn't know my name, of course," Sonny muttered. "Some of them might take my money and whisper my name. That would be bad."

"Not cricket," Hawksley agreed.

They settled on a figure of twenty thousand Hong Kong, which had to be adjusted up a couple of thousand when one of the captains on the force proved to be greedier than Hawksley had estimated.

Since then Hawksley had learned a great deal about the Scarlet Team, and he had passed much of what he learned right back to Sonny. Various people had tried to betray Wu Tai Kwong, of course, and they had disappeared from Hong Kong, never to be seen again. A few people thought they could become police informants, one or two wanted to explain about sabotage plans.

At one point Hawksley knew so much he began to fear for his life. He wrote down what he knew, made a copy, then gave the copy to Sonny with a remark or two about the original.

Sonny had merely smiled, raised the money to twenty-five thousand a month.

Still, Hubert Hawksley begin to think seriously about early retirement and a return to England. He mentioned these plans to Sonny one day, and Sonny tried to dissuade him.

"I know too much," Hawksley told the gangster.

"Not at all. Anyone in your position is going to learn a great deal, and you are a reliable man. The next man might not be. Stay awhile, see this through. Earn all the money you can. Leave Hong Kong a wealthy man."

He stayed, of course.

And now, in the wee hours of the morning, the WB cell phone given to him by a woman trying to avoid prosecution for theft squawked into life, waking Hawksley from a sound sleep. He knew the significance of the message. Afterward he lay awake in the darkness thinking about what was to come.

Today, he decided, was going to be an excellent day to call in sick.

All over China the special cell phones rang, stimulated by a WB signal piggybacking on the signals of every television station in the country, and all over China the owners of the cell phones listened with mixed emotions.

For some, the message was a signal for a mission that had to be accomplished on an agreed timetable. For others, the signal meant to wait a little while longer. For all, it was a message heralding the coming of a new day.

The single-sheet flyers were piled willy-nilly on street corners, in subway, store, and office building entrances, and in the entrances to the endless blocks of government-owned apartment buildings. The headline on the front page trumpeted: BANK RECORDS WIPED OUT IN MASSIVE COMPUTER FAILURE.

The story began:

A massive computer failure last night at the Hong Kong bank clearinghouse wiped out the computerized records of member banks, which are all the banks in Hong Kong. Sources say that the computerized account records of the borrowers and depositors of the affected banks have been destroyed and will have to be reconstructed from backup tapes where they exist, and by hand from written records, which all banks maintain, before the banks can again open for business. The task will take weeks.

It is common knowledge that various high government officials have demanded and received personal loans at ridiculously low interest rates from Hong Kong banks, which were the only banks affected by the clearinghouse computer failure.

The story continued, citing no sources but implying that the government had willfully destroyed the bank records to hide official corruption.

Very little of the story was true, a fact Rip Buckingham had pointed out to Wu weeks ago when he was asked to write it. "The government," Wu said, "has told so many lies that people are ready to believe the worst. The goal is to put government officials on the defensive. The story in the flyer must create doubt in people's minds."

The story did more than that, though. It called for a general strike and a mass demonstration in the Central District today to protest the malfeasance of the government.

Lin Pe was up at first light. She had been rising at that hour ever since she could remember and saw no reason to change at this stage of her life. She used the early morning hours to work on her fortunes or the books of the Double Happy Fortune Cookie Company, occasionally to correspond with friends. Every few weeks she had to sign all the company checks that her accountant had prepared, payroll and suppliers and utilities and the like. The checks were there on the table, but since the bank collapsed, it was ridiculous to sign them.

This morning she got out the fortune book and sat reading while she waited for a good idea to arrive. When inspiration was hard to find, as it often was, she would wait patiently. If she didn't think about too many other things a good idea would show up eventually.

She had a lot on her mind these days: Wu, the frozen accounts at the Bank of the Orient, her daughter Sue Lin, Rip, whether she should sell the cookie company to Albert Cheung....

Sue Lin knocked, then came into the room carrying a flyer.

"Mother," she said, "all the banks will be closed."

Lin Pe read the story, then laid the flyer aside and sat looking out the window at the great city. "I can't meet my payroll," she said softly.

"Oh, no one will expect to be paid," Sue Lin said dismissively. "Too much is happening." She sat down facing her mother and told her about Wu's kidnapping.

Old Lin Pe listened to everything her daughter had to say and asked no questions. When Sue Lin ran out of steam she sat silently looking at her mother, who rubbed her hands together, then smoothed her hair.

"Wong will kill him after he gets the money," Lin Pe said finally.

"Maybe not," Sue Lin said, unwilling to cross that bridge. She felt so helpless. "What can we do?"

Her mother sat staring at the wall, saying nothing.

As Jake Grafton walked the streets to the ferry landing in the hour after dawn, he had to thread his way around the citizens of Hong Kong, who were engrossed in the flyers that littered the streets and sidewalks.

Jake had tried to get some sleep on the couch in Tiger Cole's office, but he had tossed and turned, unable to stop thinking about his wife. He had dropped off for a few minutes, only to have a nightmare about her, which woke him and left him unable to get back to sleep.

At one point Tommy Carmellini came in, wanting to tell him what he had heard on his listening devices. About the only thing worth reporting, according to Carmellini, was a call Kerry Kent got earlier in the evening. "She said yes, paused, yes again, paused, no, then another yes and hung up."

"So?"

"I don't know who called her, but it wasn't a social friend."

"Doesn't sound like it," Grafton agreed.

As the sun rose he had stood at Cole's window watching the traffic on the street below and the people on the sidewalk reading the flyers.

Cole wasn't there. He had gone out at some point. No doubt he is off leading the charge, Jake thought gloomily.

He couldn't shake the thought that this mess was Cole's fault.

If the bastard had minded his own business, stayed in California getting rich making magic technoshit for robots and the like, Callie would be safe and sound, not in danger of being murdered by a goddamn Asian gangster.

That thought made him angry. There would be plenty of time later for recriminations, but now was the time to figure out how to rescue Callie.

That's the mission, Jake, and it's high time you put the brain in high gear and got cracking.

He decided that he should go back to the hotel. If by chance Callie had been released, perhaps she would go there. The chances were small, but still . . .

"Goddamn it!" He had said the words aloud, then stood there grinding his teeth.

He needed a bath, a shave, and a change of clothes.

If Sonny Wong has any sense, someone will be waiting to ambush me as I walk out the front door of the consulate.

With that thought in mind, Grafton went out the back of the compound in a truck that had just delivered a load of fresh vegetables. When the truck stopped for a light two blocks down the street, Grafton raised the rear door and jumped down, then lowered the door and slapped it twice.

Now, walking through the streets, he was struck by the number of youngsters and the elderly out and about on a weekday morning. They weren't the dressed-for-success business types who filled the Central District office towers during weekdays. These folks wore jeans and cotton pants and T-shirts. They carried backpacks and sacks of food.

The damn fools are going to the big demonstration!

Governor Sun Siu Ki read the news of the clearinghouse computer disaster in the flyer labeled *The Truth* as he dressed for the day. An aide had brought him one of the sheets.

"Is this true?" he demanded, waving the offending paper at the aide.

"Yes, sir. The director of the clearinghouse called us with the news at three this morning. The entire clearinghouse staff is working now to determine the extent of the damage."

Sun was not the swiftest civil servant in Hong Kong, but he wasn't stupid. "How did the writers of this flyer get the news so quickly, get it printed and onto the streets?"

"Sir, we do not know. These flyers were thrown out of trucks all over the S.A.R. as early as five A.M."

"This computer failure the story speaks of, could it have been sabotage?"

"We do not know."

"Find out," Sun snapped. "Immediately," he added and shooed the aide out.

The story was libel, of course. Well, probably libel.

Sure, there were grotesquely greedy men in government—there had been misfits and rogues in every government in every age since the world began. And of course some of these misfits might have twisted arms in the Hong Kong banking community. But to suppose that these people, if they did owe money to the local banks, would destroy the banks so they wouldn't have to pay it back? The whole thing was preposterous, pure poppycock.

And even if the story were true, this rag should never have printed it. The sole purpose of such a story was to lower the people's respect for the government and the men who made it function.

Mao would never have tolerated such disrespectful diatribes from anyone, Sun told himself primly, and certainly he should not.

Regardless of what the bureaucrats in Beijing thought, the time had come to take off the gloves with these people. Show them the government's steel backbone and this type of libelous misbehavior will stop.

Sun was capable of applying the pressure, of crushing enemies of the state. He didn't have many skills, but at least he had that one. He picked up the telephone on his desk and told his secretary to call General Tang.

Tang came to City Hall by car to confer with Sun. The two of them ate a hurried breakfast of rice and fish at Sun's desk while they waited for a call to Beijing to be returned. An aide came in and told them that the subway trains refused to operate this morning. "It is the doors," the aide said. "The administrator of the system says the doors will not open on the trains."

"Can't they be opened manually?"

"Yes, but then they cannot be closed. The chief engineer blames the fluctuations in the power grid."

When the minister in Beijing called, he was obviously distraught. "First Hong Kong, now the nation is under attack. We do not even know who the enemy is, and he is wounding us seriously."

Sun didn't have a clue what the minister was talking about. He made noises anyway.

The minister explained: "Several hours ago our ballistic missiles exploded in their silos, starting horrible fires that threaten to contaminate large areas. Last night the Hong Kong and Shanghai banking systems collapsed, the stock exchanges cannot open, the railroad dispatch computer refuses to come on-line, refineries all over the country have had to shut down to prevent dangerous conditions progressing to explosions and fires . . . and every air traffic control and GCI radar in the country is mysteriously broken. The nation is wide open to an aerial invasion, and we won't know it is coming until enemy troops arrive at the gates." His voice rose an octave here.

The minister paused to get himself under control. "Obviously the nation is under cyberattack. The telephone network has been used to sabotage critical computers. The premier has decreed that the telephone system be shut off on the hour, in ten minutes, until such time as the critical systems can be brought back on-line, our enemies identified and rendered harmless, and future attacks of this sort guarded against."

Sun couldn't believe his ears. He pushed the mute button on the speaker phone and asked General Tang, "What is a cyberattack?"

"Computers," Tang replied.

The minister was still going on, about how Sun should notify Beijing immediately of any change in the situation in Hong Kong, and then he hung up, leaving Sun staring at the little telephone speaker on his desk, quite unable to grasp the import of what he had just heard.

"They are turning off the telephone system?" he asked General Tang.

"So he said."

"The Taiwanese," Sun said bitterly. "I have argued for years that China must bring those rascals to heel. Events will prove me right."

"I suspect the Japanese," General Tang shot back. "They are our natural enemies."

They finished eating in silence, each man deep in his own thoughts.

When they pushed the plates back, they discussed the situation. They were on dangerous ground and they knew it. The nation under cyberattack from unknown enemies, the power of the government being tested here in Hong Kong . . .

The right course of action was unclear. Still, they were the men who would have to answer to Beijing for inaction as well as action.

When he had heard Tang out, Sun issued his orders. "Today many unhappy people will congregate in the Central District. They will once again attempt to embarrass the government." The British legacy was still causing problems, Sun thought sourly. "That challenge to the government's mandate to rule is, in my judgment, our most important problem. Put your troops in the downtown and refuse to let the demonstrators in."

"The subway problems will keep people from coming into the Central District," Tang remarked. He assumed that most of the city's citizens would want to demonstrate against the government, an assumption that Sun didn't challenge.

"The time has come to be firm," Sun declared. "We must show the people the steel of our resolve. Show them the might of the state they hold in such contempt."

Lest there be a misunderstanding, Sun added darkly, "I abhor the useless effusion of blood, but if we do not hold our ground now, that failure will cost more blood."

"We will give the order to disperse, then enforce it."

"We must tell the people," Sun told the general. "Go from here to the television studio. Stand in front of the camera and tell the people to stay home. Tell them the nation is under attack, but we shall prevail because we have the resolve of a tiger."

"Only one television station is still operating," the senior aide informed them. "The others have had power outages or equipment failures."

"All?" Sun demanded.

"Yes, sir. During the night they went off the air, one by one."

"Sabotage," said Tang. "Could this be related to the nuclear weapons disaster?"

"Impossible," the governor opined. "Here in Hong Kong we are dealing with criminal hooligans."

Had the brain trust in City Hall asked about the situation with the radio stations, they would have been more alarmed. Of Hong Kong's dozens of stations, only one was still on the air. The morning DJ at this station atop Victoria Peak was a Hong Kong personality named Jimmy Lee, easily the most popular man on the south China coast.

Lee was funny, irreverent, crazy, with it, and cool, a combination that delighted the young people and brought smiles to the faces of everyone else. Listening to Jimmy Lee was always a breath of fresh air.

Jimmy Lee wasn't himself this morning, though. The man was constitutionally unable to keep a secret—it wasn't in him. Everything he knew eventually slipped out, usually when he least wanted it to. Normally this trait didn't do him any harm since his off-kilter personality was his stock-in-trade. For the past two weeks, though, Jimmy Lee had been the possessor of a huge secret, one that had grown heavier with each passing day.

He had joked so much about Wu Tai Kwong, the phantom political criminal, that Wu had concluded Lee could be an ally. So one morning one of Wu's lieutenants was waiting when Lee finished his morning show.

At first Lee didn't believe the man knew Wu Tai Kwong, as he said he did, but the man's serious demeanor and his anti-Communist sentiments assuaged his doubts. The man returned to the station for private conversations week after week for months. Lee finally realized that the man wasn't a government agent and that he indeed knew Wu Tai Kwong.

Eventually the man enlisted Lee to become a spokesman of the revolution. Two weeks ago he was told about the upcoming battle of Hong Kong, presented with a cell phone, and told about the message that he would receive on the designated day.

Jimmy Lee had not told a soul this fantastic secret, which was a remarkable testament to the supreme effort he was making to control himself. He had thought deeply about it for two weeks, brooded upon it, had nightmares about it. The reality was that the revolutionaries wanted him to commit treason . . . when the telephone rang.

Treason! If the revolution failed, Jimmy Lee's life would be forfeit. The government would hunt him down and execute him publicly.

This morning Lee was almost incoherent on the air. He played songs but babbled nonsense when he had to speak. He had never been able to resist food, was almost a hundred pounds overweight, yet this morning he was unable to eat. Sweating profusely, nauseated, able to talk only in monosyllables, he was questioned by his producer . . . and he told everything.

The producer refused to believe Lee. He was unaware that this was the last radio station on the air in Hong Kong. He knew nothing about the disasters in the stock market, the airport, the subways . . . none of that had been published by the government, which like all Communist governments was loathe to admit or discuss problems.

Lee talked on. He produced the cell phone. He told about meeting a friend of Wu Tai Kwong's, told about how the army would be confronted today, about the explanations he was to make over the radio . . . and then he produced the cassette.

The producer put the cassette into a player and listened to a minute or two of it while Jimmy Lee hyperventilated.

The male voice on the cassette was as calm and confident as a human can be, calling for people to rally behind the freedom fighters, obey the revolutionary leaders, and kill PLA soldiers who refused to surrender.

The producer turned off the cassette player and sat chewing his fingernails while he considered what he should do. The first thing, he decided, was to let the New China News Agency censor listen to this tape. The man worked for the government, knew how things worked. He would know what to do about the tape.

Lin Pe was not thinking of resolve, although she had as much as the governor and then some. She was thinking of the strange ways human lives are twisted by chance, or fate, call it what you will.

She dressed in her newest clothes, brushed her hair, made herself look as nice as she could. In her purse she put her notebook—so she could write down any fortunes that crossed her mind in the course of the day—two rice cakes, and a bottle of water. She ensured the house key was already in the purse, then went to find her daughter, who was giving the maids their daily instructions. The television was on—General Tang was telling people to stay home.

When Sue Lin finished with the maids, she told her mother, "Rip wanted us both to stay home today. He said the streets will be dangerous, there may be shooting." Her mother would respect Rip's opinion, Sue Lin knew, more than she would her daughter's, for her mother had not lost her lifetime habit of deference to men.

"I think the rebellion will begin today," the old lady said calmly. "Today is the beginning of the end for the Communists."

"Richard Buckingham is paying the money today, Mother. Wu Tai Kwong will probably be home this evening."

Lin Pe merely nodded. Then she went out the door and along the street toward the tram, which would take her down the mountain to the Central District.

The matter was quite simple, really. Her son thought this struggle was worth his life. That being the case, it was worth hers, too.

CHAPTER FOURTEEN

At the Victoria ferry landing, people were streaming off the overloaded ferries from Kowloon and patronizing a small army of food vendors, who were selling fish and shark and rice cakes as fast as they could fry it. Not many children, considering. Here and there Jake Grafton saw people reading sheets of *The Truth,* sometimes three and four people huddled together looking at the same piece of paper. The people looked somber, grim, though perhaps it was just his imagination.

Not many people were interested in going to Kowloon, so there was no line. Jake went right aboard the ferry *Star of the East.*

As the boat approached Kowloon he could see the sea of humanity waiting to board the ferries to Victoria. With the subways out of service, this crowd was to be expected. The terminal was packed, with a large group of people outside on the street, waiting to get inside.

As soon as the boat tied up, Jake was off and walking at a brisk pace. Outside the terminal the crowd swallowed him. He thought about getting something to eat in McDonald's, which was about fifty yards away, but it too was packed full, with people waiting to get into the place.

For the first time since he had arrived in Hong Kong the sheer mass of China threatened to overwhelm him. People everywhere, densely packed, all talking, breathing, shouting, pushing . . .

He made his way along Nathan Road and turned into the street that led by his hotel. Fewer people here, thank God.

The manager was in the lobby trying to calm a crowd of tourists from Germany. The common language was a heavily accented pidgin English.

So sorry, the manager explained, but the airlines had canceled all flights; daily bus tours of Hong Kong were canceled; trains to Canton, Shanghai, and Beijing were not running; telephone calls to Europe were not going through; credit cards could not be accepted for payment of bills; money-changing services at front desk temporarily suspended. So sorry. All problems temporary. Not to worry, all fixed soon. So sorry.

Behind Jake he heard an elderly British male voice say with more than a trace of satisfaction, "Bloody place is falling apart. *Knew* it would! Wasn't like this in the old days, I can tell you."

In the corner an American college student was trying to comfort his girlfriend. In the snippet he heard, Jake gathered that the girl was worried that her parents would be worried.

Jake waited until the manager made his escape from the unhappy Germans, then waylaid him. He told him his name, reminded him of the trashed room, wanted to know where his luggage was.

The manager signaled for a bellhop, then spoke to the uniformed man in Chinese.

Jake was escorted to the elevator and taken to the top floor of the building. They had laid out his and Callie's luggage in a three-room suite, the best in the house, probably. The sitting room and bedroom both had balconies.

The crowd was so dense it intimidated Lin Pe, and she had lived in dense Chinese cities much of her life. There was an intensity, an anticipation, that seemed to energize the people.

She fought against the flow of people and managed to get aboard a ferry to Kowloon, as it turned out the last one, because the authorities demanded that the Star line stop carrying demonstrators to Victoria and forced the crews off the boats.

In Kowloon Lin Pe began walking. On Nathan Road she caught a bus and rode it north for several miles, then transferred to a bus going to Kam Shan, near Tolo Harbor. She got off the bus at Shatin and walked a quarter of a mile through town. Shatin was huge, with more than a half million people living there now. Lin Pe remembered when it was just a small town, not many years ago.

She stopped at a small corner grocery where she knew the proprietor. After the usual polite greetings, she found a seat on an empty orange crate under a sign advertising scribe services. The letter writer would not be here for hours, but people with little to do often passed the time by sitting here, so no one would say anything.

From her perch on the orange crate she could see the entrance to the main PLA base in the New Territories. Nothing much seemed to be happening on the base, which was good.

From her bag Lin Pe extracted her WB telephone. She turned it on, then called in and reported that she was in position. Then she turned the phone off to save the battery.

Jake Grafton took a shower, shaved, and put on clean clothes that fit; Cole's were too large. He strapped the Smith & Wesson to his right ankle and put on the shoulder holster containing the Model 1911 Colt .45 automatic he had requisitioned from the marines at the consulate. Over this he donned a clean sports jacket. He put a hand grenade in each pocket. Just another happy tourist ready for a day of fun and games in good ol' Hong Kong.

He checked with the hotel operator to see if he had any messages. Yes, a voice mail. He listened as the senior military adviser on the National Security staff told him that his mission was canceled, he could come home anytime.

He tried to return the call and got as far as the hotel operator. All lines overseas were out of service. So sorry.

So Tiger Cole and the Scarlet Team had isolated the place.

He turned on the television. Only one channel was still on the air—the others were showing test patterns or blank screens.

Oooh boy!

Jake Grafton went out on the bedroom balcony, which also overlooked the police station. Not many troops on the lawn. He could hear a helicopter circling overhead, though he couldn't see it.

There was a division of troops in Hong Kong, Tiger said, China's best...with tanks, artillery, and twelve thousand combat-ready soldiers.

Jake's attention was drawn to the street in front of the hotel, eight stories below him. A convoy of trucks had pulled up alongside the hill and wall of the police station, and people were streaming from every truck.

In thirty seconds the street was a sea of people. A van-type truck was sitting at the main gate, the driver talking to the guard.

On the street the people were removing ladders from the trucks. My God! They were armed. Assault rifles, it looked like.

The ladders went against the wall, people swarmed up them.

As they reached the top of the wall, they got off the ladders, walked along the wall. There must be interior ladders or stairs, Jake thought.

The driver was out of the truck at the gate, holding a pistol on the guard. People ran by the truck into the compound.

Jake had a grandstand seat. In less than a minute, several hundred armed civilians were running through the compound.

Shots! He could hear shots! Some of the soldiers were shooting! And being shot at!

The reports rose into a ragged fusillade, then slowed to sporadic popping.

A dozen or so soldiers wearing green uniforms lay where they had fallen.

Now a convoy of trucks came streaming through the main gate.

In two minutes all the shooting stopped, even the occasional shot from inside the administration building. Several of the trucks were backed up to a loading dock, and a small human chain began passing weapons out of the building. As fast as one truck was loaded, it pulled out and another took its place.

Jake Grafton looked at his watch. The time was 8:33 A.M.

Welcome to the revolution!

He had to get to Victoria while he still could. Cole had said the Scarlet Team intended to confront the People's Liberation Army with Sergeant Yorks. That would be the acid test. Either the Yorks could stand up to trained troops or the revolution would be over before lunch.

But all those people heading for the Central District—Grafton wondered if he had what it takes to sacrifice innocent people for the greater good. He thought of Callie and concluded that he didn't.

The New China News Agency censor assigned to Jimmy Lee's radio station listened to the Wu Tai Kwong cassette tape with a growing sense of horror. Jimmy Lee was sitting on a nearby stool near collapse—the producer had taken his place at the microphone. The tape sounded authentic. Any doubts the censor had were wiped away by the conviction in that taped voice . . . and the call for people to kill PLA soldiers who refused to surrender their arms.

The censor called his superior officer on the telephone, but no one answered. Too early. His superior wouldn't come to work for another hour yet, and with the subway out, maybe not then. The man lived way up north in the New Territories.

The censor swallowed hard and telephoned City Hall.

He ended up with an aide to Governor Sun and began telling him of the tape and the upcoming battle in the streets.

Callie Grafton awoke stiff and sore from her beating the previous evening. Places on her face were blue and yellow, and one side of her face was severely swollen. Sometime during the night she stopped shivering . . . thankfully, but her ordeal had drained her.

Still, she was in better shape than she thought she would be. When those thugs were pounding on her she thought she might die.

She had awakened on and off during the night, waited fearfully for the men to return, to drag her off for another interrogation or session in the meat locker, but it didn't happen.

Perhaps this morning.

She tried to recall everything she could remember about the Vietnam prisoners of war she had met or read about. The men she had known were ordinary men who had endured torture, starvation, and beatings for years and somehow survived. One looked at them expecting them to be different somehow—and no doubt they were on the inside—but the difference didn't show in the facade they presented to the world. They looked ordinary in every respect.

Perhaps the lesson was that they were ordinary yet had somehow found extraordinary courage. Or maybe that courage is in all of us and we just don't know it. Or need it.

I am as tough as those guys, she told herself, thinking of the POWs. She wanted to believe that even though she didn't.

"He wants me to implicate Cole in murder," she told Wu Tai Kwong. He nodded.

"What does he want from you?"

"A confession that he can give to the Communists, one that he can use to justify a fat reward for my capture."

"He will turn you over to the government?"

"I'll be dead by then. He'll give them my corpse and demand a huge reward. The confession will be the . . . how do you say it? The sauce upon the cake?"

"Icing on the cake."

"Knowing Sonny," Wu continued, "he has demanded money from everyone, Cole, the government, everyone. He keeps me alive so he can prove that I am alive, should that become necessary. Then he will kill me and sell my corpse."

"Do you really believe that?"

"He cannot set me free. I have many friends. I will find him and kill him, no matter where on earth he goes to hide. He knows that. He will kill me."

"Are you frightened?"

"Of what? Death?"

"Dying."

"Yes."

"But not of death?"

"I have achieved my dream. The revolution has begun. The regime is crumbling and the revolution will speed its collapse. Sonny Wong can do nothing to stop it. The government can fight, delaying the day of its doom, but it cannot prevent the inevitable."

A terrible smile spread across the face of Wu Tai Kwong. "I have won," he whispered. "I have undermined the levee—the sea *will* come in."

Despite the fact that she was no longer cold, Callie Grafton shivered. "When the regime collapses, what will happen then?" she asked.

"The people will execute the Communists. That is inevitable. And fitting. That is the fate of all dynasties when they fall. The Communists will go like the others."

Jake Grafton went out the main door of the hotel and turned right, headed for Nathan Road and the ferry landing. Two men who had been lounging against the wall followed him.

He glanced back just before he turned the corner—they were keeping their distance.

Rounding the corner, another man stepped away from the wall with a pistol in his hand. It must have been in his pocket.

Jake didn't think, he merely reacted. He dove for the pistol, seizing it and wrenching it away from the man.

No doubt Grafton's sudden appearance had startled the man, who must have thought that the sight of the weapon would freeze Grafton, make him stand still in the hope of not being shot. In any event, the American's move was so unexpected that it succeeded.

Jake Grafton's adrenaline was flowing nicely. With his assailant's pistol in his left hand, he hit him with all his might in the throat and dropped the man to the sidewalk, gagging.

Now he ran, fighting the crowd, toward the waterfront.

Soldiers were spread across the pier in front of the ferry landing.

They've stopped the ferries!

Jake veered right, toward the small basin beside the huge shopping mall for cruise ship passengers. In this basin small boats normally took on and discharged passengers for harbor tours.

There were a handful of tour boats tied to the pier, all of them sporting little blue-and-white awnings to keep off the sun and rain. Jake ran along the pier until he saw a man working on one. The engine was running, although the boat was still securely moored.

By now Jake had the pistol in his pocket that he had taken off the man in the street. He was going to have a nice collection of these things if he lived long enough.

He looked behind him. The people who had been following were apparently lost in the crowd, which filled most of the street.

He pulled out his wallet, took out a handful of bills, replaced the wallet in his hip pocket. He jumped down into the boat and waved the bills at the boatman, who was in his early thirties, with long hair that hung across his face.

The boatman said something in Chinese. Jake gestured toward Victoria. "Over there," he said and offered the money again.

The boatman ignored the money. He pointed back toward the soldiers and shook his head.

Okay.

Jake looked at the boat's controls as the boatman showered him with Chinese. The throttle was there, a wheel, a stick shift for a forward-reverse transmission . . . the boat was idling.

"Out. Get out!" Jake pulled the pistol just far enough from his pocket for the boatman to see it, then pointed toward the pier.

Frightened, the boatman went. As he did, Jake Grafton jammed the money he had offered into the man's shirt pocket. Must be my genial expression, Jake thought as he ran forward to untie the rope on the pier bollard.

With it free, he made his way aft as quickly as he could.

Where are the men who were following me? Did they lose me in the crowd?

That must be it. They're probably searching frantically right this minute.

With the bow and stern lines loose, Jake scrambled back to the tiny cockpit and spun the wheel while he jammed the throttle forward. The boat surged ahead, caroming off the boat moored in front of it.

He didn't waste time but headed for the entrance to the basin.

There, on the pier! The men who followed him from the hotel! They stood watching. Now one of them removed a cell phone from his pocket and made a call.

There was a nice breeze and a decent sea running in the strait, so the little tour boat began pitching the moment it cleared the mouth of the basin.

Some soldiers around the ferry terminal were shouting and gesturing at him, so Jake turned his boat to the northeast, away from Hong Kong Island. *Those guys are itching to shoot someone,* he thought and decided to get well out of rifle range before he turned south to cross the strait.

———

In the helicopter circling over the police station, Hu Chiang also looked at his watch. The assault on the police barracks had gone like clockwork, for which he was supremely grateful. Wu Tai Kwong was supposed to be in the left seat of this chopper running the show; the others had insisted that Hu Chiang take Wu's place.

As he watched the trucks loading small arms at the police barracks, Hu Chiang wondered just where Wu was . . . and Sonny Wong. No one had seen Sonny in days.

He had almost refused to take Wu's place as the tactical leader. Generalissimo Hu Chiang—the thing was ridiculous. If the choice had been his he would have declined. Yet he remembered what Wu had said, so long ago when the revolution was just a dream: "The cause must be bigger than we are, worth more than we are, or we are wasting our lives pursuing it."

"We cannot make a utopia, fix all that is wrong with human society," he had told Wu.

"True, but we can build a civilization better than the one we have. To build for future generations is our duty, our obligation as thinking creatures."

Duty. That was Wu's take on life. He was doing his duty.

So Hu Chiang was in the chopper this morning, half queasy, trying to keep his wits about him as the faithful stormed the police barracks on the southern tip of the Kowloon peninsula.

From this seat a few hundred feet up he could see much of Hong Kong harbor, which was dotted with dozens of moored ships from all over the earth and squadrons of lighters and fishing boats. He could see the airport at Lantau, the Kowloon docks and warehouses, the endless high-rises full of people with hopes and dreams of a better life, the office towers of Victoria's Central District, and the spine of Hong Kong Island beyond.

The most interesting portion of the view was to the north, toward mainland China, hidden this morning in the June haze. Hong Kong was but a first step, then the revolution must go north, with or without Wu Tai Kwong or Hu Chiang. . . .

The radio sputtered again. The leader of the barracks assault was checking in. "Mission completed," he said, so proud he almost couldn't get the words out.

"Roger," Hu Chiang replied and directed the chopper pilot to circle over the entrance to the highway tunnel under the strait.

The army had it blocked off this morning, of course. Forty or so troops were visible, a truck, and . . . a tank!

Yep. There it sat, right in front of the harbor tunnel entrance, squat and massive and ominous.

Hu Chiang picked up the mike and began talking.

Another helicopter, this one belonging to the PLA, was circling over Victoria's Central District and the southern tip of Kowloon. General Tang was in the passenger seat. He had had the chopper pick him up at City Hall and was now looking the situation over.

He had certainly not expected the crowds that he saw coming toward Victoria's Central District from the west and east. Connaught Road was crammed with people, as were Harcourt Road and Queensway, an endless stream of people coming from the Western District, Wanchai, and Happy Valley, all headed toward Central.

He had his troops deployed in the heart of the Central District and around City Hall, with his headquarters in the square in front of the Bank of the Orient.

The troops there seemed to be properly positioned, but the size of the crowds stunned Tang. This massive outpouring of people in defiance of the government he had not expected. It was almost as if . . . as if the people *expected* to swallow the troops.

For the first time, General Tang wondered if Sun Siu Ki or the party leaders in Beijing understood what was happening in Hong Kong.

A cry for help from the Kowloon police barracks snapped General Tang back to unpleasant reality. He motioned to the pilot of the helicopter, who swung out over the strait and flew toward the southern tip of Kowloon.

The pilot pointed out another chopper to General Tang, who had trouble seeing it at first.

"A television station helicopter," the pilot said over the intercom. "I have seen it many times before. They must be taking pictures for the television."

That, of course, was the last thing that General Tang wanted. Television pictures of this mass outpouring of antigovernment sentiment would shake the regime to its foundations. The people in Beijing had no idea, none at all!

Tang waved angrily at the television helicopter. The pilot looked directly at him, then looked away.

"Can you talk to that pilot?" Tang demanded.

"Yes." The army pilot changed the channels on the radio and called the helicopter.

Hu Chiang didn't hear the army pilot's call because he was talking on a different frequency to the squad leader in charge of the trucks carrying the weapons from the police barracks. These trucks had to get through the tunnel to Victoria, so the tank and army troops were going to have to be neutralized. Hu's pilot heard the call, though, and told Hu about it on the intercom.

"Trouble," the television station pilot said. "If we ignore him too long, he will have everyone in the world shooting at us."

"Let's do it to him first," Hu said and pointed west toward the harbor as he spoke into the microphone on his headset. The pilot took the TV chopper in the indicated direction.

Tang forgot about the civilian helicopter when he got a glimpse of the police barracks and the uniformed bodies still sprawled upon the lawn, which had been used as a campground. Tang knew corpses when he saw them, and those men looked real dead.

He saw the trucks, which must be loading the weapons Tang knew were stored in the barracks.

He directed his pilot eastward.

The streets of Kowloon were packed with cars. With the tunnel to Victoria closed, there was no place for the Hong Kong Island traffic to go, so a massive traffic jam was the result. Traffic in the city was always bad, yet today it was impossible. People had abandoned the cars in gridlocked intersections. The weapons thieves were fools to assault the police barracks with the streets impassable.

They certainly weren't going to make a fast getaway in all this traffic. His order to close the tunnel, he thought with a bit of pride, may have proved their undoing.

He again spoke to the pilot, who took him east a half mile until the machine was over the entrance to the harbor tunnel.

The troops were where they were supposed to be, the tank was there. . . . They just needed to be told that there were armed criminals in the vicinity . . . to be ready!

He consulted the printed frequency list his staff had given him this morning, then dialed the radio to the proper channel. He keyed the mike and began speaking. When he did so he naturally looked down at the people he was talking to, the soldiers surrounding the tank.

He was three words into his message when the tank exploded.

The explosion was not a massive fireball: but a cloud of smoke that jetted from the side of the thing, then seemed to envelop it.

As if it were hit by a wire-guided antitank weapon, General Tang thought, then realized that was exactly what had happened.

Out of the corner of his eye he saw a streak of fire in the air, not large. Before he could react a loud, metallic bang shook the chopper, followed by a severe vibration, then a slew to the right.

"We've been hit," the pilot shouted over the intercom. He wrestled with the cyclic and collective, trying to gain control, even as the helicopter spun faster and faster to the right and began falling.

Michael Gao was a thirty-six-year-old security analyst with a finance degree from Harvard. He worked for one of the large American mutual funds that regularly invested in the Hong Kong market . . . when he was working. Just now he was engaged in high treason against the government of a sovereign nation. Dress it up any way you like, he thought wryly, shooting down an army helicopter with a Strella missile is going to be difficult to explain away in court. Ditto popping a tank.

He had wrestled with these issues a thousand times in the past year and always came back to the fact that he personally wanted the Communists out of power in China. He believed it would be better for everyone, including himself, if some form of democratic government were installed in Beijing. And he believed the conversion worth a major national convulsion. That being the case, it logically followed that he should personally commit himself to making it happen. So he had.

No going back now, he told himself as the helo competed the last few revolutions of its out-of-control spiral and smashed onto the top of a gravel dike around the tunnel entrance.

The chopper didn't explode or burn. After the dust from the impact settled, just a wisp of smoke rose from the crumpled wreckage. No one emerged from the cockpit—no doubt the crew was dead or dying.

No one rushed to their aid.

Michael Gao realized with a start that he was hearing the popping of small arms. He looked down from the top of the building where he stood and watched his friends snipe at the troops around the smoking hulk of the tank.

With a gut-wrenching certainty, Michael Gao knew that if there had been any men in the tank, they too were now dead. The armor-piercing sabot he had fired raised the temperature of the metals it penetrated so high that the materials forming the tank's interior would spontaneously ignite and cook the crew, if by some miracle they survived the initial concussion and thermal shock.

The soldiers near the tunnel entrance were lying in the street or trying to find cover. Bursts of automatic rifle fire created sparks where the bullets ricocheted off concrete and little puffs where they impacted. This was ridiculous! The rebels didn't have time for this.

Gao leaned over the edge of the roof, shouted to the man who was on the roof of the lower building across the street, the one facing the tunnel entrance. "Use the loudspeaker!"

The man picked up the microphone. "PLA soldiers! Lay down your arms. You are surrounded. We will kill you all unless you lay down your arms and surrender."

One by one, the demoralized soldiers threw their assault rifles on the street and raised their arms in the air.

When the general's helicopter went down, Hu Chiang told his pilot to circle back over the tunnel entrance. He arrived in time to see the last of the soldiers guarding the tunnel throw down their arms.

The problem was the cars and trucks that filled the streets from curb to curb . . . and the tank that smoldered in the tunnel entrance. In their planning sessions the rebels had anticipated both problems. They had two solutions, both painted yellow and made by Caterpillar. They were on flatbed trucks parked in the rubble of a building being demolished. Now they came clanking onto the street with their blades down.

Vehicles that couldn't move were bulldozed out of the way. Trucks were pushed up onto sidewalks, cars were stacked one atop the other.

All this was accomplished in a bedlam of people running, screaming, protesting, begging the armed rebels not to ruin their cars . . . all to no avail. The bulldozers pushed and shoved and made a way, and soon the first truck carrying weapons taken from the police barracks armory was waiting near the tunnel entrance. The truck was covered with armed rebels hanging on every available protuberance.

One of the bulldozers backed up to the tank, and a cable was hooked to the thing. Then the dozer began pulling, dragging the tank out of the way.

When it was clear, the other bulldozer raised its blade and led the trucks into the tunnel.

Governor Sun's secretary thought the New China News Agency weenie on the telephone was some kind of flake. This story of Jimmy Lee falling apart, worried about committing treason . . . Jimmy Lee? The top one percent of the top one percent of cool?

He put the radio censor on hold and told his colleague at the next desk, "Another nut case. This one wants to talk to the governor."

"The governor will refuse."

"I know."

"He will be angry you asked."

"What should I do? Perhaps the man is telling the truth."

The man at the next desk surrendered. "Tell the governor. Let him make the decision."

At Lantau Airport Ma Chao and his fellow fighter pilots were directed to don their flight gear and wait in the ready room, which they did. Apparently during the wee hours of the night Beijing had ordered a full alert.

Unfortunately, no amplifying orders had been received over the military radio communications net. The telephone system was down, silencing the faxes and computers. An old Bruce Lee movie was playing on the television.

The ready room was abuzz with speculation. Everyone seemed to have an opinion—the more outlandish, the louder the proud possessor proclaimed it. They argued, wondered, gestured, and guessed. The

Americans and Taiwanese were invading. The Japanese had declared war. There had been a coup in Beijing.

Ma Chao and his friends sat silently, taking it in, saying little. They thought they knew what was happening, but without explanations or verification from headquarters, they couldn't be certain. Nor was there a need for immediate action.

Patience was needed, and Ma Chao had plenty. Like all the pilots, he was wearing a sidearm. He had the flap unbuttoned so he could get it out and into action quickly.

As he listened to the fantastic scenarios that were being paraded before the group as quickly as they were concocted, he thought about the commanding officer and his department heads, all Communists, all loyal to the regime, as far as Ma Chao knew.

When the crunch came Ma Chao and his three fellow conspirators were going to have to take charge, and that probably meant they would have to shoot some of the senior men. Ma Chao sat in the ready room wondering if he could do it.

He had assured Wu Tai Kwong that he could. "I am a soldier," he said. "I have the personal courage to do what must be done."

"You could shoot men you have served with for many years?"

"I do not know," he finally replied, truthfully.

"Ah, my friend, on men like you the revolution will succeed or fail. You must use your best judgment, but you must not surrender. You must face unpleasant reality and do what the situation requires of you."

He had nodded, knowing the truth of Wu's words.

Wu always told the truth. All of it, never just a piece, and he never sugarcoated it. You got bald reality from him.

"Chinese pilots are poorly trained," Wu told him and explained how Western air forces trained their pilots. "You Chinese pilots fly straight and level, relying on the ground controller to find the enemy and steer you to him. What if the ground controller is off the air, or the enemy refuses to fly straight and level, waiting for you to assassinate him? What then? Could you improvise?"

Ma Chao did not answer. He thought about the question but refused to state a mere opinion.

"When the revolution begins," Wu said, "you will have to weigh the situation and make the best decision you can, then go forward confidently, aggressively, believing in yourself. There will be no one to give you orders. You must decide for yourself what needs to be done, then do it. What we require of you is the courage to believe in yourself."

Ma Chow thought about that courage now as he sat in the ready room waiting for the earth to turn.

Governor Sun's secretary found that his boss was tied up with an engineer who was trying to explain the difficulty with the subway doors. "The problem is in the computer," the engineer explained.

"The computer opens and closes train doors?"

"Yes," the engineer said, pleased that Sun was with him so far. "Something has gone wrong with the software. We must find the problem before we can fix it."

"I thought you said the problem was power fluctuations?"

"Power fluxes caused the problem with the software."

The secretary went back to the New China News Agency man he had on hold. "The governor is busy. Why don't you tell me the message? I'll write it down and give it to him when he has a moment."

"This is very important," the censor said. "The message is too important and too long to be written down."

The secretary rolled his eyes. "I'll have the governor call you. How is that?"

"I will await his call." The censor dictated the telephone number at the radio station, then hung up.

The secretary threw the call-back slip into the governor's in-basket.

The soldiers on duty at the Victoria end of the Cross-Harbor Tunnel heard echoes through the tunnel of the small battle in Kowloon. They also saw General Tang's helicopter crash and assumed, correctly, that it had been shot down.

They waited in nervous dread for what might come next. There were only a dozen of them, a small squad, manning a police barricade in front of the tunnel entrance. They were young, the oldest a mere twenty-four, from rural villages far to the north. They had joined the army to escape the drudgery of the rice fields. Only four of them could read the most basic of the Chinese ideographs.

They were armed with old Kalashnikov assault rifles and one machine gun. When they heard the clanking of the bulldozer coming through the tunnel, they assumed it was the tank that they knew had been positioned at the Kowloon end.

Relieved, they relaxed and the sergeant in charge walked down the tunnel to meet the tank coming the other way. He went about fifty yards and waited.

When he realized he was looking at a bulldozer, and behind it trucks, the sergeant knew something was happening that no one had told him about. He turned and scampered back up the tunnel, shouting to his men.

Unsure of what to do, the men waited for direction.

The uncertainty ended as the bulldozer emerged from the tunnel. Two men atop the dozer opened fire on the soldiers standing about.

The other soldiers might have killed these two men and some of the men following the dozer on foot if they had been given a chance, but they weren't. A machine gun atop a nearby building swept the tunnel entranceway with a long burst, sending the bullets back and forth, knocking the standing soldiers down like bowling pins.

The three-second burst was enough. Men emerging from the tunnel shot the survivors as the bulldozer rolled over two bodies. The trucks turned into the crowded streets and stopped. Men inside the truck beds began passing out assault rifles and ammunition to the crowd of young men and women who had been lounging there.

At the biggest television station in Hong Kong the atmosphere was strictly business as usual when Wei Luk and three other rebels walked in. There were no guards in the lobby, armed or unarmed, and no guards in the reception area; just two potted palms and large photos of the station's news stars. One of the stars was a man named Peter Po, who, like Wei Luk and his friends, had bet his life that communism could be successfully overthrown.

Wei Luk glanced at the smiling picture of Peter Po and then stepped over to the receptionist, a beautifully made-up young woman with an expensive coiffure and long, painted nails. She gave Wei and his friends a dazzlingly professional smile.

Their pistols were in their pockets, so they looked presentable enough. Wei Luk smiled, told the girl that he had an appointment with Peter Po.

"And these other gentlemen?"

"Them too."

She picked up the phone, pushed a button, waited a bit, then asked his name. He gave it.

"At the end of the hallway take a right," she told him after she had talked to Mr. Po, "then it's the third door on the left."

The girl pointed toward a green steel door with a small window. She unlocked it with a hidden button as Wei Luk pushed.

Po welcomed them into his office. He was wearing the television uniform, a suit and tie.

"I thought there was a guard," Wei Luk said.

Peter Po nodded. "I told him today would be a good day to stay home sick, and he agreed."

"Okay."

Peter Po looked at his watch. "When do you think?"

"I don't know. When the truck delivers weapons and more men, then and only then."

Fortunately Governor Sun had not yet realized that the rebellion had begun, so no one at City Hall had sent police or troops to secure the one operating television station or shut it down. A rebel broadcast would cause them to cure this error as quickly as possible, however. Until an armed force could be resisted, the rebels thought it wise to hold their tongue.

Yet the rebels were now inside and the police and army were out. Peter Po had a script and knew how to run the equipment in the building so that the rebel leadership could talk to the people of Hong Kong.

Wei Luk's orders were to ensure that the police and soldiers stayed out of the building, to the last man. "Fight until there are no bricks left stuck together," Wu Tai Kwong had told him.

"Take your places," Wei told his men now. He directed one of the men to go back to the lobby and sit with the receptionist.

"Let no one else through the door. Call when the truck arrives."

The crowd in the Central District of Victoria chanted antigovernment slogans, sang snatches of songs, surged along the streets carrying everyone with them, a giant human river.

The crowd came to a stop against the ring of PLA troops that surrounded the Bank of the Orient square. There were five hundred soldiers in the streets around the plaza, all armed with assault rifles and wearing riot-control shields and face masks. The trucks that had delivered them there were parked on the streets inside the military perimeter.

At the four corners of the plaza the officer in charge, Tang's number two, Brigadier General Moon Hok, had ordered machine guns placed in nests built of sandbags. In the center of the plaza he had placed two tanks. Between them sat a command car bristling with radio aerials.

General Moon was in the command car when he learned that General Tang might have crashed. While the PLA was attempting to verify why their helicopter had ceased all transmissions, Moon got out of the vehicle and stood looking at the sea of soldiers in the square and the huge buildings that surrounded it.

From a military point of view, the position was not a good one. The buildings were man-made high points that would afford an enemy excellent positions from which to shoot down into the square, creating a killing zone.

He called a colonel over, told him to assign squads to search each of the buildings adjoining the square. The colonel walked away to make it happen.

As Moon Hok listened to the noise of the boisterous crowd echoing through the urban canyons and the radio noise emanating from the command car, he decided to use his troops to push the crowd back one block in all directions, thereby putting the buildings that faced the square within his perimeter. Tang had told him to bring no more than five hundred men this morning because the square wouldn't physically hold any more; now he was contemplating holding nine blocks with the same five hundred men. They would be thin, very thin.

What if the crowd rioted, got completely out of control?

Could Tang be dead?

The noise of the crowd made the hair on the back of Moon Hok's neck rise.

He got on the radio and called for another five hundred men to join him. It would be hours before they arrived from Kowloon, but better late than never.

When Virgil Cole designed the Sergeant York units, he realized that the volume of data flowing from the sensors would require that each unit be individually monitored. Since a network was only as good as the data its sensors fed into it, he didn't trust a computer to make life-or-death decisions. The U.S. Army planners didn't want people completely removed from the loop, either. Consequently, part of the York system was a mobile command and control trailer where the people who monitored each unit sat at individual stations. Here a mainframe computer checked the sensor data and suggested possible courses of action to the human operators.

The trailer had also been on the C-5 Galaxy that delivered the York units and was now parked in an alley three blocks from the Bank of the Orient. Despite the fact that power cables led to it from mobile power units parked nearby, the trailer was gaily painted with surprisingly good graphic art. A sign on the side proclaimed the trailer to be a mobile museum exhibiting the latest in computer technology, sponsored by a well-known philanthropic organization dedicated to the education of the world's children.

Cole had huddled with the Scarlet Team members this morning, telling them what he knew of other team efforts throughout China. He repeated the litany of woes that the minister in Beijing had recited to Governor Sun, ticking them off on his fingers. "The government is inundated with troubles this morning," he said in summation. "The population is getting out of control in most of the major Chinese cities. Beijing is beginning to suspect that revolution is in the wind. When the people see how fragile the government's control is, the rebellion will spread."

"Wu Tai Kwong has done his work well," someone commented.

"We must do ours equally well," Cole shot back and went to check the sensor data feeds from each York unit. Six monitors were arranged in a row, all six labeled from left to right: Alvin, Bob, Charlie . . .

Kerry Kent stood beside him, comparing her handheld tactical controller with the main monitor.

Satisfied, she stood back, took a deep breath.

"Worried?" Cole asked.

"Only about Wu," she replied. "This will go fine. You'll see. You built good stuff."

Cole waved the compliment away. "I won't authorize a transfer of money to Wong's account until Jake Grafton sees Wu and Callie Grafton in the flesh and calls me—they leave together when the Swiss have got the loot."

"Does Wong know that?"

"I told him when he called earlier. The bastard threatened to hack off more fingers, but we have no choice. We must be tough, insist on fair dealing, or the son of a bitch will take the money and kill them, sure as shootin'."

Kerry Kent took a deep breath. "When?"

"Tomorrow night is the earliest I could set up the wire transfer. We have to do it while the Swiss bank is open; they don't stay late for anybody."

The two-way radio had been busy all morning. Now the man monitoring it signaled to Cole. "The convoy has cleared the harbor tunnel."

"Cleared the tunnel, aye," Cole acknowledged.

He keyed the intercom mike on his headset. "The convoy has cleared the harbor tunnel. All units check in."

The operator at each monitor sang out, "Alvin ready," "Bob ready," and so on, in order.

Kerry Kent took control. "We are ready, Mr. Cole."

Since Kerry Kent was going to be fighting a revolution this morning and her boyfriend was a guest of Sonny Wong's, this should be a good time to search Kent's apartment, Tommy Carmellini thought. He used the stairs for this visit—the elevator was out of service—and picked the lock to get in.

He checked the small bathroom and closet to ensure that he was the only person there, then strolled slowly through the place taking inventory.

He had no idea what he was looking for. Kerry Kent, SIS double agent, revolutionary, anti-Communist warrior . . . maybe she had Mao's little red book under her pillow. He picked up the pillow and looked.

Well, no book, but a businesslike little automatic. He picked it up, checked the caliber. .380. She didn't use this on China Bob Chan.

The bed was as good a place as any to start. He put the pistol on the dresser, began stripping sheets. He examined the mattress inch by inch to see if it had a compartment for documents or the like. Apparently not. Nothing under the mattress, in the box springs, in the frame of the bed.

He piled the mess in the center of the bed and worked around it. Kerry's dresser was next.

The sea breeze and swells running in the strait this morning distracted Jake Grafton for a moment and made him smile. The salty wind cooled the perspiration on his forehead and filled his nostrils with the pungent scent of the Pearl River, flowing from deep in China. The pitching, bucking little tour boat was a handful and forced him to think about how he was going to bring the boat into the pier on Hong Kong Island.

Just which pier he should use was a problem. Who were the men on the sidewalk? Who hired them? Whom did the man call on the cell phone? They were undoubtedly watching him now, waiting to see where he landed.

He wanted to go back to the consulate, avoid the disaster that was about to happen in the Central District. When the shooting started the crowd might stampede, killing hundreds of people, perhaps thousands. Cole, you damned fool, getting smack in the middle of someone else's war!

The engine of the tour boat hummed sweetly. That was a lucky break. Thinking about possible observers, Jake took the boat in close to the shore and turned east. He motored along for five minutes before he found what he wanted, a low pier with empty cleats. Someone used this boat to make a living; Jake Grafton didn't want to deprive him of it.

He brought the boat in smartly toward the pier. Although he didn't own a boat, he had watched sailors handle small boats for years. With the prop engaged and the engine idling, he leaped onto the pier with a rope in his hand and dropped it over a cleat. Back onto the bucking boat as it kissed the tire hanging at the waterline, reverse the prop, let the bowline spring the boat in . . . When he had the boat tied up fore and aft, he killed the engine.

The rock-solid pier felt good under his feet. He walked off the pier thinking about the thugs in Kowloon, wondering if they had been working for Sonny Wong.

CHAPTER FIFTEEN

Sergeant Loo Ping was told to search the Bank of the Orient tower, which stood on the north side of the square. He picked four men and went to the front door, which was locked. With his face against the glass, shielding his eyes with both hands, he could see that the bank lobby was empty.

He fired his rifle into the door lock. After three shots he pushed experimentally on the door. It gave, but a piece of the deadbolt still held it. He had two of the men put their shoulders against the door and push. The glass cracked, the broken lock gave way, and the door opened.

Sergeant Loo led his men inside. Of course the major hadn't told him what to look for. "Search the building," was all the major said, as if the object of the search was self-evident.

"People," Loo Ping told his squad now. "Look for people. If we find anyone, we will take him outside to the command vehicle for interrogation."

The soldiers moved off. One went to the basement, the others went to the elevators and pushed the button. Nothing.

Loo Ping led them to the staircase and they started up.

"What if we find money?" the youngest soldier asked, which amused the others.

"You think they leave money lying around?"

"This is a bank, isn't it? Perhaps there is money. They must keep it somewhere."

Loo Ping was a rice farmer's son himself and had never had a bank account. Of course there was money in a bank, even a failed one. Perhaps the major really wanted the soldiers to search for money.

"Money would be locked away in safes," one of the soldiers remarked now, which made sense to Loo Ping. The bankers certainly wouldn't leave money lying around.

The second floor was a huge open room, carpeted, full of desks, with a computer on each of them. The lights were off, so the only illumination came through the windows on the sides of the grand room. The soldiers stood at the door, marveling. Imagine what the room must be like when the lights were on and people were seated at every desk, counting money!

This morning there were no people, so after a bit the soldiers let the door close—amazing how the door silently closed by itself—and climbed another flight of stairs.

The third floor was like the second, a vast office full of desks and computers and wonderful white machines that did God knows what, and . . .

Something was standing in the center of the room, near the window overlooking the square.

It looked like a big man.

Loo led the way, the other three behind. All had their rifles in their hands so that anyone could see they were men with authority who must be obeyed.

The man at the window was huge! He turned to watch the soldiers walk between the rows of desks toward him. He had dark skin and was completely naked.

Loo Ping's steps slowed.

It wasn't a man.

No.

A machine? Nearly seven feet tall, the neck consisted of three flexible stalks. The head was narrow at the chin and top, widest at the eyes, with a stalk or flexible tube coming out the top. The legs reminded Loo Ping of the hind legs of a dog; he thought the feet looked like those of a chicken, with three prominent toes. And that tail! Something from a movie?

No!

A *robot!* That is what it must be!

One of the men whispered to Loo, tugged at his sleeve. "It has a weapon," the man said.

"Hey!" Loo Ping called, still walking forward, but slower.

He halted ten feet from the thing and looked it over. The letter C was visible high on its shoulders. Its hands were claws, and they held a launch tube for a wire-guided antitank missile. Another launch tube lay on the floor.

Now Loo realized the head was lowered a few degrees, so the eyes—they were really some kind of lenses—were looking right at him. One of them had a circular lens turret in front of it, and now the turret rotated, stopped with a click, then rotated again.

Nervous, Loo took a few steps sideways.

The head followed.

For the first time Loo Ping noticed that a multibarreled weapon of some kind was mounted on the right side of the robot's torso. Now the barrels began spinning, emitting a high-pitched whine, barely audible in this quiet room.

Loo Ping tightened the grip on his rifle, glanced at his three troops. They were still there, although they looked like they were going to run.

"Hey!" Loo Ping said again, facing the robot and moving the barrel of his rifle a little, so it pointed more at the robot. He searched for the safety with his right thumb.

"The gun is pointed right at you," the closest soldier whispered to Loo Ping. He was right. The spinning barrels of the weapon were pointed at Loo Ping's chest. He took another step to the right. The barrels followed.

"Ooooo . . ." he began, but he never completed the sound.

The robot's weapon fired, and Loo Ping felt the impact of the bullet as it hit him dead center in the heart. His blood pressure dropped to zero, and he was dead seconds after he hit the floor.

The robot swung its weapon and fired one bullet at the nearest soldier, then the next, and the next. Four individual aimed shots in less than a second.

The four empty cartridges ejected from the minigun's breech rattled like hail against the window glass, then fell to the carpeted office floor while the barrels of the minigun freewheeled to a stop.

The soldier Loo Ping had sent to search the basement walked through the door just as the minigun fired. As the reports echoed through the room, he dove back through the door and scrambled down the staircase.

"Someone is escaping," Kerry Kent said. She was watching the monitor intently, listening to Charlie York's audio in her headset.

"Let him go," Cole said. "He's no threat." He wiped his mouth with the back of his hand. Four uneducated kids dead in a heartbeat. His mouth was watering badly, like he was going to puke.

Charlie York turned back to the window. The turret on his right camera clicked to another lens, bringing the video of the plaza below into focus on Kent's monitor.

She checked with the other units. All okay, all ready.

Jimmy Lee, the King of Cool, was still babbling incoherently about Wu Tai Kwong and treason and not wanting to be executed. Lee's producer and the government censor stood wringing their hands.

Governor Sun hadn't called and in truth the producer doubted if he would. Still, Jimmy Lee was a celebrity of sorts, so he might.

The censor tried to place a call to Beijing but the operator said the lines were down. "This is a government emergency," the censor shouted, then wished he hadn't. The possibility that Jimmy Lee had gone off his nut and was babbling nonsense crossed his mind for the first time. He wondered just how hard he should press to get though to someone important.

He didn't have to worry. The operator told him that government business or not, the telephone lines out of Hong Kong were still out of order.

"Call army headquarters," the producer suggested.

"Why don't we just broadcast the news?" the censor replied. "Everyone will hear. What better way is there to warn the authorities of the plot?"

"What if Jimmy is crazy? Huh? Have you considered that? Maybe he's on drugs. The fool has used them before, remember?"

"All the telephone lines out of Hong Kong are down," the censor retorted. "The banks are closed, the subway isn't running, the airport is closed. . . . Jimmy says the rebels are attacking the computers. There is going to be an attack on the troops in the Bank of the Orient square. That sounds like truth to me."

"Okay, okay," the producer said. He eyed Jimmy, tried to decide if he was up to talking coherently. No.

He went into the studio and sat on the stool in front of Jimmy's mike. As he waited for the current song to end, he thought about what he was going to say. Tell it straight, he decided. Don't try to jazz it up like Jimmy would. Just act like a man with all his marbles.

Don't panic, people, but this is a rumor that may have some truth to it. Authorities, take action. You heard it first, folks, right here on the Jimmy Lee show.

The song came to an end. The producer flipped the switch to make his microphone hot and began speaking.

The people in the mobile museum trailer parked three blocks from the Bank of the Orient had a radio tuned to the Jimmy Lee show and a television showing the only station left on the air. Popular music had been coming from the radio and a Chinese soap opera from the television.

Someone called Kerry Kent's attention to the voice that came over the radio. A male voice, talking about the revolution that was just beginning, a revolution to overthrow the People's Republic. Troops were going to be attacked this morning in the Central District by armed rebels, who were trying to cause a major riot, a riot that was supposed to engulf City Hall and lead to the arrest of the authorities there.

"That isn't Jimmy Lee's voice," the man told Kerry ominously.

She looked at her watch. This wasn't supposed to be happening now.

"Have the people who are to guard the radio and television stations reached there yet?" These people could not be armed until the weapons came through the Cross-Harbor Tunnel.

"They are on their way. They haven't called in."

"What is going on at the radio station?"

No one could answer that.

Virgil Cole was watching now. Kerry Kent called Hu Chiang, who was still circling over the Central District in a helicopter. The feed from the chopper's television camera was displayed on a monitor in the trailer.

"You're over the bank square?" Kerry asked.

"Yes. I'm ready when you are."

Kerry turned to Cole. "The television and radio station guards are not yet in position, but a premature announcement is coming over the radio."

"Anything on television?"

"No."

"Are we ready?"

"We are waiting for the television and radio guards. When the hammer falls, we have to deny the government use of the media and keep it for ourselves."

"Is the army listening to Jimmy Lee?"

Kerry Kent stared at the monitors, which showed her what each of the Sergeant York units was seeing. Then she checked the computer-generated composite. "If they are, they haven't taken alarm yet," she said.

"Call the people on the way to the TV and radio stations. Get an estimated time of arrival. All they have to do is get there before the PLA does."

Kerry Kent nodded at one of the computer technicians, who picked up a WB phone and began dialing.

"Two hours," the radio operator told Moon Hok. That was how long the colonel at the barracks in the New Territories estimated it would take for the troops Moon requested to be loaded on trucks and transported to the Bank of the Orient square. Neither the barracks colonel nor Moon Hok yet knew that the Cross-Harbor Tunnel no longer belonged to the army, nor were they factoring in the gridlock conditions that prevailed in the streets of southern Kowloon. Still, Moon Hok knew the estimate was optimistic.

From where he stood he could hear the crowd chanting an antigovernment slogan, something about no more stealing.

Once again, Moon Hok thought bitterly, Tang and the governor had placed the army in an impossible situation. The crowd was definitely hostile and growing with each passing minute. In the streets leading to the square the people were packed to standing-room-only density.

Should they be allowed to remain where they were, or should he push them back and expand his perimeter?

While he was mulling his options, the radio traffic continued about the helicopter in which General Tang had been riding. It had crashed, according to an army officer who said he had witnessed the disaster from a vehicle a half-mile away. The helicopter had fallen near the Kowloon entrance to the Cross-Harbor Tunnel. Another officer chimed in, claiming he saw the missile that downed the chopper.

"It was shot down," he said on the radio net.

Shot down!

If the hostile population was now shooting at PLA helicopters, the entire situation had changed. This bank square was militarily indefensible. Perhaps he should load the troops in the trucks and get them out of here. Of course, that move would have political repercussions.

He decided to dump the whole mess in the governor's lap. He directed the radio operator to get Governor Sun on the radio.

But time had run out. Some of the civilians in the crowd outside the military perimeter were listening to the only radio station in Hong Kong that was on the air. These people were being entertained by Jimmy Lee's producer, who was describing the horrible, treasonous uprising that was about to take place in the Bank of the Orient square.

At first the people who were listening laughed. Then they stood looking at each other, wondering if this diatribe were true.

To a crowd that was already rowdy, the radio voice seemed to be describing the perfect way to vent their anger at the myriad of frustrations and injustices that were their lot in life.

The shouts became loud, angry, and the people began pushing forward toward the soldiers in the square.

Virgil Cole saw the crowd surge on the monitors. He pushed a button on his control panel so that the audio from the York units was in his headset. Now he could hear the angry chants.

"If the soldiers feel threatened, they'll fire tear gas or bullets, and the crowd will panic," he said to Kent, who was mesmerized by the unfolding spectacle. "Let's do it now."

The soldier who had witnessed Loo Ping's death at the hands of Charlie York stood now in front of General Moon, pointing at the Bank of the Orient building. He explained about the robot.

"A monster ten feet tall shot my sergeant and the other three men in my squad. Up there, on the third floor."

The general listened to this drivel, then walked away. The junior officers could handle the man. Monsters!

The man kept pointing at the third floor.

When he heard glass breaking, Moon Hok involuntarily glanced in the direction the soldier was pointing. He saw glass showering down . . . from a third-floor window.

Moon was about to tell one of the staff officers to have the soldier lead him to the monster in the bank when the nearest tank exploded. The explosion burned the general and tossed him through the air. He landed in a heap on the pavement, too stunned to move.

The York robot called Charlie dropped the empty launch tube for the wire-guided antitank missile and picked up another. While it was bringing the weapon into firing position, the second tank exploded. Dog York, in the building on the south side of the square, had fired that round.

Charlie aimed this missile at the command vehicle, then squeezed the trigger.

The missile pulverized the van, showering the men lying on the pavement with sheet metal and radio parts.

Having fired both the antitank missiles Charlie York had carried into the Bank of the Orient, Kerry Kent decided to have Dog York fire a rocket-propelled grenade at the machine gun nest on the far right side of the square. The York control screen was a Windows-based system—point and click—so in seconds she had a rocket screaming across the square. It struck the ammo feed on the side of the tripod-mounted heavy machine gun and destroyed it.

Seconds later Dog destroyed another machine gun on the far side of the square.

The tanks and two machine guns were out of action. Thirty seconds had passed, and every PLA soldier in the square was flat on his face or huddled behind a concrete planter wall.

The sounds of the explosions echoed through the urban canyons and were heard by more than a hundred thousand people standing and sitting in the streets. The energy level in the crowd soared as people craned their necks, trying to see in the direction of the square.

When the truck screeched to a halt outside the Victoria Peak television station, Wei Luk was standing in the doorway. With a huge sigh of relief, he watched a dozen university students with assault rifles pile out of the back of the truck and pass down a machine gun. They set up the machine gun where it had an excellent field of fire along the main street leading to the station, then took up positions around the building.

Wei Luk went back inside. The receptionist stared at him in wide-eyed amazement when he pulled a pistol from his pocket and directed her to unlock the door. Dazed, she pushed the button.

Wei Luk and his colleagues walked down the hallway toward the main studio, where they saw Peter Po and gave him the high sign.

Less than two minutes later the station had the feed from the camera in Hu Chiang's helicopter on the air. Peter Po began a voice-over, explaining to the television audience that the first battle of the revolution had begun.

In the museum trailer three blocks from the Bank of the Orient square, a cheer went up when the television began playing the aerial feed.

Virgil Cole turned to the shortwave radio that sat on a bench behind him. In less than a minute he began receiving reports from revolutionaries in television stations all across China that had picked up the Hong Kong signal from the satellite and were rebroadcasting it the length and breadth of the nation. With the program on the air, the revolutionaries would then abandon the stations, forcing all the personnel out and locking the doors of the buildings. When the authorities reacted, as they eventually would, they would have to break into the buildings to stop the broadcasts. And there would be no one there to arrest.

By then the damage would be done. The news would be out, the credibility of the government severely damaged.

Virgil Cole leaned back in his chair with a sigh of relief. *Finally,* he thought, *we have crossed the threshold. There can be no turning back.*

Alvin and Bob York were in a locked room in the basement of the building that stood on the west side of the square. The door was locked to discourage any soldiers who might be ordered to search the building. Now Alvin broke the lock with a twist of the door handle. Both units climbed the stairs toward the street level. The staircase was narrow with a low ceiling, with barely enough room for the robots when they tucked in their appendages and curled their backs.

Kerry Kent checked the video feed as the two units climbed the stairs to ensure all was well, then used the mouse to activate Easy and Fred.

Behind her Virgil Cole helped himself to another cup of coffee. He had spent five years of his life overseeing the design of the York units and had a huge financial stake in the company that manufactured them, so he should have been nervous about the Yorks' first operational trial. He wasn't. He had used up all his juice fretting the success of the nationwide television broadcast, which he thought more critical than the performance of the York units to the eventual success of the revolution.

He sipped the coffee and glanced at the monitors and wondered if he should have absolutely refused Wu Tai Kwong's demand to confront the PLA in front of an audience. He had confidence in the York units, but crowd psychology was a huge unknown—a stampede could kill thousands.

As he watched he remembered Wu's words: "Revolutions are made by people—the Yorks are just things. The people of China must see that others are willing to fight. We can give them something to fight for, but they must find the courage in their own hearts."

As the four York units that had been in hiding came running from the buildings, Charlie and Dog leaped through the broken glass of their respective third-floor windows. They used their hands and feet to cushion the shock of their landing on the concrete street, then they began running toward the center of the square.

Now all six Yorks were transmitting video and audio to the central computer in the museum trailer; in seconds the computer had transformed the six data streams into a three-dimensional picture of the square, the trucks, the decorative planters, trees, light poles, smoldering hulks of tanks . . . and the armed men who were rising from the pavement with their weapons in hand, staring wild-eyed at the huge, running robots, which attacked the crews of the two remaining machine guns.

Inevitably a few of the soldiers snapped their rifles to their shoulders to shoot, and instantly the system directed a York to engage. An onboard CPU slewed the minigun onto the target and triggered a round. Just one round per target, because unlike humans, the Yorks didn't miss.

The ring-laser gyros inside each York fed data to a separate maneuvering computer that kept it upright and balanced, the onboard sensors gathered data that was processed internally by the weapons-control computer and passed to the mainframe via UWB, and threats were identified and engaged in the order set by the controller before the battle began. In addition, the weapons-control computer passed information to the maneuvering computer so that it could move the unit to minimize the danger posed by low-priority threats, or threats the York had not yet had time to engage.

The computers and sensors operated seamlessly. Each unit engaged targets that threatened it and ran, leaped, swerved, and bounded to throw off the aim of opponents it had yet to engage.

The result was mass confusion. Officers shouted and pointed, gesturing wildly at the Yorks, which were leaping from truck to truck, running across the square, leaping up on the sides of the buildings and executing turns in midair while their miniguns hammered out aimed shots.

Soldiers who raised their rifles to aim at the sprinting Yorks were shot down, those who did nothing were not harmed.

One soldier threw down his rifle and stood erect in the center of the square with his hands in the air. One of the junior officers drew a pistol and pointed it at the erect soldier. He was immediately shot by two Yorks.

Other soldiers threw down their rifles, first a few, then many.

The firing slowed to an occasional shot, then stopped altogether.

The running Yorks slowed to a walk, then came to rest. Each one stood with its head turning, its sensors scanning, and the barrels of its minigun spinning, ready to fire. They were ominous, fearsome.

A cheer went up from the watching civilians, who ran into the square.

Burned and groggy from the concussion of the tank that had exploded nearby, General Moon Hok managed to get to his feet. He stood swaying, looking uncomprehendingly at his soldiers with their hands up. Then he took his first good look at the closest York, Alvin, whose sensors were scrutinizing him in return. The minigun followed his every move, but the shot didn't come.

The helicopter carrying Hu Chiang settled into the center of the bank square and Hu stepped out. The cameraman, his camera still going, piled out the back and focused his camera on Hu, who looked around, then walked over to General Moon Hok and demanded that he surrender his command to the revolutionary forces of China.

The civilians were running into the square now, many of them armed with weapons liberated from the Kowloon police barracks. They were taking weapons from soldiers and passing them to unarmed civilians. A few of the newly armed revolutionaries aimed their weapons skyward and pulled the trigger, just to see if they would shoot.

The Yorks nearly shot these people. Cole suspected what was coming and warned Kerry Kent, who safetied the Yorks' firing circuits just in time.

Moon Hok was in no mood to do or say anything to the people who had killed his soldiers and humiliated him, and Hu Chiang wisely decided that Moon's silence was good enough. He ordered one of the armed revolutionaries who had appeared nearby to jail Moon and his officers.

All this made excellent television. It got even better: From his hip pocket Hu removed a written speech that he and Wu Kai Kwong had drafted for Wu to give at this moment. Since Wu wasn't here, Hu read the speech to the unseen audience behind the camera as the cheering crowd gathered around him.

"We hereby proclaim the goals of the revolution: China shall become a free and democratic nation with a written constitution guaranteeing the rule of law, with leaders regularly elected by popular vote, a nation free of graft and corruption, a nation that protects its citizens from criminals, a nation where everyone shall have an equal opportunity to earn a living, a nation with free speech and freedom of religion, a nation that can take its place as a proud member of the world's family of nations. . . ."

The last half of the battle in the square was broadcast all over Hong Kong and mainland China. In Canton and Shanghai, in Beijing and Hunan Province and in villages all over the nation, people who happened to be near a television saw the Yorks standing in the center of the bank square surrounded by PLA troops with their hands in the air. Then the cheering crowd flowed into the square as if a dam had burst.

In Hong Kong City Hall someone called Governor Sun to the television. He was not in time to see the Yorks in action, but he watched as Hu Chiang landed in the square in the television station's helicopter and walked over to General Moon. He saw Hu accept General Moon's sidearm and he saw the first of the deliriously happy civilians stream into the square, hugging Hu Chiang and the surrendered soldiers and each other and gazing in awe at the York units.

"Radio Beijing," Governor Sun ordered peremptorily. "A revolution is underway in Hong Kong and we need more troops immediately to stabilize the situation."

The aide went off to do as he was told, leaving Governor Sun rooted to the spot, still staring at the television.

Nothing happened instantly in China, Sun well knew. It would take days for the government to reinforce the division of troops that were already here. Perhaps several weeks.

For the first time, Sun admitted to himself that he had misjudged the situation here.

His next epiphany followed immediately: The rebels would probably execute him if they could catch him. Chinese revolutions had never been bloodless affairs. This one wouldn't be either.

Jimmy Lee's producer stopped talking into the radio microphone when he realized that someone was standing beside him with a pistol, a pistol that was pointed at his head. He stopped talking in midword.

The pistol jerked, ordering him out of the chair.

A young woman of eighteen or nineteen years, an inch over four feet tall, took his place and began speaking into the microphone. "The Chinese revolution," she announced simply, "has begun. The island of Hong Kong has been liberated from Communist control."

Lin Pe watched the celebration in the Bank of the Orient square on the small television the Shatin grocer kept above his soft drink cooler. She watched as the cameraman inspected a York unit at close range— the thing towered a foot over everyone there and its head never stopped scanning—and the smoking hulk of a tank.

Hu Chiang appeared on television, behind him the crowd milled around, every now and then someone fired a shot into the air . . . the scene was festive, gay. No one even bothered to guard the unarmed PLA soldiers, who wandered through the crowd aimlessly, without direction.

Wu should have been here to see this, Lin Pe thought. He worked for a dozen years to make this happen, this *first step*!

The long journey had finally begun. She didn't know whether she should be happy or sad. She went back outside and sat down on the orange crate where she could see the gate of the army base and thought about everything.

She would tell Wu of this. In this life or the next.

In City Hall the governor and his staff were mesmerized by the televised spectacle, by the aerial shots of the crowd surging into the plaza, and by the simple, infectious joy that was apparent on every face.

They huddled around the television, which alternated between shots from the square taken with a handheld camera and aerial shots from the helicopter, which had taken off again. Through it all Peter Po gave the voice-over, as calm and collected as though revolutions were a weekly occurrence.

Hu Chiang's speech broke the spell in City Hall. Never known for an even temper, Sun exploded as he listened. He cursed Tang and Moon and the other PLA officers as incompetent, defeatist traitors. A call was put forth to the navy base. Sun demanded that all the gunboats steam up the strait and use their guns on the rebels celebrating in the Bank of the Orient square. The commander had caught the tail end of the televised debacle, and he agreed. Without much enthusiasm, Sun noted darkly.

Next he called the Su-27 squadron at Lantau. He got the squadron commander on the phone and demanded that armed sorties be flown against the rebels in the square.

"Drop bombs, strafe, shoot rockets . . . *kill the rebels! Stop the rot right here, before it spreads.*"

The colonel made him repeat the order to ensure he understood. "We will use a cannon to kill mosquitoes, eh?"

"Will you obey or must I call Beijing and have you court-martialed?"

"Bombs in the square will do a lot of damage, Governor. I just want to ensure you understand that. Afterward will be too late to complain."

"Kill the rebels."

"Bombs don't care whom they kill, Governor. Rebels, bankers, children, women, tourists, soldiers, policemen, whomever. That is what I am trying to explain."

"Obey my order!"

Next he called the chief of the metropolitan police and demanded he muster his officers and engage the rebels in armed combat. The police chief wasn't enthusiastic. Unlike the navy and air force commanders, he knew his men would be face-to-face with the robots he had seen on television.

"What are those things, Governor? What are their capabilities?"

"I do not know. Bullets will stop them, however."

"The army didn't seem to have much luck with bullets. What makes you think the police will do any better?"

"I have given the order," Sun said icily.

"So you have. But I tell you now, my men are police, not soldiers. They are trained in traffic control, not armed combat. I make no promises."

"Lead them yourself, coward!"

"If I am killed, whom will you blame for our defeat?"

Before Sun could give that disrespectful question the answer it deserved, he discovered that the chief of police had hung up.

Sun slammed down the phone. His chief aide was right there by the desk.

"Governor, you must report this matter to Beijing, but first, you must think of getting off this island."

"What are you saying?"

"Sir, the rebels will come for you, walk in the front door. The three or four policemen on duty out front cannot hold off armed rioters. You must not be here. You must not let them make a spectacle of you."

"You're right," Sun said, with more than a little gratitude in his voice. He telephoned the army base in the New Territories, asked for a helicopter to pick up him and his key aides on the roof of City Hall as soon as possible.

On the way to the roof, he stopped in the radio room. The operator called Beijing on the scrambled voice net.

Sun tried to quickly summarize the events of the morning. He told Beijing of his orders to the army and navy. "We need military reinforcements now," he pleaded with the minister.

The minister made no promises. "You must resist with the forces you have at your disposal," the minister said. "The rocket forces have had a horrible disaster, the trains cannot run until the computer systems get sorted out, the nation's electrical grid is experiencing spot failures, the telephone system is sporadic at best. We cannot get troops to you for some days."

"Air support? Could we have two more squadrons of MiGs or Sukhois?"

"The maintenance personnel, spare parts, and weapons all must be moved by road," the minister in Beijing informed Sun. "The move will take several weeks. I will give the order, but until they arrive, you must hold out with what you have."

Hold out with what we have.

Perhaps that is possible, Sun thought as he made his way up the stairs to the roof of City Hall. *If we can hurt the rebels in the square, then keep the remnants of the rebel forces on this island, prevent them from crossing the strait, perhaps it can be done.*

The chief of police was too old a dog to go running after every stick. He sat behind his desk at police headquarters watching the rebels celebrate on television.

After he read the flyer this morning, he ordered his policemen to stay away from the heart of the Central District. Apparently they had obeyed him, because he didn't see a single police officer on any of the camera's sweeps of the crowd.

A cop learns many things about the people he serves: who drinks to excess, who has a drug-addicted son or a pregnant teenage daughter, who takes bribes, who doesn't . . . who is fucking whom. In a society in which everything is for sale, everything has a price. A cop quickly learns to survive or he is eaten by the sharks.

The chief was busy surviving right now.

He tried to ignore politics when he could. Sonny Wong told him a year ago that rebellion was brewing in Hong Kong. Of course Sonny wanted to profit from that fact—that was a given. The rebels wanted change, Governor Sun and the Communists wanted to keep the status quo. One would win, one would lose.

Whoever won would need the police. And the police would need a chief.

This chief had no intention of ending up like China Bob Chan, with a fresh hole in his head and everyone in town breathing sighs of relief. Sure, China Bob made lots of money, got rich, had the big house and hot women and all the trimmings . . . and now he was sleeping in a hole in the ground because he knew too much about too many things.

Actually Sun wasn't a bad sort. The chief wondered now if he should have told the governor to get out of Hong Kong; the rebels would kill him if they caught him. Surely the man is bright enough to figure that out for himself.

The chief reached for the telephone, then thought better of it. He owed the governor nothing.

Michael Gao was on the roof of the building near the entrance to the Cross-Harbor Tunnel when he spotted the PLA helo running low, at treetop level, headed for City Hall on Hong Kong Island. He had a Strella launcher at his feet, so he lifted it, squeezed the trigger to the first notch to try for a heat lock-on.

And got one. He squeezed the trigger and the missile roared out of the launcher.

Away it went in a plume of fire. Straight across the street into the top story of the next building over.

He had another launcher, but he waited. Perhaps he would get a better shot. If he could get onto the sea wall . . .

The chopper settled onto the roof of City Hall. Sun and three aides came running out. When they were aboard, the chopper rose into the air just enough to clear the railing on top of the building, then tilted into the wind.

The pilot turned to fly out over the strait, then he turned east.

Michael Gao ran with the missile launcher in his arms. People scurried to clear a path. He came to the sidewalk on the sea wall and hurriedly threw the launcher to his shoulder. The helo was speeding east over the strait, at least two miles away and low, no more than fifty feet above the water.

The missile's guidance unit refused to lock on to the helo's exhaust. The distance was just too great, the angle too large.

Gao lowered the launcher and watched the helo fly away.

Tommy Carmellini systematically examined every item in Kerry Kent's apartment, disassembled the lamps and clocks, took the television from its shell, examined the works. Did the same with the clock radio. Tapped along the floorboards, scrutinized the light fixtures, used a knife to slice the stuffing from the easy chair near the window, picked through every single item in her dresser . . .

Tommy Carmellini knew how to search an apartment and he searched this one. He found absolutely nothing that shouldn't be there.

Two hours later, discouraged and tired, he dropped his trousers and lowered himself onto Kent's commode. Before he did so, however, he lifted the lid on the back and examined the workings. Looked precisely like a commode should. Then he felt behind the tank to ensure that nothing was taped to the back.

As he sat answering nature's call, he picked up a magazine that Kent had arranged on a nearby stand. Flipped through the pages, looking to see if anything had been inserted. No.

A newspaper. He picked it up, shook it. Nothing fell out. He was about to put it back on the stand when he paused, looked again. *The Financial Times*, a week-old edition. Kent had it folded to the stock listings.

Idly Carmellini ran his eye down the listings. Column one, two . . .

Huh! There was a tiny spot of ink under the Vodafone listing, as if she rested the tip of her pen there for a moment.

He held the page up, scrutinized it carefully. Here was another spot, and another. Six in all.

Stocks. Investments. A portfolio. Well, even civil servants had portfolios these days. Hell, he had a little money in the market himself.

But he couldn't recall seeing anything about her portfolio in the apartment. Not a monthly statement, a letter from her broker, nothing.

Odd.

There should be something, shouldn't there?

CHAPTER SIXTEEN

Major Ma Chao and his three coconspirators were standing in the back of the ready room when the commanding officer and his department heads came in. Someone called the people in the room to attention.

"We have orders," the CO announced. "Governor Sun has directed us to bomb the rebels in the Bank of the Orient square in the Central District, and headquarters in Beijing has confirmed. We will launch four airplanes with four two-hundred-and-fifty-kilogram bombs each. Fortunately, the weather is excellent. We will coordinate the attack with a shelling by two naval vessels, putting maximum pressure on the rebels."

In the silence that followed this announcement the television audio could be heard throughout the room. The pilots had watched Hu Chiang make his speech, had seen the York units and the happy, joyous crowd that filled the square. They had listened to Peter Po explain the significance of the revolution, why the overthrow of the Communists was of the gravest national importance.

Now this.

There was certainly much to think about, including the fact that no pilot in the squadron had ever dropped bombs from a J-11. Although the plane was a license-built copy of one of the world's premier fighters, it had no all-weather attack capability; visual dive-bombing was the only option. Unfortunately the Beijing brass thought the risks of dive-bombing training too high, so it had been forbidden.

Major Ma turned sideways so his right side was partially hidden and drew his sidearm, a semiautomatic. He held it low, beside his leg.

"Sir," Ma asked, "did you verify the governor's identity? Agents provocateurs may be giving false orders."

This comment was grossly insubordinate and the commanding officer treated it as such. "*I* am completely satisfied that the governor issued these orders and that headquarters concurred," he said, daring anyone to contradict his statement. "The time has come to separate the patriots from the traitors," he added ominously. "I intend to follow orders, to bomb the rebels as directed by the government. Who will fly with me?"

The senior officers raised their hands, but not a single junior.

"You traitors are under arrest," the commanding officer snarled. "Now clear the room."

Ma Chao raised his pistol, pointed it at the CO. "It is you who are under arrest, Colonel. Drop your sidearm."

The CO was a true fighter pilot. He grinned broadly, then said, "We thought something like this might happen, Ma Chao, but we never suspected you. Some of these other little dicks, yes, but you surprise me. Too bad." He raised his voice. "Come in, Sergeant, come in," he called and gestured through the open door to people waiting in the hallway.

Three senior noncommissioned officers walked in. They were carrying assault rifles in the ready position.

The CO gestured toward the rear of the room. "Major Ma and those junior officers. Lock them up until we can interrogate them and find how far the rot has spread."

The NCOs pointed their rifles at Ma.

This was *it*! Now or never. Use your best judgment, Wu had said.

Ma steadied the front sight of his automatic and pulled the trigger. The bullet knocked the CO down.

"Anyone else?" Ma said, looking around.

The senior NCO grinned at Ma, then pointed his rifle at the department heads. "Your pistols, please. You are under arrest."

The lieutenant beside Ma couldn't contain himself. "I thought the sergeant was going to shoot you!"

Ma Chao thought the sergeant was on his side. He said he was last week, yet every week the earth turns seven times. Ma breathed a sigh of relief and walked toward the front of the room to see how badly the CO was hurt and to take charge.

When the trucks filled with troops left the PLA base, Lin Pe telephoned a number she had memorized. She recognized the voice that answered, a nice young girl who attended Hong Kong University. "Seven trucks have left the base."

Five minutes later Lin Pe called again. "Ten trucks filled with troops. They drove away through Shatin."

"Very good. Thank you for the report. We would like you to go back to Nathan Road and walk along it. Report any strong points that you see under construction."

Lin Pe said good-bye to the grocer, who had let her use his restroom, and walked through Shatin toward the bus stop. Her bag was heavy and she was tired, so she made slow progress.

Her son, Wu, had told her of the dangers of spying on the PLA. "They will shoot you if they catch you talking about them on the cell phone. They may arrest you because they are worried. They will be frightened, fearful men, and very dangerous."

"I understand," she replied.

"They may beat you to death trying to make you talk. They may kill you regardless of what you say."

"I understand," she had repeated.

"You do not have to do this," Wu told her.

"Someone has to."

"Ah . . ." he said, and dropped the subject.

Where in the world could Kerry Kent hide the information about her stock portfolio? Tommy Carmellini stood in the middle of Kent's kitchen thinking about that problem. He could have sworn he had searched everything there was to search, peered in every cubbyhole and cranny, pried loose every baseboard, looked in all the vents. . . .

The pots and pans were piled carefully against one wall. He had even peeled up the paper she had used to line her shelves.

Her attaché case wasn't here. Must be at the consulate.

The notebook . . . a spiral notebook had lain on her bedroom table. He had flipped through it, but . . .

He found it again, sat down in the middle of the bathroom floor in the only open space and went through it carefully. Halfway through the notebook, there it was. A page of multiplication problems, seven in all, and a column where she added the seven answers together. She hid it in plain sight.

He compared the numbers in the problems to the stock listings in *The Financial Times*. Okay, this stock closed at 74½, and here was the problem, 74.5 × 5400. Answer, 402,300.

He checked every problem. The correlation with the six stocks highlighted with a tiny spot of ink was perfect. One stock he couldn't find; only six were marked.

The total . . . £1,632,430.

A pound was worth what, about a buck fifty?

Wheee! She wasn't filthy rich, but Kerry Kent was certainly a modestly well-off secret agent, which was, as any self-respecting gentleman would tell you, the very best kind.

Almost two and a half million dollars.

On a civil servant's salary.

Perhaps her grandparents were loaded and left her a bundle. Perhaps she had a rich first husband. Then again, perhaps she was the world's finest stock picker and had done more than all right with her lunch money.

Or perhaps, Tommy Carmellini thought as he pocketed the worksheet and financial page, just perhaps, Kerry Kent was crooked.

Elizabeth Yeager's apartment was a walk-up in a small village setting on the south side of the island. As the taxi driver settled in to wait, Jake Grafton made his way past the craft shops that catered to the tourist trade, only some of which were open today, to the stairs of Yeager's building. Ivy and creeping vines covered the walls.

There were four mailboxes. Yeager's was Apartment Three. He pushed the button.

"Yes." An American woman's voice, tired and angry.

"Elizabeth Yeager, I have a message for you."

"What?"

"For you personally."

"Come on up." She buzzed the lock open.

The former consular employee opened her door just a crack. Jake Grafton slammed the door with his shoulder, and it flew open, nearly bowling her over. There was another woman sitting by the couch, a dumpy, middle-aged woman with graying hair.

"Who are you? What do you want?"

Yeager's eyes were red from crying.

"You're Yeager?"

"Yes."

"Some questions for you." He looked at the other woman. "If you wouldn't mind."

Yeager nodded at the woman, who glared at Jake as she swept past.

"It's a crime to break into people's apartments," Yeager said as she perched on the edge of a chair. "Don't forget, my neighbor, Mrs. O'Reilly, can identify you."

"That was the woman who was just here?"

"That's right."

"Ms. Yeager, I wouldn't be talking about crimes if I were you. Stealing passports, forgery, treason, kidnapping . . . If you ever go back to the states you may wind up spending the rest of your life in a cell."

"You're Grafton, aren't you?"

Jake nodded.

"I've nothing to say, so get out."

"Or what? You'll call the police?"

She merely glared at him.

"Perhaps you'll call Sonny Wong and he'll send someone over to run me off. There's the phone—call anyone you like."

He sat in the chair facing her.

"Bastard."

"Where's my wife?"

"I don't know." Yeager hitched her bottom back in the chair and looked obstinately away.

Jake Grafton tried to hold his temper, which was getting more and more difficult. If Yeager only knew. "My wife has been kidnapped," he explained patiently. "Her life is at stake. I think you know a great deal about Sonny Wong, where he can be found, where he stays, where his men operate from. I want to know all that. I'm not going to tell anyone what you tell me. I won't report it to the United States government. It'll be strictly between us, absolutely confidential."

She turned to face him again. "You're an officer in the United States navy. You can't touch me. *I know my rights!* I have nothing to say!"

He pulled the Colt .45 from under his sports jacket, pointed it at her head, and thumbed off the safety. As she blanched, he turned the muzzle a few inches and pulled the trigger. The report was like an explosion, overpowering in that enclosed space. The bullet smacked into the wall behind her.

He leaped for her, grabbed a handful of hair, put the muzzle against her nose.

"Your rights don't mean shit! Where is my wife, goddamn it?"

She swallowed hard. "I don't know." That came out a squeak.

"We're having a revolution in Hong Kong, Ms. Yeager. The police have crawled into holes and the army has its hands full. No one cares about you. I can break every bone in your miserable body. I can shoot you full of holes and leave you here to bleed to death and nobody on this green earth will give a good goddamn. Now I'm going to ask you one more time, and if you give the wrong answer, we're going to find out how many bullets it takes to kill you. *Where is my wife?*"

Elizabeth Yeager's eyes got big as half-dollars and the color drained from her face. She tried to speak; the words came out a croak. Then she passed out cold. At first Jake thought she was faking it, but she went limp as linguine.

"Shit!" said Jake Grafton, more than a little disgusted with himself. Scaring a woman half to death.

"Shit," he said again, and released his hold on Yeager. She slid off the chair onto the floor like a bundle of old rags.

He kicked the coffee table. It skittered away.

He had his chance last night. He should have stuck that revolver up Wong's nose and told him he was going to blow his fucking head off if he didn't produce Callie in a quarter of an hour.

Yeah.

He slammed the door to the apartment on his way out.

He had the taxi take him back to the consulate so he could watch the revolution on television. Since Cole had submitted his resignation and was technically no longer an employee of the United States government, Grafton probably shouldn't be in his office. In any event, no one had suggested he leave. He turned on the television and settled behind Cole's desk.

The thought that he should be doing something to find Callie gnawed at him. Just what that something was he didn't know.

When the time came, Sonny would produce Wu and Callie to collect his money, but once he got it, he had to kill them all. Wu, Callie, Jake, Cole, everyone who had firsthand knowledge of the kidnapping. If he didn't he was a dead man.

Sonny Wong would have enough shooters in the area to ensure no one escaped. You could bet your life on that.

Jake's thoughts wandered. Callie had a brother in Chicago, married with two kids in college. Her mother was in an independent living facility near her brother, and her father was dead.

Her father had spent his career on the faculty at the University of Chicago. Professor McKenzie. What a piece of work he was! It wasn't that the old man believed in Marxism, with its dubious theories of social change and mind-numbing economic twaddle—the feature he liked was the dictatorship of the elite. The professor was an intellectual snob. The great failing of the common man, in McKenzie's opinion, was that he was common.

Jake wondered just what the prof would have thought of the collapse of communism all over the world.

He snapped off the television and sat down behind the consul general's desk in the padded leather executive chair that usually held Tiger Cole's skinny rump. There was a yellow legal pad on the desk, so he helped himself to a pen and began writing a report to the National Security staff on the situation in Hong Kong. Fortunately the consulate had radio communications with the State Department, so the staff could encrypt the report and put it on the air as soon as Jake finished it.

He was scrawling away when the secretary stuck his head in. "Ahh . . . Admiral." He frowned, perhaps offended that Jake was using Cole's office.

"Yes," Jake replied, and kept going on the sentence he was writing.

"There's a telephone call, sir. Mr. Carmellini."

Jake picked up the instrument. "Grafton."

"Carmellini, Admiral. I'm over here at Kerry Kent's apartment checking her cupboard. It seems she has a sizable stock portfolio somewhere."

Jake stopped writing. He had the telephone in a death grip. "Tell me about it."

Carmellini did. He gave Jake the names of the companies he thought she owned shares in, the number of shares, and the values. He also gave Jake the information on the seventh stock, though he didn't know the name of the company.

"Anything else?" Jake asked.

"That's about it, unless you are interested in the brands of her clothes."

"Should I be?"

"Well, they strike me as expensive duds, better than I am used to seeing on government employees, but she's British and a hell of a lot richer than me. . . ."

"Better come on back to the consulate."

"Is the ferry still running? I know the subway is dead and the tunnel is closed."

"Hire or steal a boat," Jake said, and hung up.

He pushed the intercom button to summon the secretary. When he appeared, Jake told him, "I want to call the Pentagon on the satellite phone."

"Those circuits are all in use by the staff, sir, for official business. They are giving the National Security Council and State real-time feeds on the situation here."

"Terrific. I want to use a line."

"Who are you, sir? Really? I mean, I know you are an admiral on active duty in the navy, but using the consul general's office and—"

"I don't have time for this," Jake snapped. "Get me a line, and now. After you do that you call the Secretary of State's office and complain to them."

The secretary was offended. "I'll have the call put through. You can use the phone on the desk. Wait until it rings."

Okay: China Bob Chan was smuggling money and high-tech war equipment into Hong Kong. And he was a conduit for Communist money being given or donated to American politicians in the hopes of getting favorable export licenses. Sonny Wong was a professional criminal with ties to criminal gangs all over China. Cole was an American agent supplying money and highly classified weapons systems to the rebels.

And Kerry Kent? A British SIS agent, either covertly assigned or playing hooky. Cole's weapons system operator, WSO, wizzo in U.S. Air Force terminology. Screwing the head rebel. With money in the bank . . .

Cole didn't trust China Bob, so a CIA agent bugged his office and was killed before he could retrieve the tape. Then somebody shot China Bob Chan, and the whole tangled skein became a mare's nest.

Callie listened to the tape and heard . . . nothing.

She heard hours of conversation, much of it one-sided because Chan was on the phone, and probably all of it relevant if one knew more about Chan's business . . . but not otherwise. For Callie it was just noise.

Then she was kidnapped.

Money?

Wong threatened Cole. Callie could convict him with her testimony, he said.

How would he know? He didn't hear the tape.

What if he were assuming the tape contained something it didn't?

Ahhh . . . !

The phone rang.

Jake picked it up and found himself talking to the Pentagon war room duty officer. He identified himself and asked for Commander Tarkington.

Twenty seconds later Toad was on the line.

"Are you sleeping there?"

"Up in the office. I was down here loafing, hoping you'd call."

"Got a job for you."

"Yes, sir. Fire away."

Jake gave Toad all the information he had on Kent's stock portfolio. "This is a straw we are trying to build with," he told Toad. "See what the NSA computer sleuths can come up with. The account probably won't be under her name. I would think it's probably with a London brokerage or the Hong Kong office of a London brokerage. This woman may have had access to stolen American passports from this consulate. If she has contacts in the Hong Kong underworld, she may have passports from anywhere, genuine or faked." Jake gave Toad a physical description of Kent.

When Toad had finished writing down the description, he told his boss, "I've been talking to the CIA. They say SIS is well aware of Kent's status with the rebels, though they refuse to admit anything. Officially the Brits say they never even heard of her."

"Forget that. Find the money. Find where it came from. An inheritance, divorce settlement, whatever."

"Heard anything from Callie?"

"No."

"I asked for permission to come over there to help you, but the President nixed it. Said he doesn't want any military personnel going in-country for any reason."

"I figured he'd say that."

"I've talked to the chairman." The chairman of the Joint Chiefs, Toad meant. "We shouldn't have a problem getting cooperation. When I find out anything, I'll call you."

"I'll be sitting right here," Jake Grafton said.

At that moment Callie Grafton was telling Wu Tai Kwong, "We need an escape plan." She had inspected every inch of the small stateroom where they were being held, as well as the tiny bathroom. She had looked at the door hinges, the window, the air vent, the beds, and didn't have a glimmer of an idea.

"Yes," Wu agreed after a moment's reflection, "a plan would be good."

"Do you have any ideas?"

"No." Wu raised his hands, then lowered them. The sheet strips around his arm were blood-soaked, but the bleeding seemed to have stopped.

She found the situation infuriating. She balled up her fists and shook them. "I don't understand you. You say they will kill you, yet you don't seem to be worried. You aren't figuring out how to get out of here. You're just sitting there."

"What else is there to do?"

She made an exasperated noise. She had been married so long she judged all men by her husband. Jake Grafton wouldn't be sitting calmly, waiting for the inevitable. Not Jake. He would be scheming and planning until he drew his very last breath.

She missed him terribly.

"Figure a way to get us out of here," Callie told her fellow prisoner. "There must be a way. We're on a ship, a small one I think, docked I believe, maybe anchored. When they come for me again—or you— we'll both jump them. Fight, claw, do whatever we have to. Get out. Get free. Stay alive. Let's find something we can use as a weapon. Anything."

Wu waited a while before he spoke. He had that habit, she noticed, and she didn't much care for it. He said, "You would like my mother, I think. She is much like you. She struggles with life, seeks to conquer it."

"And you don't?"

"We all do to some degree. My mother more than me. You are more like her, I think."

"You are supposed to be a revolutionary. By definition, revolution is struggle."

"Quite so. I struggle to change the world as man has made it. But life? When the rain comes, it does not matter whether you welcome it or hate it—the rain falls upon your head regardless."

"Everyone dies, too," Callie said acidly. "I don't know about you, but I'm not ready. I have a lot of good years left in me. I'm not going to be robbed of life by some hoodlum, not if I can do anything to prevent it."

"That's the rub," Wu said softly. "Preventing it."

The Luda-class destroyer, Number 109, came steaming west through Victoria Strait between the island of Hong Kong and the Kowloon peninsula. She had been ordered by the commanding officer of the naval base to sortie immediately and shell the rebels in the Bank of the Orient square, pursuant to the orders of Governor Sun.

Lieutenant Tan was the officer of the deck when the order was received, and he protested. The commanding officer was not aboard, the ship was not ready for sea. His protests fell on deaf ears. "Sail with the men you have aboard and shell the rebels as ordered," the base commander said.

Of course, the base commander was having his own troubles. A riot had broken out in the enlisted mess hall, probably instigated by the rebels. The officers who attempted to turn off the base television system had been met with sticks and garbage pail lids. The rioting sailors were making threats against the officers' lives.

Actually two destroyers had sailed, but Number 105 had gone dead in the water with an engine room casualty before it cleared the base breakwater. Sabotage, Lieutenant Tan suspected, but he didn't say so with the quartermaster and helmsmen within earshot. These two were surly, doing their duty with the minimum acceptable professional courtesy. No doubt they sympathized with their rioting mates and perhaps with the rebels in the bank square.

Number 109 steamed on alone.

Lieutenant Tan began thinking about the professional problem he faced. The gun to use for surface bombardment was the twin 130-millimeter dual-purpose mount on the bow. There was a similar mount on the stern, but it was out of service for some critical parts.

The bow gun would do very well. Unfortunately in this ship the Sun Visor fire control radar that was designed for this gun was never mounted, so the gun had to be aimed visually. The gun had an effective range of eight or nine miles; that was no problem. In fact, the ship was within maximum gun range now.

The problem, Lieutenant Tan told himself as he stared at the chart of Hong Kong on the navigator's table, was going to be putting the shells into the square. He was going to have to lob them in with the gun elevated to a high angle. Maximum elevation angle was eighty-two degrees.

If he missed the square and started scattering 130-millimeter, 33.5-kilogram high-explosive shells around the downtown, there would be hell to pay later. Regardless of what they said now, the governor and base commander would want pieces of his hide then.

Of course the designated gunnery officer was not aboard. Lieutenant Tan was the only officer qualified to lay the gun, and he also had to con the ship.

He was so nervous his hands shook. He laid the chart on the table so it wouldn't rattle and consulted the range and elevation charts for the gun. Shooting at a hidden urban target was going to be a challenge, perhaps an impossible one.

He put the binoculars to his eyes and studied the buildings in the Central District. The ship was about five miles from the downtown, he estimated. Needless to say, the buildings did not appear on his chart of the area's waters. If he could remember which buildings were which . . .

He asked the helmsman for the speed.

"Eight knots, sir."

He was studying the chart, measuring, when he heard the lookout.

"Bogey on the starboard bow."

What?

"Jet airplane, sir, looks like he's lining us up for a low pass."

Lieutenant Tan looked.

A fighter, two of them. They were completing the turn to pass the length of the ship, bow to stern. Dropping down, one trailing the other, not going too quickly, maybe three hundred knots . . .

Suddenly he knew. "*Air attack!*" he screamed. "Open fire!"

Flashes on the wing root of the lead fighter . . . the water in front of the ship erupted. Quick as thought, the shells began pounding the ship, cutting, smashing.

The glass in the bridge windows shattered, the helmsman went down, shrapnel and metal flew everywhere.

The attack ended in a thunderous roar as the jet pulled out right over the ship, and the next fighter began shooting.

Screaming . . . someone was screaming amid the hammering of the cannon shells . . .

Fire! Smoke and flame.

When the shooting stopped, Lieutenant Tan tried to stand. The ship was turning to port, out of the channel. The helmsman was lying on the deck, his head gone. Tan spun the helm to center the rudder, bring the ship back under control.

"Arm the see-whiz," he shouted, meaning the CIWS, the close-in weapons system that the Chinese navy had purchased from the Americans.

Behind him he heard the talker repeat the order. The talker was huddled on the floor, bleeding badly from a wound that Tan couldn't see.

Tan looked aft. Something was burning, putting out smoke. He rang for full speed on the engine telegraph, a bell that was answered. The ship seemed to accelerate noticeably as the gas turbine engines responded.

The jets were on a downwind leg, high out to the right over Kowloon.

"Forward turret, fire at will at the enemy planes," Tan ordered. "CIWS on automatic fire."

This time as the planes dove, the ship was going faster, perhaps twelve knots. The forward turret opened fire unexpectedly. Of course the gun crew was shooting visually, using an artillery piece to shoot at a fly, but the noise and concussion helped steady Tan. He huddled down behind the helm station as the fighter's cannon shells slammed into the base of the mast and bridge area.

The noise had become beyond human endurance—the twin 130-millimeter mount was hammering off a shell every two seconds. There was a pause as the first jet roared overhead, then the gun began again. Despite that racket Tan clearly heard the chain-saw roar of the 20-millimeter Gatling gun of the Phalanx close-in weapons system when it lit off, spitting out fifty tungsten bullets per second.

Then, suddenly, the guns fell silent. Only the roar of a jet engine changing pitch, then nothing. Tan rushed to the side of the bridge in time to see a man ejecting from a stricken fighter. Then the fighter rolled inverted and dove into the choppy water of the strait.

Pulling out, climbing away after his second strafing run, Major Ma Chao also saw his wingman eject and the plane go into the water.

The destroyer was on fire, smoking badly from the area behind the bridge.

The crew would probably forget about the mission to shell the square as they fought to save the ship.

That was enough.

Ma Chao's commanding officer had a bullet hole in a lung, and one of the squadron's planes had been shot down—status of the pilot unknown.

And so we begin.

"A good beginning." Rip Buckingham used those words as the title for the story he wrote for the Buckingham newspapers. He told the story as completely as he could, leaving out the Sergeant York robots, concluding with the surrender of General Moon Hok in the bank square. When the story was finished he printed it out, then went to his den. He had an antique cabinet in one corner, one that he hinted to the maid contained liquor, which was why he kept it locked.

Inside the cabinet was a shortwave radio, an unlicensed ham set, the existence of which was unknown to the Chinese authorities.

Rip plugged the radio into a wall socket and connected the antenna lead. He used the wire that held up the awning on the roof patio for an antenna. Rip checked the time and ensured that the radio was tuned to the proper frequency.

He plugged in a hand microphone, then pushed the key and transmitted. "Hey, Joe? You there?"

"I'm here."

"Got a story for you."

"Wait until I get a pen and paper."

The man who monitored the radio would take down the story in shorthand, transcribe it, and send it via E-mail to Rip's father, Richard. Tomorrow it would be in the Buckingham newspapers worldwide.

"I'm ready."

"Okay," Rip said, and began reading aloud.

The televised celebration in the bank square was still going on hours after General Moon's surrender. Jake Grafton wondered why the giant block party had gone on so long because he knew that Cole and the rebels must prepare for the next battle, the real Battle of Hong Kong. What he didn't realize was that the rebels had lost control of the crowd. It was now a mob.

Beyond the range of the television cameras, the mob began seeping away down the side streets, flowing toward City Hall, which was on the waterfront.

The four policemen in front of City Hall stood their ground when the rioters first appeared by the dozens. By the time the crowd numbered several hundred, they were nervous. Not a single soldier was in sight.

As the crowd swelled into the thousands and began packing the streets, the four policemen walked away. They merely took off their hats and gloves and walked off into the crowd.

The jets diving on destroyer 109 and the thunder of the guns galvanized the crowd, which had a ringside seat. When the pilot of one of the jets ejected the crowd fell silent, but when the destroyer, smoking badly and in obvious distress, turned and limped away to the east, the crowd cheered wildly.

As fishing boats along the shore rushed to rescue the pilot in the water, the television helicopter circled low over City Hall, transmitting the scene to the station on Victoria Peak, which broadcast it. Television stations in at least a dozen southern Chinese cities were still retransmitting the broadcast. Pictures of the mob around City Hall and the wounded destroyer retreating after an aerial attack, accompanied by Peter Po's professional voice-over, stunned audiences that had been allowed to hear nothing of the civil troubles in Hong Kong.

An hour and a half into the pirate show the mob stormed City Hall. No one led it, no one advocated it, it just happened.

Governor Sun was not there, of course, but three prominent Communists were. One was a Beijing appointee to the Court of Appeals, the other two were officials in the government of the Hong Kong Special Administrative Region. All three were dragged out of City Hall and beaten to death in the street as the camera filmed it from a hundred feet overhead.

Hu Chiang, Cole, Kerry Kent, and the rebel leaders were holding a council of war in the trailer in the alley when they were called to witness the storming of City Hall on television.

No one had much to say when they realized the crowd was beating the Communist officials to death.

"I hope the world gets a good look," Cole said to no one in particular.

"What do you mean?" Kent asked.

"That mob has just driven a stake through the argument that the Chinese are happier and better off under communism. We've heard the last of that crap."

The defeat of Moon Hok meant that the PLA had to temporarily abandon all hope of reinforcing its forces on Hong Kong Island. PLA radio traffic revealed that they were well aware that the Cross-Harbor Tunnel was in rebel hands.

The New Territories garrison was frantically appealing to Beijing for help. The government had plenty of problems of its own, most of which had been created by Cole's cybertroops. Still, given enough time the Communists would move additional troops from mainland China to Hong Kong. Eventually overwhelming military power would be brought to bear on the rebellious population of the former British colony. Obviously the rebels could not allow time to become their enemy's ally.

"We are in a life-or-death struggle," Hu Chiang told the rebel leaders when they gathered again around the map of Hong Kong mounted on the wall of the trailer. "We must never lose sight of that fact even for a moment, or all is lost.

"As we speak the PLA is constructing fortified positions and strong points beyond our perimeter at the tunnel exit. Our watchers report that tanks are being arranged as a defense in depth.

"Despite this, we still expect the PLA to assault the tunnel entrance to see how strongly it is held. If the resistance is weak, we anticipate they will press until we crack. On the other hand, should resistance be stronger than anticipated, we believe they will drop back and wait for us to shatter ourselves on their strong points."

Hu Chiang paused here, surveyed the faces of his audience. "The government in Beijing is pressing the local commanders for immediate action. The Communists see the revolt in Hong Kong as a political disaster that must be crushed before it spreads. Nor can we afford to wait. The government has an overwhelming military advantage and given enough time to marshal its forces, would crush us. We must convince the Communists that the real crisis is political, induce them to rush into action and fail to properly employ their military advantage.

"The fighter squadron at Lantau will keep the Chinese air force and navy off us for a few hours. While we enjoy air superiority, we will attack. Tonight, as planned."

No one objected.

"Let us proceed," Hu Chiang continued. "The York units will be moved through the tunnel and take up hidden positions outside our perimeter." He indicated those on the map that hung behind him on the wall. "We have weapons for almost a thousand soldiers now, counting those captured today. We have a dozen heavy machine guns and several trucks full of tear gas canisters, if we need it.

"We are organizing our supporters into military units and using these units to reinforce our tunnel perimeter in Kowloon. When we are ready to push our entire force through the tunnel, we will open our assault by attacking the strong points with the York units. Are there any questions?"

Cole broke the silence. "The PLA might attack before we are ready."

"They could. If a fireball like Wu Tai Kwong were leading them, they would. Fortunately, the division commander is dead and the deputy commander is our prisoner. I listened to their radio traffic, and I did not sense a burning desire to fight. They are being ordered to fight. Beijing is making dire threats."

"How would you characterize the morale of the common soldier?"

Hu Chiang paused a moment before he spoke. "We have interrogated some of the soldiers captured this afternoon. They are not Communists. They want the same things every Chinese person wants—a job, money to feed and raise a family, a better life. Make no mistake, many will fight fiercely, and others will refuse to fight or defect. We hope the Sergeant York units sapped some of their fighting ardor. They are confused. Too much has happened too quickly."

Cole grinned, and so did the others. "Let's keep them confused, shall we?"

For Jake Grafton the tension was nearly unbearable, the waiting hell. Soon the sun would go down behind Victoria Peak and all of the Central District would be in shadow.

He paced like a caged lion and paid partial attention to the television while he worried about Callie. Was she still alive? Would Sonny Wong release her tomorrow when Cole paid off? Was hunting her tonight the right thing to do?

When Tommy Carmellini knocked on the consul general's office door, Jake waved at him to come in. He sat on the couch.

"Did you swim the strait or what?"

"I persuaded a ferry captain to bring a whole boatload of folks over, kids wanting to enlist, mostly."

"Did you bribe him?"

"A little bit. I think he would have done it for nothing, but I wanted him to have some drinking money."

"Have you been through her desk and files downstairs?"

"A cursory look, yes."

"Go look again. I want to know everything there is to know about that woman."

Fifteen minutes later the telephone rang, and Jake jumped for it. Almost two hours had passed since he spoke to his aide, Toad Tarkington, in America over the satellite circuits.

"Grafton." He spit out the word.

"You were right, Admiral," Toad said with triumph in his voice. "There is an account belonging to an American woman, same age and physical description as Kent, at the Hong Kong office of a London brokerage. Turns out the American woman has been dead for six months, but her passport has never been turned in."

"How'd she die?"

"Traffic accident in Hong Kong."

"Her name?"

"Patricia Corso Parma." Toad spelled it, gave Jake the social security number, date of birth, and passport number. "She may be dead, but she opened the account four months ago and has been depositing money in hundred-thousand-American-dollar chunks."

"The way I figure this," Jake said, "Kerry Kent is somehow tied in with Sonny Wong. He's the guy who kidnapped Callie and Wu Tai Kwong, the rebel leader. I'm going to sweat her, see if she knows where Wong might be holding Callie. If she doesn't know, she might know somebody who does."

"Okay, boss," Toad said.

Jake looked up and realized that Tommy Carmellini was standing near the desk, looking out the window. He must have just reentered the room.

"If anything happens to me," Jake said into the telephone, "I want you to make damned sure Wong and Kent don't have fun spending any of this money. Have the CIA screw with their bank records. Okay?"

"You got it, boss," the Toad-man replied. "But you be careful, will ya?"

"Yeah."

"When you see Callie, tell her that she's been in my thoughts, mine and Rita's."

"Yeah."

"Take care," was Toad's good-bye.

When Jake replaced the telephone on its cradle, Carmellini tossed a passport on the desk in front of Jake. American, with the blue cover. He opened it. Patricia Corso Parma. Staring at him from the page, however, was an excellent picture of Kerry Kent.

"Where did you find this?"

"Taped inside the air return ducting in Kent's cube, downstairs. I found a screwdriver in her desk and went looking for something to unscrew."

CHAPTER SEVENTEEN

"We need to talk," Jake said to Tiger Cole. He and Carmellini had just gotten through two circles of armed guards around the museum exhibit trailer and had been allowed to enter. Cole was watching the video from the York units, which were being positioned in preselected hiding places in Kowloon. Kent was at the main control panel. Beside her sat a Chinese student from Hong Kong University whom Cole thought brilliant.

"Give me two more minutes," Cole said.

"Where are you putting those things?"

Cole kept his eyes on the computer monitors. "In shops and basements, just getting them out of sight."

"This will be the acid test, huh?"

"They were designed for night fighting in urban areas. The official designation is AVSPU, for Assault Vehicle, Self-Propelled, Urban. The army put them in a class with hummers and armored personnel carriers."

When the last York was in place, Cole turned to Jake. "What can I do you for?"

"A short talk with you and Ms. Kent. Got a private place?"

"There's a tiny office at the end of this trailer."

"That'll do."

Cole spoke to Kent, and she got up from the control panel and followed Cole and Jake. Carmellini hung back, then followed her.

She glanced around at him, didn't say anything. She was wearing tennis shoes, jeans, and a pullover today; Carmellini had never seen her in anything but a dress or skirt. Her abundant hair was pulled back in a ponytail, making her look like the girl next door.

The office was small, with just a desk and two chairs. Jake snagged one and motioned Kent into the other. Cole stood. Carmellini waited until the door closed on the three of them, then went looking for Kent's purse.

Jake laid the passport on the small desk. "Explain this," he said to Kerry Kent.

She didn't reach for it. Jake passed it to Cole, who opened it, flipped through it, then tossed it back on the desk.

She nipped on her lower lip, but not a trace of emotion showed on her face.

After about ten seconds, she reached for the passport. She spent at least half a minute examining it, then laid it back on the desk.

"I never saw it before," she said.

"Wrong answer," Jake Grafton said sourly. "I know a lot and can guess at a lot more. Believe me, your future depends on how clean you come, right now."

"I'm a British citizen. I work for the SIS. I don't have to tell you anything."

"Another wrong answer," Jake said.

They were interrupted by a knock on the door. Cole opened it and Carmellini passed in a shoulder purse. Cole made room for him.

With another glance at Kent, Jake opened the purse, looked in. "Aha." From its depths he removed a Derringer, a small two-barrel single-action .22 caliber. "Would you look at this."

He opened the action. Loaded. Snapped it shut and passed it to Cole. "Want to talk now?"

"Why?" she said. "You don't know anything."

"You should have gotten rid of the gun. Do the British still hang people?"

"It was given to me."

"By whom?"

"Wu Tai Kwong."

"Wrong answer again. How about Sonny Wong?"

She leaned back in her chair and looked in every face. "You don't have proof of anything," she said. "Carmellini must have planted that gun in my purse."

Jake stood. "Tommy, stay here with Ms. Kent. Don't let her touch anything, call anyone, speak to anyone. We'll be back."

He walked through the door and Cole followed him.

"What was it about the pistol?" Cole asked as they walked to the York control console.

"Wasn't that CIA agent, Harold Barnes, shot with a twenty-two?"

A look of surprise crossed Cole's face. "I can't recall."

"I can," Jake Grafton said. He paused behind the York master control panel. "I read the report. Twenty-two slug at point-blank range above the right ear. The Hong Kong police turned the bullet over to the FBI."

"Kent?" He sounded skeptical.

"Perhaps. I'm guessing, but it fits. Now tell me, what would happen if someone changed some of the lines of the code that the Yorks use to separate the good guys from the bad guys?"

Cole pursed his lips thoughtfully. He went over to the keyboard and began typing. He spent two minutes studying lines of software code. "Looks okay," he muttered and came back to the control menu.

"But if one of the Yorks started shooting our guys, I would see it. I'm right here."

"That problem could be easily solved with a bullet."

"We've got to trust people," Cole responded. "There's no other way to do it."

"Wake up, Tiger. Kerry Kent and Sonny Wong aren't on the same sheet of music that you and Wu have been singing from. A wise man surrounds himself with people he trusts and checks on 'em constantly."

"You're right, of course."

"Where's your television helicopter?" Jake asked. "You and I need to take a ride."

"It's back at the TV station. The PLA would gladly pot it over Kowloon tonight."

"Call the station and have the pilot fly it down here. You and I need to borrow it."

"Want to tell me what's going on?"

"Not yet. Like she said, we need some proof. Call the station and get us a chopper."

The helicopter, a Bell 206 JetRanger, landed in the street. The pilot was a small man in his mid-twenties. As the chopper was making its approach, Jake turned to Tiger Cole and said, "We better take assault rifles, just in case."

"Okay." He borrowed rifles from two of the men guarding the trailer.

The pilot flew the helicopter between the office towers of Victoria, then dropped to fifteen feet above the waters of the strait. They flew over the trucks and armed rebels who were guarding the tunnel and kept going. Cole pointed to a building, and the pilot slowed to a hover over the street in front of it. He let the chopper descend straight down, cushioning it at the bottom, until the skids kissed. Cole got out and led the way.

They were in front of a laundry. Not many civilians around, although heads peered out windows all along the block. With Cole leading, the two men went through the laundry, out the back, and down an alley. Forty feet or so down the alley, they knocked on a back door. It opened a crack.

Cole said something in Chinese, and the door opened.

A York unit, Alvin, stood near the front of the building, which was a shoe shop. A curtain hung between it and the shop door. It stood facing the curtain, a belt-fed machine gun in its hands and an electric cord hanging from its back. "We're charging the battery," Cole explained, gesturing at the cord.

"Yeah. Are there any access panels on this thing?"

"Yes. Three, actually. One in his abdomen under the UWB radar, one in his back above the electrical socket, and one in the back of his head."

"Open 'em up. Let's take a look."

Cole didn't hesitate. From a trouser pocket he produced a small cloth bundle. He unrolled it, revealing four tools. One looked to Jake like a plain Phillips screwdriver. Cole used it to open the panels.

From his shirt pocket he produced a penlight. "This is a regular flashlight or a red-light laser. I use it to check the sensors. Use the white light." He showed Jake the control.

Jake peered into the back of Alvin's head. It was full of wires, contacts, and component connections. "Take a look," Jake told Cole and held the penlight for him.

"What are we looking for?"

"Anything that isn't supposed to be there."

"Looks okay to me."

"Next panel."

Of course, they found what they were looking for in the last panel, the one on the abdomen. Cole almost missed it. A tiny bare wire, no more than an inch long, protruded from the top of a solid black plug-in component.

Cole used his fingers to remove the connection, then began tugging on the bare wire. It turned out to be six inches long, a small antenna, and was connected to a small radio receiver, a AAA battery, and a blasting cap buried in about three ounces of malleable plastique explosive.

"A bomb."

"If it went off, what would it do?"

"Destroy the main power supply. The York will just stop, wherever it is. Think Kent did this?"

"She had access and motive."

"How did you know it was here?"

"Someone paid Kent a lot of money in the last four months," Jake replied. "A million and a half pounds. I'm betting it was Sonny Wong. He then kidnapped Wu and Callie and demanded fifty million American from you and ten from Rip, Wu's brother-in-law. He's your security chief, and he's dirty."

Cole used a pocketknife to cut the wires leading to the head of the blasting cap, which protruded from the plastique.

Jake continued. "Either Sonny Wong is going to kill you, Wu Tai Kwong, and the folks loyal to Wu, then take over the rebellion and lead it himself, or he sold the rebellion to the Communists. They pay him, he wipes out the rebel leadership—at a profit, which he pockets—and disables the Yorks. The PLA defeats the rebel army and hangs a couple hundred traitors as an example to everyone. Voilà! everything is once again copacetic in Communist heaven."

"We've kept a tight rein on everything."

"You're planning a goddamn revolution involving hundreds—for all

I know thousands, maybe tens of thousands—of people all over China and you think the Communist leadership didn't get wind of it? Maybe in Oz, baby, but not in the real world. Hell, man, the folks in Silicon Valley are selling high-tech secrets to anyone with money. You know that! Cash is king! Sonny Wong may be a patriot, but he can be bought. Kent's a chippie; you could buy her for pocket change."

"Okay, okay." Cole shook his head. "Yeah. Okay."

"You better visit all these Yorks and see what Ms. Kent was up to in her spare time. I'll take the chopper back to the barn and have a little chat with our lady friend from SIS."

"Okay," Cole said. "Send the chopper back for me. I'll meet him where it is."

"Give me the bomb." Jake held out his hand. Cole handed it to him. "When you get back, Carmellini and I are going to need some weapons. What have you guys got in inventory?"

"A little bit of everything for the Yorks."

"I need two silenced submachine guns, a couple of silenced pistols, and two fighting knives."

"You going to get Kent to tell you where Callie is?"

"Uh-huh."

"Don't do anything you'll regret."

"I intend to get my wife back alive," Jake Grafton said. "Whatever happens to anybody who gets in the way is their tough luck."

Tommy Carmellini and Kerry Kent were still seated in the small office at the end of the museum exhibit trailer. "Any problem?" Jake asked.

"She offered me some money."

Kent was staring at a spot on the wall, her face a mask.

"Anybody talk to her, she talk to anybody?"

"No, sir."

Carmellini got out of the chair and Jake sat. "I don't have a lot of time," he said to Kent. "I'm not going to fool around. I want the truth and I want it now."

She didn't say a word.

"You understand that you're never going to see a dollar of that money. It's history. Forget about it. The SIS will confiscate the account. What we're talking about now is your life."

Jake Grafton leaned forward and stared across the desk into Kerry Kent's eyes. In spite of herself, she found she couldn't look away. "Tell me where my wife is. If I get her back safe and sound, you live. If I don't, you die. It's that simple."

She said nothing.

"Carmellini," Jake said. "Get me a roll of duct tape."

The CIA officer went through the door.

Almost too quickly for the eye to follow, Kent lashed out at Jake Grafton's throat with the cutting edge of her hand. Jake took the blow on his forehead and went for her with both hands. He got his left hand around her neck, his thumb on her windpipe, and squeezed for all he was worth while he used his right to pop her hard in the nose.

Cartilage shattered and blood spattered everywhere.

The fight went out of her. Grafton released his grip.

She sat dazed, bleeding freely, then her eyes focused again.

She held her shirttail to her nose, exposing her bra. Jake didn't take his eyes off her. Amazingly, he felt better.

"Asshole," she hissed. "Hitting a woman."

Carmellini opened the door, then paused. Jake stood up and took the tape.

"We'll tape her to this chair. Put her in it."

That didn't take much wrestling. Jake began wrapping tape around her. "Put her hands behind her."

"What about her nose?"

"Never heard of anyone dying of nosebleed. If she croaks we'll put her in the medical textbooks."

Kent screamed. Jake punched her again, medium hard, and she stopped.

"One more time," he told her. "I enjoyed that."

He used almost the whole roll of tape on her. "Now," he said, removing the bomb that had been in Alvin York from his pocket. "Here's how we're going to do this. You are going to tell me where my wife is, and Mr. Carmellini and I will go get her. If we return with Mrs. Grafton, we'll come in here and disarm this bomb. If we don't return . . . well, I guess you'll die when Sonny pushes the button to pop the Sergeant Yorks."

Carefully, with her watching, he twisted the wires that ran to the blasting cap back together. "There."

"You're an American naval officer," she whispered. "You can't do this to me."

"Everyone keeps telling me that. Actually, I was thinking of taping this bomb to your head. What do you think, Tommy?"

"Asshole," she hissed. The blood covered her mouth and shirt. She was a hell of a mess.

"Get the WB phone out of her bag."

Carmellini did as he was told.

"I doubt if she memorized the phone number. Look for something with phone numbers written on it, a little pad, her checkbook, anything."

Kent's eyes widened.

"You were supposed to blow the Yorks with the cell phone, weren't you?"

She lost control of her face.

Jake continued. "We'll just tape the bomb to your head. If anything happens to Callie, I'll call you. How's that?"

Her eyes narrowed. She wiped the blood on her mouth off onto her shoulder.

"She doesn't think you'll really kill her," Carmellini said.

"I won't have to," Jake told him. "All I have to do is tell these people how she betrayed Wu and them. If Wu dies, she won't live another ten minutes. They'll kill her with their bare hands."

Her head was down now. Blood still flowed from her nose.

"He's holding them on a yacht, the *China Rose*." Her voice was a husky whisper. "It's at the Kowloon docks."

Jake Grafton lifted her head. He looked straight into her eyes. "You'd better pray we find them alive and get back here. Without me you're dead. Understand?"

They put tape over her mouth and punched a small hole in it so she could breathe. Then they left her, locking the door behind them.

"Sorry about that," Jake said to Tommy Carmellini as he used a rag to wipe blood from his hands. "When you left the room she turned wildcat, so I punched her in the nose."

"Glad it was you and not me. I knew Harold Barnes. He didn't deserve what he got."

"Cole is going to give me some weapons. I don't know what is on that ship. Maybe two people, maybe fifty. You want to come along?"

"Yeah."

"Ain't in your job description. When you're dead the story is all over; the movie ends right there. If you've got a woman somewhere and big plans, I understand."

Carmellini shrugged. "Going places people don't want me to go is what I do."

Jake tossed the bloody rag in a corner. "I'm going to kill anybody who gets in my way," he said. "No questions asked, no hesitation."

Carmellini glanced at the closed office door. "And Kerry Kent gets off with a busted nose."

"Oh, I doubt it," Jake said, sighing. He gestured to the people conferring in front of the map and checking the computer monitors. "She betrayed these people. If they don't kill her, Wu Tai Kwong will."

When the helo brought Tiger Cole back from Kowloon, he had five more small bombs with him. "Okay," he told Jake Grafton, "you've convinced me. She sold us out. There was a radio-controlled bomb in every one of the Yorks."

"Only one?"

"God, I hope so. I inspected them as carefully as I could. We could take them out of service for a week or so and disassemble each of them into a pile of parts and check every goddamn nut, bolt, and screw, but . . ."

"She says Callie and Wu are being held in a yacht tied up at the Kowloon docks."

"She being cooperative now?"

"That's probably not an accurate statement."

Cole snarled, "By God, I have a few things I'd like to ask her."

"Hey, she isn't going to tell you anything you don't already know. She did it for the money."

Virgil Cole shook his head, rubbed his eyes. "I just don't understand people like that. Maybe I've had too much money for too long. . . ."

"You were never that poor, believe me," Jake said. He handed Cole the sixth bomb.

"You said you wanted weapons?"

"And the use of your helicopter. I want to find this yacht before the light fades."

"Wong has a yacht?"

"Kent says he does. *China Rose.*"

Cole's eyes lit up. "I've seen it! An older ship, steel, about two hundred and fifty, maybe three hundred feet long, with a little bridge and a massive salon aft. White with red trim." He looked at his watch. "The sun sets in about ten minutes. Go find that thing while I round up some weapons and clothes."

"Black."

"Today's your lucky day. Black is our uniform. I've got a truckful of black shirts and trousers. I'm trying to convince my friends that night is the time to fight."

Jake settled into the copilot's seat of the Bell and the pilot immediately lifted it into a hover. When he was above the power lines, the pilot eased the nose over and let the machine fly between the buildings toward the harbor.

They stayed low, the skids almost in the dark water, as they worked their way northwest up the Kowloon docks. Scanning the ships with binoculars, Jake fought down the sense of panic that welled up within him as the sun dipped below the horizon. Time was running out.

Coasters, tankers, container ships, tramps, fiber-optic cable layers . . . ships of every kind and description. They were Russian, Chinese, Japanese, Greek, American, and flag-of-convenience ships from all over the globe. Grafton hunted through them as the light faded slowly, inexorably.

Lin Pe worked her way along the nearly deserted streets of Kowloon. She was very tired and her feet dragged.

Unable to go farther, she sat on the sidewalk against a building, her bag clutched in her hand.

She had never seen the streets this empty. Those people who were out walked purposefully, determined, with quick glances up and down the street.

There were soldiers, of course. PLA trucks drove along the streets with soldiers sitting on the fenders, rifles in hand. At street corners soldiers directed traffic, waving civilian cars off the streets to make way for trucks.

And tanks.

Three tanks rumbled by Lin Pe, huge beasts with long, clumsy barrels protruding from their turrets. Their treads chewed up the pavement.

She got up and followed them, walking as quickly as she could. The tanks were faster than she was, but they didn't disappear from sight.

The three of them came to a halt at the intersection of Nathan and Waterloo roads. The intersection was about a mile north of the southern tip of the peninsula. One tank went through the intersection, then turned in the street. Gingerly the drivers maneuvered. One tank came to rest in the intersection, its nose and the cannon pointed south. One tank was parked on each side of the intersection, slightly back. The tankers on each flank pushed the barrels of their cannons through the glass windows of the corner buildings so they could also command the street and remain half hidden by the buildings. Two trucks stopped to discharge soldiers, who took up positions behind the tanks and the parked cars that lined the side streets.

Owners of parked cars came pouring from adjacent buildings. They scrambled to move their vehicles, some of which were already blocked in by the tanks. Shouting and pleading with the soldiers did no good. One officer pointed his rifle at several civilians and ordered them to leave. In seconds the last car that could be moved was gone, and the sidewalks were empty.

Lin Pe walked another block and found a store whose owner had yet to lock the door. He protested as she entered, but she insisted, talking loudly, refusing to leave. When the owner went back in the store to summon his wife, Lin Pe took out her WB cell phone and dialed the number she had memorized. It took her but thirty seconds to report the location of the tanks.

"Climb," Jake said to the helicopter pilot. He was desperate. There was little light left, and the *China Rose* was eluding him.

"If we climb the PLA may knock us out of the sky."

"Climb," Jake repeated, his voice hard and urgent.

The pilot hoisted the collective and the helo bounced upward; Jake fought against the downward G-force to hold the binoculars steady.

The pilot leveled at a thousand feet above the water. "Fly the whole waterfront again," Jake Grafton ordered, "especially the area by the amusement park."

But *China Rose* wasn't there. The haystack contained no needle.

Just when he was ready to admit defeat, he saw it.

"*There!*" He pointed. "Closer. Go closer."

The pilot turned the Bell and closed the distance.

Yes. There was just enough light to see the red trim, the small bridge, and the windows of the salon. A small boat hung on davits behind the stack. The yacht's name . . . he couldn't make it out. It must be *China Rose*!

The yacht—actually a small ship—was moored to a pier, the last of three large yachts on the north side. Three more were moored against the south side of the pier, which was at least two hundred yards long.

At the head of the pier stood a wire fence with a closed gate. On the quay itself were pallets of boxes, some Dumpsters, stacks of fifty-five-gallon drums, forklifts, trucks, some people walking. . . . Ocean-going general cargo ships were berthed at piers to the north and south.

"Over the quay." Grafton pointed out the direction he wanted to the pilot. He had to see how he was going to get onto the quay from the street.

In the last of the light he got his landmarks.

It was completely dark when he tapped the pilot on the shoulder and jerked a thumb toward Victoria. The helo turned and dropped the nose and accelerated out over the harbor. The pilot didn't turn on the exterior lights until he was approaching the shoreline of Hong Kong Island.

"Where did you see *China Rose?*" Jake Grafton asked Tiger Cole as they hunted through the clothes littering the floor of the truck for a pair of pants that might fit him.

"At a pier in Kowloon. Across from the yacht of a friend of mine, the *Barbary Coast*."

"For Christ's sake, why didn't you say so two hours ago? I damned near didn't find it before the light faded."

"It just slipped my mind, until you asked. I saw it but paid little attention."

"Well, it's still there, on the end of a pier. If we had the time we could get a delivery truck, fake up some invoices, drive through the gate at the head of the pier and motor right up to Wong's gangway. No time, though. We gotta go as fast as we can get there."

"Why don't you land on my friend's yacht? Nikko Schoenauer. He's right across the pier. Has a helo pad on top of the salon."

"This guy German?"

"American as a hot dog."

"It must be nice having all these filthy rich friends."

"Nikko Schoenauer flew A-4s in Vietnam. He told me that he decided to get into a business that would always be popular, didn't pollute or use up scarce resources, with a product that people paid for with discretionary income, something nice to have but not necessary. His yacht's a whorehouse. He fills it with Japanese businessmen and sails off for weeklong parties and writes a fat check to a bank on the first of every month."

Jake glanced at Cole, who looked absolutely serious. "Whores 'n' More, eh? Tiger, you never cease to surprise me."

Jake pulled the shoulder holster containing the Colt on over the black shirt. Tommy Carmellini was waiting outside the truck with two silenced submachine guns and five magazines of ammo for each. He also produced a couple of marine fighting knives, one for each of them, and two sets of night-vision goggles. "First-class stuff," Jake said to Cole after he gave them a quick brief on the goggles.

Jake and Tommy put on the goggles, turned on the power. Idly Jake asked Tiger, "So you were visiting Schoenauer last week?"

"Yeah. The girls are kinda cute."

"I thought you were dating China Bob's sister?"

"Naw! China Bob was a snob. He wanted his sister married off to a decent husband. I was just another dude he was doing business with."

"Schoenauer's got a floating whorehouse, huh?" Carmellini asked. He had been standing outside the truck listening to Grafton and Cole.

"California girls mostly," Cole said. "They come and go. Refugees from suburbia and bad marriages. When they've gotten their batteries recharged, off they go back across the pond."

"Live in a yacht at the side of the road and be a friend of man."

"Something like that."

"We'll land on his boat and troop across the pier," Jake said, "if you don't think we'll be interrupting anything."

"I'm sure he won't mind," Tiger rejoined. "He can't get underway until he gets another load of clients, which won't happen until the airport reopens. Tell him I sent you."

Jake Grafton looked at his watch. "You ready?" he asked Tommy Carmellini.

"Yes, sir. Let's do it."

They stowed the weapons, ammo, and night-vision goggles in a drawstring bag, which they slung over their shoulders.

"When does the war start?" Jake asked Cole.

"In about two hours," Tiger replied, "unless the PLA kicks off the ball sooner."

"We'll be back by then," Jake muttered.

"Or dead," Carmellini added.

"You still got a handle on the electrical grid?"

"Yep."

"How about killing all power to that pier, or that area, in twenty minutes?"

"Sure. Hang tough, shipmate." Cole shook both their hands, then went back into the museum exhibit trailer.

"You scared?" Carmellini asked Jake as they walked to the helicopter, which was sitting in the street with the engine off.

"Hell, yes, I'm scared," Jake shot back. "That's a fool question. Why'd you ask it?"

"I wanted to make sure I wasn't the only one."

The helo pilot made sure both men were strapped in, then he pushed the starter, and the Bell's engine wound up with a whine.

Jake lied to Carmellini; he wasn't scared. He had been too busy worrying about Callie to be scared.

"Rip, Mother isn't here."

Rip Buckingham looked up from his PC. He was doing an in-depth piece on the revolution for the Buckingham Sunday editions.

"The maid said she left this morning and hasn't come back," Sue Lin said.

"Maybe she's at the cookie company."

"I called there. No one answers."

"Well . . ."

"Rip! She could be killed out there. If the government finds out she is Wu's mother, they'll throw her in prison. She'd die there. *Rip!*"

"For God's sake, Sue Lin, she's a grown woman, this is her town. She can take care of herself."

"But she can't!" Sue Lin sagged into a sitting position and began weeping. First her brother, now her mother. She was trying to be brave, but she just couldn't.

Rip cradled her head in his hands. "Sue Lin, your mother wanted to help. She wanted to be a part of what was happening."

"Why didn't you tell me? Why didn't you say no?"

"What right did I have to tell her no? She's Chinese—this is her country. These are her people."

"I'm your *wife*." She struck his hands away.

"Indeed. And it's time you realized that the future of China is more important than we are."

"What do you mean by that?"

"I mean it's time you realized that your happiness is not the most important thing in your mother's or brother's life."

"Is it the most important thing in your life, Rip? Answer me that."

"Don't ask me a foolish question, woman. You may not like the answer."

She rose from the floor and walked to the window. With her back to Rip she said, "You had no right to let her go without telling me."

"You would have said no. She wanted to go. What would you have me do?"

"If you love me, you will find my mother and bring her home."

He turned off the computer and stood. "You don't understand what love is. You think it is possessive, and it isn't. Sometimes you have to let go of the things you love the most."

He took a few steps toward her, then changed his mind. "I will try to find Lin Pe and help her do the job she volunteered to do. When it's over, if we're alive I'll bring her here."

Sue Lin didn't turn around.

He walked from the room and headed for the stairs.

This, Governor Sun Siu Ki thought, was without a doubt the worst afternoon of his life. His friends in Beijing had shouted, sworn, second-guessed, cajoled, and threatened him. He had been accused of being a dupe, a fool, a liar, and an incompetent imbecile. He tried to explain that the afternoon debacle was the fault of General Tang, now dead, and General Moon Hok, now a prisoner, but to no avail. The truth was that if those two soldiers had obeyed his orders to vigorously enforce the law and lay the wood to the outlaws, these riots would not have gotten out of control. They were afraid to use the military power the nation gave them. They were cowards.

Then the television showed the mob beating government officials to death. If that wasn't bad enough, the ministry in Beijing said that treasonous criminal spectacle had been seen by a large percentage of the urban population of China. It had even run on a television station in Beijing, the outraged minister told him, as if the failure of the media officials was Sun's fault.

So when his aide passed him a note saying Sonny Wong was on the phone, Sun Siu Ki was in a savage mood.

"Carrion-eater. Double-crosser. Traitor." He used all three of these phrases on Sonny when he picked up the telephone.

"Whoa, Governor. I know you're having a bad day, but there is a way out. I've told you that. I couldn't single-handedly stop these criminal combinations, but I can save the day."

"For money?"

"Of course, for money. I have a large organization that I support at my own expense, and we have done what the government could not—we have penetrated the rebel organization. Pay me the money and I will give you their heads."

"Beijing has not authorized the payment," Sun protested.

"I find their attitude beyond understanding. They are faced with a genuine rebellion that is getting worldwide press and inciting treason throughout China. The rebels are waging cyberwar against the nation. Government officals are being beaten to death by mobs, a spectacle played on every television on the planet"—this was only a small exaggeration—"and the government dithers over whether or not to pay me one hundred million American dollars to put a stop to all this. What are you people thinking?"

"Beijing has faith in the PLA," Sun explained. "Beijing is a long way from Hong Kong; from there they see the backs of ten million soldiers. Ten million soldiers are ten million soldiers. These traitors are causing huge problems, of course, but no ragtag mob is going to crush the PLA."

"You saw the robots on television today. Those robots are not a ragtag mob."

"Beijing was not impressed. You cannot extort money from them with movie props."

"Sun, you are as stupid as a snail. Wait until tonight. Tonight the robots will be in action. Tonight is the Battle of Hong Kong. When the PLA is losing, think of me. You know the telephone number." And Sonny hung up.

CHAPTER EIGHTEEN

Callie Grafton awoke with a start. She had been dozing, lost in despair, and suddenly she *knew*. The knowledge brought her wide awake. She sat up in her bunk.

"He's coming for me," she said to Wu, who was also awake. She said it first in English, then had to translate.

"Who is?" Wu asked.

"My husband. He is coming. I know it."

Wu didn't believe her, of course, but he had grown to like this strange American woman and her delicious accent.

"Us. He's coming for us." The faux pas of excluding Wu occurred to her now, and automatically she spoke again, correcting her error.

"How do you know he is coming?"

"I just know." She searched for words. "I can feel it. I can feel his presence, the fact that he is thinking of me, the fact that he is coming."

"Soon?"

"I do not know."

"Tell me of your husband," Wu said, to humor her.

Callie looked at him sharply. "You don't believe me and I don't expect you to, because I wouldn't if I were you. But Jake is coming. Perhaps I know it because I know the man."

She wrapped her arms around her legs. "All this time I have been worried because I didn't have an escape plan. Ha! I've got Jake Grafton."

"The knight in shining armor," Wu said.

"Laugh if you like. He'll come."

She was still sitting like that when they heard someone outside the door, then a key in the lock. Two men entered with weapons drawn.

"Come with us, Wu. Time to do some more work on your confession."

They handcuffed his hands behind him and took him away.

Two minutes later the key turned again.

The Russian, Yuri Daniel, stood in the open doorway looking at her. "You too, Mrs. Grafton. Your statement is ready to sign."

"I gave no statement."

"That wasn't a problem. I wrote it for you. Come."

Since he knew where he was going this time, the helicopter pilot kept the Bell JetRanger low, just above the water. He weaved around several junks and a fishing boat, then flew parallel to the coast for several miles. When he was on the extended centerline of the pier that held the *China Rose* and *Barbary Coast*, he turned for it.

"Wind's out of the north, a bit east," the pilot told Jake. "I'll land into the wind on the helo pad on the *Coast*."

"Yeah."

"Guns in or out?" Carmellini wanted to know.

"In the bags, I think. Don't want to scare 'em to death. But be ready, just in case."

The pilot kept the chopper so low that he actually had to climb to land on the *Barbary Coast*. A night landing on a tiny platform on a small ship, even one tied to a pier, was certainly not routine. The pilot's expertise was obvious.

As the helicopter settled onto its skids, Jake was looking across the pier at the *China Rose*. A few lights were on: on the bridge, over the gangway, and in a few of the portholes. The main salon aft was dark.

Safely on deck, the helicopter pilot shut down his engine. Jake and Carmellini got out, bags in hand.

Just in time to meet a man coming out the hatch from the bridge. He was about Jake's age, tan and graying.

"My name is Jake Grafton. Virgil Cole said you wouldn't mind if we landed on your boat."

When he heard Cole's name, the man extended his hand. "Name's Schoenauer. How long you going to be with us, Mr. Grafton?"

"Not long, I hope. Let's get off this weather deck and I'll explain."

Nikko Schoenauer led them to the bridge. He poured them coffee while Jake talked. Carmellini went straight to the pierside corner of the bridge and stood looking at *China Rose* through binoculars.

"Sonny Wong is rather a nefarious character, but this is the first time I've heard he indulged in kidnapping."

"I heard him ask for the ransom, so there is no doubt he's in it."

"I believe you, Mr. Grafton."

"It's Admiral Grafton," Carmellini said without turning around. "I'm just the civilian help."

Jake reached into his bag for the silenced submachine gun. "We're going over to get my wife back, if she's there. If it goes well, we'll return and ride the chopper off the pier. If it doesn't, friend Wong may pay you a visit."

"Hmm," Schoenauer said, looking at the submachine gun.

"If you have any weapons aboard, you might want to dig them out."

"Well, we do keep some old AKs, just in case we run into pirates. Pay off customs with a few bucks and they let us by. They know me, of course."

"Say, would you have any Vaseline and shoe polish around? Black shoe polish."

"I buy Vaseline by the quart. Shoe polish is another thing entirely— these days everyone wears tennis shoes—but I'll check."

While Schoenauer was gone the lights went out on *Barbary Coast, China Rose*, and the pier. In fact, the lights went off all along the waterfront.

Jake and Tommy got out their night-vision goggles and studied the *Rose*. "They had an electric eye rigged at the top of the gangway. Probably have a pressure pad too, so an alarm rings somewhere when you step on it. They're off until someone starts a generator."

"How many guys do you think?"

"I saw two before the lights went out. One was on the bridge. One walked along the main deck."

"I'd bet my pension there're more than two."

"Probably closer to twenty."

"Can we get aboard without using the gangway?"

"How about that stern mooring rope? It's in shadow. That'll be about it from the pier."

"Okay."

"I got this creepy feeling," Carmellini said, "that those sons of bitches know we're coming."

"Maybe. Just shoot first and it won't matter."

Schoenauer returned with two women. Jake couldn't tell much about them in the dark, but they were definitely Americans. He also had Vaseline and shoe polish. Jake smeared Vaseline over his face, neck, and hands, then applied the black shoe polish.

"Jake Grafton," one woman said as he smeared away. "It's a pleasure to meet you. Virgil told me about you. He said you were his very best friend on this earth."

Jake didn't know quite how to respond to that. "I'm sure he was just being polite."

"Oh, he didn't mean that he was your best friend, but that you were his, if that makes sense. He said you saved his life once."

"Long ago," Jake muttered, more than a little embarrassed.

"He said that Jake Grafton was the one man on this earth he would trust always to do the right thing, regardless of the stakes or the consequences."

Cole said all that? The crazy bastard!

"Hurry up," Jake urged Carmellini, who was also smearing himself with shoe polish. "They'll start an engine or generator to get power while we're standing here socializing."

As they were leaving, Carmellini asked Schoenauer, "You got an address or something where I can write to you?"

"Got a Web site," Schoenauer replied and told him the name.

"When I get some time off . . ."

They paused under a sheltered overhang on the main deck and used the night-vision goggles to check out *China Rose*. The small ship was dark, without a single light. Not even a battle lantern on the bridge. And no one was visible.

Due to the widespread power outage, only a glow of light from the sky enlivened the darkness.

"What if your wife isn't aboard?" Carmellini asked.

"We'll cross that bridge when we come to it," Jake said, trying not to panic. The CIA officer had hit squarely on the problem.

If she wasn't there, they would probably kill her unless he got to her quickly. And how would he ever find her in this city?

"So what do you want to do?" Carmellini asked.

"What I'd like to do is march straight across the pier and up the gangway and shoot anyone we meet, just go right on through them."

"Well, hell, why not?"

"Because we don't know where they are holding Callie or Wu, and Sonny Wong just might have someone guarding them with orders to kill them at the first sign of a commotion."

"Double ditto for Wu," Carmellini remarked. "Okay, what's your second option?"

"Walk down the gangway, turn right, go aft to their stern line, and up it. I'll climb it while you watch, then I'll watch while you climb. How's that?"

"I'll go first up the rope," Carmellini said. "I don't know what they told you about me, but sneaking around is my thing. I'm a burglar by trade."

"How in the world did you get in the CIA?"

"It was the CIA or prison. I'll tell you all about it sometime over a beer."

"Let's go," Jake said, and led the way down the gangway.

They walked along the pier, in no apparent haste, their weapons in bags over their shoulders. This was the most difficult part so far, Jake thought, as he willed his feet not to run.

When they reached the stern line bollard, Jake squatted behind it and donned the night-vision goggles. He saw no one on the *Rose.* Two people were visible on the bridge of the ship moored nose-to-stern of the *Rose,* but they didn't seem to be looking this way.

"Go," he whispered to Tommy Carmellini. The CIA officer already had the straps of his weapons bag over his shoulders, so he immediately crouched under the line, which was Manila hemp about three inches in diameter, and launched himself up it hand over hand. He kept his heels hooked over it behind him. In seconds he reached the rat guard, a platelike metal dish that surrounded the line and was supposed to constitute an insurmountable obstacle for rats trying to go up the line from the pier. Hanging on the line with one hand, Carmellini used the other to explore the catch that held the guard on the line, then release it. He dropped the guard in the water and continued up the line to the rail, grabbed it with both hands, swung a heel up, and clambered over.

Jake was taking his goggles off when the *China Rose*'s lights came on. The pier was still dark, as were the other ships. Someone had started an emergency generator, probably in the *Rose*'s engine room.

With the goggles back in the bag and the bag looped over his shoulders, Jake Grafton took a deep breath, then grabbed the line and swung out. As he suspected, the physical effort required was very high. Heart thudding, breathing like a racehorse, he was stymied by the rail and probably wouldn't have gotten over it if Carmellini hadn't grabbed him with hands like steel bands and literally lifted him over the rail onto the deck of the *Rose*. It was then Jake realized that Carmellini's buff physique was indeed rock-solid muscle; the thought had just not occurred to him before.

"You take the port side, work your way forward to the bridge," Jake whispered as they huddled out of sight under the rail. "I'll find a way down. Meet me below."

Carmellini's head bobbed.

Jake removed the submachine gun from his bag, made sure it was cocked and ready, then took the safety off. He pulled another magazine from the bag and held it against the forearm of the gun with his left hand. Carmellini already had his weapon in his hands. Now he went forward along the port side of the ship.

The little ship seemed deathly quiet. Almost too much so. Jake listened intently and heard the faint sounds of television. At least it sounded like television—a male voice, racing along in the up-and-down lilt of Chinese, allowing no breaks for conversation. He slipped up to the salon entrance and put his ear against the bulkhead.

A slight vibration—perhaps the generator?

He went forward along the starboard rail, walking as quietly as he could.

The first hatch he came to was a ladder down. He could hear television coming up the ladderway.

He looked down as much as he could without sticking his head down the hole. There didn't seem to be a passageway, so the ladder probably dropped right into a lounge of some kind. And that was where the people were.

Well, he could drop a grenade down the hole—he still had a couple the marines had given him—then go charging down after it went off, but everyone aboard would hear the explosion.

There had to be another way.

He walked on forward, looking for another ladder.

A lit cigarette arced out of the open bridge window toward the pier below. Tommy Carmellini saw it go and knew instantly what it was. The butt hit the concrete pier in a shower of tiny sparks.

He couldn't see the man who had tossed it. No, wait! He was walking in front of the open door at the top of the ladder. Now he was gone, back toward the helm in the center of the bridge.

Carmellini moved forward, almost a dark shadow.

He took a deep breath and exhaled slowly, silently.

You had to admit, this was living! Others could have the eight-hour days and houses in the suburbs; Carmellini liked living on the edge. He was certainly in his element now, although if he weren't very careful he could end up a corpse. That didn't worry him much. In fact, it added to the danger, so it added to the thrill.

He was thinking about the thrill when he got to the bridge ladder. He examined it for alarms, then experimentally put his weight on the lower step. Now the next.

The door at the top of the ladder was open, which Carmellini decided was a lucky break.

Or a trap.

He had had that feeling earlier, that they knew someone was coming. Was that just nerves?

Whatever, there was the open door, the dark bridge, and the man waiting up there.

He thought about sticking his head around the corner, then rejected that. If the man was expecting him, he would be in no position to shoot. He thought about jumping through the door, hoping he was faster on the draw. That option didn't seem so great, either. If the man was waiting for him he was dead meat.

Ah, I've watched too many movies, read too many thrillers. These guys are smugglers, thugs.

He decided to go in the third way, the tried-and-true Tommy Carmellini special way. He would sneak in, glacially slow, his weapon at the ready. And shoot the smuggler dude when he got a shot.

Up the last step, ever so carefully, weight balanced, weapon in left hand, so the barrel went around the edge at the same instant the eye passed it. . . .

There he was, by the navigator's table on the far side, bent over something. . . .

Slow as melting ice, Tommy Carmellini stepped onto the bridge, the gun leveled, his finger on the trigger. Carefully, purposefully, he scanned his eyes to ensure there was no one else on the bridge.

Just the one man.

Shoot him now or move closer?

Less chance to break a window with the bullets if I get closer.

Step . . . step . . .

Close enough. Sorry, pal!

He pulled the trigger. The gun coughed a short burst. Three shots in the lower back, to ensure he didn't punch one through the bridge window, breaking glass.

The man half turned and fell. Carmellini stepped forward to shoot him again in the head to finish it.

Something smashed him across the arms, ripping the gun from his grasp. His arms were numb! He couldn't feel his hands.

Another blow, this time across the back. The bag containing the night-vision goggles and spare ammo helped cushion the blow, but still he fell forward, sprawling on the deck. There was a room off the bridge, the captain's cabin. This guy must have been there!

"That twit!" a man's voice said conversationally. "I told him you'd be along sooner or later, and the fool wouldn't listen." The lights snapped on.

That voice . . .

"I heard about you, Carmellini. Harold Barnes told me."

Carson Eisenberg.

Another mighty blow across the shoulders. A pipe or a baseball bat. Eisenberg smashed Tommy across the ribs, over the head, almost broke his arm when he raised it to protect himself.

Carson Eisenberg was going to kill him. He was going to beat him to death with the pipe.

"You . . . cost . . . me . . . my . . . life . . . fucker!" Eisenberg accented every word with a blow.

Tommy Carmellini fell to the floor, reached for the gun, but his hands were too numb to hold it.

Whack! *"Bastard!"*

Desperate, Carmellini lashed out with a foot. And caught Eisenberg on a knee.

The ex–CIA officer lost his balance, and the pipe made a metallic ring as it struck something.

The knife! Carmellini realized he had it on his belt! Could he hold it with his numb hands?

He forced his right hand to curl around the handle. He got it out of the scabbard. And lost it.

Eisenberg was trying to scramble up from the deck. Carmellini kicked him again, this time with more force behind it. And again. Now Carmellini levered himself erect and aimed a kick at the man's chin.

He caught Eisenberg with his head coming forward and bobbing down as he prepared to shift his weight aft, over his legs. Eisenberg's head snapped back from the force of the kick. He went over backward and lay still.

Sobbing, Carmellini sank to his knees. His hands . . . he kneaded one with the other, felt along the forearms where the pipe had struck him. It was a miracle bones weren't broken. His shoulders, ribs, on fire . . . Eisenberg had given him a hell of a beating.

Can't stay here. . . . Gotta get the gun, get the knife, move on. To stay here is to die. Can't stay, can't stay, can't stay. . . .

He got the gun in both hands, checked it over as well as he could, then picked up the knife.

His forearms felt like they were broken, but they weren't.

Carson Eisenberg lay absolutely still, the back of his head touching his spine, his eyes open wide.

Carmellini wiped his eyes on his sleeve, smearing shoe polish, Vaseline, and blood, and staggered to the bridge door.

There was a light switch on the bulkhead, and he snapped it off. He waited until his eyes adjusted to the gloom before he stuck his head around the bulkhead and looked at the deck below.

Empty.

Where was Grafton?

The blood flowing from Kerry Kent's smashed nose gradually slowed to a drip. Her shirt and jeans were covered with it. She was thinking of all the things she would like to do to Jake Grafton when the door opened and one of the Chinese York controllers stuck his head in. He looked the situation over, then stepped into the room and pulled the door shut behind him.

She tried to talk, but all she got past the tape were grunts.

The man squatted in front of her and ripped the tape from her mouth. She almost screamed.

"Wow," the man said, staring at her nose and the blood.

"Cut me loose, goddamn it. Hurry."

As the controller slashed with a penknife at the tape that held her to the chair, she demanded, "Where in hell have you been? Why did you leave me sitting here bleeding?"

"Cole just stepped out to the porta-potty. He's been in front of the monitors continuously."

"Do you have a gun?"

"In my pocket."

"Hurry. Before he decides to ask more questions."

The controller jerked the tape away in great wads. Everywhere it touched her skin it tore the tiny hairs out. She bit her lip until it bled.

"What did you tell them?" the controller asked.

"Nothing. I told them nothing. They knew a lot without a word from me."

When the last of the tape came clear, she stood. There was not a rag in the room, nothing made of cloth. She pulled off her shirt and used it to wipe the worst of the blood from her face, then threw it on the floor.

"Give me the gun." She held out a bloodstained hand.

The controller passed it over. It was a 9-millimeter automatic, a fairly small one.

Kent checked the chamber to ensure it had a cartridge in it, then let the slide close. She pointed it up and thumbed off the safety.

"We're leaving," she said and jerked open the door.

Cole had just reentered the trailer and was standing ten feet away in front of the master York console when, out of the corner of his eye, he saw the office door fly open and Kerry Kent come boiling out. When he saw she had a pistol he dove behind the only desk in the place, so Kent's shot at him missed.

She knew that everyone in the place was armed. A shootout in here could end only one way, and Kerry Kent had no intention of dying for anybody's cause except her own. She ran. As she charged past the York control equipment she snapped off a shot into the main monitor and saw glass shatter, then she was flying out the door as fast as her legs would take her, the controller right behind.

One of the guards with an assault rifle tried to block her exit. She shot him in the chest and ran into the crowd before anyone else could get off a shot.

The main ladder to the belowdeck spaces in *China Rose* was in a thwartship passageway abeam the gangway. It was more of a staircase than a ladder. Jake Grafton eased himself down to the deck and looked as far as he could along the passageway. There were lights on down there and he could hear that television coming up the stairwell. It seemed to him probable that this passageway ran aft to the lounge where the television was located. Stateroom doors opened off both sides.

On the other side of the thwartship passageway was a closed hatch with a porthole in it. That probably was a ladder that led belowdeck to the crew's quarters and engine room spaces.

Okay.

He stood, grasped the long handle that rotated the dogs of the forward hatch, and put pressure on it.

The dogs rotated and the hatch came loose, ready to open.

As carefully and quietly as he could, he opened it, took it to its full one hundred and eighty degrees of travel, and hooked it over the latch that held it open. Yes, there was a regular ladder down.

He listened.

Voices.

And he was going to have to go down this damn ladder feet first!

He grasped the submachine gun with sweaty hands.

Maybe he should do the other side first.

Come on, decide, goddamn it! Callie is on this boat and her life—and yours—is on the line.

Forward. Then aft.

He stepped in, put his right foot on the first rung of the ladder.

The good news was that he had climbed ships' ladders all his adult life.

With his heart in his mouth, he went down as quickly as he could, swinging the gun barrel as he dropped below the overhead.

A short passageway with two doors off it, one port, one starboard, then another ladder down, and a door leading forward. He went to the open hatch and looked. Lights. Voices. The engine room spaces.

But first these compartments. Callie just might be in one of them.

The port door opened as he twisted the knob. A small stateroom, empty. The door to a tiny head stood open and he could see in. Also empty.

He tried the starboard door.

Locked.

He put the silencer right against the doorknob and pulled the trigger once. A ripping sound as the bullet smashed through the innards of the door lock.

He twisted the knob savagely, and it opened.

Another empty compartment. But wait!

The bunks were made up in this one.

He went back to the port compartment. Two messy bunks, wadded-up blankets . . . blood!

Had they held Callie here?

The door leading forward, this had to lead to the owner's stateroom. *Please God, let Sonny Wong be there right this very second.*

Grafton put his ear to the door and heard nothing.

Now he turned the doorknob.

Locked.

He used the gun on the lock. Instead of one shot, he accidentally triggered three.

This was the master stateroom, all right, complete with four port-holes—two on each side of the ship—a king-sized bed, and Jacuzzi, but the stateroom and adjoining bathroom were empty.

Goddamn these sons of bitches.

He sensed that time was running out.

Hurrying, he descended the waiting ladder into the engine room.

Two men were fifteen feet aft, and they turned their heads as he came down the ladder. He hosed half a magazine at them, dropping them both.

Turning, going forward, hustling along, through a door into the accessories compartment.

Empty!

Aft again, running, checking for people . . .

There were another two men working on something on a workbench between the large diesel engines in the extreme after end of the ship. They saw him running toward them between the fuel tanks. One dove sideways to cover and the other pulled a pistol.

Jake managed to drop the gunman before he pulled the trigger.

A burst of Chinese came from the alcove where the other man had taken shelter.

Grafton didn't hesitate. He couldn't leave people alive behind him, or he and Callie and Wu and Carmellini would not leave this ship alive. He squirted a burst into the alcove as he ran by, then stopped and fired again, emptying the magazine in the gun.

Changing the magazine, he stalked forward, back through the engine room, past the bodies of the first two men he had killed. Even though he didn't want to, he looked to ensure they were dead. His stomach churned as if he were going to vomit.

Up the ladder he went, gun at the ready.

Jake Grafton saw the shadowy figure in the thwartship passageway as he climbed the ladder and almost shot him. At the last second he realized he was looking at Carmellini, who was swaying as if he were drunk.

"What happened?"

"Ran into an old colleague. He damn near killed me."

Blood was running down Carmellini's blackened face from a cut on his scalp.

"I've been forward and into the engineering spaces," Jake whispered. "Callie has got to be aft, down this staircase."

Carmellini wiped at the blood flowing from his scalp, then used a bloody hand against a bulkhead to steady himself. "Let's go," he muttered.

They descended the staircase together. The passageway at the bottom led aft to a swinging door, two actually, hinged on each side, with windows in each. There were doors—probably to staterooms or storage compartments—on each side of the passageway.

Motioning for Carmellini to hold his position, Jake walked the length of the passageway and peered through the window. He was looking into the dining facility. Four men sat there over bowls of Chinese food, smoking and watching a television mounted high in one corner. Beside Jake was a door to a refrigerated compartment. On the aft end of the dining hall was the door to the galley.

She had to be in one of these rooms off this passageway. Jake turned, went to the first stateroom door, and put his ear to it.

Nothing.

Voices at the next one, speaking in Chinese, it sounded like.

The next one nothing.

Carmellini motioned to him. He was checking the starboard doors. He was pointing to one. He came to Jake, whispered right in his ear. "English, a woman's voice."

"Chinese in this one," Jake said and pointed.

He went to the door Carmellini pointed out, and Carmellini took the door with the Chinese speaker. They looked at each other, then both turned the knobs at the same time and opened the doors.

The first thing Jake saw was Callie, facing him across a table. A man sat facing her with his back to the door. Otherwise the room was empty.

He couldn't shoot the man in the back because he might hit Callie.

The look on her face galvanized Yuri Daniel into action. He rose, spinning, reaching for a pistol in his belt, all at the same time. And found himself staring into Jake Grafton's face.

The Russian got the pistol clear of his belt when a burst from the submachine gun caught him under his chin and knocked him backward. Another burst, this time full in the chest, caused Yuri Daniel to collapse across the table.

"Oh, Jake, *thank God!* They have Wu in the—"

He had her then, jerking her through the door into the passageway, in time to see Tommy Carmellini empty a magazine through the open doorway of his compartment.

Carmellini charged through the doorway. Jake pushed Callie forward toward the staircase and ran aft, toward the dining hall, the gun leveled at his waist.

A glance through the door—three of the men were still watching television, though one was looking toward Jake. Perhaps he heard something.

Jake dug in his pocket, pulled out a grenade. He pulled the pin and let the lever fly off. He pushed the swinging door open a couple of inches and tossed the grenade.

The explosion made the doors swing on their hinges.

Then Jake stepped in and emptied the magazine at the men sprawled amid the tables.

As he changed magazines, the cook came running from the kitchen, shooting with a pistol.

The first shot thudded into the bulkhead as Jake was going down, the second hit a chair while he struggled to get the Colt .45 out of his shoulder holster.

Before the cook could fire a third shot, Tommy Carmellini killed him with a burst of submachine gun fire.

"Let's go, Admiral," he roared from the doorway. "We got 'em. Let's get outta here."

Jake finished changing magazines, then scrambled up. "Go, go, go!" he yelled.

Tommy Carmellini led the way with Callie and Wu right behind. Jake Grafton followed.

Jake called to Tommy, "Get them aboard the other ship and warm up the chopper. I'll be right along."

He ran up the nearest ladder to the topmost deck, above the salon, and went to the lifeboat, which had a canvas cover protecting it. Jake used his knife on the cover.

Sure enough, in the bottom of the boat was a can of gasoline that might contain two or three gallons. He shook it. Full, or nearly so.

Jake went to the hatch that led down to the engine room and emptied the gasoline can into the compartment.

From the foot of the ladder leading topside, he tossed a grenade, then scrambled upward.

He was nearly up when a jet of hot gases tore at him, almost causing him to lose his grip, as the explosion shook the ship.

Trying not to breathe the flames that singed his feet and hands, Jake scrambled for the gangway.

He was across the pier and up the gangway on the *Barbary Coast* when another explosion tore through the *China Rose* and flames jetted from her hatches.

"Are you all right?" Jake demanded of Callie.

"Yes, yes! Are you all right?"

Before he could answer the adrenaline aftershock hit him like a hammer and he vomited. He leaned against the passageway bulkhead aboard *Barbary Coast* and whispered, "Sorry about that," to Nikko Schoenauer, who was standing guard with an AK-47.

"Hey, forget it," said Nikko, who had overdosed on adrenaline a few times himself.

"Oh, Jake, I love you." Callie hugged him as tightly as she could while staying away from the shoe polish. She drew back. "You look like the wrath of God."

He took a good look at Callie under the *Barbary Coast*'s lights, which were brilliantly lit by the ship's emergency generator. "They really pounded on you," he said bitterly.

"It's over. Get me to a hot bath."

Wu and Schoenauer had a short conversation in Chinese. "Why not take a bath here?" Schoenauer asked the Graftons. "The helicopter can take these two—" he jerked a thumb at Wu and Carmellini—"to the Central District and come back for you in an hour." He turned to Carmellini and examined the cut on his head. "You need to have that stitched up."

Jake nodded his agreement.

Wu paused and rested a hand on Jake's shoulder. "Your wife save my life, maybe," he said in heavily-accented English. "She very strong woman."

He smiled at Callie and nodded once, then turned to follow Tommy Carmellini.

When Callie was up to her neck in bathwater, Jake told her, "For a while there I thought I might never see you again. When I saw the blood smears in that stateroom, I thought I was too late."

"I knew you'd come, Jacob Lee. I've never been so happy in my life as I was when that door flew open and I realized that terrible blackface apparition standing there was you."

While the Graftons cleaned up in *Barbary Coast*'s owner's stateroom, *China Rose* burned at the pier. No one came to fight the fire, although the crews of nearby ships gathered on deck to watch her burn.

Flames gradually spread throughout the ship. Finally the aftermost line securing her to the pier burned through, and wave action and the tide swung the stern well away from the pier.

When she sank an hour later in a welter of steam there wasn't a whole lot left. The black water of the harbor extinguished the last of the flames.

CHAPTER NINETEEN

The Cross-Harbor Tunnel was jammed when Rip Buckingham picked his way through it. People by the hundreds lounged against the wall and sat in the traffic lanes. Most were armed with weapons taken from the police barracks armory or soldiers who had surrendered in the afternoon, but there weren't enough weapons to go around.

Appointed officers were busy trying to organize the crowd into military units. To facilitate this process members of each unit were issued distinctive badges that attached to their clothes with Velcro. The plastic badges were in a variety of solid colors and simple shapes, such as circles, squares, triangles, and the like. The rebel organizers, Rip noted, stood in front of their groups and emphasized that everyone in the group must wear the group's badge, although they never told the volunteers why.

Rip knew. The badges allowed the York units to quickly recognize the wearer as a good guy, thereby freeing up York processing capability for other things.

The enemy would eventually catch on, of course, but by then the recognition patterns would have been routinely changed.

The tension in the air was palpable; it was impossible not to feel it. As Rip walked and listened to the excited conversations, which were echoed and magnified into an infinite chorus by the walls of the tunnel, the power of the moment almost overwhelmed him.

There was nothing these people could not do. They would pound at the rocks and shoals of the tyrant's forces like an angry sea and sweep them away, winning in the end, as inevitably as the spinning of the earth.

He reached the mouth of the tunnel and walked into the black night. The rebels had killed all electrical power in Kowloon. Looking north one could see the occasional glow of lantern light in a window, but that was all. The Kowloon skyline had completely disappeared. Members of the Scarlet Team were here at the mouth of the tunnel, working by flashlight with items on a long table.

Rip walked over for a closer look. Michael Gao was preparing a tiny radio-controlled airplane, a "bat," for flight. He held it in his hand, a black toylike thing with a wingspan of eight inches. With a two-bladed prop driven by a minuscule electric motor, the four-ounce bat could fly at about thirty miles per hour for several hours.

Gao nodded at a colleague in front of a control panel, who pushed a button, starting the bat's engine.

The controller waggled a stick; the ailerons, elevators, and rudder of the plane wriggled in sync. As Gao held the bat at arm's length, both men studied a monitor on the control panel.

Inside the bat was a miniature infrared television camera that continuously broadcast its signal. This signal gave the controller a real-time look at what lay beneath the bat. The signal was also processed by the York network, increasing the situation awareness of the York units.

When all was ready, Gao tossed the bat upward into the air at a thirty-degree angle. In seconds it disappeared into the darkness, and he reached for another one of the dozen that sat on the table.

"How close is the enemy?" Rip asked.

"They have a few scouts within a couple hundred yards," Gao told him, "but their combat units are about a mile back. They are building fortified positions in depth across the peninsula. We are trying to learn what is behind the leading edge of their forces. Are they or are they not going to attack us?"

"What do you think?"

"I don't know. The bats should tell us soon, then the brain trust will make some decisions."

"Okay."

"Have you heard? Wu Tai Kwong is back!"

Rip Buckingham hadn't heard. Relief flooded through him. His legs felt weak. He grinned and slapped Gao on the back.

"Did Sonny Wong release him?"

"No. He was rescued. I don't know much more than that. He landed in a helicopter moments ago."

"My mother-in-law is out there," Rip said, gesturing beyond the perimeter. "I am going to go find her."

"The PLA is out there, too. Do you want a weapon?"

"Have they started shooting civilians yet?"

"I don't know."

"I'll take my chances."

"Good luck," Michael Gao said, and held out his hand.

Rip Buckingham shook it, then walked away into the darkness.

"Losing the main monitor is no big deal," one of the controllers told Virgil Cole. "We'll just use another monitor for the primary display. I can't understand why she wasted a bullet on it."

Cole took a deep breath and exhaled carefully. He consciously tried to think like Jake Grafton. "She just wanted us to keep our heads down while she got the hell out of here, that's all."

"She might have caused real trouble if she'd taken the time to empty a clip into the CPU."

"And someone would have shot her," Cole muttered. "She ain't sacrificing any goddamn skin for the cause. Sonny Wong doesn't have enough money to buy that epidermis."

Wu Tai Kwong stood in the corner surrounded by his lieutenants, the Scarlet Team. He listened as they all tried to talk at once, smiled and said a few words now and then, then finally sent them back to their posts. Then he came over to Virgil Cole. A few minutes sufficed to tell the American of his adventures. The cuts on his arm had been stitched and bandaged, and he had been given an antibiotic for the infection. The stump of his finger seemed to be healing properly.

"We couldn't stop the revolution to turn Hong Kong upside down trying to find you," Cole explained.

Wu waved it away. "You did precisely the right thing, the same thing I would have done in your place."

"Your return saved me fifty million dollars."

"And I know you need the money," Wu said with a grin.

"Is Callie Grafton okay?"

"She is bruised but intact. Her spirit is unbroken. She is a warrior's wife. They wanted her to sign statements implicating you in many crimes, and she refused."

Cole didn't understand. "Why did she refuse?"

"She thought she was protecting you, doing the honorable thing. She would not have signed to save her life." Wu Tai Kwong's head bobbed as he thought of Callie. "With a thousand like her I could conquer the world."

"Jake Grafton and Carmellini?"

"Bloody but still on their feet."

Cole passed a hand across his forehead, then moved on. He gestured toward the monitors. "We are intercepting PLA radio traffic. Beijing has approved the use of heavy artillery. Governor Sun wanted a barrage laid on the tunnel entrance. We think the PLA is now positioning the guns at the army base preparatory to a barrage. We have launched bats to see where the guns are and estimate when they might open fire, but the question is: Should we keep our forces in the Cross-Harbor Tunnel while the barrage is underway or move them out now?"

The two men studied the computer presentations of enemy positions and the locations of the York units, then referred to the map on the wall. They were joined by a half dozen of the key lieutenants, who listened silently to the discussion.

"The PLA will probably attack after the barrage," Wu said after he had looked at everything. "Let's get the people out of the tunnel and position them in front of the PLA strong points. If we can do it without the PLA learning of the movement, they will think we are in the tunnel entrance rubble when they attack."

The orders went out immediately on the WB cell phones, and the volunteers in the tunnel began walking forward, into Kowloon.

Wu continued to study the map. "The winner of this battle," he said, "will be the side that controls the subway tunnel."

Cole looked at Wu with raised eyebrows. "That's very perceptive. I couldn't agree more. Your colleagues have been arguing with me about it."

"What do they say?"

"That the tunnel is too narrow and dark to get many people through, that the PLA won't bother with it."

"It will be difficult, certainly, but it is key. Most of the PLA officers are good soldiers—they will think of the subway. That is why I want them on our side."

Cole nodded vigorously. "We put a York in the tunnel at the Central Station. It's got four or five dozen men with it, which was about all that can follow efficiently. I was afraid to give them rocket-propelled grenades or antitank weapons for fear they might hit the York."

"You have done well, Cole," Wu said and bowed a millimeter. "I will go through the subway tunnel behind the York. I will have a WB cell phone, so keep me advised."

The artillery barrage, when it came an hour later, fell like Thor's hammer on the area around the entrance to the Cross-Harbor Tunnel, which was east of the Tsim Sha Tsui East reclamation project, a district of luxury hotels, restaurants, entertainment, and shopping complexes designed to profit from the tourist trade.

Nearby buildings absorbed direct hits from major-caliber shells, which began reducing them to rubble. Shells tore at concrete streets and abutments and gouged huge chunks from the levee. What the shells didn't do, however, was kill anyone. The rebels were no longer there.

Everyone in Kowloon heard the guns and felt the earth tremble from the impact of the shells. Windows rattled and broke, crockery fell from shelves, dust sifted from every nook and cranny.

Lin Pe was sitting in the entrance to an alleyway on Waterloo Road, a block west of the three-tank strong point at the Nathan Road intersection. Parked cars lined the side streets, including the one Lin Pe was on.

Ten minutes into the barrage a long column of troops marched south on Nathan Road and came to a halt behind the tank that sat in the intersection. The soldiers were eight abreast, all wearing steel helmets and carrying assault rifles and magazine containers.

The men stood nervously in line, peering about them in the darkness at the storefronts, looking up at the blank windows looking down on them, looking at each other and the tanks and the officers, who huddled together for a moment as they gestured and pointed at the buildings around them. The officers broke up their meeting in about a minute and began pulling squads of troops out of line and pointing to various buildings. The troops trailed off under NCOs. Then at least a hundred men peeled off and trooped down the steps into the Yau Ma Tei subway station, which was dark, without power.

Lin Pe removed her WB cell phone from her bag. When it synched up, she dialed the number she had memorized.

Whispering, she told the person who answered of the troops, where they were and what they were doing, how many she estimated there were. "They are going into the buildings, up on the rooftops, and down into the subway," she told the woman on the other end of the line.

Then she hung up.

An officer was staring at her.

She palmed the cell phone, pretended not to notice him.

He was wearing a pistol. Continuing to stare at her, he began toying with the holster flap as artillery shells rumbled overhead and the earth shook from their impact.

The man couldn't hold his feet still. All that dancing brought him a few steps closer, and he continued to toy with the holster. Now he pulled the pistol, took his eyes off her long enough to check it over.

When he looked again at Lin Pe, the officer still had the pistol in his hand. He seemed to be trying to make up his mind about something.

Would he search her? Shoot her?

She stood, turned to the nearest garbage can, took off the lid, and began rummaging through it as the artillery continued to pound.

Several minutes later she half turned so she could see him. His pistol was in his holster and he had his back to her as he talked to another officer.

Lin Pe bent over the next garbage can.

As the barrage hammered the entrance to the Cross-Harbor Tunnel, Bob York led Wu Tai Kwong and fifty other men through the subway tunnel under the strait. They had entered at the Central District Station; now they walked as quickly as they could given the unevenness of the rails and ties and the fact that the only light came from flashlights.

The third rail was not hot, which was a blessing since people occasionally stumbled against it. Wu had almost refused to let them use the flashlight, but with the York leading the way, no PLA soldier was going to surprise this little band.

The impact of the artillery shells could be felt rather than heard, a series of thuds that made the rails vibrate.

"What will we do if the electric power comes back on?" one soldier asked Wu.

"We have it turned off. It will not come on."

"But if it does, a train might come through here."

"You must trust me," Wu told the nervous man, "as I trust you. We hold our lives in each other's hands."

Ironically, no one mentioned what Wu knew to be the worst aspect of the small, narrow tunnel: Any bullets fired in here would ricochet viciously. With its concrete sides and dearth of hiding places, this tunnel was a horrible place to fight.

Moving along, carrying two machine guns and a half dozen antitank rocket launchers, the rebels made good time. Still, Wu breathed easier when he felt the floor of the tunnel tilt upward and they began the climb to Kowloon.

They passed the southernmost subway station on Kowloon, Tsim Sha Tsui, and kept going. The next station was Jordan Road, and there they would stop. Beyond that was the station at the intersection of Nathan and Waterloo roads, Yau Ma Tei. Wu thought that PLA troops were somewhere between those two stations.

Twenty minutes after the barrage began, it was over. The rubble around the tunnel entrance was covered by a dense cloud of dirt and concrete particles, and there had been one casualty: a woman near the Tsim Sha Tsui East shopping development who went outside to watch and was hit by a sliver of flying metal. None of the other spectators was even scratched.

Breaking the silence following the barrage was the sound of running feet pounding the pavement. Four thousand troops of the People's Liberation Army charged through the streets toward the tunnel as fast as they could run.

The Alvin York robot stood behind the curtain in the shoe shop where it had been placed. In its hands it held a water-cooled machine gun. Belt after belt of ammo was draped over its shoulders. All of its sensors were in operation at the moment, but only three were feeding data to the network: the UWB radar in its chest and the infrared sensor in its face, both of which looked through the curtain that obscured him and the glass of the shop window, and the audio sensor. The main York processing unit used data from all the Yorks to update the tactical situation. In addition, the net was receiving data from the ten reconnaissance bats that were still circling unseen over Kowloon and feeding real-time infrared video into the system.

All this information was displayed in two- and three-dimensional form on the master control monitors. Cole and the York technicians watched intently and waited. The waiting was growing more difficult by the second. Cole wanted to hit the troops after the leading edge of the assault was well past in the hope that the Yorks could disrupt the rear, which would panic the people in the lead.

"They are coming down Nathan and the Wylie-Chatham roads," one technician said. "No doubt they will push down Austin, aiming for the tunnel."

"We've got the Yorks positioned well enough," Cole said. "They can't win the battle for us, though they will help. We're going to have to win it for ourselves." He turned to the man at another panel and said, "Call the field commanders and tell them where the enemy is."

Finally he touched the York operator on the shoulder. "Okay," he said. "Do it."

The operator slid the mouse over the Alvin York icon and clicked once.

Alvin reached out its left hand and tore the curtain down that hid it from people in the street. Only when the curtain was completely out of the way did it put its left hand back on the machine gun. Then it pulled the trigger, sweeping the gun back and forth, hosing bullets at the soldiers in the street, shattering window glass and knocking them down.

Alvin moved forward, right through the remains of the window to the street.

When it hit the sidewalk it turned north, away from the southern tip of the peninsula, and broke into a run. Alvin ran like a halfback. In seconds the York's erratic, shifting pace was up to twenty miles per hour, a terrific dash against the bulk of the running soldiers, who were still flowing down the street toward it.

The York fired the machine gun as it ran, a shot for each target, its titanium claw working the gun so quickly that many of the soldiers thought the York was firing a continuous burst. In addition, the 5.56-millimeter weapon in the chest turret was engaging targets, different targets, in aimed single-shot rapid fire.

Several times the robot shot at soldiers that were too close to fall by the time it got to them, so it ran over them, hitting them like a speeding truck, causing their bodies to bounce away.

Here and there soldiers managed to fire shots at Alvin. A bounding York running erratically at twenty miles per hour along a totally dark street packed with humanity was an extremely difficult target, so most of the shots missed. The few full-metal-jacket bullets that hit the York spanged away after striking titanium or Kevlar.

Fred York's nearest major threat was a machine gun nest in the third floor of a building on the corner of Nathan and Jordan roads. It left the apartment where it had been stationed and climbed the stairs to the roof of the building. In addition to the built-in weapon, Fred carried two antitank rocket launchers.

Children and householders stuck their heads out of their apartments to silently watch the robot pass, its machinery softly whining and the minigun barrel on the chest mount spinning ominously. Instinctively the civilians knew to say nothing, to make no noise, and to refrain from touching, but they could not resist the opportunity to see a York up close and personal.

Fred kept its legs flexed, so by bending its head it could get through the doors. When it straightened its head, the stalk on top dragged along the ceiling.

Once on the dark roof the robot moved quickly. It crossed the roof in three strides, saw that the next roof was only one story lower, and jumped.

An alley barred the way to the next building, which was two stories taller than the one the York unit was on. Without breaking stride Fred leaped the alley and went through a window of the taller building. Shards of glass cascaded to the street below.

Without electricity or the glow of city lights outside, the office building the York had leaped into was stygian. This mattered not a whit to the York, which went through the nearest door and made its way along the hall, looking for the stairs.

Down the stairs, whining ever so gently, the hulking machine moved along the hallway toward the office suite that held the machine gun nest.

It found the people and the gun with its UWB radar. There were four men behind an office wall. One man was leaning out the window, looking at the street below, and the others were loading the gun. Fred detected the metallic sounds of the ammo belt being inserted in the gun and the chamber being charged.

"How thick is that wall?" Cole asked the operator who was monitoring Fred's progress. Cole was standing behind him, looking over his shoulder.

"A few inches, I think. Typical commercial construction."

"Have him shoot through it. If that doesn't work, have him punch a hole in it and shoot through the hole."

The robot's minigun moved to slave itself to the aiming point, then fired. The soldier leaning out the window fell forward until he was lying across the sill.

Three more shots followed in less than a second. The other men around the machine gun fell to the floor.

"We're going to need that gun," Cole said. "Have Fred bring it along."

"It won't be able to maneuver very well carrying the launchers, the machine gun, and some ammo belts," the operator objected.

"If it needs to move quickly, it can drop anything that hinders it."

Dog and Easy York fought their way along the tops of the buildings toward the tank strongpoint at the Nathan-Waterloo roads intersection, one on each side of Nathan Road. On top of the buildings the fighting machines were at peak efficiency—there were no civilian spectators and no friendly soldiers, so everyone they saw they shot.

Running, leaping from roof to roof, scrambling up or down, shooting at—and hitting—every target that the sensors detected, the Yorks covered six blocks quickly.

Each York carried an antitank rocket, so when they were in range they stepped to the edge of the buildings and brought the launch tubes to firing position. The Yorks fired their rockets simultaneously.

Flames jetted from the open hatches of the tanks as the rockets penetrated the relatively thin upper deck armor and exploded inside.

The one tank that survived was half buried inside a corner store, with its gun punched through the store and pointing down Nathan Road. When the other two tanks were hit, the commander of this tank screamed at his driver, "Go, go, go!"

The driver popped the clutch and the tank leaped forward, collapsing the corner of the building that sheltered it. It accelerated across the sidewalk and bulled through a line of parked cars.

The tank crossed Nathan at an angle and rode up on the cars parked on the left side of the road, crushing them, as the driver struggled to turn the tank to the right to keep it in the road. The turn kept his left tread on top of the parked cars, which were squashed and ejected backward as the tread fought for purchase. PLA soldiers hiding in shop doorways and behind cars ran for their lives.

Into this bedlam the Yorks began tossing grenades. One of the grenades ignited fuel trickling from a crushed gasoline tank, and soon the car was burning in the street and casting an eerie glow on the storefronts and the wreckage.

Dog York was throwing its last grenade when it was hit in the back by two bursts of rifle bullets. It spun and found two PLA soldiers running toward it, shooting. They probably intended to push or throw it over the edge of the building, but they had no chance. With bullets bouncing off its torso, the robot leaped and grabbed each by the neck with its powerful titanium claws, killing them instantly. Then it tossed the bodies off the roof.

Easy and Dog descended the stairs in their respective buildings, hunting for PLA soldiers. There was a machine gun nest in a third-floor apartment of Easy's building. It tore its way through walls, killed the soldiers, and picked up the gun. With ammo belts draped over its shoulders, the York unit went into the hallway and descended the stairs.

Someone dropped a grenade down the staircase. The thing exploded a few feet from Easy, showering it with shrapnel, but it kept going.

Out in the street it attacked the soldiers there with the machine gun and the few rounds remaining in the minigun. The tank was long gone, careening south on Nathan Road, leaving a trail of crushed and damaged vehicles in its wake.

Dog came out of a building on the other side and began working in tandem with Easy, killing every enemy soldier they detected.

One soldier huddled behind a car heard a running York coming at him and threw down his rifle. He stood with his hands in the air.

The Yorks ignored him.

Seeing this, more and more soldiers threw down their weapons and stood, almost two hundred of them.

The shooting stopped. The two Yorks came to a halt in the center of the intersection back-to-back, one holding a machine gun, their heads turning back and forth, the barrels of their miniguns spinning silently.

In the control room, Virgil Cole looked the situation over, then ordered the operator to stop the spinning miniguns to save battery power.

The runaway tank tore south on Nathan Road, forcing the PLA soldiers in the street to scurry for cover or get run over. The panicked tank commander kept the hatch open so he could look up at the buildings, spot enemies with antitank weapons.

Alvin York, running north up the street, saw the tank coming and got between two parked vehicles, out of the way. As the tank passed, Alvin chased it.

The York was capable of a sustained pace of twenty miles per hour and even higher speeds in short, battery-draining bursts. Alvin used that speed now to catch the tank.

The tanker must have sensed the York coming, for he turned and looked back just as Alvin leaped onto the back of the machine and aimed the minigun at the tanker's head. One shot in the head killed the man.

Alvin pulled the body from the hatch and threw it backward into the street.

Then the robot climbed up on the turret and descended into the tank.

The driver pulled a pistol and emptied it at Alvin. Bullets ricocheting inside the steel compartment killed the gunner, who slumped in his seat.

The out-of-control tank smashed over a line of cars, crossed a sidewalk, and buried itself inside a shop selling electronic gadgets. With the treads still spinning, the tank tore out the building's supports, causing it to collapse.

Inside the tank Alvin York reached for the screaming driver and tore his head from his body.

"Jesus H. Christ!" Virgil Cole exclaimed as he witnessed the gruesome scene on the computer monitor, two miles away. "Couldn't you just have the York shoot the guy?"

"He's on full automatic, sir," the controller responded. "The program is designed to allow him to conserve as much ammunition as possible."

"Sweet Jesus," Cole said, then turned away so he wouldn't have to look.

The Bob York robot saw the PLA soldiers advancing south in the subway tunnel toward the Jordan Road station and opened fire. It was standing in total darkness, partially hidden behind a pillar between the two train tracks. Wu had his men on the platforms on each side where they could not be hit by ricocheting bullets.

When the York opened fire, Wu shoved the muzzle of the machine gun he was manning around the edge of the platform and triggered a long burst. On the other platform another rebel did the same. The muzzle flashes lit the scene in a ghastly flickering light.

Wu waggled the barrel of the weapon, hosing the bullets into the tunnel. Up tunnel he glimpsed showers of sparks where the bullets bounced off concrete.

In that dark, closed space the din of the hammering machine guns and the strobing muzzle flashes were almost psychedelic.

Wu stopped firing when he saw Bob York leave its hiding place and begin advancing. He would like to know what the York was seeing, but the only way to find out would be by calling the command center—and the wide-band cell phones did not work in this tunnel. Wu knew because he had already tried it.

The York fired several more individual shots, then ceased. With his eyes closed, waiting for them to adjust to the darkness, Wu listened to the York until he could hear it no more. As the seconds passed he thought he could hear someone sobbing.

Well, there was no way around it. He was going to have to put his men on the track and advance.

"Let's go," he whispered and lowered himself over the edge of the platform. Two other rebels passed down the machine gun.

He had advanced fewer than fifty yards before he stumbled over the first body. He stumbled over six more bodies before he came to his first live man, who was moaning softly, begging not to be shot. Wu flipped on his flashlight. In the beam he found a PLA soldier on his knees with his hands in the air. The man's eyes were shut and he had blood flowing from a gash on his forehead.

One of the men with Wu Tai Kwong picked up the soldier's weapon and told him to follow along behind the rebels.

On the streets above the subway tunnel the PLA had ceased to be a fighting force. The soldiers were no longer under military control; they were either running for their lives, trying to find a place to hide, or surrendering.

After conferring with Virgil Cole on the WB cell phone, Michael Gao ordered the rebel assault force to advance northward up the avenues.

The firing was sporadic and dying down. Soon each rebel was carrying an armful of rifles and being trailed by a half dozen PLA soldiers.

Gao met Wu Tai Kwong at the street entrance to the Yau Ma Tei subway station near the Nathan-Waterloo intersection. They conferred briefly, decided to hold the prisoners in the center of the intersection with a few guards while the main force advanced with the Yorks up Waterloo Road toward the army base. Wu called Cole on the cell phone and told him what they wanted to do.

While the leaders conferred, people began coming out of the apartment buildings on the side streets and avenues. They were in a festive mood and proved hard to handle.

When Wu finally got his men moving toward the army base, the civilians followed. Indeed, they mixed freely with his troops, as if everyone were out for an evening stroll.

Another force of two hundred rebels, accompanied by Charlie York, advanced northeastward toward the entrance to the naval base. The rebels advanced cautiously. The command center had informed them that the naval base personnel had dug a trench near the gate to the base and were in it with machine guns, grenade launchers, and antitank rockets.

After consultation, the rebels decided to appear in front of the position and threaten it while Charlie York worked its way over the buildings to a flanking position. When it was in position, it could pin the enemy with a machine gun while the rebels made an assault.

Charlie York had no trouble getting into position. The building contained enemy soldiers, but fighting in a dark building was the forte of the Yorks. Using infrared sensors and UWB radar, the Charlie robot quickly found the enemy and exterminated them.

Standing in a fourth-floor window looking the length of the trench, Charlie opened fire with the machine gun that it held cradled in its arms. Each round was aimed, each round found a target.

The people in the trench saw only the muzzle flashes on the side of the building. With people dying all around him, one man pointed an antitank rocket launcher at the muzzle flashes and squeezed it off.

The rocket hit Charlie in the right arm. The impact ripped the arm from its socket and knocked the robot off its feet. Shrapnel from the shaped charge in the warhead damaged the minigun, rendering it useless.

"Damn!" said an exasperated Virgil Cole. "That's what happens when we sacrifice mobility, put a York in a fixed position and let people whale away at him. *Damnation!* We're going to lose a bunch of our guys carrying this trench if we don't get with the program, people! Don't let a York stand there like a statue until someone blows it into a thousand pieces! Now have Charlie jump down into the trench and get on with it."

Charlie leaped. . . . forty feet into soft earth. It fell when it landed, its left hand ending up six inches under the ground.

The robot scrambled to its feet and charged the nearest live man with a weapon. Fortunately it didn't have far to go, because without the right arm to assist in balancing it lurched badly.

The melee that followed was short and vicious. Using only its left claws, Charlie York tore at living human flesh. One man had an arm ripped off at the shoulder and began screaming, a high-pitched wail that lasted until Charlie hit him in the head, fatally fracturing his skull.

The darkness, the screaming, the maniacal superhuman thing that killed by hitting, ripping, or tearing—the nerve of many of the sailors broke. They dropped their weapons and ran, either back onto the naval base or over the lip of the trench toward the rebels.

In less than a minute it was over.

The man leading the assault group didn't learn that for another thirty seconds, when his WB cell phone rang. "You can advance now," the controller said.

Governor Sun Siu Ki listened to the radioed reports from the units in the field and watched the headquarters staff mark the positions on a table map of Hong Kong. The senior officer was Colonel Soong, a practical, down-to-earth military professional who had spent forty years in the army. He had tried to advise Sun of the reality of the military situation earlier in the evening but the governor refused to listen, replied with bombast and party slogans and quotes from Chairman Mao about being one with the people.

As the Yorks cut a swath through his combat forces and demoralized the rest, Soong suggested that Sun confer with Beijing, which he did via the radiotelephone.

The fall of the naval base was the turning point for Colonel Soong. It was then that he realized that he could not defeat the rebels with the forces he had at his disposal. He made this statement to Sun, who turned deadly pale.

After one more hurried conversation with Beijing, Sun got out his cell phone and made a local call.

"Sonny Wong."

"Governor Sun here, Wong." He took the time to exchange the usual pleasantries, perhaps as a way of composing himself.

With that over, he said, "I am calling to inform you that Beijing has decided to accept your offer. They are wiring one hundred million American dollars to your account in Switzerland."

"Rather late in the game, don't you think, Sun?"

"Governments are not like businesses—some things take time."

"I understand." Sonny let the silence build, then said, "I should wait until the money is in my account before I act, but since the hour is so late, I'll trust the government's good faith and move ahead expeditiously."

"Good! Good!" Sun said, genuinely grateful. "The government has committed to pay; it will honor its commitment, as it does all its obligations."

"Of course," said Sonny, a bit underwhelmed. "I'll let you get back to your pressing duties while I get on with mine."

When he severed the connection, for some reason Sun Siu Ki felt better.

Sonny Wong tossed the cell phone on his desk and broke into a roaring belly laugh.

Kerry Kent was sitting across from Wong. Her broken nose had been set, filled with packing, and taped into position. If she could have frowned, she would have.

"What's so funny?"

"We've *won!* That idiot Sun has talked Beijing into paying me a hundred million American."

"I told you Cole took the bombs out of the Yorks," Kent said. "We can't sabotage them. There is nothing we can do even to slow the rebels."

Sonny grinned pleasantly. "I know that and you know that," he said, "but the ministers in Beijing don't. By the time they figure out that we have done nothing to earn the money it will be too late. The money will be in my bank and they will be unable to reverse the transaction."

Sonny Wong laughed awhile, then poured himself a drink of good single-malt Scotch whiskey and lit a cigarette.

Damn, he felt good.

Too bad about Yuri. Too bad about the restaurant and the yacht. Grafton and Cole had screwed everything up and cost him some serious money. Before he left Hong Kong tomorrow he should probably settle that score.

But tonight, a drink. A laugh. One hundred million from the Communists in Beijing and ten million from their archenemy, Rip Buckingham's old man down under.

A good score, any way you looked at it.

Ha ha ha!

"Here's to revolution, wherever and whenever," Sonny Wong said and lifted his glass.

Rip Buckingham accompanied the rebels following the Yorks north on Nathan Road. He stopped to watch technicians service the Yorks, replace batteries, replenish ammo, oil and lubricate them. He looked over the herd of prisoners sitting in the center of the street—they didn't seem unhappy—then he went looking for Lin Pe.

He found his mother-in-law just where the controller said she was, in the entrance to the alley a block west of the Nathan-Waterloo intersection. The street was filled with a happy, joyous crowd, everyone talking at once. The glare of numerous small fires that the celebrants had built in the center of the streets lit the scene.

Rip sat down beside her. The old woman looked exhausted.

"We have won," he told her. "The PLA soldiers are surrendering by the hundreds, by the thousands."

"They really did not want to fight," Lin Pe said. "I could see that in their faces. Their officers made them fight."

They sat together watching the rebels stream up Nathan Road and turn east, heading for the army base. From where they sat they could see one of the still-smoking tank hulks. When the breeze gave them a whiff, the smoke smelled of burning diesel fuel and rubber, a nauseating combination.

"Why are you here?" Lin Pe demanded. "Why are you not writing this story for the world? That is your job."

"Sue Lin was worried. She wanted me to come. Since I love you both, I could not refuse."

After a moment to collect his thoughts, Rip said, "Wu was rescued earlier this evening. He is leading the rebels now. He was just here a little while ago, organizing the rebel forces. He led them up Waterloo Road toward the army base."

Lin Pe nodded. She had heard the news that Wu was alive and with the rebels earlier this evening from the girl taking cell phone calls. She didn't say that to Rip, though; she was so tired. And content.

In the midst of this raucous, happy crowd she could feel the common thread of humanity that ran down the long centuries of Chinese history from the unknowable past, through the present, into the unknowable future. Dynasties, wars, famines, babies born, and old people buried— these living people surrounding her now, filling the streets, were the sum of all that had ever been, and in their spirits and bodies they carried the future, all that would ever be.

She rested her head on her knees. With her eyes closed she could see her parents' faces as they were when she was very young, could remember the wonder she felt when she saw the sun rise on a misty morning, with the earth pungent and fresh after a night's rain. She remembered her husband, his face, the way he touched her, the feeling she had that their children were life the way it should be—these memories washed over her now, swept her along.

Lin Pe got out her notebook and wrote, "You are mankind."

She stared at the words, trying to decide if she had captured the nub of it.

Beside the first sentence she wrote, "You are the past and the future."

She gave it one last try: "Do not despair—life is happening as it should."

Sun Siu Ki's mood was just the opposite of Lin Pe's. His world was crashing in on him. The rebels owned Hong Kong Island. They had the only television and radio stations still operating in the S.A.R. and were filling the airways with their capitalist, imperialist filth. Rebels were in control at the airfield on Lantau and at the naval base. With six robots and an armed mob, they defeated the trained troops Colonel Soong had put in the field. In fact, the only real estate the government still controlled in the Hong Kong S.A.R. was the army base.

All this, Sun reflected, was a local disaster, like a fire or an earthquake. It was just his bad fortune to be here when it happened. Certainly his friends in Beijing would understand.

The only ray of sunshine in this miasma of doom was the certain knowledge that the huge Chinese army, armed with weapons featuring the latest technology—some of it purchased from the Russians and the rest stolen from the Americans—would in the fullness of time crush these rebels like a tidal wave coming ashore, overwhelming all in its path.

Six robots? Untrained civilians with captured rifles and limited ammunition? Amateur officers? They didn't stand a chance.

The sky to the east was pink with the coming dawn when Colonel Soong faced the brooding governor.

"The base is surrounded," the colonel said. "The rebels have completely encircled the perimeter of the base."

Sun got out of his chair and made his way to the map table. Grease marks on the map told the story.

"I have been begging Beijing to launch an air strike," Sun said. "Perhaps our comrades will deliver us."

The colonel didn't reply. He was fed up with wishful thinking.

"Will they attack?" Sun asked, referring to the rebels.

"Unless we surrender."

"Surrender?"

"They have not yet demanded our surrender, but we must consider it. They may attack without asking, or they ask and attack if we refuse."

"Why not use your artillery? You know where they are—hammer them into the earth."

"While we are hammering they will attack. There are too many people out there, Governor, for us to stop them."

Sun was incredulous. "What? A few thousand armed civilians against your trained soldiers?"

"We have about three thousand fighting men left on the base, counting every able-bodied man. My officers estimate there are more than two hundred thousand people outside the fence just now. Even if we set about slaughtering them with machine guns and artillery, they can push the fence down and overwhelm us before we kill them all."

Sun didn't believe it and said so. Soong took him to an observation tower to see for himself.

With the sun peeping over the earth's rim, Sun forced his tired legs to climb the stairs. From three stories up on the open-air platform near the parade ground—a structure normally used to train paratroops and review military parades—one could see the main gate and the road beyond and several hundred yards of the base fence.

The situation was as the colonel had presented it. Sun found himself staring at a sea of humanity. The people weren't under cover—they were standing and sitting almost shoulder-to-shoulder. People! In every direction, as far as he could see.

A soft moan of despair escaped the governor. He closed his eyes, swayed as he hung on to the railing.

He took time to compose himself, then said, "It would be a political and propaganda disaster if the rebels were to capture me. We mustn't take that risk. Order a helicopter warmed up."

"Governor, I don't think you understand. The rebels have the base completely surrounded. Yesterday they fired missiles at the helicopter you were in. If you try to leave, Governor, they will shoot you down."

A breathless messenger from the command center brought a ray of hope. "Bombers are inbound, sir. They have radioed for instructions. What targets do you wish them to attack?"

"The rebels around the army base?" The pilot of the leading Sian H-6 bomber asked this question of his radio operator.

"Yes, sir. That is the order. Here is the chart." The radio operator passed it forward to the copilot, who held it so the pilot could see.

The Sian H-6 was a twin-engine subsonic medium bomber, an unlicensed Chinese version of the Russian Tupolev Tu-16 Badger. First flown in 1952, the Badger was used only as a target drone or engine test bed in Russia these days. However, in China the H-6 was still a front-line aircraft in the air force of the PLA. This morning four of them were on their way to Hong Kong.

"The rebels are just outside the base perimeter," the radio operator said.

As the implications of the target assignment sank in, the pilot and copilot looked at each other without enthusiasm. To ensure the bombs fell on the rebels and not inside the base, they would have to bomb from a very low altitude. Since the navigation-bombing radar was useless at low levels, the bombardier at his station in the glass nose would merely release the bombs as the plane flew over the enemy. As long as the rebels lacked antiaircraft missiles or radar-directed artillery, the bombers should be able to strike their target. If the weather was good enough.

"What did you tell the base commander?" the pilot asked the radio operator.

"That we would try for the assigned target, sir."

"Tell the other airplanes to follow us in single file. We shall make a pass to locate the target, then bomb on the second pass."

"Yes, sir."

"We should be bombing on the first pass," the copilot objected on the ICS.

"I want to see what's there."

"We have been ordered to bomb—a first pass without bombing will merely wake up the rebels."

"When you are the pilot in command you can do it your way. Today we do it my way."

After he squashed the copilot, the pilot reminded his gunners to keep a sharp lookout. Alas, the Sian H-6 lacked a radar-warning receiver. The plane contained a single forward-firing 23-millimeter cannon and three twin 23-millimeter mounts: a remote on the top of the fuselage, one on the belly, and a manned mount in the tail. Only the tail turret was aimed by a fire-control radar.

The bombers were three miles high when they flew across the city of Hong Kong and turned eastward, out to sea, still descending. No low clouds this morning, the pilot noted, visibility five or six miles. He and the bombardier stared down into the haze as the planes flew over the city.

"I see the base," said the bombardier on the intercom.

"They should have sent fighters to escort us," the copilot said nervously as he searched the wide, empty sky.

"They did!" the tail gunner sang out. "At four o'clock, high."

The pilot looked in the indicated direction with a sense of foreboding. The briefing officer had specifically said there would be no escorting fighters. Rumor had it that the fighter pilots were politically unreliable. A civil war, the pilot told himself, was mankind's worst fear realized.

"Shengyang J-11s. Two of them." The tail gunner again.

"Uh-oh," said the copilot, who had also been told that the J-11 squadron at Hong Kong had joined the rebels. "What do we do now?"

"Those fighters may be hostile," the pilot told the tail gunner. "If they shoot a missile or line us up for a gunshot, be ready."

"Aye," said the gunner, his voice rising in pitch. Like everyone in the bomber, he knew he had little chance of hitting an incoming missile with his gun. In fact, he had never been allowed to fire his gun with real ammunition.

Ensuring he was out of 23-millimeter range, Major Ma Chow turned to get behind the four bombers, which were strung out in trail. His wingman stayed in a loose cruise formation several hundred feet behind Ma and slightly above the plane of Ma's turn.

Ma Chow was well aware of the fact that the bombers were defenseless against the two fighters, each of which was armed with four air-to-air missiles and one hundred and forty-nine 30-millimeter cannon shells. The fact that each plane was flown by a crew of his fellow countrymen also weighed heavily on him.

"What do we do?" his wingman asked over the radio.

"Let's try the radio," Ma Chow replied.

"Think they know we're back here?"

"If they don't, we'll tell them." The radios in Chinese warplanes could transmit and receive on only four frequencies, so it was a simple matter to try each of them.

Making a long, slow, descending turn in smooth air, the bombers dropped to a thousand feet above the water before they began their run westward toward the army base. Once in level flight the four bombers descended still farther, until they were only four hundred feet above the water.

Ma Chow locked up the trailing bomber with his radar and readied a missile.

"Bomber lead over Kowloon, this is fighter lead, over." The pilot and copilot of the H-6 heard the call in their headphones.

"What do we do?" the copilot asked, panic evident in his voice. "If we talk to them the authorities will call it treason."

"Bomber lead, this is fighter lead. If any of the bombers open your bomb bay doors, we will shoot you down. Please acknowledge."

The bomber pilot didn't know what to say, so he said nothing. He led the bombers around an island, then they straightened on course for the army base.

They crossed the waterline at about two hundred fifty knots, four hundred feet high.

There was no flak, of course, and no missiles. The planes flew in and out of splotchy sunshine over an immense, sprawling city. Ma Chow and the bomber pilots each wondered what the other would do as the tension ratcheted tighter and tighter.

"Target one mile," the bombardier of the lead bomber sang out on the ICS. He readied the bombsight so that he could designate his aim point as he passed over it; the sight would track that location mechanically and give him steering back to it.

Crossing rooftops, racing along a few hundred feet up with the rising sun behind them and the buildings casting long shadows ahead, the string of planes thundered toward the army base. Automatically the pilot retarded the throttles slightly, causing the speed to bleed off still more.

Then they saw the people. A horde of people, an endless sea of humanity extending for miles completely surrounded the base.

"Those must be the rebels," the bombardier said disgustedly as the lead plane swept overhead. "They aren't even armed."

"A few of them are," the copilot offered.

The pilot, also looking, said nothing. He had never seen so many people in one place at one time in his life.

When they were past the base the pilot trimmed the nose a bit higher and pushed the power levers forward. With the two engines developing ninety-five percent r.p.m., he stabilized in a cruise climb. Passing three thousand feet, he said to the copilot, "I think it's time we went home."

"They will shoot us for disobeying orders," the copilot objected.

"I saw no rebels, merely civilians."

"Those *were* the rebels," the copilot said obstinately. He was something of a fool, the pilot thought.

"You would bomb them, would you?"

"I have a wife and son at Quangzou," the copilot replied, naming the town near the airbase they left before dawn.

"Life is full of shitty choices," the pilot shot back. "Are you suicidal? If we open the bomb bay doors those fighters will swat us out of the sky."

Before the copilot could think of an answer to that verity, the tail gunner sang out on the ICS, "Number two has dropped his landing gear! He's turning out of formation. And there goes number four! They must be going to land at Lantau."

There it is! the pilot told himself. *Make up your mind.*

He retarded the throttles; with the nose in a climb attitude, the speed bled off sharply. Now he reached for the gear handle and moved it to the down position. As the hydraulics hummed and the gear extended, the pilot said to the copilot, "Better hope it's a short war."

Three of the bombers dropped their landing gear and turned for the airfield at Lantau. Only one continued to climb away to the northeast. Ma Chow's wingman went with the landing bombers while Ma Chow followed the one climbing out. As it passed twenty thousand feet he broke away.

He did a large 360-degree turn while he watched the lone H-6 disappear into the haze. When it was completely gone, he checked his compass, then dropped the fighter's nose.

Down he went toward the city below, accelerating rapidly. In seconds the plane was supersonic. He kept the nose down, let it accelerate.

Passing five thousand feet, Ma Chow engaged his afterburners. The airspeed slid past Mach two.

The tail of the fighter was hidden by a moisture disk condensing in the supersonic shock wave as Ma Chow flew across the PLA base below a thousand feet. Then he lifted his fighter's nose and rode his afterburner plumes straight up into the gauzy June morning.

Wu Tai Kwong and the members of the Scarlet Team were standing outside the closed main gate in plain sight of the PLA troops behind the gate and perimeter fence and in the observation tower when the shock wave of the racing fighter hit them like an explosion. When the crowd realized what it was, they cheered lustily.

Every person in the crowd looked up to watch the fighter disappear into the haze over their heads.

Wu listened to the fading roar of the engines and glanced at the hands of his watch, which were creeping toward seven o'clock.

At two minutes before the appointed hour, Wu nodded at Virgil Cole, who had a portable York control unit hanging from a strap around his neck. He used the unit to walk Alvin York forward and stop it next to Wu, who examined the robot with interest. This was the first time he had seen a York up close in the daylight.

When the Scarlet Team had looked it over, they stood aside, giving the soldiers on the other side of the fence their first good look. Cole walked the York to the closed metal gate, stopping it just a few feet short.

As the seconds ticked away, the crowd gradually fell silent. All that could be heard was the buzzing of the television helicopter overhead. Looking around, Cole tried to guess how many people were there. A quarter million, he thought, more or less. Most were unarmed, of course, but that was not the point. In human affairs numbers matter.

At precisely seven o'clock, Wu Tai Kwong nodded at Cole and he clicked on an icon.

Alvin York stepped forward, seized the gate, and tore it from its hinges. The robot threw the gate off to one side, then walked through the opening with its head scanning and minigun barrel spinning. Behind it walked the Scarlet Team, and behind them, all the people in the world.

The waiting soldiers threw down their rifles and stood aside. Alvin York and the Scarlet Team walked on by.

The Scarlet Team was not around when the crowd found Governor Sun hiding in a storage closet in a barracks. They dragged him outside and stripped him naked.

By the time Wu and Cole fought their way through the packed humanity, it was too late for Sun. The crowd used their fingernails to rip the flesh from his bones, then they pulled his limbs from their sockets and wrenched them from his body. He screamed some, then succumbed. Even if Wu could have reached Sun's person, it is doubtful that anyone could have stopped the mob.

The blood riot was captured by the television camera a few hundred feet overhead. Fortunately the human wave that swarmed over the base was fairly well-behaved and Wu's armed men were able to prevent wholesale looting of the military stores.

By noon the crowd had thinned considerably, and by midafternoon Wu's lieutenants began herding civilians off the base so they could see what was left.

Wu and Cole departed soon after Sun's death. They had much to accomplish and very little time.

CHAPTER TWENTY

Jake and Callie Grafton went to bed in the consul general's suite in the U.S. consulate while the rebels were fighting the PLA in Kowloon. After the television chopper brought them back to the consulate from the *Barbary Coast*, Jake merely nodded at the marines at the gate, who snapped him smart salutes, and walked through. He informed the consulate duty officer that he was expecting a call from Washington, which was an untruth of a low order of magnitude.

The duty officer was juggling telephones as he tried to coordinate the efforts of the staff, which was trying desperately to keep Washington informed of the progress of the battle in Kowloon as they learned of it. The duty officer muttered "Yessir" at Jake, who wandered off with Callie in hand. When the duty officer was out of sight, Jake made a beeline for Cole's bedroom.

They were under the covers with glasses of champagne on the nightstand ten minutes after they locked the door.

"I have a serious question to ask and I want a serious answer," Callie said.

Jake sipped champagne and wriggled his toes under the silk sheets. *Silk sheets!* God, how these billionaires lived! "Sure," he said, to humor her.

"Okay, here goes: If you were asked, would you accept an appointment as an officer in the Free Chinese Navy?"

"Have you been mulling that for the last two days?"

"I just wondered. What's your answer?"

"Hell, no. They might not make me an admiral. I'm not going to join anybody's navy unless they make me an admiral."

"What if they offer to make you an admiral?"

"I'd have to think about it."

"Really?"

"No. I'm pulling your leg. Turn out the lights and let's snuggle."

"I'm too sore to make love," she said.

"And I'm too tired. Turn out the lights, lover, and let's pretend until we collapse."

She reached and got the lights. "Do you mean it? If Wu Tai Kwong asks, you'll say no?"

"He won't ask, but if he does, I'll say what an honor it is to be asked, blah blah blah, but unfortunately blah blah blah."

"You're absolutely sure?"

"You and I are hitting the road the first chance we get. We are going back to the land of Coke and hot dogs as fast as we can get there."

"Level with me, Jake."

"You're really serious, aren't you?"

"Yes."

He thought about how he should say it. "If you hadn't been kidnapped, I wouldn't have had to kill those guys tonight. I'm not blaming you; I just don't want to have to fight this fight. This is a Chinese civil war—it's *their* problem. I'm willing to fight for my country and my family, and that's it. Sure, those guys tonight got what they had coming, but I'm not God, don't want His job. If we go home we're out of it. Do you understand?"

"Yes." She *did* understand, and she felt relieved.

"I was damned worried about you, Callie. Staring at the spectre of life without you was not pleasant. Maybe it's post-traumatic shock—I don't want you out of my sight, not for the foreseeable future."

"I was pretty worried, too," she whispered. "I kept thinking there was something I should be doing to get out, and I finally calmed down when I realized you'd come for me if you could. Jake Grafton was my ticket out."

"You're one tough broad, Callie Grafton."

"It's crazy to tell you this: I *knew* you'd come. I could feel your presence." She was going to say more, but he lowered his mouth on hers and the thought got lost somewhere.

It turned out he wasn't too tired and she wasn't too sore.

Afterward, as they lay back-to-back, she remarked, "That's the first time I ever took a bath in a whorehouse," but her husband didn't respond. He was already asleep.

An hour later the telephone rang. After he grappled with the thing, Jake managed to get it up to his ear.

"Grafton."

"That call you were expecting from the states is on line two, sir. Before you answer it . . . we just received a flash message appointing you the American chargé d'affaires in Hong Kong. Orders are coming via satellite now—tomorrow afternoon the American and British navies are bringing a half dozen ships to evacuate non-Chinese citizens who wish to leave."

Jake took a few seconds to digest all that, then said, "Who is on line two?"

"The Secretary of State, sir."

"Thanks." Jake sat up in bed, turned on the light, then pushed the button for line two.

He gave Callie the news while he dressed.

"Oh, Jake, I wanted to go home, too."

"It'll be a few weeks, at least, the Secretary said. The main thing is to get out the non-Chinese people who want to leave."

"Will that be many people?"

"Who knows?" he said as he strapped on the ankle holster. "The real question is what the Communists will do. I assume the rebels will leave Hong Kong soon. Maybe the Communists will try to retake the city. Maybe they'll sail their navy down here and assault the place. I don't know and neither does anyone in Washington. On the other hand, if the Chinese try something big the recon satellites will pick it up and Washington will give us a warning—a few hours, anyway—for whatever that's worth." He reached for the shoulder holster, decided he didn't want to wear the heavy Colt, then changed his mind and put it on.

"Some of the Americans won't leave," Callie said. "And you know that a lot of the British and Australians will refuse to go. This is their home."

"They stay at their own risk. They're betting Wu Tai Kwong and Tiger Cole can protect them. In my opinion, that isn't a very good bet."

He bent over and kissed her. "Get some sleep. If I'm going to be responsible for the way the consulate staff performs, I'd better find out what they're up to."

"I'm not leaving this city without you," she told him as he started out the door.

Jake grinned at her. "I didn't figure you would."

Callie didn't think she could get back to sleep, but she was so exhausted she soon drifted off.

The sun was up and Jake Grafton was drinking coffee at Tiger Cole's desk in the consul general's office when the rebels walked into the army base. He was on the satellite telephone to the State Department when the television showed Governor Sun Siu Ki being torn to pieces by the mob.

The power was on throughout the city, so everyone in Hong Kong who wasn't in the streets got to watch the rebels' final victory.

When the conversation with Washington was over, Jake Grafton went to the window and pulled back the drapes so that the morning sun shone full in the office. He was standing at the window looking out when he heard a voice at the door. Tommy Carmellini, sporting a bandage on his head.

"Just the man I wanted to see. Come in and drink a cup of coffee."

"I hear you're now the head hoo-ha around here."

"Yep. You're still working for me."

"I dunno, Admiral, if I'm up to it. Another night like the last one and I'll be a hospital case."

"Thanks, Tommy, for everything. You saved my wife's life when you figured out that Kent was up to her eyeballs in this mess."

Carmellini was still there when Callie came in.

"Did you get some sleep?" she asked her husband.

"No."

He kissed her and held her awhile before he told her that the rebels had won in Hong Kong. The city was theirs. "At least for a little while," he added under his breath.

The three of them were eating breakfast when the secretary buzzed and announced Cole.

He breezed in, dirty and tired and elated.

"We've won the first campaign," he told them.

"Congratulations."

"And congratulations to you," he said to Jake. "The secretary said you are now the chargé d'affaires."

"I'm moving right up the ladder. Who knows how high I'll go? How about some breakfast?"

"I'm starved. Order me some while I tell you all about it."

Jake picked up the telephone and dialed the kitchen. When he hung up, he waited for Cole to finish his summation of the night's adventures, then told him, "A federal grand jury in Washington has issued a warrant for your arrest. Washington announced it an hour ago. You are officially a fugitive."

Cole shrugged. "I volunteered. I'll live with it."

"So where do you guys go from here?"

"Shenzhen, which is a special economic zone right across the border. It's actually sort of a suburb of Hong Kong. We'll cross the bridge this evening and try to take the town. If all goes well, we'll head for Canton in a day or so."

"How are you going to get there?"

"The old-fashioned way—we're walking. We'll move the York units and our heavy weapons and ammo by truck, but the people will have to hoof it. We've got ten thousand men and women under arms, about half of them former soldiers who volunteered. With the trains out of commission, walking is our only viable option."

"Can you win?" Callie asked. "Can you really topple the Communists?"

"If we can convince the people that the Communists have lost the mandate of heaven, the right to rule, then, Yes. Mao Tse Tung always said political power grows from the barrel of a gun, and he couldn't have been more wrong. Every dictator who ever lived believed that fallacy. The truth is that power comes from the consent of the governed. So far the public reaction to the rebellion, at least in Hong Kong, has been better than anyone hoped. Wu always argued that the people were ready—events seem to be proving him correct."

"You've bet your life that he was correct," suggested Tommy Carmellini.

"Life is meant to be lived," Cole replied and helped himself to a cup of coffee.

He grinned—a rarity for Tiger Cole—then offered a coffee toast, "To life and good friends, wherever they are."

They were finishing their breakfast at the conference table by the window, enjoying the morning sun and their last hour together, when the secretary burst through the door. "Admiral, I'm sorry, but—"

He was knocked out of the way by Charlie York. The one-armed robot limped into the room and took up a position near the window, facing the three people around the breakfast table. A few wires hung from the robot's shoulder where its arm had been attached, and the minigun turret was visibly damaged. The skin was spattered with a dark substance, probably a mixture of blood and mud.

Behind the robot came Sonny Wong and Kerry Kent. Kent's nose was taped in position on her face. A portable York control unit hung from a strap around her neck.

Sonny Wong had a pistol in his hand, a nasty-looking automatic. He pointed it at Cole, then at Grafton, as he said, "Sorry to interrupt your breakfast, my friends, but we owed you a social call."

"The marines let them in, sir," the secretary squeaked, "because they thought they were with Mr. Cole."

Sonny pointed the pistol at the secretary. "If anybody comes through that door I'm going to shoot these people and turn loose the York. Tell that to the marines. Now get out!"

The man went, pulling the door closed behind him.

Kerry Kent sat in the consul general's desk chair and put the control unit on the desk. Jake saw that she was stirring the cursor around while Wong talked.

"We have both won, Mr. Cole. You have conquered Hong Kong and I have relieved the Chinese government of a great deal of money."

Sonny parked his rump on the edge of the desk, one leg dangling, the pistol negligently pointed in their direction.

"What do you want?"

"I owe this man here"—he gestured with the pistol at Grafton—"some serious pain. He killed more than a dozen of my associates and destroyed several major assets of mine, a floating restaurant and a large yacht. Capital assets worth twelve million American dollars burned or went to the bottom, Admiral, thanks to you. You are a real pain in the ass."

"You should have left my wife alone," Jake said calmly.

"Nothing personal, but I was trying for a lever to pry some money from Mr. Cole, who has more than is good for any man. He couldn't spend it in five lifetimes. I merely wished to help him with that chore."

"I should have killed you when I had the chance," Jake said, still speaking in a conversational tone.

Sonny Wong grinned. The truth was he felt damned good. "Too late now, Grafton. Too late, too late."

"Where did you get the York?" Cole asked Sonny.

"It was being repaired. Miss Kent had to shoot several of the technicians when they proved uncooperative, but the York seemed glad to see her."

Cole finished the last bite of his breakfast and put the knife and fork on the plate. Carmellini moved his feet back under his chair.

He truly is evil, Callie thought, staring at Sonny. She had never seen him in the flesh; he wasn't anything like she had imagined. Short, pudgy, a round, youthful-looking face—he didn't look like anyone's idea of a career criminal. He was, though.

"I'm ready," Kerry Kent announced triumphantly. She smiled at Carmellini. It wasn't a nice smile. "After Charlie does the admiral, he's going to do you, Carmellini, you sneaky bastard."

The coffeepot, creamer, and sugar bowl sat on a highly polished silver tray. Jake reached for the edge of the tray with his left hand, pulled it a little closer so he could reach the coffeepot better. The York unit was about fifteen feet away, staring at him.

Jake poured himself a cup of coffee and set the pot on the table, away from the tray. He then looked again at Wong, who was saying, "Tell you what, Cole. I will give you a chance to save yourself and your friends. Use the satellite telephone. Call your banker in California. Tell him to wire the fifty million to my Swiss account. There's been enough violence in Hong Kong. Pay me the money and get on with your quest."

"I don't have that kind of cash available at a moment's notice," Cole remarked evenly.

"Perhaps your banker can be persuaded to find some lying around somewhere. Miss Kent has programed the York. I am out of patience and time. We have played the game and you have lost. Step over here and pick up the phone."

Callie was staring at her husband. *He's going to kill that man,* she thought, *and regret it for the rest of his life.*

"We just want to go home," Callie said, causing Wong to look at her.

Jake reached for his coffee cup with his left hand and knocked the cup over. As he started to rise to avoid the coffee splashing across the table, he drew the Colt .45 from its shoulder holster with his right hand. He thumbed off the safety as he swung the barrel and shot at Sonny Wong.

Sonny was looking the wrong way when Jake drew and he wasn't ready, so he was a second behind, which was just enough. His shot missed Jake's head by three inches and smacked into the wall behind him.

Jake Grafton didn't miss. His shot hit Sonny in the middle of the chest. His second hit him high in the throat, snapping his head back, and his third went through Sonny's heart.

When the first bullet hit Sonny, Kerry Kent screamed and lifted the York control unit up in front of her face.

She was still screaming when Jake Grafton put his fourth shot through the control unit and hit her in the forehead, tearing off the top of her head and spraying a blood mist.

The York unit lurched forward as Kent's corpse toppled to the floor.

Jake tilted the edge of the silver tray with his left hand. The creamer and sugar bowl fell over. Jake turned the tray to catch the sun, then shined the brilliant reflection into the sensors of Charlie York. The robot froze, blinded.

Jake concentrated on keeping the reflected sunbeam in the lenses of the York's visual and infrared sensors.

"Oh, Jake," Callie murmured.

"Now what?" Jake said to Cole as he slowly holstered the pistol.

"Jesus, man, you shouldn't have shot a hole in the damned control unit."

Cole scrambled for it, picked it up, and turned it over in his hands, inspecting it.

"Oh, boy!" said Tommy Carmellini, who had dashed around the table and was checking Wong's pulse. "I don't think Mr. Wong expected that."

"Ruined the bastard's day," Jake muttered.

"Is he dead?" Callie asked.

"Pretty much," Carmellini replied, and went to take a squint at Kent. A glance was enough.

"Ruined," Cole said disgustedly, and tossed the control unit on the desk.

"Well, don't just stand there, Dr. Frankenstein," Jake said, his voice tightly controlled. "Turn the son of a bitch off."

"That's just it, Jake. Without the control unit, I can't."

"Isn't there an on-off switch or something?"

"Ah, no. The thinking was that the enemy could flip a switch as well as we could. The control unit is the only way to communicate with a York."

"Go get another one."

"Okay, but I don't think it'll do any good. Kent probably slaved the York to this unit so no one else could give it extraneous commands."

The sun was moving. In a couple of minutes Jake was going to lose it. As the beam wavered on Charlie York's face, he steadied the tray with both hands.

"Start thinking!" he said to Cole. "Gimme a plan!"

"Maybe you'd better get the hell out of here!"

"What if the damn thing then kills you people?"

"Kent said—"

"She lied to everyone—her whole life was a lie." He stared at Charlie York, trying to think. "What are the York's shortcomings, its vulnerabilities?"

"We just started the testing process when we had to stop. We ran out of time."

"No shit!" Jake took a deep breath, then exhaled. "Okay, everyone out of the room. All you people clear out, now! Go down the hall and get in one of the offices and close the door."

One by one they went around behind him and out. Callie was last.

"Jake . . ."

"Go on, Callie. I want to know you're safe."

"Jake!"

"Go! Let me think for a minute."

There it stood, a big, massive mechanical monster with one arm and a damaged minigun, blinded by the sun.

It *was* going to kill him.

Perhaps he should just sit still, refuse to be a threat.

But Kent said she had told the York to kill *him*! As the York was looking at his face, she probably designated him as a target, bypassing the threat recognition program. Or was she merely using a figure of speech? Or just flat lying?

He was about to find out. In a few seconds the sunbeam would be gone and . . .

Holding the tray as steady as he could with his left hand, he drew the Colt .45 again. The distance to the York was about ten or twelve feet. God, the thing was intimidating!

With his elbow on the table, he aimed at the York's visual light sensor behind the lens turret. Got the sights lined up, held them as still as humanly possible, and squeezed the trigger.

The gun bucked in his hand.

The York's head snapped back from the impact of the heavy .45 slug, but the sensor lens appeared intact. So did the lens in the turret.

Bulletproof glass! Of course!

He had two more rounds left, so he aimed at the left sensor, the infrared one.

The York jerked again from the impact of the bullet, yet when its head came erect the lens still appeared to be okay.

The last shell.

Another hit. Again to no apparent effect.

He gently laid the empty Colt on the table, trying not to disturb the beam of light reflected from the tray.

On the table was a squeeze bottle of ketchup. Jake picked it up with his right hand. Still pretty full.

Now!

He flipped the tray at the York and ran for the door.

The York was right behind him.

As he went through the outer office, he grabbed a chair and hurled it at the York's feet.

Like a champion hurdler, Charlie York launched itself up and over. And lost its balance on landing and fell in a crash.

Inertia caused the unit to do a somersault.

And it rolled forward onto its feet and kept coming!

Jake dashed along the hallway as fast as he could go. He risked a glance over his shoulder. The York was twenty feet back, lurching along, touching the wall occasionally with its left hand to steady itself.

Callie opened a door, pushing a chair on rollers. "In here," she urged Jake as she sent the chair flying along the corridor toward the York, who again attempted to hurdle it. This time the chair caught one foot while it was in the air, and the York landed in a thunderous crash on its head and good shoulder.

Jake slammed the door closed. Carmellini, Cole, and Callie were there along with five or six consulate personnel. "I told you people to get outta here," Jake protested.

"In line, quick," Cole said. "It'll look through the wall."

A half dozen of the quickest thinkers got into a tight knot, then they separated.

The door shook from the impact of Charlie York's fist.

"Where's the nearest swimming pool?" Jake demanded of Cole.

"The hotel, three doors down the street."

"Meet me there," he shouted as the York's left fist smashed through the door. "Bring extension cords."

He jerked open the door to the adjacent room and dashed through it just as the York ripped the door to the room he had left completely off its hinges.

The robot charged into the room, then examined the features of each person there. Clearly it was unsure which of the humans was the designated target.

Grafton was not there. With its UWB radar the York had seen one person leave, so after no more than a four-second delay, it turned and charged after Grafton, lurching as it went, slightly off balance.

As he left the adjacent office Jake had locked the door behind him. He ran down the corridor as the York smashed at the wall, punching holes in the dry wall with its fist, ramming it, making dust come out in clouds.

Jake was going for the stairs when he reconsidered. He pushed the button for the elevator and stood there waiting while the York tore at the wall behind him. A leg came through, the head, now the arm.

He could hear an elevator coming, a high-pitched whine. There were two elevators, so he looked at the floor numbers over the doors. The elevator on the left was a floor away ... stopping on this floor ... the doors opened as the York crashed completely through the wall into the corridor.

Jake wormed his way between the opening doors and jabbed the down button as the York came tearing down the hall, each leg driving hard.

The elevator door took its own sweet time closing.

If it gets its claws in the door, the door won't close!

The elevator closed in the York's face, with the hand reaching....

The York slammed its fist into the exterior door, making the whole elevator shake.

Jake's eyes went to the floor indicator. The elevator had been going up, so the up arrow was there. Before his eyes the arrow flipped to a down indication, and the elevator doors began opening.

Jake pulled out the emergency stop button. An alarm rang somewhere.

The door opened about two inches and stopped.

The York got its two claws into the opening and began tugging.

The door creaked.

If Charlie York had had two hands, the door would probably have failed. With only one hand, the robot could get insufficient leverage.

The ringing alarm bell only added to Jake's adrenaline level.

The York was right there in front of him, its head only inches away.

He pointed the plastic bottle of ketchup at the York's face and squeezed with all his strength. The ketchup squirted out, covering the York's sensor lenses.

When its vision clouded, the York withdrew its claws from the crack in the elevator door and brought its hand in front of its face. Fluid squirted from an opening in its wrist onto the sensor lenses. The doors remained frozen open about two inches, so Jake could still see the York.

With the alarm ringing steadily, Jake opened the emergency escape door on top of the elevator car and grabbed it with both hands. He swung his feet, wriggled wildly, and got one shoulder through.

The York tore at the door again. It got its hand through and used the middle joint of its arm for leverage.

It's learning, he thought. *The damn thing is learning!*

Jake got both shoulders through the opening, now his chest, then he was sitting on the side of the hole. The York had the doors open a foot now.

He swung his feet up just as the York lunged for him.

His sports coat was torn and inhibiting his movements. He jerked it off. He was about to throw it away when the stalk on the top of the York's head came up through the hole.

He tossed the coat over the stalk, forcing the York to lower itself down and use its hand to pull the coat away.

Meanwhile Jake was climbing the ladder in the elevator shaft.

He pushed the emergency exit button by the door two floors above. The door slowly opened. Jake dashed through the door, paused and looked back, just in time to see the stalk on top of the York's head disappear into the exit hole.

The York is coming!

The York will undoubtedly use the stairs, the door to which was twenty feet away.

Jake pushed the button for the elevator. He went over to the stair door, opened it a crack, and listened.

The damn elevator alarm was still going off, masking the sound of the climbing York.

Jake heard the other elevator arrive and the door open.

He turned . . .

And found himself staring at the York, which was charging him as fast as its legs would churn.

He tore open the stair door and dashed downward, taking the stairs three at a time. Charlie York was right behind.

Goddamn Cole! This fucking machine is too smart by half.

Even crippled, the agility of the York was awe-inspiring.

Jake vaulted a rail to gain a little distance, then did it again.

He slammed open the door at the bottom of the stairwell and charged through, right past two marines with assault rifles.

They turned and knelt.

As the York blasted through the door the marines opened fire in full-automatic mode.

The impact of the bullets staggered the York and gave Jake another second of lead, but that was all.

Fortunately the York didn't attack the marines. It ignored them and ran by, limping slightly, using its hand on whatever was handy to help stay balanced.

Jake ran through the metal detector at the main entrance, blasted through a group of American tourists waiting to talk to consulate personnel about leaving Hong Kong, and on out the front door.

The York was four seconds behind him.

"Jesus!" one tourist exclaimed to a marine guard. "What in hell was that?"

"A York unit," the sergeant replied.

"Who was it chasing?" the tourist's wife asked.

"That is our new chargé d'affaires."

"Oh, Lord," the woman moaned. "Why in the world did we ever leave Moline?"

There wasn't much traffic, so Jake sprinted across the street without breaking stride and ran into the next building, a huge office tower. The entire first floor consisted of a variety of shops, the interior walls of which were floor-to-ceiling glass. The effect was stunning.

Jake Grafton glanced over his shoulder, checking that the York wasn't too close, then dashed into a shop that had an exterior exit.

Sure enough, the York attempted to cut the corner and smashed into the glass, which literally exploded from the impact.

Shards of glass flew everywhere as screaming shop girls dove for cover. The York stumbled, went to its knees. Jake hit the bar for the outside door, triggering an alarm, and blasted on through.

In the center of the reception area of the next building was a large pool filled with giant Japanese goldfish. Water trickled in from a slime-covered waterfall. The whole thing was ringed with a variety of stunning tropical flowers.

Jake leaped to a small rock in the center of the pool, then leaped on across to the other side.

Charlie York tried to make the same leap . . . and fell into the pool.

With legs and arm churning, it rose, slime dripping from the barrels of its minigun, and splashed wildly after Grafton, who gained three or four seconds on the York.

The next building was the hotel. The doorman shouted at Jake as he ran toward him, but the uniformed man cleared out of the way when he saw the York coming, still decorated with green pond slime.

People in the hotel lobby ran for cover, screaming, shouting, getting behind whatever was handy as Jake ran by, looking for a sign or symbol that might indicate the pool's location.

He slowed as he went by the front desk. "Where's the pool?" he roared at the little squad of clerks in their bright red blazers.

One of them pointed toward the rear of the hotel.

Jake ran that way.

He saw a short stairs, then a double door. Aha! A sign.

Two turns, one more door, and he found himself on the edge of a large swimming pool. He went around one side, slowed to a walk. His chest was heaving. Fortunately there was no one in the pool.

The York blasted through the door, slamming it open.

It saw Jake, started for him, then slowed, its head turning back and forth, scanning.

It came to a halt two yards past the shallow end, on the side opposite Grafton.

"Smart," Jake muttered. "The damned thing is too smart."

Obviously the York appreciated the dilemma. Regardless of which way it chose to approach Grafton, he could escape by going in the other direction. He could even escape by jumping in the water.

Unless the York could swim.

Naw! Four hundred–plus pounds of titanium and hydraulic fluid, Kevlar and computer chips?

The York began moving forward, toward the deep end of the pool. It removed a pole the maintenance personnel used to vacuum the bottom of the pole from its hook on the wall.

The pole was far too short to reach. Apparently the York realized that fact, for it cocked its arm to throw the pole like a javelin. The butt end of the pole hit the wall behind the York.

Charlie York moved toward the shallow end, where there was more room to throw the thing.

Jake retreated toward the deep end. He suspected the York could heave that light pole with excellent velocity, and he wanted all the distance he could get.

He was right. The pole came like a Zulu spear and nearly got him.

When it realized the pole had missed, the York bent down and began breaking off tile with its claws. Then it backhanded the pieces the length of the pool at Jake.

He misjudged the first one, which almost got him on the arm.

The odds were with the York. It had him trapped.

How long would it keep this up? How much of a charge was on its battery?

Enough, apparently.

Jake dodged piece after piece of tile.

Then the door flew open and Tommy Carmellini and Tiger Cole came blasting through. They had power cords in their arms.

Callie was right behind them.

The two men stopped dead, sized up the situation, then began looking around for a place to plug in the cords.

The York half turned, watched them, waiting—probably—for threatening behavior, which didn't seem to be coming.

As it turned its head to check Jake's location, Callie charged the thing. She hit it in the side with her shoulder, her legs driving as if she were an all-pro tackle taking out a nose guard. She heard Jake's shout, then the force of her charge carried her and the York into the pool, where they hit with a mighty splash.

Foam welled up, obscuring the water.

Jake ran around the pool toward them. If the York got hold of her . . .

He hit the water in a running dive.

He was stroking toward them when he saw Callie's head break water.

The York had used its hand to get itself erect, its feet on the bottom.

As it stood it saw Jake swimming toward it.

And went for him.

"Get out of the damn pool," Cole shouted.

Grafton managed to turn, to stroke toward the deep end. Over his shoulder he caught a glimpse of Callie climbing from the water.

The York followed Jake, walking on the bottom.

It went deeper and deeper, reaching for the man, who couldn't see how far behind the York was.

Terror flooded him. He was so tired.

"Get out of the damn pool!" It was Cole, shouting again.

Jake got to the end, reached up for the edge with both hands, and heaved himself up, out of the water.

The York was only ten feet behind. Its stalk was the only part that protruded above the water.

As Grafton got his feet out of the water, Cole threw one end of a plugged-in extension cord into the pool.

The York kept coming. There was just too much water and too little current.

It reached the end of the pool, turned, and started for the ladder in the corner.

"The damned thing is going to climb outta there," Jake shouted. "Get that cord out of the water and bring me a female end."

Carmellini ran down the side, meeting Jake halfway. The hundred-foot cord was plugged into a socket near the door to the room and appeared to be long enough.

Jake ran back toward the York, which was slowly and laboriously trying to climb the ladder with one hand.

It slipped and fell back in.

Jake slowed, walked the rest of the way.

The York grasped the top of the ladder railing with its only hand and climbed the first two steps. Now it needed to release its hold on the top of the railing while it balanced itself and get a new hold farther back so it could complete its climb. This was where it fell the last time.

This time it slid its hand along the railing....

The damn thing had an uncanny ability to learn.

It was going to get up the ladder, onto the concrete...

Jake leaned in from the right side, the side with the missing arm, and jabbed the female end of the extension cord into the receptacle on its back.

The York froze, half in, half out of the water.

It had gone into its rest cycle.

Callie ran toward him. Jake turned and caught her as she threw herself into his arms.

CHAPTER TWENTY-ONE

"You guys have a way to go to perfect those York units," Jake Grafton told Virgil Cole as they drove through Kowloon on their way to the railroad station at Lo Wu, a mile or so from the border. The army was gathering there.

"If they were any better you wouldn't be here."

"I grant you that, but still . . ."

"Write a letter to my company, a guy named Harvey Keim. Tell him what you observed, what you think. He'll be pleased that you took the time to help."

Callie was sitting in the middle of the limo's backseat, between her husband and Cole.

"Is that all you two have to talk about? Those damn robots?"

"Well—" Cole said, coloring slightly. "I'm sorry it wasn't much of a vacation for you folks."

"I didn't mean that," Callie stated emphatically. "You guys haven't seen each other in twenty-eight years." She made a gesture of exasperation.

"It's been an exciting visit," Cole agreed.

Callie opened her mouth to speak, then closed it when she felt Jake squeeze her hand.

As they rode they watched the people walking beside the road. Many carried army weapons on their shoulders and a makeshift pack on their back. There were so many of them. . . .

"Looks to me like you have more than ten thousand troops," Jake commented.

"I was thinking the same thing."

"Be honest. How would you rate the chances of overthrowing the Communists?"

Tiger Cole thought a moment. "Fair. I think a majority of the Chinese people are ready for a change, and a revolution is the only way they're going to get it. Rebellion has busted out all over. There's fighting in every major city, units of the armed forces are refusing to fight the rebels, people are thinking seriously about what comes next. If the Chinese want change badly enough, they can accomplish anything. We'll just have to live the tale and hope it turns out well."

The driver pulled the limo to a stop as near to the station as he could. The passengers got out and stretched their legs.

The aroma of shark cooking in a deep-fat fryer wafted across them. A street vendor had set up business nearby.

The driver opened the trunk and passed out a sleeping bag and a small backpack. Jake had given Cole the Colt in the shoulder holster, which he was wearing. Now Jake helped Cole put on the backpack.

"This is ridiculous, you know," Jake said to Cole. "You're on the *Fortune* magazine list of five hundred richest Americans, and you boil your earthly possessions down to a pistol, a backpack, and a sleeping bag?"

"In the age of hypocrisy a man has to travel light."

"I've heard there is such a thing as underpacking," Callie remarked, "though I've never gone there myself."

"After a couple hundred miles I'll be down to a toothbrush and one extra pair of socks," Cole replied. "I'll give the backpack to some lucky soul who wants to make it into a hat."

Another car drove up. Rip Buckingham and Wu Tai Kwong got out, along with two women, one old and one in her thirties.

The younger woman had been crying. Rip took her in his arms and held her tightly as he swayed ever so slightly back and forth. He didn't seem to care who was watching.

"I wish you would stay," she whispered.

"I'm a newspaperman, Sue Lin. This is the story of a lifetime. I have to go."

"I know," she whispered.

Wu hugged the old woman, bent down and whispered something to her, then picked up his backpack and walked away. He looked back once, paused, then continued on into the crowd, which swallowed him.

Rip lingered. "I want you and Lin Pe to go to Australia," he said to his wife. "I mean it. No ifs, ands, or buts. I don't want to walk all over China worrying about you."

"We'll worry about you."

"That'll be enough worry for the whole family. Lin Pe, will you and Sue Lin do as I ask?"

Both women nodded.

He put them back in the car finally, murmured something to the driver. The car pulled into a gap in the passing traffic and crept away.

Rip came over to where Cole and the Graftons were standing. "Hello, Admiral. I owe you a debt of gratitude for rescuing my brother-in-law."

Jake just nodded and shook the outstretched hand. "Good luck, Mr. Buckingham. Don't be too harsh in your stories on the archcriminal Virgil Cole."

"I'll try to be objective and fair."

"I'll hold you to that," Cole said, serious as always. Buckingham winked at Grafton, shook Callie's hand, then shouldered his packs and walked away.

"How long will you stay in Hong Kong?" Cole asked Jake.

"A couple of weeks, according to the weenie at State. He's probably lying so I won't squawk too much. You know how it is—I'll leave when they tell me to go back to the states, and not before."

"I love Hong Kong," Cole said, quite unnecessarily. He stood looking around, breathing in the sights and smells and sounds. "It's a unique, magical place. Nowhere else quite like it."

Callie Grafton found herself nodding in agreement. She too found Hong Kong fascinating. "When you get back to America," she told Cole, "come see us. If you're broke, call and we'll wire you the price of a bus ticket."

That remark brought a shadow of a grin to Cole's features. "I'll remember the invitation," he said, offering his hand. Callie shook it, then Jake.

"There is one thing I still don't know," Jake said as Cole picked up his bags. "Who shot China Bob Chan?"

"Ooh," Cole said, grunting a little as he hefted his pack. "I did, of course. He knew too much."

"Why didn't the CIA tape pick up a conversation?"

"I knew the office was bugged, so I stopped in the secretary's office, and Chan stopped because I did. We discussed our business right there. He decided he wanted to show me a letter he had received, so he opened the door and walked across to his desk, me tagging along behind.

"You see, he knew everything and he wanted money, a lot of it. Even if I paid him off, I thought it probable that he'd tattle to the authorities with specifics they could check. So as I followed him to the desk I drew the pistol from my pocket and shot him in the head when he turned around. Bob didn't even see it coming. Not a bad way to check out, if you gotta go, and he did. Then I ditched the pistol in a trashcan and went downstairs and got on with the mixing and mingling."

"So you knew there was nothing on the tape that would implicate you?"

"I was pretty sure there wasn't, but the truth was that I didn't care. Still don't. I wouldn't pay ten cents for a videotape of me doing the shooting, if one existed. Sonny Wong never understood that simple fact, which tells you how bright he really was. You can tell State I shot Chan if you want to—now that the revolution has begun, it just doesn't matter."

"Doesn't sound like you're planning on returning to the states any time soon."

"I'm not." Cole sucked in a bushel of air and let it out. "Life's an adventure. I've been a high-tech exec long enough, been a diplomat, been rich, been to all the black-tie parties I can stand. Now I'm going in this direction, going wherever the road leads."

"Keep the faith, shipmate."

"Yeah, Jake Grafton. I'll do that. For you and me and all of those guys who fought the good fight in their time."

They shook hands, then Tiger Cole walked out of Jake Grafton's life.

Jake turned to Callie. "I hate to say this, but I'm up to my ears in work at the consulate. Want to have the kitchen make us a pizza and help me tackle the paperwork?"

"Yes," she said and put her arm around his waist as they walked back to the car.

AUTHOR'S NOTE

Alas, there is no "correct" way to render the Chinese language into English. Prior to the Communist takeover of China, the widely used Wade-Giles system of transliteration gave us Hong Kong, Peking, Mao Tse Tung, Chiang Kai Shek, etc. The Communist bureaucracy spawned a new system, Pinyin, to transliterate Mandarin, which the bureaucrats decreed would be *putonghua*, or "common speech," i.e., the "official" language of China. (Mandarin is the language of northern China; the language of southern China is Cantonese.)

Unlike Wade-Giles, Pinyin often fails to present phonetic clues to English speakers, or, amazingly, the speakers of any language that uses the Roman alphabet. For example, *qi* in Pinyin is pronounced *chee*. We anglicize or transliterate Paris, Rome, and Moscow, and the French, Italians, and Russians seem unruffled. Why must Hong Kong become Xianggang?

For reasons we can only speculate about, in the last two decades American and British newspaper editors have embraced Pinyin with remarkable fervor, which leads to nonsense such as "The President ate Peking duck in Beijing."

In his excellent book, *The Making of Hong Kong Society* (Oxford: Clarendon Press, 1991), Dr. W. K. Chan points out that there are at least fifty-four different ways of presenting any Cantonese name in

English. Faced with this plethora of choices, the author has spelled the names in this book in a way that seemed to him easiest for an English speaker to pronounce. Any complaints should be addressed to the Pinyin troglodyte in Peking, or Beijing, or wherever.

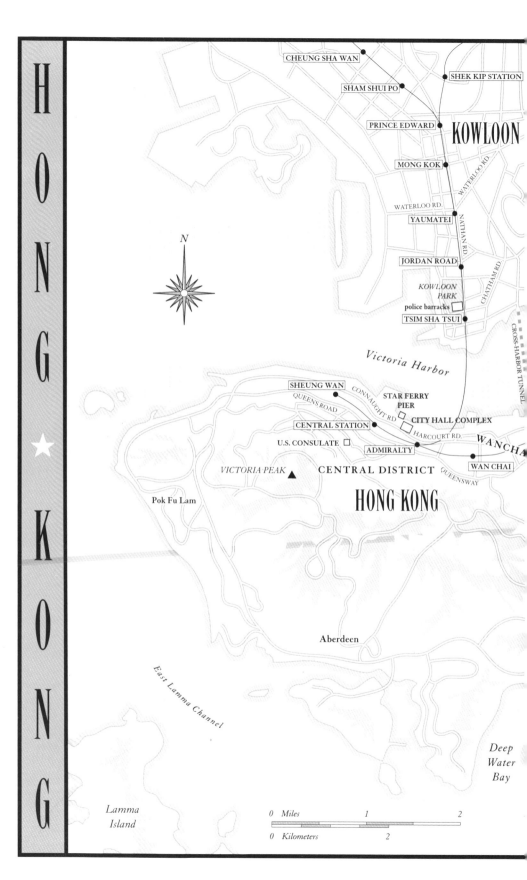